The Zoo of Intelligent Animals

D.A. Holdsworth

FOR SHINTA

1

"'Patch me through to your boss, you cretin, and this time keep your clapper shut.'"

Elizabeth finished reading the message to the two gentlemen, paused, and looked up. If anything ought to impress them, it was this.

"Hmm, interesting," the older gentleman mused, a wry wrinkle playing at the corner of his lips. He paused – all three paused – as the study windows gave an unexpected rattle in their frames. A gust of wind hurled a dense flurry of rain, which hit the glass like gravel.

"And tell me, did they use commas?"

"*Excuse me?*" Elizabeth looked back into the study a bit startled and not quite comprehending.

"Around the phrase, 'you cretin' – did they use commas?"

"Well… Well, there are commas here. On the piece of paper I've got." *Who the bloody hell cares whether they used commas or not?* "Does it matter?"

Elizabeth Belfort didn't normally do flustered, but she did now, as her attention was stretched three ways between the rattling windows, the insanely important mission she was on to bring in one of the government's most elusive advisors, and that same advisor's apparent focus on commas.

"A little perhaps, a little," the older gentlemen

replied, unruffled. "And remind me, when was the *first* signal received?"

"August 15th. About five weeks ago."

"And this signal?"

"Eighteen hours ago."

"Interesting. And you're sure it's not a hoax?"

In truth, Elizabeth had also assumed it was a hoax. It was the first question she'd asked her boss that morning, when he had called her in to see him on the other side of London. Given the overwhelming importance of the message, its tone was – *well* – a little surprising. It wasn't even, strictly speaking, a message. More of an instruction, and not a very polite one.

But her boss, 'C', was not known for his frivolity. He had assured her it was not a hoax, his face expressing all the humour of a man whose toast has just fallen marmalade-side downwards. A hoaxer would have needed a satellite with a radio transmitter at a very precise point in space a very long way away. All Earth-bound sources, including the Russians, had been discounted. Tests had been carried out, the scientists had been consulted, and 1st April was still many months away. The message was genuine.

"It's not a hoax, sir," she replied. And then immediately bit her tongue for calling him 'sir'. "They've checked. The message was received on exactly the same frequency as the previous signal. SETI are certain it's genuine."

"Do you hear that, Artemas?" the older gentleman said to the younger gentleman, who had been sitting quietly, almost unnoticed. "Not a hoax."

"Ah yes, indeed, no. Not a hoax, *haha!*" the younger gentleman replied, somehow finding amusement in the situation. "It does seem all too, hmm

– how might one say? – plausible?"

"Yes, I agree. All too plausible. Very much in character."

*

'Plausible'? 'In character'? Who are these people? And what do they know?

Dinner with this family an hour earlier had already been awkward enough. And now Elizabeth was going from *awkward* to *put-out* and she had every right to.

After all, she was the one who was supposed to be imparting startling information. Here she was – a young, trusted member of a highly secret government agency – urgently delivering to an esteemed government advisor a message that only twenty other pairs of eyes on Earth had seen. And this wasn't just your average top secret, fate-of-nations sort of message. This was more than that.

Far more than that.

This was arguably the most important message that had ever been passed to a human being.

This was the first ever message – the first ever *intelligent communication* – from an alien race.

2

"No more questions – quick, quick, children, I implore you!"

Dr Setiawan shooed his two students towards the door where his maid was waiting for them, holding their jackets over one arm.

"But, sir, you've not yet covered the—"

"Next time, Willem, next time." Dr Setiawan paused at the window of his first-floor sitting room. The rain was starting to splatter the London plane trees outside. He could sense the air pressure had dropped. The weather was going to get a lot worse before it got better. "You too, Laura," he fussed. "You're both on bicycles. I cannot have you catching your death of cold out there. What would your parents say?"

"Sir, we're postgrads now, I don't think—"

"*Look!* You didn't even bring raincoats. You're still children. Be off with you!"

The maid escorted the two protesting students down the stairs, closing the sitting room door behind her.

Dr Setiawan paused to exhale.

Then, next to the door, he straightened the *keris*, which Willem's backpack had knocked very slightly as it brushed past. He stepped back, checked the dagger was perfectly straight on its hook again – *it was* – and gently ran his finger along the ornamental markings on the sheath.

This was a room filled with colourful artefacts – fifteen years as an anthropologist had yielded collectibles beyond the average knick-knacks. But the *keris* held a special place for Setiawan precisely because it *wasn't* a souvenir. A Javanese ceremonial dagger, the *keris* had been in his family for generations beyond count, since the time of the Mataram dynasty at least. In European terms, that meant the 17th Century or earlier. The Javanese believed the *keris* possessed magical powers, including the power to confer bravery.

While Setiawan was ninety-five percent scientist, that still left five percent of his mind free to wander. In his experience, it was at the boundary of life and death that the unknown forces of the Universe were most likely to manifest. And where could come closer to that boundary than a curved, twelve-inch blade of razor-sharp, tempered steel?

Setiawan exhaled again, with satisfaction. The formal working day was at an end. He turned round to tidy up a few books that were still open on the coffee table. He often invited his brighter postgrads back to his home for a tutorial. It brought a touch of *Oxford* to his London existence.

He straightened back up and looked out the window. Willem and Laura were already wheeling their bikes down the twenty yards of garden path that led to the road, their bodies hunched against the rain. He could see an unbroken strip of Union Jack bunting left over from the Silver Jubilee gusting erratically between the trees at the end of the garden. He'd let it stay there for months, out of sentimentality. *I really must get that taken down*, he thought to himself, *before it snaps.*

From simple force of habit, he took a single step sideways from the window to the mirror that was hung next to it. He adjusted his stiff white collar, shifting its position from straight to very straight. He dusted some barely visible fluff from his jacket sleeve. Both in his speech and in his dress, Setiawan brought precision to his Englishness as only a foreigner could. High shirt collar, pinstripe trousers, black jacket. Even by the fusty standards of his friendship circle in London, he passed as old-fashioned.

But he didn't care.

A life of research among the native tribes of South-East Asia had given Setiawan a singular appreciation of traditional costume. His philosophy was simple: what you wear is a costume. When you put your clothes on, you present an image to the outside world. Some people might think they're not wearing a costume, nor presenting an image – they might dress casually, perhaps even sloppily. *My students are masters of sloppiness.* But he – Setiawan – was only going to wear the best. And the best costumes, sadly, were to be found in the past.

He picked up a small, fine comb and started to re-establish the just-off-centre parting in his sleek black hair. True, he would always be an outsider among the English upper classes. An amusing curiosity. Descended from the kings of Solo, his aristocratic status – *Raden Mas* Agustus Setiawan – had been his ticket into high society. He was quite happy to play the role of exotic foreigner. His years of fieldwork had left him perfectly comfortable with that – and if he had to park his books and bags anywhere, he was quite happy for it to be here, in London.

He loved the contrast. For nine months of the year,

the elegant bachelor; for three months, a life of pure simplicity among tribal peoples. His London friends were perpetually amazed that someone so fussy could slum it in the field. But people were essentially unknowable in Setiawan's view; and he certainly liked being a little bit unknowable. And, after all, if he didn't punctuate his life with periods of adventure, what on Earth would he talk about over dinner?

With the working day over, he started to pull his jacket off.

And then he paused.

A strange feeling shivered down his spine.

He stood there for a moment, mid-motion. Jacket half on, half off.

His years of travel in remote places had given him something of a sixth sense. Or, to be more precise – and Setiawan liked being precise – it had taught him not to ignore his sixth sense. *What was this feeling?*

He couldn't place it to begin with.

And then he did.

He felt like he was *being watched.*

He carefully hung his jacket over the back of his desk chair, composed himself, and returned to the window. He looked out at the rapidly darkening rainscape before him. He looked at the trees that formed the majority of the view, and the few houses he could see between them.

Nothing.

He went over to the other window, further along the same wall.

Still nothing.

Regents Park looked exactly how Regents Park always looked, which was what Setiawan liked so much about it. *And yet.*

Strange, he thought to himself, and decided to dismiss the feeling. *For now.* He wanted to get on with his evening. He picked up two sleeve garters from his desk and carefully slid them over his arms, each one to a position just above the elbow.

Still trying to shake the queer feeling, he headed to the staircase, making his way to the attic rooms on the fourth floor. Anthropology was Dr Setiawan's life. The way humans interacted, organised themselves, transmitted their culture – it was endlessly fascinating. If he could, he'd find a tribe of humans, shrink them to ant-size, pop them in a miniature town the size of a lab, and study them under a magnifying glass.

But he couldn't.

So he had his special hobby instead.

3

Seriously, who were these people?

Elizabeth watched as the older gentleman – the 'esteemed government advisor' – reached down into his desk drawer and withdrew a polished wooden box. He opened it, took out a pipe and a tobacco pouch and proceeded to parcel the contents of the one into the other.

Elizabeth felt exasperated by his calmness to the point of irritation. She was expecting excitement, she was expecting gasps, she was expecting disbelief. Fainting might be over the top, but it could possibly – *plausibly* – be expected. And instead, what did she find?

Bemusement.

Elizabeth thought of her own reaction when C had told her the news.

Her world had turned upside down.

She had been dimly aware of the earlier signal, the so-called 'Wow' signal. Back in August, the SETI Institute – the Search for Extraterrestrial Intelligence – had detected a signal broadcast at a frequency of 1420 MHz. The signal was strong, clear, blank, and inexplicable. Not something found in nature. And, more crucially, 1420 MHz was the exact frequency at which scientists had predicted one alien species might reach out to another. Unsure what this blank signal signified, speculation had been rife and publicity widespread. That's how Elizabeth first heard about it, the same way as everyone else.

And then eighteen hours ago, a second signal had been picked up by SETI on the exact same frequency, from the exact same source. But this time it was a message. *In English.*

Elizabeth's world had been turned upside down and, moments later, when C had invited her to imagine how the world would react if it were to find out that an alien species was in contact, her world had spun on its axis a second time.

And now – as she shared this inconceivable, quite literally Earth-shattering news with a trusted government advisor, who seemed not only to take it in his stride, but to know more about it than anyone else – who seemed to know *its context* – her world was spinning a third time.

"You don't seem very surprised?"

"Hmm?" the older gentleman replied in a distracted tone, as he bedded the tobacco down in its little wooden tomb.

"*The message.* You don't seem very surprised?"

"Oh, I'm surprised alright," he replied as he reached for his matches. "The way you are when you suspect a thing is going to happen, but don't know exactly *when* it's going to happen. It still comes as a surprise, despite all one's attempts to stay calm."

From where Elizabeth was standing, his attempts to stay calm appeared to have been entirely successful.

"It seems that you know – or at least *think* you know" – she added with ill-disguised contempt – "a lot more about this message than we do?"

"Oh, I wouldn't say *a lot more*. I wouldn't claim that," he replied, looking at her over the top of his pipe as he struck a match.

"Well, what would you claim?"

"Well, let's see now…" He paused while he started to puff rapidly on his pipe, drawing fire from the match onto the small bonfire that he was lighting at the far end. *Puff* "…I'd say I know" – *puff* – "who sent this message and" – *puff* – "why they sent it. But sadly," he concluded as he shook the match and exhaled a longer and clearly very satisfying puff of smoke into the air, "that's all I know."

Elizabeth Belfort spluttered.

She didn't want to – in ordinary life, she no more did splutter than she did fluster – but this wasn't ordinary life and she spluttered.

"How do you… Could you… What do you—"

She pulled herself together.

"Would you mind telling me how you know this?"

"Well, I could tell you," the older gentleman started, as he drew in a deep draught of smoke from his successfully lit pyre, "but I haven't yet decided if I shall."

"And why not?"

"Because I'm still getting the measure of you." He released a long draught of smoke.

Patronising git.

Even through the vapour, Elizabeth Belfort could see his eyes were fixed on her. His gaze was uncomfortably penetrating, even as his eyes sparkled with amusement.

"Let's see first how we all get along, shall we?" He sprang up from his seat with surprising agility, picked up a small silver box and stepped towards her.

"Snuff?"

"*What?* Excuse me? No… No thank you. I don't."

Not a patronising git, Elizabeth re-evaluated. *Plain git will do.*

At that moment Elizabeth was distracted by a sudden flash. Lightning illuminated the room, throwing shadows outwards from the windows. A few seconds later, a distant peal of thunder reverberated through the study, sonorous and electrical. The rain shower was turning into something more potent. *That feels about right*, she thought to herself.

She pulled her gaze back into the room and watched as he offered snuff to the younger gentleman. Artemas James. *Dr* Artemas James if the introduction was to be trusted, which she wasn't sure it was. Dr James smiled like a child who has been offered a boiled sweet and, with his right hand, took a pinch from the small silver box in front of him. He carefully released the snuff onto his left hand, depositing it on the little bend between his thumb and first finger. Closing one nostril, he then delivered his other nostril onto the small mound of powder and snuffled it up.

Elizabeth watched this small ritual unfold with a subtle combination of disgust and revulsion.

At the same time, she couldn't help noticing Dr James' fingers. They were long and fine, almost feminine. The skin was soft and lightly freckled. They didn't look like they'd done a day's manual work in their lives. They'd almost certainly never dug a potato.

The rest of him didn't look much like a potato-digger either. His frame was slight. He was just under average height, with light brown hair – tidily combed – and a light brown moustache and beard. The beard was small, pointed and carefully trimmed. *Professorial.* He was presumably in his mid-thirties – although it was hard to be sure. His face was boyish, even while his manner seemed old to the point of antique. On his nose was perched a pair of small, round, gold-rimmed glasses that were almost on trend. Although Elizabeth suspected it was 1940s fashion that had installed them there, not John Lennon.

The only thing that lent this wisp of a man any bulk were his clothes. *And how.* A heavy three-piece tweed suit, complete with a gold watch chain hanging in a loop across his non-existent tummy. *This was the 1970s for Heaven's sake, not the 1930s.* The organisers of 'Young Fogey of the Year' must have packed up shop as soon as they saw this one. *Yep, that's Top Prize wrapped up for the next decade, boys, shall we head to the pub?*

The contrast with the older gentleman couldn't have been starker. There was nothing slight about Sir Claude Danziger. He was tall and square-shouldered. He possessed a face that was lively, broad, and framed by a jawline like the bumper of an over-engineered car. It had the ruddy complexion of a well-exercised – and equally well-watered – Englishman. Beneath his nose was a steel-grey moustache, the two halves of which shot out in horizontal spikes like a pair of repelling magnets. It was a face that couldn't hide in a crowd, not even if you put a box over it.

How old? At least sixty but exuding the vitality of a younger man. He was as hard to age as Dr James but in the opposite direction. Their spiritual age, Elizabeth noted, probably met somewhere in the middle – about forty or fifty.

Elizabeth had questioned whether Dr James should be present to hear the message. She was supposed to be passing it to the 21st pair of human eyes, not the 21st and 22nd. But C had warned her Sir Claude might insist on an additional presence and told her to trust his judgement. So she'd agreed to let the younger – *older* – man stay.

"Dr James is my confidential secretary" – *whatever that is* – "and he's also my nephew and my heir." That was the full introduction. She supposed she was being told that to impress how much Dr James was to be trusted. But now she thought about it, she marvelled there was any family link between the men. They couldn't be more different. The younger one looked like he couldn't say boo to a goose; the older one looked more likely to *shoot* the goose.

The only thing they seemed to have in common was their tailoring. Three-piece tweed suits all round. Elizabeth wondered for a moment, caustically, if tailoring was a heritable trait in a certain kind of English family. And then she realised, with horror, that was probably exactly what it was. There was probably a tailor in a workshop somewhere at the back of Savile Row who even now – through no fault of his own – was being passed down the generations of this and other similarly conceited families.

"So, just to be clear, just so I know what to report back to C," Elizabeth added with a hint of menace, "you're not willing to share with me any further information regarding this message?"

"Of course, I am," Sir Claude replied soothingly. "But perhaps not right now."

"Then we appear to have arrived at an impasse." Elizabeth folded her arms.

"Ah, an impasse!" Dr James clapped his hands. "My favourite kind of place."

Elizabeth looked at the younger gentleman in confusion and wondered for the second time that evening whether he was actually a simpleton.

"I always find," Dr James continued, "something enormously productive lies on the other side. *Don't you?*"

4

The first time Elizabeth had wondered if Dr James was a simpleton was about an hour earlier, at dinner.

Elizabeth had arrived that evening on Cleremont Avenue in a taxi. Twilight was almost upon the tree-lined avenue, and the globe-shaped gas lamps had already been lighted. As she watched the increasingly grand houses pass by the taxi window, her fingers pressed protectively against the two things she was carrying in her pocket.

They were, after all, rather important.

The first was a letter of introduction. It struck her as a bit old-fashioned, but C had insisted. She would need something to establish her authenticity. Sir Claude had apparently been travelling in the Arctic Circle for months. He was due back this evening but there was no way of reaching him by phone to check.

On the face of it, her mission was simple. To appraise Sir Claude of developments and invite him – *persuade* him if necessary – to join the new committee that was being formed in response to the alien contact. This new committee would comprise the top experts in their various fields, those best equipped to guide the heads of state. *Who should reply to this strange message? What should they reply?* Only a very few experts would be in the know, and even fewer heads of state. Sir Claude was being included as a botanist, which seemed a bit strange to Elizabeth. *Why do they need one of those?* But C had had that don't-ask-questions look in his eye, and Elizabeth hadn't pressed the point. The new committee was due to meet for the first time at dawn at the Foreign Office on Whitehall.

At that point, Elizabeth's role would get more challenging. She was to act as Secretary to the committee. C couldn't entrust a role so confidential to any regular secretary. He needed a young high-flyer from within his own organisation. Someone junior enough not to mind doing some bag-carrying – but smart enough to win the confidence of the planet's most powerful politicians and some of its finest minds. Her job was to keep minutes at the official meetings, and extract as much information as possible at the unofficial ones. She was to be C's eyes and ears. He'd told her – in a slightly mysterious tone – that some of the committee members would know more than others. Her job was to find out *everything*.

Elizabeth ought to be glowing with pride at being selected. But to glow you need an audience and an audience was the one thing she wasn't allowed. This role was so confidential, she couldn't even tell her husband – and he worked in the same organisation.

Elizabeth's fingers instinctively felt again in her pocket – for the umpteenth time – for the other item. The message. *The* message. Elizabeth had an excellent memory, honed by years of training. She no more needed to copy the message down than her own name. And she worked in a profession where you absolutely didn't write things down if you didn't need to.

And yet she'd copied it down anyway.

This was the one line in her life which she didn't

want to fluff. That and her marriage vows. And she *had* fluffed those.

If any unauthorised person found the message, what would they make it of it anyway? The message was meaningless by itself. A peremptory and rather rude bit of nothing. To mean something, it needed *context*. And that was in very short supply at the present time—

"'Ere you are, Miss. Number 55," the taxi driver announced, interrupting her train of thought. He pulled back the internal window. "That'll be one pahnd fifty."

"There you go – and keep the change." Elizabeth handed him two crisp one-pound notes. Sir Isaac Newton's still unsullied face was glowering from beneath a large wig while, behind his shoulder, the celestial bodies were captured in a frozen spin.

"Ta very much. Mind 'ow you go in there, Miss." The cabbie nodded towards the particularly large house outside which they'd just stopped. "If you get lost, I won't be able to 'elp. I do streets, me, not corridors."

He winked as he wound the window back up.

Elizabeth stepped out onto Cleremont Avenue and was immediately buffeted by the wind. The temperature in London had dropped rapidly, even in the short time since she'd got in the cab. She took a moment to tighten the belt on her raincoat and gather her long hair back from her face. As she did so, she briefly contemplated the long, elegant Edwardian frontage before her.

Number 55.

It was stunning.

Just for a moment a little ray of imagination slipped like sunlight through a crack in the cold hard professionalism, that otherwise cloaked her and this mission. She briefly wondered what it must be like to live in such a building. The roofline of the house rambled in a way that was both haphazard and perfectly proportioned at the same time. Here a tall, three-storey section, over there a single-storey garage, and between them a low, inviting archway leading to a garden beyond. The windows, likewise, presented a library of different shapes and sizes, while remaining somehow coherent. There were tall windows on the ground floor, and shorter ones on the upper floors, the height diminishing according to the golden ratio. There were small round windows tucked beneath gables, a tall arched one set in front of a staircase, and – above the front door – a surprisingly large and intricate stained-glass window. Elizabeth couldn't tell what scene it depicted; the glass wouldn't yield its meaning until nightfall and a light was turned on from within.

The whole building was set back from the road by about fifteen yards. A couple of copper beeches and a few London plane trees studded the strip of garden at the front. Wind was whipping the branches back and forth in an autumn swirl, while the house sat behind, as immutable as a dream untouched by restless reality.

But Elizabeth wasn't here to admire architecture. Or dawdle. A strong squall whipped around her – almost causing her to totter – and blew on down the street like an ill omen.

She hurried up the steps to Number 55, one hand clutching the lapels of her coat, the other trying to hold down her hair. Reaching the front door, she tugged on the large bell pull. It opened and a butler appeared with a look of polite inquiry on his face. Elizabeth was about to explain her mission when another violent gust of wind blew her – literally blew her – across the threshold. The butler stepped aside as Elizabeth Belfort arrived, a little ruffled, inside the house.

*

Somehow – without seeming to have any say in the matter – Elizabeth had found herself having dinner with Sir Claude's wife, Lady Danziger.

Sir Claude, it transpired, had still not arrived back from his travels and his wife had insisted she join them for what she called 'supper'. Supper was not part of Elizabeth's plan, still less a formal dinner with a family who were waited on *by footmen*.

And that was the easy bit.

The difficult bit was that her dinner companions appeared to have no conversation.

And no interest in it either.

Two customary anxieties hit Elizabeth as soon as she had to make small talk with the wife of a contact. They always wanted to know *what* she was going to discuss with their husband. Which she was never allowed to answer. Which then lead them to wondering why – really, *why* – she wanted to see their husband. Sometimes they inquired out loud, sometimes with their eyes. Elizabeth had encountered more than a few wives of the stay-at-home variety, who had looked at her long legs and wondered precisely what could require such urgent attention.

But Elizabeth needn't have worried.

Cutlery clinked against crockery as the three of them supped on vegetable soup in silence. Lady Danziger appeared to trade neither in suspicion nor in small talk. She sat to Elizabeth's right at the head of the table. She was tall and taciturn and, for a lady presumably in her late fifties, quite, quite beautiful.

Opposite Elizabeth sat the younger gentleman, whom Lady Danziger had introduced as Dr James.

Strangely, it had been a one-way introduction. Lady Danziger seemed to think it unnecessary to pass her name to Dr James, which had struck Elizabeth as a little rude. It would be days – many days and a long adventure – before it occurred to Elizabeth this might have been a delicate consideration on Lady Danziger's part.

Right now, neither of Elizabeth's dinner companions appeared to mind the ponderous silence that hung over the room. Periodically, Dr James chortled to himself, as if some passing thought had amused him.

"Where has Sir Claude been travelling?" Elizabeth asked, hoping to spark some conversation.

"Yakutsk," Lady Danziger replied.

"Oh really? Why's that?" Elizabeth tried to place Yakutsk in her mind.

"He's been studying the permafrost in the Siberian tundra."

"In *Russia?*" Elizabeth reacted like an electrician to an exposed wire. This was 1977. People didn't just travel to and from Siberia. "They allowed him in?"

"Yes, Russia," Lady Danziger replied. "My husband is a botanist, not a spy."

"Of course." Elizabeth backed down. She tried to banish from her mind all the posh Englishmen who had betrayed their country.

The last exchange hung in the air like icy breath. Elizabeth cast about desperately for small talk to dispel it. "How long does the journey take?"

"About three or four days."

"Yes, that is a long time. I'm sure he'll be tired

when he arrives?"

"My husband doesn't get tired."

Elizabeth stared at Lady Danziger for an instant and then at her soup. Frankly, she didn't know where to look.

At that moment, a window blew open from the force of the gale. It was just above Dr James' head. Wind erupted into the room and the first burst of rain followed it in.

"Ah ha!" Dr James exclaimed with excitement. He raised a single, happy finger in the air. "A sign from the Heavens!"

"A sign of what?" Elizabeth asked, wondering for the first time if he was a simpleton. But also not caring as she relished the fresh air gusting across her face.

"I've no idea, *hmm?* But I'm sure we shall find out!"

"Close the window please, would you, Juckes?" Lady Danziger asked the butler, before turning back to Elizabeth. "You must forgive my nephew. Dr James is of the religious variety. My husband and I prefer to be guided by the light of science," she added, as if rehearsing a well-worn family debate.

"Ah yes, of course," Elizabeth replied.

"My nephew is a linguist by profession, but has made a particular study of theodicy," Lady Danziger continued in a tone that suggested neither approval nor disapproval. "He has allowed his intellect to wander in a number of different directions."

"Theodicy?" Elizabeth asked, not knowing how to react to this sudden rush of conversation.

"Yes. The problem of evil. How to justify a loving God in a world of suffering."

"Right."

"Impossible, of course."

"Of course."

Elizabeth turned from Lady Danziger to Dr James, who was smiling happily, and quite unconcerned he was being discussed. Elizabeth wondered if he'd fully mastered English, never mind other languages.

Meantime, Juckes the butler – *could anyone in this house just be called 'Mr' or 'Mrs'?* – had managed to wrestle the window shut. The brief refreshing blast of air was gone. As the soup bowls were cleared – and desperate to escape – Elizabeth asked where the cloakroom was, feeling a little pleased with herself. *Cloakroom.* It seemed to have the right tone.

"Juckes will show you."

*

Elizabeth had got lost on the way back. Just as the cabbie had predicted. But then she was scarcely in a hurry to re-join dinner.

She was emerging from a low-lit, windowless corridor, and had just sighted the main entrance hall ahead, when she heard the clear peal of a doorbell. Juckes swept past from her left, heading straight for the front door. Just before he reached it, the door opened – *blew open* would be more accurate – and a tall figure appeared.

The sound of the gale rose and then – as the door was promptly slammed shut – fell away again, like tuning past static on a radio.

Elizabeth retreated a step or two into the shadows, out of sight. She turned around, hoping to head back along the corridor, but a floorboard creaked beneath her. She winced.

"Good evening, Sir Claude. How was your journey, sir?" It was the butler's voice. She was eavesdropping by accident. She froze. She hadn't meant to retreat, but now she'd done it, she was stuck. A step in either direction and the floorboards would give her away.

"Tolerable, Juckes, tolerable," the other person – *Sir Claude* – replied. "Rather a long way to travel to look at some ice. But there you have it, needs must." Elizabeth could see nothing, but she heard the vague rustle of outerwear being removed. "Could you have one of the chaps fetch my trunks from the cab?"

"Of course, sir. Have you brought any specimens with you?"

"No. They're arriving tomorrow."

The irony wasn't lost on Elizabeth. Here was the one moment in her career when she was spying without wanting to. She looked up and saw that she had her back to a wide wooden staircase that swept up from the main hallway, passing over her head to the upstairs landing above. She was shielded from view by a large tropical plant to her right that was bursting out of a gleaming brass tub. It had luxuriant, deep green fronds and purple flowers. Beyond that, against the oak panelling on the wall opposite, she could see what appeared to be a…

A suit of armour.

Obviously.

"Will you be joining her Ladyship and Dr James for dinner?" The butler again.

"Let me think… No, let's not interrupt their meal. I shall greet them afterwards." There was a short pause, while another article of clothing was removed. Presumably his hat. "Have a fire made up in the study, if you could Juckes?"

"It's already been done, sir."

"Excellent. Well then, that seems to be everything. Except of course for the matter of our mysterious guest," Sir Claude's voice added, as Elizabeth's heart leapt into her mouth. "Perhaps she and Dr James could join me in my study after dinner?"

"Of course, sir."

"Meantime, do show her back to the dining room. She appears to have taken a mis-turn." Sir Claude crossed the entrance hall, briefly passing through Elizabeth's field of view, and – without once looking at her – passed under an archway and vanished.

And that had been Elizabeth's first introduction to the Cleremont Avenue household and its occupants.

5

Ants.

They had become more than a hobby to Dr Setiawan, almost an obsession.

Not just ants in truth, but *Hymenoptera* – ants, bees, wasps, and their many cousins.

Setiawan leaned across and carefully dropped a sprinkling of melon seeds onto the far end of a slim, twisting branch. He brushed his hands, one against the other, and hinged down the heavy glass lid. He cleaned his hands on a silk handkerchief, which he replaced in the pocket of his waistcoat, and waited for the activity to unfold.

Hymenoptera. One of the seventeen orders within the class of animals known as insects and – let it be said – the most numerous order of any animal on Earth. Not the most diverse; that honour went to *Coleoptera* – beetles. And certainly not the heaviest by biomass. But in terms of the sheer number of individuals, *Hymenoptera* – with their vast, teeming colonies – held the crown.

But to what degree could you actually think of them as *individuals*?

This point was at the root of Setiawan's fascination. When an individual is ready to sacrifice itself unthinkingly for the colony, has it not surrendered its individuality? Human cells are routinely programmed to die for the good of the organism – *apoptosis*. Following that logic through to ants, isn't the colony therefore the true organism?

Were they *intelligent?*

Of course, the individual isn't intelligent. *But the colony?* So few people seemed to ask the question. But why not intelligent? After all, no-one thinks that an individual human brain cell is intelligent, but we accept without question that millions of them networked together can be. Why could individual ants or bees, when networked together in a colony, not be considered intelligent?

True, they could never communicate as rapidly as nerve cells in a brain. But they had other advantages to compensate.

For one thing, they could be in dozens of different places at once. Returning from a forage, bees had exceptional mechanisms for communicating where to find the best sources of nectar – complex little flight dances. Information could pour in from all corners of the compass and be processed at speed within the hive and acted on. To receive information – process it – make a decision – and provide instructions. Didn't that match the function of a central nervous system? But with the added advantage of *reach*.

Setiawan watched as the first couple of sentinels were already carrying melon seeds back to the nest. Even now, they were laying down invisible chemical markers that would guide their fellow workers where to go. In a short while they'd reach the guard ants, who themselves followed a sophisticated duty roster to protect the nest.

If a colony could replicate the intelligence of a nervous system, did that mean a larger colony could be more intelligent than smaller ones? What if ants could organise into *super*-colonies that could span beyond a single nest?

And could a colony *learn?* Not learn in the sense of finding new information, but learn in the sense of findings new *patterns* of information – autonomous learning?

It was all these questions that Setiawan was studying. He looked across the attic. Previously it comprised a number of small rooms – the servants' quarters – but he'd had the walls knocked down to create a single, larger space. Within it, he had a dozen different glass cabinets, each one about five feet long, and mounted on wheels. At the end of each cabinet was a single circular hole. These holes could either be blocked or – if he was conducting an experiment – linked by Perspex tubing to the hole of a neighbouring cabinet. In this way Setiawan had started to study the interaction between different colonies: when they cooperated, when they fought.

Setiawan was playing god with his ants. He knew that. It was both a thrill – and a source of guilt.

To others, his ant hobby was a mysterious academic leap from anthropology. But to Setiawan the two complemented each other perfectly. They both came down to the same thing: how do groups cooperate, communicate, *learn.*

Setiawan watched as the second wave of ants reached the little pile of melon seeds. Not a few scouts this time, but a steady line of worker ants, following the chemical breadcrumb trail laid down by the scouts. They stretched in a long line down the length of the log

– evenly spaced, organised, numerous. Each one picked up a seed heavier than its own bodyweight before setting off back down the branch.

Setiawan stood back up and stretched. As he did so, a flurry of rain lashed against the window at the far end of the attic. He started, with uncharacteristic nerves.

Strange.

At the back of his mind, he still had the nagging sensation of being watched.

Giving into it for a moment, he walked across to the window. It was set low. He knelt down and looked out. The view looked as it always did at this hour of the evening, except wetter. The wind was driving the rain in rhythmic bursts against the window, like spray against the bridge of a ship. To one side, he could see dimly across row after row of grey slate rooftops, looking like so many waves of an unsettled sea. To the other side, he could see Regent's Park itself, a few miniaturised humans scurrying across it, their outerwear pulled tight about them.

But nothing untoward.

He tried to dismiss the uncanny feeling. Setiawan liked to stay alert to his senses, but his was a bachelor household. It didn't pay to start imagining monsters—

"Excuse me, sir – the telephone."

He started again.

His maid – young and rather in awe of her eccentric employer – had appeared apologetically on the staircase, carrying a small tray. On it was a telephone trailing a long cable.

Setiawan stood up from his eyrie and re-composed himself. He stepped carefully between the glass cabinets and took the phone from her. He seated himself on a chair next to the staircase and placed the phone on a small table next to him, that was positioned there for the purpose.

"That's very kind, Miss Wainwright, thank you," he said, settling into his chair and back into his usual manners. His maid gave a timid nod and disappeared quickly down the staircase.

He placed the receiver to his ear. "Hello, Setiawan speaking." He paused as he listened to the voice at the other end. "Ah, Sir Claude, how lovely to hear from you."

6

Elizabeth watched Sir Claude at his desk, back to the room, speaking on the phone in a low voice.

Here she still was. Still in Sir Claude's study, still at an impasse. Dinner already seemed like half a day ago. Although, in reality, probably just half an hour.

Elizabeth was perched on a low seat in the further of the two bay windows. The sound of the rain clattering against the panes drowned out anything he was saying. In any case, she'd decided against eavesdropping on the master of the house for a second time. She looked out the window. In the soot-coloured light of the storm she could see the wind driving the rain in great billowing gusts. Some distant lightning crackled over the rooftops.

Normally, Elizabeth took a secret thrill in violent weather. It was the Scot within her.

But not today.

She found it distracting, enervating. She wanted to get to the bottom of what Sir Claude knew. Except that Sir Claude was stuck on the phone and the weather was stuck at foul.

Her eye drifted back into the room. Dr James was reading some kind of report or periodical, while sunk deep into a sofa by the fire. It was a studded, green leather sofa. Very club-like, *what a surprise*. There was a large antique globe on a small table next to him and, around the walls, shelf upon shelf of books. The long wall opposite her was covered floor to ceiling in bookshelves, with only a small gap scalloped out for the fireplace. It was hosting a small log fire. Over to the left, she spied a brass spiral staircase. It wound its way up towards a mezzanine gallery, which ran along the left-hand wall and which was lined with – *yes* – more books.

Her gaze was drifting to the opposite side of the room – towards Sir Claude's desk – when her eye picked out a set of library steps. In the context of the room, they looked perfectly at home, almost camouflaged. She was about to ignore them...

Until she noticed them.

These weren't any normal set of library steps. They were unusual, ornate – extraordinary.

For one thing, they were tall. Eight steps high. Running up their right-hand side, all the way to the top, was a fluted, wooden banister. At the top, the last step was large, more like a small platform. The banister ran all the way round it and there was even a small red leather bench on one side – just wide enough to seat two. *Who needs steps like that just to get a book down?*

Thus the man, so the house.

The leather armchairs, the library steps, the study – the whole house seemed like an extension of Sir Claude. It was hard to tell where one ended and the other began. Elizabeth scoffed to herself. It was all clubby, chummy nonsense. Exactly the nostalgic, backward-looking world the country needed to move beyond.

She looked at Sir Claude – he was still talking on

the phone. With a slight moue of impatience, she stood up, stretched ostentatiously, and coughed a couple of times. Sir Claude didn't budge from his conversation. She was just getting ready to try a little impertinence – a louder cough, maybe a yawn – when something else caught her eye.

Between the two bay windows was a rare section of wall that was free of shelving. Instead, it had been covered – *predictably* – in school and university photographs. The sort she imagined were obligatory in a study like this. In amongst them she spotted a framed army photo. There Sir Claude was as a young man, seated at the centre – *predictably* – with fellow officers and troops lined up around him. She checked below. His name was printed on the mounting. He looked like he was in his early twenties, so that checked out. More or less.

Except – there was something strange about the photo, something that didn't sit right. *What was it?*

The uniforms.

They were British alright, but not typical of the Second World War. She'd seen enough of her father's old photos to know. She checked the writing above.

The date read…

…*1915.*

This was from the *First* World War. How old did that make him? She did a quick calculation.

He must be…

…*over 80?*

Elizabeth was confused. She tried to think it through. Sir Claude gave the impression of being a youthful 60-year-old, perhaps even 70 at a stretch – although not like any 70-year-old she knew.

But 80?

Not possible.

Her initial confusion started to subside. It couldn't be him. It must be his father. *Just like this family for them to have the same name.*

She noticed a reflection in the glass.

Sir Claude.

He was standing a few yards behind, staring at her, and smiling his bemused smile. She hadn't noticed his call end. She felt her cheeks redden and then kicked herself for it. She had nothing to apologise for.

She composed herself. And remembered her training. People don't give you information because they like you; they give it because you leave them no choice. She turned around slowly.

It was time to have it out with Sir Claude.

"Look," Sir Claude started, "perhaps we got off on the wrong foot, Miss Belfort—"

"I'm not a Miss, thank you, Sir Claude." Elizabeth reacted with hostile precision. She wasn't about to be bought off by platitudes.

"Ah, my olive branch seems to have been swatted away before I'd even offered it. Should I call you 'Ms' perhaps? That's the latest thing, isn't it?"

"Perhaps we could stop dawdling over introductions? We're past that stage. I would like you to share what it is you know."

"Well, strictly speaking," he replied calmly, "I believe your instructions were to ask me to join the newly formed Alien Advisory Committee? I don't believe C asked that I spill everything I might know to you?"

"Actually, Sir Claude, I am Secretary to the committee. I think we can all agree that – *for the sake of the planet* – the committee needs to work effectively. And for it to do that, all information must be shared. There can be no secrets among its members. It's my job to make sure that sharing happens. Lives may depend on it. So" – Elizabeth drew in a rapid breath for her final assault – "if we are to get along, then I suggest you start being a little less mysterious, and a little more open."

Elizabeth stopped talking.

She was breathing rapidly. She was shocked by her own boldness. But *there* – she'd said it. She was standing face-to-face with one of the government's most senior advisors, chastising him. Her heart was in her mouth. This could be career-ending.

She watched his reaction.

The smile had, sure enough, left his face. As he looked her up and down, he tilted his head. She wondered what was going through it. He was probably horrified that a woman had stood up to him. He'd probably thought it was going to be all flirtation and condescension, and now a woman had actually stood up to him, and he didn't know what to do. The 1970s, she'd decided some years back, was not proving the most gallant of decades. Men hadn't worked out whether they found working women terribly exciting or terribly threatening or – *more likely* – both.

"Why do I feel I'm being interrogated?" he asked.

"Because you are."

"Ha!" Sir Claude exclaimed and then dropped his gaze for a moment. When he raised his head and spoke again his tone had changed to pure sincerity. "There's actually a very good reason why I haven't shared more liberally."

"Which is?"

"Frankly, I doubt you'd believe what I have to say."

"Try me."

Sir Claude sighed.

"Very well, I shall – but could we at least sit?" He indicated the sofa in front of the fire.

Elizabeth was about to lash him another caustic remark about not getting too comfortable.

But just as the words were forming in her mouth, a flash of lightning shot across their eyes.

At the same time – not delayed, but at that exact moment – thunder erupted into the room. No longer thunder of the rumbling, atmospheric kind, but immediate and penetrating. The kind that makes buildings – and civilisation in general – seem suddenly frail. A bolt of lightning had earthed within a hundred yards of the house. The flames in the grate leapt and retreated again, almost extinguishing the fire.

There was no pretence of calm this time. As one, all three of them looked to the windows. More lightning crackled in the further distance.

They turned from the window to look at each other. A wordless understanding passed between them. Almost a bond. Dr James went over to close the curtains, Sir Claude re-kindled the fire, and Elizabeth sat down on the sofa.

7

"Look," Sir Claude began, as he perched on the armrest of a chair by the fire. "This message. Dr James and I thought something like this might in the offing. There have been certain... *Certain*—"

"—signs," Dr James added with a smile, as he sat back down on the sofa, next to Elizabeth.

"Certain signs," Sir Claude repeated.

"Such as?"

"Well..." Sir Claude started re-filling his pipe. "The story starts about ten years ago. *We think*. From about that time, reports started to trickle in of disappearances."

"Disappearances? What was disappearing?"

"People. In strange and not entirely explicable ways."

"Sir Claude, you're not suggesting these disappearances were—"

"I'm not suggesting anything at this stage," Sir Claude interrupted before Elizabeth could scoff. "They were simply what I said they were: reports of disappearances."

"Well, who then?"

"Ah, that's what made this interesting." Sir Claude lit another match. "Scientists and scholars. From across the Western world. From Russia and China too, for all we know. Although, of course, we never will."

He paused while he drew on the flames and re-lit his pipe. He shook the match and threw it in the grate.

"We're now aware of at least four dozen that have disappeared over that time. Biologists and physicists, a few economists, several historians. Some engineers. And doctors... Surgeons actually. And in all cases, we're talking about men – and a few women – with a successful career. In most cases, a happy homelife too. People with a lot to lose in other words. Not your regular candidates for a missing-persons case."

Sir Claude drew on his pipe and exhaled the smoke meditatively into the air. "But here's the thing. I'm talking now as if this was some well-defined narrative. *It wasn't.* At the time, no-one was joining the dots. After all, people disappear all the time. Usually suicide, but just occasionally a person is fleeing from – *I don't know* — gambling debts or an unhappy relationship. Whatever the reason, the relatives often want *to avoid* publicity. They're distraught, they fear they've let the individual down. So, to repeat, no-one realised there was a pattern."

"So how was the pattern spotted. And *when?*"

Sir Claude looked at Elizabeth through narrowed eyes. She met his gaze with sincerity.

"About four years ago," he replied, satisfied he was being taken seriously. "A wife of one of the 'disappeared' – if I can call them that – came forward to report her husband was missing. A distinguished German geneticist. Herr Doktor Yuval Nussbaum. But she claimed more than that. She claimed to have been present at the disappearance. She claimed to have *witnessed* it."

"It's scarcely a disappearance if you see it happen, surely?"

"Indeed. 'Disappearance' no longer felt like the right term."

"So what was the right term?"

"Abduction."

"Abduction?"

"Yes, abduction."

"You mean kidnapped? Abducted by criminals?"

"No, I don't. I mean abducted by..." Sir Claude nodded briefly towards the sky.

"Abducted by—" Elizabeth got to scoff after all. "Oh, *that* kind of abduction. You mean flying saucers over cornfields in Kansas? Visitations at midnight? Strange probes? Really, Sir Claude. Such speculation. And *Star Wars* hasn't even reached our cinemas yet."

Her turn to do bemusement. She landed her mockery with satisfying accuracy. In truth, she hadn't yet seen the movie – no-one in Britain had – but it was creating an almighty fuss in the US.

"Quite," Sir Claude replied equably. "That's exactly how the authorities reacted. They wanted to laugh at her – or, at the very least, suppress her claims. But there was just one problem."

"Which was?"

"She *was* the authorities. Frau Nussbaum is a Director General in the German Ministry for Economic Affairs. One of Germany's most senior government officials and – by all accounts – a straight-talking type devoid of imagination. Women of her ilk don't dream up alien abductions."

Elizabeth didn't reply. Her bemused smile starting to become a little forced.

"This is when it was brought to my attention. It was

C. *Your* C. He couldn't spend departmental time on it, of course – it wouldn't look right, not even in an organisation as secretive as yours. So he called me in. For reasons we'll get to later, he thought I – *we*," Sir Claude added, looking towards Dr James, "might be able to shed some light."

The smoke from Sir Claude's pipe hung in layers across the room. Elizabeth found her attitude softening, even while she resisted it. The truth was, the smell of the pipe reminded her powerfully of her father.

"So what did you do?"

"I interviewed her, of course. Just because someone is important, like Frau Nussbaum, it doesn't mean they can't be delusional. Or, more likely, desperately ashamed of the real reason he might have disappeared."

"So was she delusional? Or ashamed?"

"Actually, she *was* a little ashamed, yes she was," Sir Claude mused. "But not in the way you might think. She was embarrassed to report something so unbelievable. She showed me the spot. The driveway of their suburban house in Bad Godesberg. Near Bonn – on the banks of the Rhine. A rather ordinary place for such an extraordinary event. She only reported it because she felt she had a duty to tell the truth. She was – in short – a very credible witness."

Sir Claude gestured to his nephew. Or – more precisely – to the document he was holding. Dr James leaned across the sofa and offered it to Elizabeth.

"What's this?"

"The report we wrote at the time. It covers the Nussbaum case – and all the others."

Elizabeth started to leaf through it.

"I asked Artemas to go back through the records,

see what he could find. Had there been other strange disappearances? If so, when and where and how many? In short, to see if there was a pattern."

Elizabeth nodded as she leafed through the report. A black-and-white headshot had been glued at the head of each double page, showing – mostly – a well-dressed, middle-aged man. Next to it were some biographical details and a current status: 'Missing'. The facing page provided the details of their last known whereabouts.

"Dr James can tell you more. Artemas?"

"Ah yes!" Dr James exclaimed. "Yes, you see, a surprising number of disappearances from what is really not such a large community. I mean, the academic community. *Hmm?* But never so many as to arouse wider suspicions. Yes... *No.* And with increasing frequency, I'm afraid." Dr James leaned across and enthusiastically prodded the report with his finger. "Many more in the last couple of years than in the preceding ones, you see?"

"How many copies of this exist?" Elizabeth asked. The question was almost a reflex. Her eyes half-closed, she scanned the paper like a connoisseur. The clunky typography suggested an ordinary typewriter, perhaps an Olympia; the slightly blotted ink said *carbon copy*. Probably the top one.

"Just two," Dr James replied. "That's one. Your Director – *C* – has the original."

"Good..." Elizabeth mumbled. *Two copies.* In her profession, you could judge the importance of a report by *how few* copies were made. Her mind moved to another detail. "Most of these abductions... They seemed... They seemed to happen in the middle of a storm?"

"*Hmm?* Yes, strange isn't it."

"Rather convenient for the abductors," she said, trying not to think about the weather outside – trying to sound offhand, even as a shiver ran up her spine.

"Yes, yes… That's one of way of looking at it."

Before Elizabeth could start to wonder what the other way of looking at it might be, Dr James dropped his voice, conspiratorially, and leant towards her. "And would you like to know the most peculiar thing of all? *Hmm?*"

"Err, yes?" Elizabeth replied. She was confused. Her mind was half on the storm, half on the story, and half on him. He wasn't like anyone she'd ever met.

"Well, you see, not one of them turned up. Later, you see? Not one." Dr James looked at her for emphasis over the top of his small, round spectacles. At that moment, Elizabeth noticed his bright green eyes. She saw a lively wit sparkling there – *not exactly the eyes of a simpleton, Elizabeth.*

"In a pool of several dozen disappearances," he continued, "one would expect at least a few to re-surface. Yes? *No?* But not one re-appeared. No."

"So what did you conclude?"

"At this point, nothing," Sir Claude replied. "But it did get us thinking."

"I'm listening."

"Who is so interested in our brightest minds *and why?* They scarcely need our technology – or lessons from us in physics. Not if they can do what they've done. Travel where they've gone."

"What then?"

"So, they must be interested in our planet, Mrs Belfort. Or our species – *or both*. We have to assume, in short, we're at risk. *All of us.*"

Sir Claude was interrupted by the sound – the

vibration – of thunder crackling around the room. It seemingly came from all points of the compass, creating a menacing 360-degree soundscape. As if the eye of the storm was about to pass over the house.

Elizabeth felt twitchy, confused. She was listening to stories that – *logically* – she wanted to scoff at from a man she wanted to dismiss as a fantasist.

However, equally logically, she couldn't. She couldn't imagine many fantasists rising to become senior government advisors, still less ones trusted by C.

*

"Well, let's summarise," Elizabeth resumed, retreating from Sir Claude's last speculation. "On the one hand, we have a strange and unusual message from outer space. You think you know who sent it." Sir Claude inclined his head. Elizabeth was desperate to ask *who* was behind the message. But she restrained herself. The information was useless without context. "On the other hand, we have a set of unexplained abductions. But you don't know who is behind these." Sir Claude nodded again. She picked her next question carefully. "So, Sir Claude, these two phenomena – the message and the abductions – are they connected in some way?"

"Yes and no," Sir Claude replied. "Would you agree, Artemas?"

"Oh, very much so. Yes and no," Dr James nodded, as he enthusiastically agreed to – as far as Elizabeth could tell – *nothing.* "Absolutely."

"Yes and no," Sir Claude repeated, smiling.

"That tells me nothing," Elizabeth retorted. "We're too far in now, Sir Claude, tell me what you know."

She could strike fast with her tongue – she knew that – and it had served her well during her short career in seeing off all manner of inappropriate condescension. And inappropriate *attention.* The one normally followed the other.

Sir Claude drew in a deep breath and turned to face Elizabeth directly. As he stared at her, she could see the fire flickering in the grate behind his shoulder. The storm was sending erratic eddies of wind down the chimney.

"You were told that this message was the first ever communication from outer space. 'First contact', if you like. Correct?"

"Yes."

"Well, that wasn't strictly true."

Sir Claude was still staring at her, deadly serious.

"Alright. What is true then?"

"What is true? Ha! For all I know, alien races have been in contact for millennia. I can't speak for that. All I can say for certain is that today – this message – is *not* first contact."

"Sir Claude, cut to the point. As far as you're aware, when *was* the first contact?"

"1944."

"And how could you possibly know that?"

"Because it's me they contacted."

"*Why… What…*" Elizabeth stopped herself. No more spluttering. She broke eye contact and stared directly into the fire. She drew in a deep breath.

She turned back to him.

"Well, who contacted you? And why in 1944?"

"Because humanity was about to cross a threshold. A very significant threshold."

"Which threshold?"

"The nuclear age."

"Excuse me?"

"Nuclear weapons. The splitting of the atom."

The questions were gathering in Elizabeth's mind faster than she could process them. Certainly faster than she could say them. "Alright... I understand that was a big threshold... So, who was it who contacted you?"

"Let me answer you first with a question. Given this message that we've received, you accept now that other alien civilisations exist?"

"I accept, Sir Claude, the existence of another *civilisation*," Elizabeth replied, putting the word firmly in the singular.

"Well, I wish it could be that simple, truly I do. But it's not. There are alien civilisations – lots of them. They possess technologies that you could only guess at. And even then, you would probably fall short. Technologies that help them to build, technologies that help them to *travel*. And, of course, their darker cousins... Technologies of destruction."

"Are you saying that the creation of nuclear weapons suddenly made us of interest to other races?"

"Not exactly. But close enough."

"And which race contacted you in 1944? Who were they?"

"No, not a race. Just one... *person*. As things turned out, one very special person. She's been a contact ever since. It's through her that Artemas and I have learnt everything that we know about... About the wider Universe. That's why we have some context to this message that's been received."

"And why would she – this *person* – bother? Why did she want to help?"

"She wanted to warn us."

"About what?"

"About what might happen next. About how other civilisations might start to reach out to us. You see her own planet had passed the nuclear threshold some while earlier. Let's just say, it didn't work out well for them."

"And so it's through her that you know – *think* you know," Elizabeth corrected herself, "who sent the message?"

"Yes."

"Well..." Elizabeth was about to get to the question. *The* question.

Who had sent the message?

But she paused.

Every piece of information from Sir Claude half-answered one question and raised a dozen more. Her head was spinning. She felt like a hockey puck – each new piece of information sent her spinning helplessly across the ice in a new direction.

Who had sent the message?

"Who... *Who*..."

The question froze in her mouth.

A different reflex kicked in, a protective one. Another part of her training. *Disinformation.* Disinformation could do more harm than useful information could do good. *Avoid it.*

Elizabeth stopped herself in her tracks.

"I'm sorry, Sir Claude, but this could all be complete fantasy. Can you actually *prove* any of this? Not just a missing-persons report—" Elizabeth waved the dossier in her hand "—but *real* proof?"

"Indeed. I don't expect you to take it on trust. I wouldn't either. You need evidence."

"I do."

"Then you must have some."

"When?"

Sir Claude paused while he fixed her with his penetrating stare. Elizabeth could see thoughts flashing behind his eyes. And then he appeared to make a decision.

"Tomorrow," he replied at length. "Would that be soon enough?"

"Tomorrow will be fine—"

Elizabeth was cut short. The storm hurled another violent gust of rain against the house. Even behind the heavily lined curtains, they could hear the windows rattle violently. Elizabeth shuddered. A small, unwelcome voice in her brain was wondering whether this storm was of natural origin.

She dismissed the thought. She didn't want to start imagining aliens around every corner. *Ridiculous.* Her mind was going nowhere without evidence.

"About tomorrow morning," she resumed, returning briskly to the *terra firma* of practicalities. "You will accompany me to the committee meeting in Whitehall?"

"Oh, I should think so," Sir Claude replied. "What time?"

"7 a.m. I shall be here at 6 to collect you."

"An early start. I take it you will be staying the night?"

"Excuse me?"

"You don't propose travelling in this mess?" Sir Claude gestured with his pipe towards the windows. "I've already had Daniels make up a room for you."

"Thank you, Sir Claude, but no." *Here comes the inappropriate attention,* thought Elizabeth. *Another*

47

older man, trying it on. "You will permit me to use your phone? To call a taxi?"

"Are you *sure?*" he asked.

"Quite sure, thank you."

"Well, if you insist." Sir Claude shrugged his shoulders and made his way to his desk. "At least allow me to call for you." There was a black Bakelite phone next to a small writing pad. He picked up the handset with one hand and – after locating a phone number – started rotating the dialer with the other.

He was about halfway through the number when a shattering sound ripped through the room.

*

Lightning had struck the roof of the house.

It was a noise that could split logs. A noise that they *felt* more than heard. Like a mighty hammer had been smashed over the roof. As 30 million volts of electricity tried to find their frantic way to the ground through the non-conducting stone and timberwork of 55 Cleremont Avenue, the sound and the vibrations of their struggle ripped down each side of the building, before meeting again under the floor and amplifying. The lights went out instantly. A couple of bulbs in the central pendant shattered. The phone went stone dead in Sir Claude's hand.

"Good grief!"

"*What*... What just happened?" Elizabeth gasped.

"Oh! Well… How exciting!" Dr James chuckled. "I believe we've just been hit by lightning."

"I believe you're right, Artemas," Sir Claude replied, recovering most of his cool. "Well, I'll be deuced. Can't say that's ever happened before."

The room hadn't gone entirely black. The flames in the fireplace were flickering – erratic but alight.

Elizabeth made her way across the room to the curtains and pulled one back. Lightning was flickering over the city, connecting the rooftops to the roiling clouds above in jagged lines.

"We must check everyone else in the house is alright," Sir Claude continued. "First, some candles."

Elizabeth watched Sir Claude's silhouette feel about in one of the desk drawers. He pulled out a couple of candle holders. This was no surprise to her; every household was well supplied. Candles were as common as power cuts, which were very common. But what people didn't tend to have were—

Oil lamps.

Juckes, the butler, appeared at the doorway, carrying two of them. The old-fashioned kind with the pear-shaped glass bulb.

"Is everyone alright in here, sir?" he asked with calm urgency.

"Quite well, thank you, Juckes," Sir Claude replied. "Is everyone in the house alright? Any sign of fire?"

"I've sent Daniels to check in the attic, sir. I think we're alright. Meantime, I've asked Mrs Carstairs to go and light the other lamps."

"Indeed?" Sir Claude replied, as he took one of the lamps from his butler. "Best go and help her, Juckes. We don't want Mrs Carstairs accidentally to finish what the lightning started."

"Quite so, sir. We should be able to get the main corridors illuminated soon enough."

Elizabeth looked again at this man they called Juckes, who had managed to remain so calm and react so quickly in the wake of a lightning strike. She was beginning to wonder just exactly what kind of a butler he was. His face had a past, she'd sensed that as soon as she'd met him. His hair was cropped short, he was a little below average height. Even in the low light of the lamps, she could see his nose had been broken once before, possibly twice. He had the reserved look of a man unlikely to start a fight but quite capable of finishing it. Not handsome, not ugly – just self-contained.

"Will there be anything else, sir?"

"No, Juckes, don't let me detain you."

"Very good, sir."

A moment after he left, Lady Danziger appeared in the doorway.

"*Darling...*" Sir Claude exclaimed. He covered the wide space towards her in what looked to Elizabeth like two bounds. "Are you alright?" he asked, as he placed his hands on either arm and kissed her with surprising tenderness.

"Yes, quite well, thank you. What an entrance you've made, Claude," she teased. "As always." *She actually teased.* "And you? Are you well? Your journey?" She looked him up and down.

"Oh, tolerable, tolerable," Sir Claude replied, still holding her arms. "They made an awful fuss at the airport in Moscow. But they let me go eventually."

"Well perhaps we could dial down the drama from here? Might that be possible?" Lady Danziger smiled.

Elizabeth wondered at these two aloof creatures. She would have expected their greeting to have all the warmth of a pair of wooden toy soldiers leaning against each other. Instead, she saw an unfeigned pleasure. Lady Danziger seemed to have lost several of her hard edges – *although that probably leaves a dozen more.*

"An eventful evening, I hadn't expected to greet you like this," Sir Claude continued as he released his wife's arms. "A lightning strike and a mystery visitor. How much more will this evening bring, I wonder?" Sir Claude's eyes were back to their normal sparkle, as he turned to look at Elizabeth.

And there they both were, staring at her.

Just for a moment – as they stood together – they appeared to Elizabeth as a single, harmonised force, powerful and quite irresistible.

"And you, Elizabeth?" Lady Danziger asked. "I couldn't forgive myself if we sent you outside in this. You will stay the night?"

"Yes, of course."

8

Elizabeth stood at the doorway for a moment, examining the room.

She had just been shown up by one of the maids, Daniels, and as she looked at her bedroom for the night the first thing Elizabeth felt was...

Peace.

Unexpected and thoroughly welcome.

A single lamp was burning on a dressing table. Its glow illuminated a room that was small and quite lovely. Gone was all the wood panelling and burnished leather that dominated the rest of the house – replaced by simple furniture and pleasant, pale yellow wallpaper. Here was a room that even in the dark looked light.

Against the wall opposite was a single bed. Towels and a white nightgown had been laid out on it. On the dressing table next to the bed, a few simple essentials for the night had been set out tidily. It was perfect.

A flash of lightning sparked through the room, and then a peal of thunder. The sound seemed less immediate than earlier. Now Elizabeth stopped to think about it, she could barely hear the rain.

There was a window just above the bed. The curtains were still drawn back. With the darkness outside, she could only see herself and the room reflected in the glass. Elizabeth turned down the lamp until it was just a flicker and wriggled across the bed on her knees.

She cupped her hands around her face and pressed it to the window.

So that's why I can't hear the rain...

She could see now that her first-floor window didn't look onto the outside world. It looked into a conservatory. She peered left and right. An enormous, two-storey structure. It was at the back of the house. As her eyes adjusted to the low light beyond, she could see it was long as well as tall, probably stretching the whole length of the house. It was dense with plants and foliage – more botanical garden than conservatory.

She spotted Juckes below to her left. He was in a clearing towards the centre. He was lighting a number of candles and a couple of carriage lamps that were laid out on a large round wooden table. Just behind him was some kind of stove, with a green-painted flue that rose all the way up to the glass roof.

After a few moments a stout, elderly lady came to join him. She started tidying up around the table. Her movements seemed laboured. That must be the housekeeper, Elizabeth thought to herself, *Mrs Carstairs*.

It was all a little strange. They didn't look like they were clearing away for the night. They looked like they were getting the place ready. Perhaps for the morning? For breakfast?

Although that didn't explain why Juckes was lighting more lamps.

Intrigued, Elizabeth continued to watch as he started hanging the lamps from hooks on the iron pillars –

elegant, ivory-painted pillars – that supported the opposite wall of the conservatory. Elizabeth wondered at the lamps, the staff, the calm efficiency with which order had been restored after the lightning strike. *Honestly,* she thought to herself, *this house prefers to live in the past.*

As the light below gathered strength, a bewitching world of fathomless green slowly revealed itself. Elizabeth saw dense bushes with narrow paths winding between, she saw orchids and other flowers glimmering faintly. She saw the trunks of palm trees reaching up and exploding into curling green branches in front of her window, some of the fronds just touching the glass roof above.

A fluttering motion caught her eye. Not four yards away a bird settled on a branch. She gave a little gasp. It was a Major Mitchell's cockatoo, very rare. With white and light pink plumage, and a red crest, she recognised it immediately. It returned her gaze with a supercilious stare that suggested she had nothing to offer that could possibly interest it. A moment later, a second, larger bird landed nearby. Another cockatoo – mostly black, it was barely visible in the low light. A flash of red beneath its eye gave it away. The black palm cockatoo.

She had picked up birdwatching from her father. She would study the books for hours as they waited in their hide for a rare glimpse of a goshawk or a honey buzzard. But these cockatoos – she had only ever seen pictures. As the light increased, Elizabeth stared in awe at the black cockatoo in particular – individuals had been known to live to over a hundred years.

She smiled to herself. People bought curtains with this kind of aviary designed on them. But she was looking at the real thing, right here in front of her bedroom.

And then her eye caught another movement. She shrank back. Sir Claude had entered the conservatory. Like some cat in its jungle, he was stalking along one of the paths towards the clearing at the centre.

Had he spotted her? She watched as he passed beneath her window and approached Juckes purposefully. The two started talking.

Elizabeth decided she'd done enough spying for one day. She withdrew slowly from the window and pulled the curtains shut.

*

"I think you should get underway now."

"I agree, sir."

"Take the Daimler. And take extra care," Sir Claude cautioned. "Dr Setiawan likes to chat. Don't let him. I rather suspect events are about to accelerate. We need him here."

"Very good, sir. I shall be off," the butler replied. "Unless there's anything else?"

"Actually, just one thing... Our guest. What do you make of her? Can she be relied upon?"

The butler paused to think, his impassive face giving little away. He chose his words carefully.

"I reckon she knows how to look after herself, sir."

"Ha! Yes. I was rather coming to that conclusion myself. But I'm not sure she's entirely taken to us."

"Give her a little time, sir. She'll come round. I feel sure of it. If I may speak plainly?"

Sir Claude waved his hand.

"She's a young lady in a man's world. I've seen this

before, sir. A few times. She's not feeling sure of her position, she wants to prove herself. We're probably seeing the worst of her."

"Ha. Possibly. Possibly."

9

Elizabeth turned off the tap and glided the hand towel over and between her ringless fingers. The smell of the soap lingered in her nostrils. It was exquisite – like a botanical garden. Replacing the towel on its little brass holder, she crossed the room to the dressing table.

She sat in front of it and picked up the hairbrush that had been left out. There wasn't much, but all the essentials were here. Everything Elizabeth needed. She wasn't one of those women who had to bring half her bathroom with her just to spend a night away.

Which was just as well, because there had been so many nights away. As she started to tug with the brush at the knots in her hair, she looked in the mirror and reflected on the demands her job made of her. *Of her marriage.* There had been so many nights away, sometimes a night at home felt more like a night away from being away.

She wondered if her husband was missing her.

She wondered if she was missing *him.* They were rather unconventional for such a conventional couple. On the face of it, a perfect match. He was the brilliant student, the athlete, the golden boy. And in the same profession as her, the star of their class. For her part, she was nearly as good an athlete, nearly the star of their class. And she was streets ahead of the other girls. Well, *the other girl.*

So there it was. She had a husband who was perfectly matched to her, and one she could look up to. That's what every girl wants, surely? To be with someone who's self-possessed, a husband who can play it cool. What an improvement on the second-rate fools who mooned after her.

But was her husband too cool sometimes?

Did he even need her?

The truth was, things had gone wrong in the marriage. It had turned sour. Or stale. Or something. And now she and Charles were going through a 'trial separation'. Elizabeth hated the phrase, *hated it.* She hadn't told a soul and nor had Charles. Not her mother, not his parents, no-one. That at least they could agree on. Two months ago, he had taken a short-term let on a one-bedroom flat a couple of miles across town. And here they now were.

The day-to-day differences in her life were small. Almost laughably small. He was away – she was away – she occasionally saw him in their flat before – she occasionally saw him now.

But it was agony.

Two decisive people caught in a state of indecision. She tilted her head and started working through the knots on the other side of her long, auburn hair. They were waiting for a judgement on their marriage. A decision. *Do we stay – or go?* Their lives were balanced on a fulcrum like two children on a seesaw that must surely pivot one way or the other – but hadn't yet. A judgement would have to be made. But how it was going to be made – or when or by whom – she had no idea.

And so, although she would never admit it to Sir Claude, she was glad to be away. Glad not to return to a home that was barely a home. It didn't matter much anyway. It was the sort of flat you could return to after a night away – after a fortnight away – and find unchanged.

*

Lightning flickered around Elizabeth, forcing its way in at the edges of the curtains and through the small gap between them. Thunder followed it through. Stripped of much of its noise by the extra layers of building that insulated the room, Elizabeth experienced the thunder more as vibration than sound. And it seemed all the more elemental for it.

The storm turned Elizabeth's thoughts to home. Her *first* home. Scotland. She tilted her head further to the side and started working through the knots at the lower end of her hair. The rambling lodge in the Highlands, rain-drenched, where the temperature was never more than ten degrees if you were more than ten feet from a fire. And yet it was filled with warmth. Games of hide-and-seek that would last until lunchtime, her father searching up one staircase, while she and her sister crept down the other. She started to wonder how much was left of that little girl, Elspeth MacBey?

'Elspeth' was the first to go. Through childhood, it seemed as natural as her own hair. Her grandmother named her that as a baby, the Scottish diminutive for Elizabeth. But on arrival in London, she started hearing it through other people's ears. Old-fashioned – faintly ridiculous. Elizabeth was the name in her passport (her *real* passport). That worked better.

Next to go was MacBey. Eighteen months after the move south. She and Charles decided they were right for each other and got through the formalities quickly. Some working women were starting to keep their maiden names – but she sensed he would've been disappointed. Belfort she became.

And lastly her accent.

It had started disappearing at her Scottish boarding school, where posh English accents were the rule. She was already sensitive about being a scholarship girl; she didn't want to provide another excuse for teasing. And now, after her five years in London, quite without meaning to, she had mostly lost it. Just a faint lilt gave her away – and even then, only to a fellow Scot.

And so somehow – by degrees – and with no deliberate plan – Elspeth MacBey had become Elizabeth Belfort.

And here she now was.

The knots in her hair had long since cleared. Reluctantly, she replaced the brush on the dressing table. She looked up at the mirror.

It was such a serious face staring back.

Pale, too pale. The fine, light dusting of freckles around the bridge of her nose was more visible than before. She ran a critical finger down one cheek. The rosy flush had gone and so had her girlhood prettiness. Age 28. Her aquiline, almost classical nose was a little more prominent than before. Her features were regular – still attractive perhaps. Or maybe *handsome* was the right word. In any case, grown up. So grown up. She didn't look like someone who was about to suggest a spontaneous trip to the beach, or a night out on the town.

But still she kept her hair long.

She'd insisted.

It was wildly impractical for the job she was in, but some small and stubborn voice deep inside demanded it. She knew what it was of course. Even as her job became more and more serious, and her life moved further from the Highlands, and she saw less of her family, and her marriage faded, she was clinging to an old part of herself. Something essential. Something that reminded her of the girl who used to play all day among the heather.

*

Elizabeth extinguished the lamp and slipped into bed.

Lying there, in the dark, she found herself – to her surprise – not thinking about the mad revelations of the past twelve hours. What was the point? Either Sir Claude could produce evidence, at which point it was worth dwelling on. Or he couldn't, in which case it never was.

She found herself wondering instead about the house she was in – about the *household* – and all its contrasts.

Her thoughts gathered into a single observation: nothing was quite what it seemed. There was a butler who seemed to be far more than a butler. There was his master, who seemed like a bounder but had a surprisingly tender relationship with his wife. And the wife, who seemed like an ice queen, but wasn't.

And the house itself. During dinner, she'd first assumed the place to be backward-looking and moribund. *All Silver Jubilee and no Sex Pistols.* And yet it possessed a strange and lively energy – and not just from the bolt of lightning.

Although that probably helped.

And then her thoughts turned to Dr James, the final contradiction. The simpleton with the PhD. She found herself thinking again about this strange creature. She'd never met anyone before who seemed able to smile at everything that happened. Literally *everything*. Do you have to be a simpleton to reach such a state of simplicity? Or something else? *Face the facts, Elspeth, the man has a PhD.* Whatever had creased a smile permanently round the corners of his mouth, it wasn't stupidity.

And then Elizabeth realised, with the force of a revelation – a revelation that shook the sleep out of her – that she had stopped smiling at anything.

When did that happen?

How did that happen?

Elizabeth pondered this realisation with dismay. She wondered how she'd ever sleep.

But – as surely as fatigue follows a caffeine rush – her restless mind sank unwittingly below the ebb of consciousness.

10

Juckes eased down on the accelerator and brought the car to a stop.

In this part of town, the thunder and the lightning had intensified. Propelled by the wind, the rain was arcing towards the windscreen of the old Daimler like tracer. Juckes peered towards Dr Setiawan's house. It was set back about twenty yards from the kerb, barely visible through the rain and darkness, even at that short distance.

Juckes knew exactly why Sir Claude wanted him to take this car. Dr Setiawan was a little old school; a 1949 Daimler in burgundy red was the sort of carriage he'd appreciate.

But it was more than that.

This car was large, strong and – in any other weather – had excellent visibility. Juckes looked again through the large vertical windows on all sides of the car, spying for danger.

But he had little chance of spotting anything. Water was falling, sluicing, splashing, bouncing; lightning was periodically splitting the sky. The foul weather gave the strange sensation that everything was in motion and, at the same time, nothing was. No-one was out and nothing stirred. The only untoward thing

Juckes spotted was an old strip of Union Jack bunting. It had snapped in the middle and the two loose ends were fluttering violently from the branches to which they had been tied.

Juckes tightened his mac at the waist and reached across to the passenger seat to retrieve the umbrella he'd left in the footwell. He paused to take a deep breath. And then – leaving the engine running and the wipers at full speed – he opened the door, slammed it shut behind him and made a dash for the porch.

Back under cover, he gave a ring on the bell pull.

The door opened instantly. It was Dr Setiawan's maid, Wainwright – the shy, pretty one. She must've been waiting by the door. She and Juckes nodded to each other in silent acknowledgement. She stepped aside and Juckes saw Dr Setiawan behind her in the hallway. He was sitting on a chair, knees together, hands folded carefully on his lap – as tidy as a mannequin – with a large leather travelling valise on the ground next to him. He was wearing an expensive-looking grey overcoat, with a dark, fur-lined collar.

"Good evening, sir." As Juckes doffed his bowler hat, water dripped from the rim to the floor.

"Juckes – you poor man. What awful weather."

"Yes, sir. A bit soggy out. Do you have everything you need?"

"Yes, I'm quite ready, thank you."

"Very good." Juckes paused a for a moment. "Sir Claude instructed that—"

"Yes, I'm quite aware," Dr Setiawan interrupted. "I'm not to engage you in idle conversation and I'm not to dawdle – and especially not outside!" He held up a single finger like a well-drilled child.

"Very good, sir." Juckes permitted himself a hint of

a smile. Replacing his hat on his head, he stepped into the house and reached for Dr Setiawan's valise. He set it back down in the porch for a second, while he opened the umbrella. He then picked up the valise in his left hand and raised the umbrella in his right. "Shall we?"

Dr Setiawan stepped forward under the umbrella. Juckes wanted to ask him to run – or at least jog – down the path. But he checked himself. Something about the man just didn't look rush-able.

Brisk was the most Juckes could hope for. He angled the umbrella into wind. The two of them stepped out into the rain and started making their way down a pathway of drenched gravel.

*

And then it happens.

Something brutally hard and unyielding knocks against Juckes' shoulder, sending him spinning downwards.

He's already sprawled over the lawn before he starts to gain awareness of the violent new reality.

He hears a strangled yelp from Setiawan.

As Juckes tries to pull himself onto his knees on the sodden grass, he sees the umbrella skipping across the garden – its shape deformed – pushed along by the wind – or the force of the knock – or both. He sees the valise has opened, some of its contents strewn across the sodden grass.

He has quick reactions, Juckes, very quick. As a young boxer, he could recover his senses from a knockdown quicker than most.

But not quick enough, not this time.

He looks up. He sees something disappearing into the sky, moving with speed *and force*. He thinks he hears another yelp or scream – maybe – and then gone.

Dr Setiawan has vanished. Back on his feet now, Juckes turns around and looks in all directions. But sees nothing. The foul weather and the darkness have closed back over the incident as mercilessly as the sea closing over the top of a sinking yacht.

All that is left is a little flotsam and jetsam. An umbrella caught in a hedge, a bowler hat on the lawn next to an open suitcase.

11

A sudden crash.

Elizabeth started from her sleep. Bits of her brain began firing immediately, but completely out of sync with other bits which weren't. Her mind raced and fumbled like a drunk trying to run.

Another bolt of lightning?

That's not possible, lightning doesn't strike twice? Or maybe it does?

Elizabeth shook her head and sat upright in bed. *Glass.* There was definitely a sound of shattering glass. A lot of glass. *Does lightning strike glass?*

No. And if it was lightning where was the sound of thunder.

What else could it be?

An intruder?

She sat still in bed, listening, trying to pull herself out of a deep sleep she hadn't even realised she'd fallen into.

The house was quiet again.

She stayed very still.

Nothing.

Slowly she reached out in the darkness for the matches. She fumbled, they dropped to the floor. She cursed herself quietly. *Think, Elizabeth.* Then act.

Leaving the matches on the floor, she pulled the curtain back a fraction and looked into the conservatory below. A single carriage lamp was burning dimly on the round wooden table. She spotted two figures in the dark – indistinct in the low light – and she immediately let the curtain fall back into position.

Intruders? Possibly. *Or members of the household?* Also possible. But there was something furtive about them. And it was Heaven-only-knows-what hour of the night.

Much more carefully – her mind awake now – she reached down and picked up the matches. She slipped out of bed. Under the pressure of her weight, the floorboards creaked. It was a noise that was imperceptible by day but, in the dead of night, went off like a firework. She winced and slid her feet into the slippers that had been left out for her. She crossed the room – each footstep going off like an echo of the first firework – and pulled a dressing gown from the hook on the door. She felt for the lamp and, without lighting it, reached for the door handle.

She pulled back her bedroom door and listened for noises in the corridor.

Nothing.

Nothing except the sound of her own pulse in her throat. She paused. She tried to remember her training. *Panic is your enemy.* Keep your breathing measured – focus on what you can control – picture a successful outcome.

The mantra almost worked and her pulse beat a little slower. She stepped into the corridor, leaving the door ajar behind her.

The corridor was pitch black. She saw a large trunk

against the opposite wall. She set her lamp down and lit it. Further along the trunk, she spied a brass telescope, fully extended. *Unconventional, but it'll do.* She picked it up and carefully collapsed it back inside itself, until it was just a foot-and-a-half long, heavy and dangerous. She started advancing down the corridor.

She had moved forward about five yards when the sound of creaking floorboards reached her ears.

She stopped – her pulse racing again – hoping the creaking was from her own feet.

But it wasn't.

Elizabeth hurriedly put the lamp down on a chair next to her and extinguished it. She crouched low and waited, telescope in hand.

The creaking continued. It was followed by the quiet – *loud* – rattle of a doorknob. A door ahead to her right opened. She could just make out the movement as her eyes readjusted to the dark. A figure stepped into the corridor.

Elizabeth's fingers squeezed tight around the telescope. The brass was slippery beneath the sweat of her palm.

And then a voice. A quiet – *very loud* – voice.

"*Hmm... Let me see... Matches, yes, matches.*"

Dr James.

He must've been sleeping in the next-door room. He was trying to light his lamp while holding it.

"*Oh dear.*"

Elizabeth heard his box of matches drop to the ground.

Her pulse started to calm a little. She put the telescope down on the same chair as her lamp. She reached into her pocket and, with hands that were shaking a little less, she lit a match.

"Dr James, it's me," she said, as she struck it. "Please let me help you." Despite her relief, a tremble was still audible in her voice.

"Oh, how very kind, thank you," Dr James replied, with all the anxiety of a man who's run out of breadcrumbs while feeding the ducks.

Elizabeth stepped forward and, while he held the glass bulb aloft, she carefully lit the wick.

"That's really very kind, hmm. Thank you, Miss, err, that's to say Ms…"

They'd just run into each other in the dark, there was very likely an intruder in the house, and the man was worrying *how to address her?*

"It's Mrs Belfort," she said, and then immediately regretted sounding so formal.

"Ah yes, I see Mrs—"

"My first name is Elizabeth," she interrupted hastily. But immediately regretted that too. It was far too *in*formal. He'd never use it. *Why can't there be something in the middle?*

"Ah yes, I see…"

"My maiden name was MacBey," she blurted out on an impulse.

"Excuse me? Did you say Mrs Vey—"

"No, with a 'B', Mrs—"

"Mrs B?"

"No, I said—"

Elizabeth stopped and did something she hadn't done all day. *All week.* She laughed. A quiet, suppressed laugh – almost a giggle – that slipped out despite herself into the quietness of the dark corridor.

"You know what?" she said. "Mrs B will do fine."

"Oh? Really? Well, very good then. *Mrs B*. Shall we?" Dr James gestured in a general *onwards* kind of direction.

"Yes, let's," Elizabeth replied, as they set off into the dark.

As physical protection in a dangerous situation, Dr James was about as reassuring as a rolled-up newspaper.

But on some other level his presence was entirely reassuring. Somehow it felt like nothing really bad could happen while she was with this man.

Elizabeth forgot to fetch the telescope from the chair.

*

A minute or so later, Elizabeth wondered for the first time – as she extinguished the lamp and put it down on a side table – why Dr James was fully dressed? It was she-had-no-idea-what hour of the night.

They had reached the ground floor. They crossed a small drawing room and advanced towards a glass double-door that led into the conservatory. Elizabeth pressed herself against the side of the door frame, minimising her profile, as she peered in.

"Why are you doing that?"

"Well… Well, I think there's an intruder in there."

"Oh no, no. *Haha*," Dr James chuckled. "I mean yes, there is someone there. But scarcely an intruder."

"But what about the smashing of glass earlier?" Elizabeth was starting to feel a little foolish.

"Ah yes, yes. *That.* Yes, that was a little clumsy," Dr James replied. "Probably a navigational error of some sort."

"A navi—" Elizabeth stopped herself. "Well, who is it then?"

"Ah… Yes, that might take some explaining."

"Well then, I intend to find out," Elizabeth replied, reasserting control, and stepping into the conservatory carefully but with determination.

"Yes, of course," Dr James muttered, as he set off behind her. "But best not to rush. You might be a little, err… You might find it a bit—"

Elizabeth put an index finger to her mouth to shush him. They were behind a large, abundant shrub. The single lamp that she'd seen earlier was still some yards away – maybe fifteen or twenty. The path in front was laid with woodchip. *That should be quiet underfoot*, Elizabeth calculated. Keeping close to the bushes, but not so close as to brush the pendulous leaves, she stepped with light feet along the path for about five or ten yards. She spotted the trunk of a palm tree and slipped behind it.

The palm had two trunks, joined at the base. Peering through the vee-shaped cleft between them, she now had a better view of the figure with his back to her.

It was Sir Claude.

Once again, Elizabeth found herself snooping on the master of the house. And once again, she experienced the same strange – unaccustomed – freezing. She couldn't move back and she couldn't move forward. Either would reveal her presence.

Again, she had nothing to apologise for – she was with his nephew, they were investigating a strange noise in the night, she was actually doing *him* a service.

But there it was. She froze anyway.

Beyond Sir Claude's right shoulder, she could just glimpse the edge of a head – the person he must be talking to. Was he – *she?* – wearing a green hat?

And then a voice becomes audible.

It's a female voice. The tone is not unpleasant, but the accent is unusual.

"…we've identified the threat. And it's not who you think. We believe the people really behind these disappearances are…"

The voice trails away.

Elizabeth strains to hear. *Are they whispering?*

"You can come out now, Mrs Belfort," Sir Claude calls out suddenly – clearly – without even turning. "And you too, Artemas."

Elizabeth steps out from behind the shrubs, sheepish, confused. Sir Claude stands up and turns around to face her.

"Allow me to introduce" – Sir Claude steps aside as he talks – "my guest."

Sir Claude continues the introduction, but to Elizabeth his resonant voice has just become a distant muttering. She doesn't hear it. He says something about his guest accidentally breaking some of the conservatory windows on arrival. But she doesn't hear that either. She doesn't hear anything. She only sees. She sees a head – a face – green, with three nostrils. A long neck. Like nothing of this Earth. *Not* of this Earth. Elizabeth sees it for a moment at one angle and then, as her body starts to fold beneath her, from another angle.

And then her body collapses. She passes out.

Pfft.

Gone.

12

A dull throbbing in her head was the first thing that started to drag Elizabeth from dreamless oblivion back to painful reality.

Her eyes blinked open effortfully.

They took in greenery – plants – low lighting reflecting against glass. She closed them again and waited for the throbbing to abate. She became aware of talking. The gentle hum of several people in quiet discussion.

She reopened her eyes.

She saw her legs were laid out flat in front of her, with a blanket across them. She was on some kind of reclining chair. Her body felt comfortable, cushioned – a few undefined aches were coming from somewhere she couldn't pinpoint yet – but mostly fine.

Except for her head. Which really hurt.

Something was pressing cold against the pulsing above her right ear. She realised it was a bag of ice. Her thoughts started trying to arrange themselves.

What's happened? Why does my head hurt?
Where am I?

She turned and saw a table – a large round wooden table – and several people seated at it. There were a few lamps around the table and beyond that the dark windows of the conservatory. *The conservatory.* Fragmented pieces of the mad night started arranging themselves in a haphazard jigsaw in her still-fogged mind.

"Ah! The patient returns to us!" a loud and rather too resonant voice declared.

"Sssh! Not so loud," a firm but much kinder voice admonished, from right next to her. "The poor girl's head must be throbbing."

It was Lady Danziger. She was seated at the round table with the others, but she was turned away from them to tend to Elizabeth.

Lady Danziger? The realisation jolted Elizabeth back into the room. Not Lady Danziger the ice queen, but Lady Danziger kind, attentive, *warm.* Even while holding ice.

"You should not have let her meet Za-Farka that way, Claude," Lady Danziger chided, as she removed the ice and gently dabbed a towel on the bruise that lay beneath Elizabeth's hair. "You could've warned her, given her time to prepare herself." She spoke into Elizabeth's ear. "I'm just trying to bring down the swelling, my dear. You took quite a tumble." The ice was wrapped in a tea towel; she reapplied it to Elizabeth's head.

"How are you feeling now, Mrs Belfort?" another voice asked.

Elizabeth squinted through her headache. It was Juckes.

"I'm fine, I think," she replied. "Really, you don't need to make all this fuss, I'm sure I'll be alright."

"Take your time, ma'am," Juckes replied. "When I first met Za-Farka – that's who you saw earlier – I had a similar reaction."

Elizabeth didn't believe him for a minute. But it was kind of him to say it.

"And when Za-Farka first met a human," Sir Claude started chuckling, "she probably found it pretty strange. Pink skin, two nostrils – can you imagine? I dare say she fainted too."

"Well, if it was you, I'm not surprised," Lady Danziger shot back.

"Very likely, very likely. I'm apt to make women swoon."

"*Urgh* – ignore him," Lady Danziger said to Elizabeth with a sparkle in her eye. "He needs me, Mrs Belfort," she continued in a loud whisper, "I'm the only one who can put up with him."

Elizabeth smiled. Clearly the pair lived for this kind of sparring.

"Just be glad you didn't meet any of her compatriots," Sir Claude resumed. "You know some of her species grow a second head?"

"You're teasing me?"

"Actually, he isn't," Lady Danziger replied. "Her species is kind and social. As a response to severe trauma, an individual sometimes develops a second head."

"Somewhere to store their negativity," Sir Claude added cheerily.

Elizabeth nodded, not sure how to respond. She looked round the table instead. Juckes was sitting one side of Sir Claude, Dr James on the other. And Daniels, the maid, was there. Seated next to her was an elderly, matronly figure, with kind, watery eyes – Mrs Carstairs again, the housekeeper. There they all were. The whole shooting match. All of them fully dressed, all of them looking at her with concern.

Elizabeth felt self-conscious. She looked at the blankets that had been laid over her legs – she looked at her dressing gown – and back at the table. She felt like an aged invalid. And she was probably the youngest in the room.

She shifted on her reclining chair. "Thank you, Lady Danziger, you've been very kind. Let me hold that," Elizabeth said as she took the ice pack from her hostess. She slid her legs down from the reclining chair and started to stand up.

Blood rushed from her head. She momentarily felt faint. Small stars sparked in her head in a prism-burst of colours. She staggered.

Lady Danziger sprang to her feet with surprising athleticism and placed two steadying hands on her shoulders.

"Are you sure you're alright?"

"Thank you, Lady Danziger – but yes, quite sure," Elizabeth replied, clearing pain from her head through simple force of will. She moved towards the one spare seat at the round table, between Dr James and Mrs Carstairs.

"So," she said, as she started to sit down, "am I allowed to know what's going on here? Is your... Is your *guest* still here, Sir Claude?"

"No, no, dear," Lady Danziger replied first. "Don't worry. She's left already."

"Za-Farka had to return quickly," Sir Claude continued. "In case she was missed."

"So who... Who exactly is she? If I'm allowed to ask?"

"Of course. I think you've earned that much. Za-Farka is my source. The one I mentioned when we spoke earlier."

"*Alright*... So why did she come?"

"She came to share something with me. Two things actually."

"Which are?"

"Well, the first thing she shared is that most precious commodity of all." Sir Claude smiled a knowing smile at Elizabeth. "The one you'll know well from your job."

"Information?"

"Indeed."

"And?"

"Well... The good news is that we now have a clearer picture of the situation. We now know who is behind the abductions. Za-Farka came as soon as she learnt. She doesn't have much detail about them yet, but she'll gather it as quickly as she can. We can expect a second visit."

A hundred questions were suddenly jostling to reach Elizabeth's mouth. So many, they were blocking each other. She fell back onto something simpler.

"That's the good news. So what was the bad news?"

"The bad news is that we have very little time," Sir Claude replied. "We're going to have to leave this house in the next two to three hours, preferably sooner."

"What? *Why?* Don't tell me something else has happened?"

"I'm afraid it has."

"In this house?"

"No, elsewhere. A friend of mine, Dr Setiawan. An expert on South-East Asian forest tribes."

"Well, what's happened to him?"

Sir Claude looked at Juckes.

"He's been abducted, ma'am."

"Really? *Another* abduction?" Elizabeth retorted. "Are you quite sure—"

"I was there," Juckes interrupted. Not annoyed, just firm. "We can fill you in later, ma'am."

"Events are starting to accelerate, Mrs Belfort," Sir Claude resumed. "We have to assume that whoever's behind these abductions will be able to extract information from Setiawan – what he knows, *who* he knows. Which means we're not safe here anymore." Sir Claude paused to look round the table. From their faces it was clear they had all agreed this and more. "We're fine while we're indoors, *we think*. And certainly now, while we're together. But not otherwise."

"Surely whoever's doing these abductions – they have the technology to *get indoors*," Elizabeth replied. "If they can travel across galaxies, I rather think they can make it into your conservatory, Sir Claude – with or without breaking any glass."

"Of course," Sir Claude smiled back, unruffled. "But discretion is still very important to them. That's our one ally in this situation. They don't want to make any more fuss than they have to."

"Discretion? *Fuss?*" Elizabeth replied. "How can you possibly know what they do or don't care about?"

"Actually, we do have a reasonable idea of what they care about. Za-Farka has been very helpful."

Elizabeth wanted to open her mouth to argue the point – to ask more questions – to scream – anything to avoid silence. Anything to avoid confronting the sheer incomprehensibility, the sheer out-of-controlness of the situation.

But nothing came out.

This group had already had their conference and

made their plans. So, while one voice in her mind was screaming incomprehension, another voice – a voice she wasn't at all used to – was telling her to let go. There are times when you can steer the raft, this quieter voice told her, and times when you have to let it run the rapids.

"Listen," Sir Claude resumed, leaning into the table and spreading his hands wide. "We've discussed this as a group. There are three simple conclusions. One. We have to get Setiawan back. Him and – as far as possible – the others… Two. These can't be random abductions. We don't know why the abductors are so interested in the Earth, but it scarcely looks innocent. We have to assume our world is threatened…"

"…our world is threatened…" Elizabeth repeated half-hypnotised.

"Yes. We'll leave it at that for now. But since we know this and we might have a chance – however remote – of doing something about it, we have a responsibility to try. And thirdly" – he continued quickly, before any of the questions screaming inside Elizabeth's badly bruised head could escape – "and thirdly, we're going to need to get away. Quickly." Sir Claude cast a glance towards his nephew and his wife. "Somewhere we can be safe, somewhere we can—"

"—do a little thinking—" Dr James continued.

"—and work out our next steps," Lady Danziger concluded.

"Well, where then? Where is safe?" Elizabeth asked.

"O – r – m – i – l – u," the three of them replied more or less as one.

The name seemed to carry some kind of finality. Silence descended, as words left the table like a flock of departing pigeons. And as they left, the bare landscape they revealed was filled with such awesome and terrifying questions, Elizabeth was stunned into silence too. *Where is Ormilu? How would they get there? How could they possibly rescue someone who's been abducted by aliens?*

And on and on.

Elizabeth felt like the mental raft she was in had started spinning and plunging through the canyons of this landscape. The riverbank was moving by too fast to grasp, everything was too bewildering to relate to.

When, at length she spoke, her question was almost childish in its simplicity.

"What's the time?"

"About 4:30. In the morning."

"Ah…" Of course it was. *Why would anyone need to sleep?* "Just now…" Elizabeth continued speaking without even knowing what her mouth was going to say until it said it. "Just now… you said Za-Farka shared something else with you. What was it?"

"This." Sir Claude replied. He picked up a small black object that was sitting on the table next to him.

"What's that?"

"That's how we're going to get to Ormilu."

"I… I don't understand?"

"This is a spare part that I need to power a craft. A special craft."

Elizabeth stared at him blankly.

"It's not for an airplane, if that's what you're thinking. And Ormilu is not… is not in Scandinavia, if that's what you're also thinking."

Where else isn't Ormilu? Elizabeth wondered. She wanted to ask but the words stuck in her throat again. The likely answer terrified her.

And excited her.

"I must ask you, Mrs Belfort," Sir Claude started, his voice gentle now, "will you come with us? I appreciate we haven't given you much to go—"

"Correction. You've given me *nothing* to go on."

"Quite true. But the fact is, we cannot guarantee your safety if you stay. We cannot guarantee it if you come with us either, but—

"But *what?*"

"Well, it'll be an adventure." Sir Claude spread his arms wide and leaned back in his chair, like a man who's finally got to the rub of an issue. "And I've got this feeling that given the choice between going on a risk-filled adventure or staying stuck in London and *still* being at risk, you'd probably prefer the former?"

He had that right, of course, Elizabeth thought to herself. But it wasn't that easy.

"What about C? What about my job? *My husband?* Sir Claude, my mission was to bring you in, not to run off with you." She turned quickly to Lady Danziger, alarmed. The trouble her tongue could get her in. "Excuse me, Lady Danziger."

"Honestly, if only someone *would* take him off my hands," Lady Danziger replied. "He's only been back a few hours and look at the mess we're all in." Everyone round the table chuckled, including Sir Claude.

Including Elizabeth.

"We've thought about that, Mrs Belfort," Sir Claude continued. "Daniels will take a message back to C that we've been otherwise detained. You, me, all of us. She'll tell him the basics. He'll understand."

"But will C accept Daniels' word?"

"I should hope so. She worked for him for years after all."

"Bu... But..." *There*, Elizabeth was spluttering again. "But won't she – I mean Daniels – I mean—"

"You can call me Jane," Daniels said kindly.

"Won't you be in terrible danger if you stay in London. If it's not safe for me, why is it for you?"

"When I go to meet C, I will travel in a car. I will get into the car in a garage, I will get out of it in a garage. I won't be exposed at any point," Daniels replied fluently. "And once that's all done, I can stay holed up in this house. I'll be fine." She smiled.

"Which I suspect is scarcely an option for you?" Sir Claude continued.

Elizabeth looked again at the group. They looked back at her with a kind, almost compassionate look. *Who are they all? What is this household?* Her head still hurt from the fall. She was dizzy. Disorientated. The raft was spinning faster than ever, she could feel the waterfall approaching.

But one thing was certain.

She was going with them – over the waterfall – *to Hell if necessary* – but otherwise to Ormilu.

Wherever that was.

*

"That's right, dear, just climb up onto the bottom step. This is how we'll travel." Lady Danziger gestured to Elizabeth, coaxing her forwards.

They were back in Sir Claude's study. Two hours had passed. Two frantic hours during which Elizabeth had watched the household gathering kit, packing, stowing, planning. Now dawn was about to break and she was dressed again.

Tentative, like a gazelle approaching a waterhole,

she stepped forward towards Lady Danziger. She felt light-headed. Her mind was spinning on an axis stretched between two poles. Either this was all a complete nonsense, a hoax.

Or it was deadly serious – the moment of total commitment.

There was only one way to find out.

She took a single step up towards Lady Danziger

"Well done, Elizabeth. You're on board. But just to be safe, come a couple of steps higher."

Elizabeth looked up. Lady Danziger was holding out a hand to her. Behind Lady Danziger was Juckes, the butler. Beyond him, Dr James and Sir Claude. All of them were dressed in cold-weather gear, like they were about to go hiking in the mountains.

Was she being hoaxed or was she stepping over the threshold to the great unknown? The usual words, the usual scepticism, stuck in her throat.

At any other time of day, at any other moment in her life, Elizabeth would not have agreed to do what she was about to do. Not without questions, not without knowing.

Elizabeth loved an adventure, yes, but mostly because she was curious. She was just about the most curious person she'd ever met. She was someone who just had to *know*.

And right now, she didn't know anything. She didn't know where Ormilu was, she didn't know *what* Ormilu was. She didn't even know why they were going there.

Above all, she didn't know why she was being asked to climb onto a set of *library steps.*

But she had given up trying to control events. Well and truly. She took Lady Danziger's outstretched hand in her own and moved a couple of steps higher.

"That's right, my dear. Now just sit down. This won't take long."

13

Elizabeth was the last to wake up.

She was roused by a hand on her shoulder – a gentle shaking – a kind but firm voice.

"We've arrived, ma'am."

Juckes.

She blinked awake. Just behind Juckes' shoulder, a storm lantern was visible, hanging from a low timber ceiling. Its flame was guttering and dancing as if recovering from a passing draught. To her left was a wall of tidily stacked logs. To her right, she could see an old wooden door and a small window on either side. She was in some kind of woodshed.

She looked down at her body. She was slumped uncomfortably on some wooden steps. A blanket had been laid across her. *Again.*

"We've arrived, ma'am," Juckes repeated, his voice arriving from a million miles away. "Would you mind terribly if you were to bring in the last box?"

"Not at all," some part of her brain replied. She recovered just enough wits to spot Juckes pointing to a wooden crate at the foot of the steps. Then, picking up a crate of his own, he opened the small wooden door and disappeared through it.

As the door opened and shut, cold and light and

snowy brightness flooded like a wave into the shed and retreated again. *Snow*. Outside she had glimpsed a landscape of pure, brilliant snow.

*

Elizabeth closed her eyes again to gather her thoughts.

For the last twelve hours she had been caught in a strange flux between wakefulness and oblivion – waking hours filled with revelations that had the consistency of dreams – followed by brief hours of sleep, devoid of dreams – followed by more impossible revelations. The conscious and unconscious worlds were jumbled, reality and illusion intertwined. Sleep seemed to take her to the real world and wakefulness to an illusory one. It was as if her whole body and being had been flushed down some kind of tunnel and she was tumbling and turning and blacking out and coming to and whenever she emerged from this tunnel, if ever she emerged, nothing in her life would ever be the same again.

She drank in the fresh, frozen air that stung her lips and throat with a much-needed pinch of reality.

Where am I? How did I get here?

She went back to the last thing first. She was being asked to get on a set of library steps. She was going to travel to Ormilu. It was either some fantastical hoax or Ormilu really was in… *This really was…*

Elizabeth couldn't bring herself to say it. *Yes*, she had definitely left 55 Cleremont Avenue. But it was possible she had simply been drugged and taken somewhere. *Abducted.* To Scandinavia, say – or Scotland.

She decided to compartmentalise.

Reflection could come later. Right now, she had a crate to carry and a group to re-join. She stood up. She briskly folded the blanket and left it on the small bench at the top of the steps, crouching low to avoid hitting her head on the low ceiling. Then she walked back down the steps, picked up the crate, and made her way out into the snow.

*

About thirty yards away, she could see a log cabin. She glimpsed Juckes shaking snow from his boots before disappearing through its doorway. She started tramping through the snow after him, the wetness seeping through her shoes.

Her eyes were starting to adjust. It was more a sunset kind of light, not the harsh brightness she first thought. She scanned her environment as she walked.

Ahead of her, beyond the cabin, were tall pine trees. Or what looked like pine trees. Over to her left still more crested upwards in a gentle curve. She was in some kind of forest clearing; it was perched on a small plateau halfway up a hillside. Because what really caught her attention was the view to her right, where the land fell away. Here, she could see over the tops of the disappearing trees to the far distance. It was a snowy landscape. It stretched in fold after fold of low, silhouetted hills to a vapourous, fathomless horizon.

It was breathtaking.

*

She reached the cabin door. She turned back around to shake the snow off her shoes. She was facing the woodshed, which looked from the outside exactly as she expected. Beyond it were more trees. She really could be back home, somewhere in Scotland.

Except for one detail.

Emerging above the line of trees in front of her, she saw a moon. But this wasn't the moon that she knew, distant and monochrome. This was large – very large. A luminous, verdant, blue-green world filling much of her field of view. She could see textured detail on its surface, she could see oceans and mountain ranges and weather systems. It felt almost intrusive. Like looking into your neighbour's house at night, when the lights have been left on and the curtains open. Elizabeth released a small, involuntary gasp – of awe and amazement and confusion.

But one thing at least was clear to her.

She was no longer on Earth.

14

Elizabeth entered the wood cabin in several states of wonder.

She was thrilled by the moon she had just seen – she was confused to conclude that she had travelled to an alien world – she was warmed by the sight of a log cabin that was in all other respects very earthly – and she was surprised to find that same cabin a hive of activity.

She flicked off her snow-sodden shoes by the door and placed her crate down next to the others, on a counter in front of her. She was in some kind of kitchenette. She looked out over the counter into the open-plan space beyond.

Why are they all so busy?

Lady Danziger was standing at a table on the far side, her tall slim figure curved over charts of some kind, which she was studying intently. Gone was her stilted, stately manner – she was radiating a quiet, dynamic energy. Gone too was her elegant clothing and finery, replaced now by a sheepskin waistcoat over a pale blue jumper and dark trousers. Previously her clothes had lent her elegance; now she lent it back. Her athletic, still-supple frame made her simple workwear seem fashionable.

Sir Claude had changed too. He was busy shuttling between his wife and an old wooden chest from which he was extracting various instruments. He had done away with his tweeds and was wearing a Norwegian-style sweater.

Over by the window, Juckes was carefully cleaning something in the fading light. Elizabeth soon recognised the actions: he was oiling a gun. A service revolver. The components were all laid out in front of him on a white cloth on the windowsill; he was alternately rubbing each part and holding it to the window to inspect it in the fading sunlight. A second revolver was sitting on the windowsill awaiting his attention. He was wearing black trousers and a black polo neck. No longer the butler, he looked like the quiet man of action Elizabeth had always suspected him to be.

But what the Hell was going on?

Over to Elizabeth's right, at the far end of the room, was a large open fireplace. Only Dr James remained the same person she'd met on Cleremont Avenue. Still wearing his tweed suit, he was kneeling down and attempting to lay a fire. She watched him fumble with the kindling and felt an unaccustomed—

"You've seen Ormil-ah."

Elizabeth started.

It was Sir Claude.

"From the expression on your face. You've seen Ormil-ah?" he repeated without looking up. He was staring intently at a notebook, running his finger down a column of figures.

"Ormil-ah?"

"Ormilu's sister planet. Up there in the sky. Don't worry, she has that effect on everyone." Sir Claude finally looked at Elizabeth and smiled.

"Err, yes. Absolutely. Ormil-ah."

"I'm glad she's showing for your visit." Sir Claude smiled again and resumed his work.

"How do you mean?"

"The two planets orbit each other, ma'am," Juckes explained, while he squinted down the barrel of the revolver with a critical eye. "A bit like the Earth and the Moon," he added, briefly reappearing from behind the gun. He picked up a cloth and pulled it through the barrel. "Except with a much stronger gravitational pull."

"Of course."

Elizabeth wanted to ask why they were all so busy. This strange sense of urgency in the room. And yet they worked around each other with such a calm, practised rhythm, she found herself unable to interrupt. She felt like she had accidentally opened the back of a beautifully tuned clock and was watching the cogs tick and rotate with their own mysterious precision. To interrupt them would be like poking it with a toothpick.

And, anyway, she was getting just a tiny bit better at letting go. They were up to something; they would tell her when they were ready.

She looked around for any way of helping that wouldn't involve questions. Her eye fixed on Dr James. The one cog that wasn't turning like the others.

She saw he was laying the fire the way he might approach the crossword. He was inspecting every twig from several angles before placing it carefully into a little teepee of kindling. Very tidy – quite useless.

Elizabeth walked across and knelt down beside him in the manner of an elementary teacher joining the underperforming group. "Would you allow me to help you?" she asked, while taking hold of the topmost newspaper from a pile next to the fireplace. It was a yellowing edition of *The Times of London*.

"Yes, well... Yes. That would be very kind, err, *Mrs B!*" Dr James seemed very pleased to have landed on her name. Or at least his version of it. "Thank you."

"Not at all." She gave Dr James an apologetic smile, before collapsing the teepee of twigs and setting them to one side. She pulled off the front and back page of *The Times*. She found the familiarity of the paper strangely comforting. It was dated February 1972 – five years ago. She could never help glancing at the newsprint while laying a fire, the older the more interesting. The front-page photo of this edition was striking, "President and Mrs Nixon visiting the Great Wall of China..." Then she scrunched it into a tight ball and placed it in the centre of the grate.

Elizabeth briskly layered the fire – paper, twigs, and a few small logs – while Dr James watched in fascination. Then she gently took the box of *Swan Vestas* from his hand, lit one, and touched it to a corner of the paper. Small flames started to quest and probe around the paper, sparking in a kaleidoscope of colours as they consumed the ageing newsprint.

*

For a few minutes they sat in companionable silence, watching the fire gradually take hold, enjoying the smell of it. Elizabeth found it similar to back home, but more aromatic. Almost like pipe smoke.

All the while, she remained conscious of the others, continuing their noiseless and mysterious work behind them. Just the occasional question-and-answer passed between Sir Claude and Lady Danziger. Their voices were low and brief and urgent, in the manner of two people who can communicate with five words where others need ten. Over by the window, Juckes had finished with the two revolvers and was moving quietly about the cabin gathering various items into a black holdall.

The fire had established itself. Elizabeth's instinct to be up-and-doing took over. "Is there anything else I can help with, Lady Danziger?"

"Please call me Adelaide," she replied, smiling. "But, no, I think we're done. And ready to leave." She patted the side of her legs with her palms and stood up. "Claude? Juckes?"

"Yes – the sooner we get you underway, the better," Sir Claude replied.

"Yes, ma'am. All ready from my side."

Elizabeth looked at them in confusion as they gathered up the last remaining essentials and headed back towards the door. The few precious minutes of fragile peace had been shattered. "You're leaving already? I mean, we've only just arrived. What about the idea of... *What was it you all said*... To plan next steps. *That was it*. To do some thinking."

"Oh-ho," Sir Claude retorted, turning round at the door as he put his coat on, "you and I and Artemas, we shall have time for all that. But first we— Here, take this." Sir Claude pulled a thick fur-lined coat from a hook near the door and handed it to Elizabeth. "But first we need to see Adelaide and Juckes on their way."

"On their way? But... But *where?*" Elizabeth stumbled over her words and feet, as she picked her way through a small forest of boots to a pair of plausible size. She saw Juckes and Lady Danziger were already tramping through the snow, back towards the woodshed.

The sun had fallen below the treeline and the light had faded to a crepuscular glow.

"You would like to know where they are going?" Sir Claude asked, as he abruptly turned around to face Elizabeth.

"Yes. Actually, I would."

"They're going on a scouting expedition. *Naturally*."

"Scouting?"

"We know where the humans have been abducted to. As I mentioned earlier," Sir Claude added with the slightest shiver of impatience. "So, before we all head merrily off on a rescue mission to an unknown planet, we need to send a scouting party first."

"I see—"

"And for that, there is no-one better than Juckes. Adelaide pilots, Juckes scouts. Does that answer your questions?" Sir Claude concluded in the manner of a busy man, who's given more than enough of his time.

"Err, yes. Yes, of course." Elizabeth was taken aback by his tone. And just when she thought they were making progress.

"Good. Well, if you'll excuse me, I need to help them run the final checks. Do shut the door behind you, Artemas. Keep the warmth in," Sir Claude hailed his nephew over her shoulder and headed off across the snow.

Elizabeth waited behind for a few seconds, while Dr James pulled on a pair of boots. Above the woodshed opposite, Ormilu's neighbour had risen clear of the tree line. In the gathering darkness of the night, it shone with increasing brightness, in hues of aquamarine and teal and shimmering white-grey clouds.

She looked from this to the one character who never seemed to be in a rush. She smiled at Dr James and he smiled back. A few moments later, they tramped side by side towards the steps.

*

"…Service revolver?"

"Check."

"Ammunition?"

"Eight clips – check."

"Beacon?"

"Check."

"Relativity watch and chain?"

"Check and check."

"First aid kit?"

"Check."

"Short-wave radio, two handsets."

"Check and check."

"Good – that's the full list," Sir Claude concluded as he ticked the final items.

"Shall I close up, sir?" Juckes asked. He was standing next to the steps, next to an open panel in its wooden side.

"Yes, close it up."

Sir Claude turned towards his wife, who was kneeling on the topmost step. The seat of the small bench was hinged backwards. She appeared to be working on some controls concealed inside. "Are the coordinates entered?" he asked.

"Yes – they're ready for checking."

Elizabeth watched as Sir Claude joined his wife on the small platform at the top of the steps and knelt down next to her. Elizabeth hugged herself and gave her arms a brisk rub to stay warm. She was standing in the open doorway of the woodshed. Even in her thick coat, this wasn't weather to stay outside in. She looked at Dr James to her left. He was wearing only his tweed suit – apparently no more concerned by the cold than he was by anything else.

"Right, that's it, you're ready," Sir Claude announced, as he retreated down off the steps. "Good luck, Juckes," he said, giving his butler a firm handshake.

"Thank you, sir."

Sir Claude moved round the side of the steps towards his wife. He reached up with his hand between the banisters and gently touched hers.

"Good luck, my darling. I'll see you in a week."

"What are you saying? I'll see you in a few hours," she replied in a gentle, teasing tone, that made no sense to Elizabeth at all.

Sir Claude smiled weakly as he stepped back towards the wall of the shed, keeping his eyes locked on his wife.

Lady Danziger – still smiling at her husband – pulled on a lever.

For a few moments, nothing.

And then...

Pfft.

The library steps had dematerialised.

Gone.

The guttering flame of the storm lantern was the only evidence they'd ever been there.

15

"You can help me unpack. We're going to be here for a few days. Might as well learn where the things go," Sir Claude grunted. "Unless you plan on me doing all the cooking?"

The words probably formed in his mouth as a joke, but the humour got lost on departure. They had re-entered the log cabin a few moments earlier – shaken the snow from their boots and hung their coats. Elizabeth could see from his movements that he was distracted, out of temper.

She had been wondering what might make this man lose his cool. She just hadn't expected it to be a parting from his wife.

"I'm not sure I understand, Sir Claude. You say a few days, but just before Lady Danziger left—"

"You can call her Adelaide," Sir Claude half-barked. "I assume I may call you Elizabeth? Have we reached that point?"

"Of course." Elizabeth was confused. She wasn't sure if the ice between them had finally been broken – or just got thicker. "Before she left, *A-d-e-l-a-i-d-e*" – Elizabeth pronounced her name like it might bite – "said that she would see you 'in a few *hours*'. I don't understand?"

Elizabeth had joined Sir Claude in the small kitchen area of the log cabin. On the worktop in front of her were three large crates filled with stores. Sir Claude was starting to unpack them into the various cupboards and drawers.

"Relativity," he said bluntly, pausing with a tin of baked beans in his hand. "Time moves at different speeds on different worlds. Here – take this," he said thrusting the tin into her hand. "It goes in that cupboard there, under the sink." He pointed with his elbow. "You unpack the tins and dried food. I'll do the fresh."

Elizabeth – who had never felt so glad to see a tin of baked beans – started wracking her brains to dredge up what she could on relativity. Her degree was in chemistry. But she'd picked up a little physics along the way. She was dimly aware that time – *in theory* – could pass at a different speed on different heavenly bodies. If they were travelling at very different speeds. But she'd never paid much attention. *Why should she?*

"Is this to do with the relative speed that the two planets are travelling at. Ormilu and... and wherever Juckes and Lady Dan— *Adelaide* are going. Is that it?" she asked, as she delivered an armful of tins into the cupboard.

"Exactly so, Elizabeth. Exactly so." Sir Claude paused to look at her, a bag of apples in hand. "Ormilu is travelling much, much slower through space. Which means time is passing much, much faster here. Look." He placed an orange on the counter in front of them. "Imagine this orange is Ormilu. And *this*" – he placed an apple next to the orange – "is planet Earth."

Elizabeth paused to watch, relieved the edge in his voice had lost a fraction of its sharpness.

"So... Here's the orange – *that's Ormilu* – moving

through its twenty-hour day." Sir Claude pushed the orange a few feet across the counter in a straight line. "In that time, the Earth – *our apple* – only moves through a single hour." Sir Claude pushed the apple in the same direction, but only a fraction of the distance. "You'll forgive me for using space – *this counter* – to describe the passage of time. But the concepts do become rather interwoven. We're talking about space-time after all."

"I think I get it… And what about the destination planet. Where Juckes and Adelaide have gone."

"Ah… *there*. Time passes even slower there." He picked up an onion and moved it an even shorter distance. "For every twenty hours that pass *here*, only half an hour passes *there*. Or to put it differently…" Sir Claude had laid aside the vegetables now and was staring straight at Elizabeth. "For every hour that Adelaide and Juckes experience, forty hours pass here. Two Ormilu days."

"My goodness, *forty hours*…"

"And so we've agreed their scouting mission can only last two-and-a-half hours, maximum three."

"But that means if there's any catch on the destination planet… If there's any problem, they've got our only means of transport and— I mean, what if they get held up even by a day or two? What if they get *captured?* Then—"

"—years could pass on Ormilu. And I wouldn't see my wife in a very long time."

Elizabeth suddenly realised what she was making him say out loud. Of course, this man had thought about the risk. It was his wife after all. "I'm sorry, Sir Claude, I didn't mean to upset you, I was just—"

"No, you're right to ask the question. The risks are

large," Sir Claude conceded. "Against that, if we were to blunder onto the destination planet without first scouting it, disaster wouldn't be a risk. It would be a certainty."

Elizabeth sensed some kind of understanding was now established. Whatever he had needed to get off his chest, he had done so.

"Sir Claude..." Something had occurred to Elizabeth. If she didn't ask now, she might never get a chance. "Could it be that... in your past... Have you stayed on a planet where time was travelling much *slower* than on Earth?"

"Ha!" Sir Claude smiled and resumed the unpacking. He stretched past her to unload the apples into a large bowl under the window behind her. "You're thinking of the photograph in my study, aren't you? You're thinking I look a little young for a veteran of the Great War. Am I right?"

Elizabeth nodded, as she also resumed the unpacking.

"Hang on. Cereal in that cupboard to the left," Sir Claude said, re-directing her. "But yes, it's true. There have been a few trips. For research. Always with Adelaide and Artemas."

"Don't forget Vega C!" Dr James called from the sofa.

"*Vega C?*"

"That's right. That was our longest trip. About a year. Or at least what *we* experienced as a year. A lot more time than that passed on Earth. Nine years to be precise."

"Oh yes," Dr James called out from the sofa, "we missed most of the Sixties!"

Didn't you just, Elizabeth thought to herself. "So

you're biological age is—"

"—about seventeen years less than our passport age," Sir Claude replied. "Correct."

It all made sense now. The age discrepancy. The antiquated household. The old-fashionedness.

"What were you researching? C told me you were a botanist."

"Ha! Is that what he called me?" Sir Claude looked amused. "I would call it more…"

"More?"

"*Geophysiology.*"

Elizabeth looked blank.

"Let's go with ecology then. Anyway, enough idle chatter. *Chop-chop* – can't hang around!" Sir Claude barked, about ten times more cheerful than he'd been ten minutes ago. "We're expecting a guest tonight." He scooped a packet of spaghetti from Elizabeth's hands. "I'll be needing that."

"For your guest?"

"Correct. She's due to arrive shortly. Or possibly later. Things can be a little uncertain in space-time."

"Here – on Ormilu? Spaghetti? *A guest?*" Elizabeth was wondering why time never stood still around this man.

"I'm surprised that you're surprised. You struck me as a perfectly sociable sort. In any case," he smiled, "you and she are already old friends."

16

The landing spot was acceptable. Good even.

They were surrounded on all sides by thick foliage – not exactly trees, more like large shrubs with intertwining fronds and putrid-smelling flowers. The edge of the forest – if that's what it was – lay twenty yards ahead. Through the dark red foliage, Lady Danziger could just make out Juckes, inconspicuous in his black clothing against the forest floor. He was lying in the prone position, propped up on his elbows, scanning the landscape beyond with a pair of field glasses. She could see the dark outline of the service revolver that he had holstered at the back of his waist.

The scouting was Juckes' job. Hers was to protect the steps. *At all costs.* She turned away from Juckes to look into the cluttered, copper-beech-red of the forest interior. If danger was to come, it was just as likely to be from behind.

On arrival – as soon as they'd both recovered consciousness – the pair had set about cutting foliage to camouflage the library steps. The air was close and humid. At that moment, nothing stirred in the sultry heat, but Lady Danziger had few illusions. It was guaranteed their arrival had been noted. The question was only by whom? Or *what?*

She checked her watch. Ten minutes since arrival. *Already*.

She carefully hinged back the small bench on which she had been sitting. Inside were a set of elegant brass controls. They were already glistening with a thin sheen of moisture. Next to them was a small open box filled with a variety of mysterious-looking instruments. On top of them was her husband's notebook. She flicked it open at the page marked with a paperclip.

With the index finger of her left hand sitting underneath a set of coordinates, and her right hand on the brass dials, she alternately looked between the two as she started adjusting the controls. She was setting course for their next destination. Juckes might need to flee at a moment's notice. And she had to be ready.

*

Juckes' eyes picked carefully over every detail of the area before him. Ten yards ahead he could see a fence, about twelve foot high. The perimeter fence. It looked poorly cared for. There was some rust on the posts and the wire was starting to curl and warp in a few places. He scanned it for any signs of additional security – cameras or electrification – but didn't spot any.

Either side of the fence a ten-yard border of ground had been roughly cleared. It meant anyone trying to scale or break through would be exposed. But again, there was some slackness. A few shrubs had been allowed to grow, some of them reaching two, even three feet high. Juckes spotted one that was growing both sides of the fence. *Useful*.

Whoever was running this facility clearly wasn't overly concerned about perimeter security.

But their lack of worry worried him.

He hadn't gained Sir Claude's trust through complacency. If the perimeter security was slack, it might be because the authorities were slack. *Or* it might be because their security protocols inside the facility were so intense that no-one would be stupid enough to try to enter. Or leave.

He adjusted his position slightly on the ground and checked his watch. A quarter of an hour had passed since arrival. T+15.

And counting.

He raised the field glasses to his eyes to scan further out. Beyond the fence, and beyond the exposed ground, was an area of scrub, where bushes and shrubs had been left to grow to maybe five or six feet. At this point, the land fell away steeply, offering Juckes a far-reaching vista of the wider landscape and a perfect view of the facility.

He tried to commit every detail to memory. At the centre was a building that commanded attention. About a mile away, it must've been seven or eight hundred yards high. It was white, thin, and conical in shape – tapering to a single point at its apex. All the other buildings in the facility were low rise, making this one seem all the taller.

Only one detail disturbed its bright white surface. At various intervals, black bands ran around the building in perfect rings. It seemed more obelisk than building. Juckes wondered about its purpose. *Religion perhaps? An observation tower?*

Or both?

Juckes trained his binoculars on the base of the obelisk. It stood at the centre of a large, open plaza. The plaza was defined by a circular ring of low-rise buildings around its edge. Within the plaza, there seemed to be a throng moving around. They seemed to be exhibiting normal crowd behaviour. Too irregular to be military personnel, too crowded to be prisoners. It looked more like some kind of town square...

Which makes no sense at all.

But the longer Juckes looked, the more his attention was drawn away from the obelisk, and away from the plaza and the crowds to something quite different.

Walls.

He didn't spot them at first – dwarfed as everything was by the obelisk. But there they were. Huge, austere, grey concrete walls that snaked out from the edge of the plaza into the surrounding countryside. About eight or ten walls, each one maybe four or five storeys high. Quite unscalable. But what made them different from your regular prison walls – apart from the height – was the length. And the apparent zig-zag shape. They didn't follow the typical straight lines and right angles of prison walls but meandered across the countryside. And as Juckes followed the walls out across the landscape, he saw them looping back round on themselves, penning in large areas of land. Some of the penned-in areas were perhaps just a square mile in size, but others maybe five or ten square miles. Each of the areas was covered by different vegetation. *Maybe this was some kind of farm?*

But one of the areas looked like a desert, which didn't stack up.

And there was more.

A short distance beyond the furthest wall, maybe five or six miles away, Juckes could see something else on the horizon. Some kind of megastructure. Straining his eyes, he could make out gantries and towers; a cloud of smoke or steam billowing from its base. He couldn't be sure, but if he had to guess, it looked like a launch site. A launch site for a spacecraft, a very large—

Something moved.

Out of the corner of his vision, in the small gap between his eyeball and the eyepiece, Juckes sensed a flicker of movement.

Unrushed, he lowered the field glasses, and turned his head towards the movement. As soon as he had arrived and seen the colour of the undergrowth, he had chosen his camo paint and smeared it in irregular stripes across his face. He was unlikely to be spotted.

An infra-red camera, however, or a sniffer animal, would be a different matter.

About two hundred and fifty yards away to the left, someone – *something* – was approaching along the line of the fence. On the opposite side of it. The slow-ish speed and the style of movement suggested a perimeter patrol. More importantly, the land away to the left was lower than the high ground on which Juckes and Lady Danziger had landed. In a few more yards, the patrol would disappear out of sight for a minute or two. Juckes quickly trained his field glasses in that direction and adjusted the focus.

It was…

…*a human being.*

Yes – a human being. Almost certainly a man. On his own.

Unhurried – inexplicable – *a man.*

What's he doing here by himself? Is he a guard? A sentry?

Juckes' brain performed a lightning-quick calculation. If he could rescue this human, it would be a platinum opportunity to gather information on the facility.

Against that, some instinct told Juckes this one might not be cooperative. The way he was moving so calmly in such a sensitive place. He looked as if he was at ease. As if he was *trusted*.

Juckes' brain continued to race. If this man was trusted, then he might be even more valuable.

Either way it was an opportunity.

He made his decision.

In a flash, he slithered away from his lookout point and was back on his feet, sprinting the short distance to the library steps, twisting and ducking past the vegetation.

He saw Lady Danziger, crouching low on the upper platform, watching him.

Juckes brushed aside the foliage covering the side of the steps and started running a finger along the edge of one of the panels. He located the hidden catch, deftly flicked it, and the side panel sprang open.

Juckes looked up briefly. "An unexpected opportunity, ma'am." She nodded back. And then Juckes – in a single fluid movement – had pulled the wire cutters from the hidden compartment and was already running back towards the edge of the forest.

He was back at his lookout position a little more than thirty seconds after leaving it. Bending low, he scanned left and right. *Nothing.* Sure enough, the sentry – *if that's what he was* – had passed out of view. *Temporarily.* He had one minute, maybe ninety seconds, to do what he needed to do.

Crouching as low to the deck as he could, he sprinted across the ten yards of open ground to the perimeter fence – to the point he had identified earlier, where the small bush was growing next to the fence. Putting the bush immediately to his left, where it provided the faintest of screens, he knelt down. He moved the heavy-duty wire cutters into position, placing the cutting blades either side of the wire at its lowest point.

He muttered a brief prayer – braced himself against the sound of alarms or the lightning flash of electricity – and made the first cut.

Nothing.

A moment's relief, but Juckes was sweating now. He could see the wire was buried deep underground. He would have to cut along at least two axes. He moved the cutters along to the next piece of wire, just to the right of the first cut, and snipped again.

And again.

Each cut was taking about two seconds. Maybe three. His brain started calculating at warp speed, even while his hands moved automatically from one cut to the next along the ground. He needed to cut a flap open, get through it, get across the open ground on the other side of the fence, and then lie in ambush in the shrubs on the far side.

Maybe this man would be cooperative, maybe he wouldn't – but Juckes didn't plan to take chances. Take him by force first, ask questions later.

He probably had forty-five seconds to a minute left. And another fifteen or so cuts to make.

He could do it. If he was quick, he could do it.

His hands were starting to tremble. Partly the pressure. Partly the weight of the damn cutters. These weren't garden-centre cutters, these were industrial-grade, escape-from-Stalag-Luft-III cutters. They weighed a ton.

He had cut far enough along the ground, horizontally. He moved the cutters to the next piece of wire vertically above, to start creating a flap he could crawl through.

His brain kept racing. He briefly wondered if he still had time to back out. But if he ran back, he might be spotted. The gap he'd cut might be spotted. The mission would be blown.

He pressed forward. He was committed.

Don't blow it, Juckes, don't blow it. He looked at the gap he'd cut. Still too small. He might get snagged on the wire, crawling through.

Three more cuts vertically should do it.

Two more.

One.

Snip.

Done.

Juckes shoved the cutters into the low bush and dropped flat on his belly. He levered himself forward on his elbows and knees. Moving in a lizard zig-zag, he pushed the wire flap open with the top of his head. The wire was stiff, but it yielded. As soon as his thighs were through the gap, he drew himself up onto his haunches.

He was through.

He looked left. Still no sign of the patrol. There might be just enough time to get across the open ground to the bushes on the far side.

Only he couldn't.

As his legs made to run, he heard the telltale rending of fabric. His trouser leg had snagged on the wire and started to rip. And worse. It remained snagged. And then his worst nightmare came into view.

The sentry.

He had been spotted.

Sure enough, it was a human. A man. About thirty yards away. First the head appeared, then the rest of him. His clothing was prison-like: a light-grey shirt and charcoal-grey trousers. The trouser leg on the left side was a few inches shorter than the right; just beneath the hemline, Juckes spotted some kind of chunky metal tag around his ankle.

The sentry quickened his step. Juckes could see his face had already creased into a look of outrage and he was starting to shout.

Juckes braced himself. He had had close scrapes before. He had a simple mantra: don't give up until it's absolutely over.

And this wasn't over.

Not yet.

Only the suspense was over. As the decisive moment arrived, a strange calmness came with it.

The figure was now twenty yards distant. There was a chance – with the bush in the way – that he hadn't seen exactly what Juckes was doing. Snagged as he was on the wire, Juckes' own body was shielding the gap he'd just cut.

He'd see if he could brazen this one out.

Meantime he slipped his right hand behind his back. His fingers reached for the cold hard grip of Sir Claude's service revolver, where it lay clipped in the holster.

The figure was now just five yards away.

His index finger felt for, and found, the clip which kept the gun holstered. He popped it open.

Juckes had come here to help rescue humans, not kill them. But he was not going to let the team down, not without a fight.

*

"Was ist hier denn los?"

German?

Probably any language would have surprised Juckes at that moment – *but German?*

Juckes had a passable knowledge of it. In his special-forces days, he had been the languages guy in the patrol. But that was years ago. He hadn't spoken German in a decade.

The figure strode aggressively forward, looking down with disgust at Juckes' black polo neck. He looked up again, his eyes on a level with Juckes', his face just a few inches away. He stabbed a single, teutonic finger deep into the cleft below Juckes' left shoulder. It was surprisingly painful.

"Wo ist Dein Hemd?"

Something about a shirt.

Juckes was confused.

In his black clothing and camo-painted face, he looked about as much like a saboteur as it was possible to look. Yet this German was acting with a strange combination of aggression and naivety. *Does he think I'm one of the other sentries?*

Even more confusing than that, Juckes was pretty sure he *recognised* the German.

The German placed his thumb on Juckes' chin and rubbed off some of the camo paint, which he proceeded to examine with seven degrees of disgust.

"Was ist dieser Schmutz um Gottes Willen?"

Why are you so dirty, for God's sake?

That bit translated itself. The figure was looking at him with the face of a sadistic boarding school master in front of a pupil who's failed to clean up after rugby. The face was a subtle mixture of outrage and pleasure at the punishment to come.

"Wasch Dich mal – so daß Du nicht aussiehst wie ein Schwein!"

Juckes nodded at the German and smiled apologetically. He was the image of polite contrition.

Meantime, he relaxed his grip on the revolver behind his back and re-configured his fingers into a tight fist-shape.

As Juckes' army boxing instructor, Right-Hook Norton, had always told him: when a gift horse comes along, you don't *look* him in the mouth—

—you punch him.

*

Juckes surveyed the German, where he lay sprawled unconscious on the ground, and his first thought was: *exactly my size.*

17

"*'Patch me through to your boss, you cretins, and this time keep your—'*" Za-Farka stopped before she reached the end of the message. "So rude!"

"I know, *right?*" Elizabeth smiled at Za-Farka and Za-Farka smiled back.

Elizabeth's second meeting with Sir Claude's alien contact was going better than her first. She'd even managed not to faint. She watched as Za-Farka took a tidy mouthful of spaghetti and then turned to Sir Claude.

"So which race *did* send this message?"

"They're called the Golgothans," Sir Claude answered.

Elizabeth tilted her head. "The *who?*"

"No, no. Not *them*. Haha! You youngsters. No, the Golgothans."

"And who are they?"

Sir Claude nodded towards his nephew.

"*Hmm?* The Golgothans?" Dr James looked up from his food, startled. He was wearing a large white linen napkin, tucked into his collar and spread expansively across his tweed waistcoat. His dexterity with spaghetti, Elizabeth had noticed, was limited. As he looked up, a strand slithered from his fork, like a fleeing snake. He cast a look of resigned disappointment in the direction of the pasta, as if they were somehow always fated to misunderstand each other, and then looked back at her. "You were saying? *Ah yes!* The Golgothans. The Golgothans are, you see, the financiers to the Universe."

"The *whole* Universe?"

"Oh yes, pretty much. They've rather, err, cornered the market as you might say. Not a very nice bunch, alas. If the Golgothans get in touch, it's a fair bet they have some outlandish financial proposal. Do you see?"

"Such as?"

"Oh, you know. *Please sell us your planet.* That sort of thing, *hmm?*"

"You mean they want to own the Earth?" Elizabeth asked in alarm.

"No, no, they don't want to own the Earth – that would be silly." Dr James' voice was all reassurance. Elizabeth relaxed and took a mouthful of food. "No, they want to buy it *for someone else.*"

Elizabeth gave an involuntary spasm, nearly unleashing a mouthful of bolognaise across the table.

*

In truth, Elizabeth had been slightly surprised by the menu choice. *Spaghetti bolognaise.* It seemed a strange dish to serve an alien guest. But then, to be fair, what could possibly count as *un*strange? As Sir Claude had explained, while they cooked together, in his experience a calorie was a calorie on any planet. And bolognaise, in point of fact, was Za-Farka's favourite dish.

He had gone on to explain more about Ormilu and

Za-Farka – and why she was visiting. Ormilu, it turned out, was her 'safe planet' and this was her safe house. An off-the-grid location where any members of her network could come and hide out. It was maintained by a small but capable group of caretakers from her home planet – shy individuals who had their own reasons for choosing a reclusive life. They even looked after a team of huskies, Elizabeth was astonished to learn – in a pen in the woods. The caretakers themselves stayed in a small hut at the back of the main cabin.

"So why is Za-Farka visiting us a second time?" Elizabeth had asked.

"To bring us more detailed information on the abductors," Sir Claude had replied. "Hopefully some books. Something on their language, their culture."

"Books? Do you mean…*books?*"

"I do indeed. Printed pages. Cover, front and back. Books."

"But doesn't she have… Well, more sophisticated technologies?"

"Oh, for sure she does. But *we* don't. Za-Farka has a strict rule, Elizabeth. She doesn't introduce new technologies to other planets unless absolutely necessary. And quite right too – we have enough trouble managing the ones we've created."

"What about the library steps?"

"The exception that proves the rule."

"Alright…" Elizabeth had conceded. "So who are these books about? Am I allowed to know the name of these abductors, *finally?*"

She was.

The *Zailans*.

*

"Alright, I'm beginning to get this now." Elizabeth looked around the dinner table and started to summarise. "So now we know who sent the message – the Golgothans. And we know who they're working with – the Zailans. The abductors. And we know what they want – to buy the Earth. Presumably as some kind of cover for the abductions. But we don't know the *why*. Why they're abducting humans. Is that it?"

She looked towards Dr James for confirmation, but his attention had already wandered back to his plate of pasta, where another round of hostilities was about to commence.

"Exactly, well done," Za-Farka replied in the sweetest of tones. They looked at each other approvingly. Za-Farka was eating her spaghetti like an Italian. Elizabeth watched as she carefully pressed her fork to her spoon and winched the spaghetti on board with barely a strand awry.

"But we do know one more thing," Za-Farka continued, as she elegantly put her napkin to her lips – dabbing, not rubbing. "The Zailans have taken all the humans to a single facility on their planet, Zil. I believe you've sent a scouting party to the coordinates I gave you?"

Sir Claude nodded.

"Let's hope they find out what goes on there," Za-Farka continued, "no-one else seems to. For such a populous race on such a large planet, the Zailans are secretive. *An enigma.* They keep themselves to themselves. I've managed to gather some more information this time" – she gestured to the books on the kitchen counter – "I'm sorry I didn't have them when I came to London. Of course, that was when you and I met for the first time—"

"Oh that!" Elizabeth interjected, embarrassed. "I'm so sorry, I can't believe I behaved that way."

"Oh, please don't worry," Za-Farka replied prettily. "I do understand the shock, really I do. It's scarcely your fault if you faint. It's not something you can control."

"Even so – it was inexcusable on my part," Elizabeth replied, somehow getting drawn into a politeness contest with an alien. But Za-Farka really was very pretty. Yes, she had green skin and three nostrils and a confusingly long neck, but she was undeniably feminine. *Elegant.*

"So, what *is* your best guess about these abductions?" Elizabeth asked

"We have to assume," Za-Farka replied in a low voice, "it's for some kind of... *research.*"

Research for what? The table fell silent. Either because they weren't ready to contemplate what 'research' might involve. Or they were but weren't ready to tell her about it.

Elizabeth tried a different tack.

"And the Zailans?" Elizabeth broached this tentatively. But she needed to know. "What are they like?"

Another silence.

"Come on," Elizabeth started, "they can't be all that—"

"I'm afraid they're rather psychopathic, Mrs B," Dr James said, without taking his eyes from his plate.

"What? *All of them?*" Elizabeth scoffed. Scoffing seemed preferable to trusting at that moment.

"No," Sir Claude replied evenly. "Not all of them. But about ten percent."

"Alright. Doesn't sound too bad?"

"We probably better tell her about the Caucus?" Sir Claude looked at Za-Farka.

Za-Farka nodded and closed the cutlery on her plate and sighed like a parent who's reached the unavoidable moment. "The Caucus, Elizabeth, is the political entity that governs Zil. Membership is voluntary. But it dominates all aspects of life on their planet."

"How so?"

"Well, as we understand it, all political and administrative roles on Zil are filled by Caucus members. They dominate the senior military and commercial positions too. So anyone remotely serious about their career has to join it. They get all the best privileges."

"If membership of the Caucus is open to all..." Elizabeth started, feeling her way forward, "and the privileges are so great... Why wouldn't everyone join?"

"To be honest," Sir Claude replied, "I found the Caucus a bit confusing too. When Za-Farka first described it. But then I thought of a parallel on our own dear planet and it started to make sense. Think of the one-party states you find in human history. Germany shortly before the war perhaps. Or the modern communist states. Something like that. They all had – or *have* – a single political party. The Nazi Party, the Chinese Communist Party – or the Soviet one – and so on. Something like that."

"Alright... But, leaving aside politics, there's still a huge incentive for everyone to join the Caucus. Why don't they?"

"Because," Za-Farka replied, "it comes with certain expectations—"

"Because they're psychopathic," Dr James repeated, while jabbing his fork at a loose strand of pasta.

"Correct," Za-Farka continued. "The psychopaths tend to concentrate in the Caucus. It makes sense, it's their natural home."

Elizabeth was puzzled. The word just brought to mind Alfred Hitchcock movies. "Thank you for explaining, Za-Farka. But I thought psychopaths mostly have a violent criminal personality. How can you put people like that at the centre of power?"

The other three erupted into laughter – to Elizabeth's consternation. Even Za-Farka, with her exquisite manners, put a forelimb politely to her mouth as she failed to suppress a guffaw.

"Ah, Elizabeth," Sir Claude replied, recovering from his mirth, "psychopaths and power have long been bedfellows. Still, this is more my nephew's terrain. He's made a study of this. Artemas?"

"Ah yes, yes, psychopathy!" Dr James said enthusiastically, looking up from his plate with relief. "Or sociopathy if you prefer?" Elizabeth didn't. "You see on Earth about one, perhaps two, percent of the population are psychopathic, *hmm?* Now with a rough upbringing, their worst characteristics come to the fore. Selfishness, impulsiveness, *violence.* Lots end up either in prison or – if they're lucky – *the army. Haha!* But!" Dr James interrupted himself, holding up a single index finger. "Many aren't violent at all. No – yes, they're not. If they're given a more educated upbringing, taught some basic self-restraint – if they're *middle class* in other words – they can often do rather well in adulthood. *Hmm?* Uncle – did you say it was trifle for dessert?"

"Yes, yes, Artemas. A Mrs Carstairs special," Sir

Claude replied, waving his hand. "Finish your point."

"Oh wonderful." Dr James turned back to Elizabeth. "That's it, you see? The middle-class psychopath. You won't find him – *or her* – in prison. Far from it, they hide in plain sight. Having reined in their worst excesses, they find their remaining traits are actually, well, *rather helpful*. For their career. Do you see? They watch how life works, they treat it like a game with a set of rules – and then set about trying to win that game. Which generally means stretching every rule and manipulating every player. *Haha!* Oh yes, they're very good at profiting from the trust of others. And so, you see, psychopaths often end up filling the positions in society that are most respectable, most senior" – Dr James held up his finger again – "*most powerful.*"

Elizabeth listened in mute fascination. The idea that her middle-class world might be infiltrated by psychopaths – *governed* by them – was new to her. "So…" she started, "as our society becomes more educated, more middle class…"

"…we have less violent psychopaths and more middle class ones," Dr James concluded. "Perhaps it's why fewer wars are being fought, *hmm?* The psychopaths are moving out of the army and into boardrooms, *haha!*"

"Oh, that's very good, Dr James, well done!" Za-Farka placed her hands together in a genteel clap.

Sir Claude leaned back and tapped the table in appreciation. "History as the long slow process of turning psychopaths from warriors into corporate directors... Really, Artemas, you should write a paper on that." Sir Claude leaned back into the table and eyeballed Elizabeth. "Against that, perhaps society needs a certain number of them? Don't you think? To fill the leadership positions and take the tough decisions? If everyone's too nice, you might end up with a highly lovely, cooperative society like... Let's see now, like..." Sir Claude paused while he tried to think of a highly lovely, highly cooperative society on Earth. "Like err…"

"Tibet?"

"Yes, thank you, Artemas. *Tibet*. And, of course, we know what happened there. It got—"

"—eaten."

"Yes, exactly. *Eaten*."

There was a pause in the conversation. Elizabeth pushed her bowl away. She was losing her appetite.

"So, these are the creatures we're up against? Some unrelenting psychopaths with a special line in abducting intelligent life forms?"

"I'm afraid we are," Za-Farka said. "And we haven't even mentioned the hermaphrodite issue."

"The *what?*" Elizabeth asked.

"Ah yes, *that.*" Sir Claude looked uneasy. "Who's for trifle?"

*

"Technically, it's actually known as 'patriarchal hermaphroditism'," Za-Farka started, as she received her bowl of trifle from Sir Claude. "Every Zailan has both male and female gender parts. They can't impregnate themselves, but they are – in principle – able to perform either role with any other Zailan."

"What do you mean 'in principle'? Oh, thank you, Sir Claude," Elizabeth said as she received her bowl.

"Because – *in practice* – Zailans are on a spectrum," Za-Farka replied. "At one end, you have very, shall we say, *masculine* Zailans. Their female body parts have atrophied, while their male ones are, well, enlarged—"

"They're often the psychopaths," Dr James chipped in.

"At the other end of the spectrum..." Za-Farka continued, "you have the Zailans, whose male body parts are somewhat shrunken, while their female parts are more developed. They tend to do the child-bearing and child-rearing. They're known as the 'submissives'. So even though the species appears hermaphroditic, they're actually remarkably—"

"—patriarchal?"

"Just so."

Elizabeth took a first spoonful of trifle. She recoiled at the slightly stale taste of the *hundreds and thousands* that Mrs Carstairs had sprinkled on it. And the artificial cream. And the tinned fruit. And the jelly.

And then Elizabeth chided herself. She was *in space* for Heavens' sake.

"Look, it says here ..." Dr James piped up. He was browsing one of the books on Zil that Za-Farka had given them a short while earlier. "It says, 'the same Zailan can move along the gender spectrum within their own lifetime.' How might that, err... *work?*"

"Well..." Za-Farka started. "If a Zailan experiences a career setback, for example, it's not uncommon for their male body parts to shrink and their female ones to increase. Conversely, many a Zailan has developed increasing masculinity as their career has progressed within the Caucus. And I'm not talking about secondary sexual characteristics – dominance and so on – but primary ones. Their actual body changes."

"So what *do* they look like?" Elizabeth asked.

"I'm afraid they're not very pretty to look at—" Za-

Farka released an involuntary burp. "Oh, I do apologise."

"Oh please, don't worry," Elizabeth shot back. "I'm sure I'd burp if you fed me alien food."

"You're too kind."

"In some cultures," Sir Claude added, "burping is exactly what one *should* do after dinner. To express appreciation."

"Oh really? Where?"

"In China, for example."

"Well, thank the Heavens for China then," Za-Farka replied prettily. "*Wherever that is.*"

"What did you mean, Za-Farka, when you said they're not pretty to look at?" Elizabeth returned to her earlier question. "What do Zailans in fact look like?"

18

Well, I'm sure their mothers love them, Juckes thought to himself as he got his first proper look.

He didn't want to dismiss a whole species as ugly. After all, he didn't consider himself much of an oil painting – or, at least, not after his nose got broken for the second time – but it's hard to suppress a first impression.

And his first impression of the Zailans was *ugly*.

Juckes had reached the plaza proper. He was standing in a discreet corner, tucked into the shadows of a low-rise building, drawing in information through his eyes.

The strange white obelisk – gleaming and pristine – towered over everything. It was about a hundred yards away. At this proximity, he could see it was a building after all, not a monument. The black bands around it, which he had spotted earlier, were formed of darkened windows.

The obelisk was keeping him oriented.

Because everything else was bewildering. He was thrown. Disorientated. He tried not to be, but he was.

The atmosphere of the plaza in front of him was one of frantic enjoyment. The crazed mania people go into when they've paid a lot of money and expect a lot of fun.

So, standing here, his first thought was… *Resort.*

Some kind of resort.

But what kind?

Around the large, crowded square, there were kiosks dotted all about. They appeared to be selling food and toys and knick-knacks. There were Zailans of all ages – older ones, younger ones, families – thronging, mingling, running, ambling. There were young couples and old couples; there were large groups and small; there were parents, children and babies. There were other races too. Species in shapes and forms that made his eyes goggle.

Trying to master his bewilderment, Juckes focussed on the Zailans, imprinting their features and movements.

Height: five to five-and-a-half foot. Body morphology: similar to a human, large head, short thick neck, two arms, two legs, pot-bellied. Body covering: clothing, like humans. Body movement: bipedal gait, but slow and awkward; arms longer than humans' – probably capable of moving on all fours. Skin: coarse, light-ish, almost Caucasian in colour, but with deep, dark creases. Hair: a light covering of flaxen hair all over the skin, otherwise bald on the head.

What really drew Juckes' attention, however, were two things: their hands and their mouths.

He had been briefed on their hands. They were the stand-out feature of the Zailan race. Eight digits on each hand, arranged around a circular palm. Two of the digits, positioned opposite each other, were thumbs. Multi-jointed, like the body of a snake, the Zailan hand and fingers were both dexterous and powerful. Originally a tree-dwelling species that walked on all fours, Zailans had a grip so strong, they could fall asleep hanging from a branch. They had even been known to die in this position – their grip so tight, their fingers had to be sawn off to release them. *They're sensitive,* Za-Farka had told him, *they hate to be reminded about their tree-dwelling past.*

And then the mouth. It undulated across the broad landscape of the Zailan face like a river canyon. Their mouths were so broad, they seemed capable of expressing several emotions at once, depending on which bit you looked at. And as Juckes studied the throng now, pretty much every emotion was available to view. Laughter – excitement – over-excitement – frustration – exhaustion – anger.

*

Before heading to the plaza, Juckes had discussed the risks with Lady Danziger.

Infiltration.

Sir Claude had given them two clear objectives. One. Find out the *purpose* of the facility – what goes on there, why humans are being abducted. Two. Find a safe landing spot for the main group, a base. Preferably inside the facility.

Theoretically, they could complete their mission without attempting to infiltrate.

Infiltration was high risk, high reward. The circumstances had to be perfect. One slip-up and the whole mission could be wrecked. Sir Claude had sent him and Lady Danziger scouting on previous adventures – this wasn't his first rodeo – but only once before had they tried to infiltrate.

The problem on this occasion was that they still had

no idea what they were dealing with. No matter how long Juckes stared through the field glasses, the facility remained a mystery. *What was it for?*

True, Juckes now had a captive. Dr Nussbaum no less. The 50-year-old German, whose abduction was the first to be witnessed and reported.

But he wasn't much help unconscious. And, if he was as brainwashed as Juckes suspected, he wasn't likely to be much help when he woke up.

When Juckes had dragged his limp body through the forest towards her, Lady Danziger immediately guessed what he had in mind.

Try his clothes – see how they fit, she had suggested.

Wordlessly, they had stripped off his clothes until he was down to his underwear. That and the mysterious tag around his ankle. While Lady Danziger bound his hands and feet and gagged him – *just in case* – Juckes tried on Nussbaum's grey trousers and shirt.

They fitted fine. Like he thought they would.

Juckes had cleaned the camouflage paint from his own face. Then he then took off his watch and slipped it into his pocket. The German hadn't been wearing a watch. Juckes wouldn't either.

He was starting to look the part.

The German was still slumped unconscious at the bottom of the steps. They were in no doubt, they'd have to take him back to Ormilu with them – they couldn't risk him being found out here. So they grabbed him under the arms and hauled him onto the steps. It was during this moment of clammy intimacy, Juckes noticed a tiny device in Nussbaum's left ear. Flesh-coloured, he might easily have missed it.

He fished it out gingerly.

"A micro radio receiver?"

"Possibly…" Lady Danziger replied. "But probably not. It looks like the one we saw last time…"

"A translation device?"

"That's my guess."

"Perfect."

Juckes cleaned off some German earwax with a handkerchief and placed it in his ear.

Next Lady Danziger reached down into the compartment under the bench and retrieved a mysterious-looking, circular object. It was a metallic, matt grey – about four inches in diameter – flat on one side and dome-shaped on the other. Juckes slipped it into his pocket.

He was all set.

Almost.

Juckes' major anxiety was the metal tag, still strapped around the German's ankle. A single small green diode on it was flashing. It's on/off state matched Juckes' own trepidation. *Infiltrate – don't infiltrate.*

Either it was some kind of control device – perhaps delivering an electric shock if the wearer approached a perimeter cordon. Or it was a tracking device. Or both.

Juckes rationalised. The device was so ostentatious, so unnecessarily large, he was ready to bet it was the first option. If the authorities wanted to track, they could use something small and hidden – perhaps they *were* using something small and hidden. *But this device?* This was designed to be seen – to connote low status – to humiliate.

He couldn't be sure of course, but in the game Juckes was in, sometimes you had to go with your gut or you'd never go at all.

So he took the plunge.

He extracted some tools from the storage

compartment under the steps. He successfully detached the tag from Nussbaum's ankle and the flashing diode went out. Quickly, he placed it round his own ankle. He hinged the two open ends back towards each other and they clicked together tidily. After a heart-stopping pause, the flashing light turned back on.

The tag was working again.

So far so good.

He pulled his watch from his pocket. T+25. He told Lady Danziger to wait no longer than two hours. If he wasn't back by then, she was to return to Ormilu with their hostage.

Lady Danziger nodded. She knew his mind was set, there was no point trying to dissuade him.

In a final gesture, Lady Danziger held out one of the radio handsets. But Juckes shook his head, as she expected. It was too bulky – it would give him away.

Without any further delay – giving himself no time to change his mind – Juckes had headed back out of the forest. He slipped across the open patch of land, crawled back through the hole in the perimeter fence, and darted into the scrub beyond. From there he made his way down towards the plaza.

Infiltration it would be.

*

Juckes steeled himself.

He couldn't continue to loiter at the edge of the plaza indefinitely. In the spying game, standing around trying to look inconspicuous was about the most conspicuous thing you could do.

He needed to start moving and he needed to look purposeful. That was the key.

He had the beginnings of a plan. The tall white obelisk looked to be a central gathering point. The crowds were pouring in and out of the ground floor. Perhaps it was some kind of information centre? Or ticket office? Either way, if he could get in there, and make his way to one of the upper floors with a window, he'd have a chance of finally getting a proper view of the facility.

But how to get in there without attracting attention? Without breaching some unknown protocol?

A hint of an opportunity blinked at Juckes.

Four Zailan guards strode past him in a box formation. At their centre was a prisoner, whom they were parading around the plaza. Juckes only glimpsed the prisoner from behind – definitely a human. A small forlorn figure in a suit.

What caught Juckes' eye, however, was what was happening around these five figures. There were about a dozen humans – all dressed identically to him – helping to clear a path through the crowd for the guards and the prisoner. This was his opportunity.

Juckes folded into their slipstream.

He observed their behaviour and gestures. They were walking sideways, facing outwards with their palms outstretched, gesturing to the crowd to stay back. Juckes edged himself into the back of the group and started imitating the actions.

It worked.

He blended in.

The Zailan guards at the centre of the group were oblivious to him. A couple of the other humans threw him a look or two, but their eyes conveyed curiosity more than suspicion.

Juckes' brain raced. The prisoner was clearly high

value in some way. If he could find out where he was being taken, that might give him a clue as to where Setiawan and the other academics were being kept.

As they continued around the outer edge of the plaza, Juckes noticed another human. She was dressed differently. *Very differently.* She was wearing *animal skins.* They were coarsely stitched together, with a single strap over one shoulder. She was also behaving differently. She was picking up litter with her hands and dropping it into a wicker, or rattan, basket on her back. Her hair was long and messy. He tried to get a glimpse of her face – see if he recognised her from the dossier. But no chance. When she looked up, he saw dirt smeared across her face like camo paint. She had been deliberately turned into the cartoon image of a cavewoman.

He started seeing other humans like her. First just a few, and then dozens of them – all dressed the same way – all doing menial tasks. Cleaning and portering. Some were supplying goods to the kiosks in the plaza; others were cleaning them back off the ground as the crowd discarded them.

Juckes made a mental note. There were two kinds of humans here – slaves and supervisors.

The entourage passed by the front of a giant archway at the edge of the plaza. The crowd were ambling in and out of it. He tried to see what lay beyond, but there were too many bodies in the way. He looked up briefly at the arch itself for a clue, but he was too close to make out the detail. He glimpsed colourful illumination – pictures of some kind – and then he was already past.

He could see other giant archways – in a horseshoe around the edge of the plaza. But then the group turned inwards. They started heading directly for the Obelisk at the centre.

Forty yards later and they reached the outer edge of the obelisk. The crowd was at its thickest here. The Zailan guards started shouting at the onlookers. Juckes' earpiece started to crackle – and then came to life. It *was* a translation device. The guards were telling the crowd to *make way*. It was just for show, of course. The crowd started showing much more interest in the prisoner now they were being shouted at.

The entourage passed up some steps and, a moment later, through the glass doors of the obelisk. The whoosh of air conditioning sent a cooling blast across Juckes' face as the group started crossing the crowded foyer.

A few seconds later and they halted. They were at the elevators. The other human supervisors started to melt away as the four guards and their prisoner waited in front of a pair of glass doors. Juckes hung back.

This was it. This was his chance to find out where the prisoners were being kept.

Should he get in the elevator with them?

Too risky.

If he could just get close enough, perhaps he could *hear* where they were taking the prisoner? He could see the guards were talking. But saying *what?* The earpiece was inert – too far away. And the crowd had started to close round the front of him. Meantime, the elevator had arrived and the glass doors were opening.

Juckes edged urgently forward, pushing between some of the crowd. Between their heads, he could see the prisoner and his four guards enter the elevator.

Now at last, the earpiece started to crackle. It started picking up a voice – one of the guards – but it was indistinct, the translation garbled. There was still a line of visitors in front of him. Juckes muscled his way right to the front. It was a risk – Juckes knew he was being reckless – but he'd never get another chance like this.

"...what do you... where... high-value suite... 55th... won't be long... spectacle this eve—"

The glass elevator doors closed and the earpiece cut out. But Juckes was euphoric. *The 55th floor.* They must be talking the 55th floor. An instant later, the guards and their prisoner turned to face the way they had come.

Juckes froze.

His gaze was locked onto the prisoner.

And the prisoner's gaze was locked onto him.

As the glass lift started disappearing upwards, the face of Dr Setiawan disappeared with it.

19

Elizabeth felt fantastic.

She hadn't slept that deeply since… She stopped for a moment to think. *Since her last trip to the Highlands.* And possibly not even then.

Day 2 on Ormilu.

She yawned and stretched her arms indulgently. The loose, heavy sweater, which she'd just thrown on, rode up her forearms and collapsed back down them again. She looked out of the cabin window and saw the others seated round an outdoor table, eating breakfast under the crisp morning sun.

How had that happened without waking her?

She looked back up at her sleeping quarters. Elizabeth had been allocated what looked very like a hayloft. While Sir Claude and Dr James were using the twin room – the only available bedroom – she had slept on a kind of mezzanine floor above the dining area. It was accessed by a ladder just to the left of the fireplace. The near end of her hayloft was completely open to the rest of the cabin. There was only enough room to stand at the very centre, under the apex of the roof rafters. Her bed was nothing more than a thick sleeping bag laid out on what looked like a judo mat. Opposite the loft, there was a small dormer window recessed into the roof, which had provided a view last night of Ormil-ah. It also provided a fresh supply of air through the ill-fitting window panes.

In short, her loft was cramped, uncomfortable, draughty, severely lacking in privacy – and *utterly perfect*.

She loved it.

She looked again through the ground-floor window at the others. They were duffled to their chins and deep in conversation. She could see the salt and pepper pots and a couple of mugs had been marshalled on the table to explain some point or other. *How very Sir Claude.* Elizabeth smiled to herself.

She ought to have been feeling embarrassed to be so late down. But she was feeling much too relaxed to feel anything other than relaxed.

She pulled her hair behind her head and gathered it briskly into a simple ponytail. She went over to the coat rack next to the cabin door, pulled off a heavy coat at random from the large number that were growing off the pegs, lifted the latch of the cabin door, and went out to join them.

*

"...so that's what they're after. The thing the Zailans really want." Za-Farka leant back a little as she said this, bringing emphasis to the point.

"Admission to the IGC? *Of course.* Fascinating." Sir Claude smiled. "That's always the trick. Find out what your enemy *really* wants – and use it against them."

Elizabeth slid onto a spare seat at the table.

"What's the IGC?" she asked.

"Ah!" Sir Claude swivelled towards her. "The explorer from the realm of sleep has joined us. Welcome to the waking world. Is it to your liking?"

"Entirely." Elizabeth smiled back.

"Do help yourself. There's still coffee in the thermos and a few slices of toast. Grilled over the fire not 30 minutes ago. A little cold now, but you'll find Mrs Carstairs' marmalade livens it up no end."

"Thank you." Elizabeth reached for a piece. "And you're quite sure this is the waking world? Honestly, my dreams last night seemed more real." Elizabeth took in the vast, spectral shape of Ormil-ah, hanging in the crisp blue sky above Sir Claude's shoulder.

"Haha, yes! Well, you should be pleased with today's agenda. It should ground us again. I propose that after breakfast" – Sir Claude spread his hands wide – "we start our training."

"Training?"

"Oh, this is going to be good." Za-Farka exchanged a smirk with Dr James. "Welcome to bootcamp."

"Yes. You know," Sir Claude replied, "fitness – weapons handling – the basics of navigation. When we head to Zil, we need to be primed and ready. Are you game?"

"Certainly," Elizabeth replied. She considered her fitness and her competence with weapons to be better than average. But she was happy to play along. "Delighted."

"Splendid. We'll make a start after breakfast." Sir Claude rubbed his hands together with boy-scout enthusiasm. "Now, to your question. What's the IGC? It does rather bring us to the nub of the issue."

"If you wouldn't mind?"

And so Sir Claude and Za-Farka started to talk. And

Elizabeth – who was full of surprises for herself this morning – started listening. Not listening in her usual way, with questions and scepticism and more questions, but *just listening*. She let the information come to her, in the speed and shape it wanted to travel.

And so it did.

She learnt that there was order in the Universe – *political* order – and that the IGC, the Intergalactic Council, was the guarantor of it. She learnt that it was chaired by a race known as the Za-Nakarians, and that its membership was comprised of the so-called 'advanced civilisations'. The ones with the most sophisticated technologies. In a universe where the technologies of destruction had become so potent as to render all war pointless, they together enforced the three unbreakable rules of the IGC. That no civilisation should ever attack another. Nor colonise. Nor take slaves or forcibly abduct.

She learned that there were also 'advanc-*ing* civilisations' – ones that had acquired nuclear technology and the basic ability to travel in space. They were bound by the rules of the IGC, but not members of it. All of them were desperate to join the IGC – and none more so than the Zailans.

And finally she learned about 'emerging civilisations'. Planets which hosted an intelligent species, but still lacked the advanced technologies to join the intergalactic community.

Elizabeth soaked up this new information matter-of-factly. She had become numb to amazement. In her calm, accepting state, the information broke over her like waves on a sandy beach. Only later, when the tide was out, would she go back and pick through the shells and seaweed, and assess just how much the shoreline of her understanding had shifted.

*

"So can I try to summarise…" Elizabeth started.

Sir Claude waved his pipe. "Please."

She reached for Mrs Carstairs' jar of marmalade. "First, we have the Za… The Za-Nazari—"

"—Nakarians."

"Sorry, Za-*Nakarians*. The Chair of the Intergalactic Council. The overlords. A bit lazy, a bit exploitative themselves – but perhaps fractionally more decent than the others?"

"Just so."

"Next we have the Golgothans," she continued, pushing her own coffee mug to one side of the marmalade. "Another 'advanced civilisation', so-called. Rude, mercenary, interested only in money. They've been hired to initiate purchase negotiations for planet Earth. Purchasing planets being the legitimate – *legal* – way of exploiting them?"

Za-Farka smiled sadly and nodded.

"Alright, I think I'm getting it…" Elizabeth took hold of Sir Claude's ashtray and pulled it into a tidy triangle with the marmalade and the mug. "Then we have the Zailans themselves, the ones who want to buy our planet. They're an advancing civilisation, desperate to join the IGC, desperate to move beyond a past where the more sophisticated civilisations exploited them." Elizabeth paused for a moment. "The Zailans… Bitter, exploited – exploitative – *psychopathic*."

"I think she's got it," Sir Claude exclaimed.

"And lastly, us." She picked up an apple from the fruit bowl and placed it precisely in the centre of the triangle. "We've been thrown into the middle of these three. The Earth. Re-classified shortly after the Second World War from an emerging to an advancing civilisation—"

"Exactly."

"—but no-one officially told us about that. So we're now deemed competent to look after ourselves, even though our leaders have no idea what's going on. Is that right?"

"I'm afraid it is," Za-Farka replied.

"And as to the rules of the IGC… They ought to protect us from exploitation – *from these abductions*. But in practice, a prosecution can only be brought by a member of the IGC and why would any of them bother looking out for a minor planet in a little visited galaxy?"

"*Ha!*" Za-Farka exclaimed. "You're a quick learner, young lady."

"Great, I get it now," Elizabeth replied, leaning back. "And what a mess."

*

A moment's silence descended on the table as they contemplated the mad, dangerous landscape into which the Earth's fate had been thrown.

"So why are you helping?" Elizabeth asked Za-Farka.

"Because my own planet was purchased by the Golgothans. And things…" Za-Farka hesitated. "Things didn't turn out well."

"They *smoked* it," Sir Claude grunted.

"You don't want to know the detail," Za-Farka continued. "Let's just say they exploited the planet until… until our ecosystem collapsed."

"Goodness…" Elizabeth's brain reeled. "But why did your leaders ever agree to sell?"

"Why does anyone ever? The buyers tell you how great it's going to be, they exploit divisions, quietly bribe the decision-makers. It's all too easy I'm afraid."

Za-Farka looked down, overcome by sadness.

"Since then," Sir Claude picked up the thread, "she's been reaching out to contacts on vulnerable planets to warn them. She first contacted me in—"

"—1944."

"Well remembered, Elizabeth. That's when I formed the Council. A small group of people in the know. Artemas is on it, of course, and Dr Setiawan too. And so is your boss – *C* – by the way."

Elizabeth's eyes widened. Everything was starting to fit together. She looked back at Za-Farka. "So where do you get your information from?"

"Ah, now you're asking! Well, I'm based on Za-Nak. Let's just say I have an occupation there that's close to the IGC. It's low-level – but trusted."

*

And so they continued talking and Elizabeth continued learning about Za-Farka and her job and her secret network and the IGC and about the worlds beyond her world. Until eventually, when Ormil-ah had disappeared beneath the treeline and the coffee had turned cold in the thermos and fully two hours had passed since breakfast started, Za-Farka said her farewells, wished Elizabeth good luck for the training with a wink, and departed.

20

Those two hours on Ormilu passed in the space of three minutes on Zil. Three minutes that would turn Juckes' world – and his body – upside down.

After learning where Dr Setiawan was being taken, Juckes had felt triumphant. *The 55th floor.* This was intelligence gold. Cold, hard, actionable.

Not quite able to believe his luck, he drifted into the open doors of the next elevator along. He had no intention of going to the 55th floor – that information he would take back to Sir Claude. His focus now was to get higher in the building, to somewhere with a window. He wanted to get a proper view of the facility and confirm its purpose.

So – with his mind rotating about lots of things, but none of them connected to his immediate surroundings – Juckes stepped into an elevator just to the left of where he'd seen Setiawan.

Mistake.

He couldn't know it, but he had just entered an elevator reserved for the facility's managers. For the elite. Unaccompanied humans were not supposed to use the elevators at all – *that's what the stairs were for* – and certainly not this one. The second thing he couldn't know was that he had just entered it behind the Controller of the facility. *The boss.* Him and his entourage.

If he was going to break elevator protocol at any point, this was precisely not the point at which to do it, nor the people to do it with.

The Controller's pot-bellied entourage looked up at Juckes with outrage. As one, they turned to their boss for guidance.

A moment later, as they erupted with questions, Juckes' earpiece starting spitting English at him like venom.

"Shall we electrocute him, sir? Or just have him killed?" was the general gist.

Juckes froze. The glass elevator doors had closed behind him – but the elevator hadn't moved. Not one inch. And now everyone was staring at him, both those inside the elevator and those outside. He had done the last thing he wanted. He had made himself conspicuous.

The Controller – a relatively athletic and extremely busy Zailan, whose head at that moment was full with quite different matters – looked at Juckes with irritation. He started casting about in his pockets for something which he failed to find. A moment later, an underling passed him a handheld device, a bit like a remote control, but smaller and with a single red button on it. The red button was covered by a transparent plastic casing.

Juckes had a premonition of the device's purpose. A sickening chasm opened up inside him where his stomach used to be. He turned to flee but the glass doors remained shut.

The Controller took the pad, flipped the plastic catch, and pressed the ostentatious red button in the

143

middle.

Nothing happened.

He held it down for several seconds.

"What's wrong with it? The damn thing's broken." The Controller tossed it aside, while the underling who had given it to him looked mortified, his long mouth undulating in several shapes of career despair.

"Get me another!"

Instantly, another five control pads appeared under the Controller's nose. He took one with a sigh, flipped the plastic safety catch and thumped hard against the red button.

This one, alas, was working.

And how.

Juckes dropped to the floor of the lift as his legs crumpled beneath him and pain blossomed around his ankle like an exploding firework. His brain tried to order his hands down to rip the ankle tag off. As if that might work. But the highly charged electrons, which were thundering along his nervous system looking for somewhere to earth, threw aside his own nerve messages like so many paper darts in front of a freight train. Juckes' body twitched and writhed helplessly as his muscles spasmed at random. The only message passing reliably along his nervous system was *pain.* But the intense screamful of it that he wanted to release remained merely a horrible thought as his throat gurgled pathetically and his lungs failed to either draw in air or expel it.

Juckes had been electrocuted before.

It was one of the less enviable rites of passage on his special forces training. The part of the course designed to prepare them for torture.

But practising agony – as Juckes was now learning

somewhere within his fried brain – doesn't improve it.

"Ah, that's better." The Controller sighed with momentary satisfaction. The sight of a sentient creature in extreme distress was a refreshing, albeit transient, release for a Zailan burdened by near-infinite bureaucratic responsibilities. Taking their cue from the boss, the entourage started pressing their pads enthusiastically. As they watched Juckes twitch and spasm, they broke out into shrill, aggressive giggles.

"Hah! Make him squirm."

"Yeah, *scum*."

"Hey – if more than one of us presses at the same time, does that double the pain?"

"Might work – we're using the newer model. What kind of tag is he wearing? Can anyone—"

"Just *do it!*"

Juckes heard their chatter through his earpiece as in a nightmare, his body spasming and his lungs suffocating. It was if the lightning that had struck 55 Cleremont Avenue had been bottled and re-released into his body. Not just one, but multiple strikes – again and again and again—

"Cut it out already," the Controller's voice rose above the others. "Don't *kill* him. Or at least not here. *We're not animals.*"

"Sorry, boss."

"Yeah, sorry boss – wasn't meaning to kill him. Just thought—"

The electrocution stopped as abruptly as it had started. One of the underlings thumped on the panel and the elevator doors reopened. Juckes felt a couple of feet connect with his numbed body, as he was booted from the lift. He heard them still muttering apologies to the Controller as the doors slid shut again.

When he looked up, the passers-by were ignoring him. Feverish, trembling, his body stiffening into a kind of living *rigor mortis*, he made a mental note to himself. A human entering a lift causes a scene. But a human being electrocuted to within an inch of his life? *Not interesting.*

Juckes staggered to his feet, making his muscles work through sheer force of will.

Just ahead he saw another human – a supervisor – open a door leading to a staircase. It was to the left of the lifts. The supervisor held it open. Juckes made his way through and collapsed against the wall on the other side. He nodded his thanks, but the other man had already gone.

Still trembling, Juckes' whole body started to relax from the strain. That group of Zailans weren't interested in him anymore. They'd done all they needed to do.

He started to breathe again. He took stock.

He was alive – his body was damaged but not broken – and he had infiltrated their headquarters.

He was still in the game.

21

Elizabeth was lying in the hayloft.

The fire in the grate below had not yet burnt itself out. She was enjoying the residual heat as it gathered under the roof and mixed with the draughts and eddies that circulated there.

Lying on her back, propped up on her elbows, she stared through the dormer window opposite. The bottom left quadrant of Ormil-ah was visible. The light was on in the neighbour's house again. She saw the planet in glorious technicolour, its presence so large, she could almost feel its gravitational pull – a strange and exciting energy drawing her upwards from her solar plexus.

She knew she ought to feel tired, but she didn't remotely. Ormilu was a planet devoid of electricity and all the energies of civilisation. And yet despite that – or perhaps *because* of it – Elizabeth found the very atmosphere of the place crackled with energy.

Elizabeth's mind wandered back to the conversation at breakfast. She found she had perfect recall. Even without using her memory techniques – the ones that allowed her to remember a 100-digit encryption key with only fifteen minutes' effort – she could bring every detail to mind.

The details were all clear – Za-Farka and her network, the Intergalactic Council, the Za-Nakarians, the Zailans and the rest – but what to make of them? How could she possibly get her head around what she had learnt?

She couldn't.

Not yet.

Her thoughts wandered on again.

After Za-Farka had left, Sir Claude had taken her on a training run. Fifteen miles. They stayed on a trail deep within the forest, where the snow cover was lightest. The pace was brisk. The old dog was annoyingly fit, of course, and she started falling behind over the final few miles. But, after the madness of the preceding 24 hours, the run had grounded her again – just as Sir Claude had said. Time had slipped by.

She wasn't surprised to find Sir Claude was in peak condition. But she was surprised to detect in him only the faintest traces of the condescension he had dolled out on Cleremont Avenue.

Or maybe he was just the same, and she was the one who had changed? Maybe she had stopped caring what he said – or at least stopped taking everything so personally. *So seriously.*

Elizabeth released her elbows and lay back in her rudimentary – but wonderfully warm – bed. Her thoughts lingered over Sir Claude.

There was more to him than met the eye. And – she grudgingly acknowledged to herself – there was already plenty that met the eye. She reflected that, to a certain type of lady, he must be devastatingly handsome. *Just like my husband.* Ageing well, groomed well – handsome, capable, rich – and with more than a hint of mystery in his past. A whole wardrobe full of it.

She was equally sure, however, that she was not that sort of lady. She was too self-reliant, too independent. She didn't want to be in anyone's shadow. Be anyone's appendage.

So, what do I want?

She mulled the question idly, played with it in her head... And found she didn't have an answer.

I'd like my father back, she said to herself half in jest.

Her thoughts wandered across to him. To the void he had left behind. *The ache.*

Aged nineteen and fatherless. She hadn't realised how much she needed him – until he wasn't there anymore. She had spent four joyless years at university. She felt like a vine, which had lost the trunk round which it had climbed. With him, she had reached higher, seen further. Without him, possibilities collapsed, horizons shrank.

Healing had come eventually, of course, as it always does. And with that healing, another realisation. Something that had been obvious to her mother all along. Her father had needed *her* too. Her and her sister. At home among his books, or his daydreams – or among wildlife – he avoided the society of other men. It was his family that sustained him. He *needed* them. All the way until the heart defect, which he had kept hidden from them, removed all needs and wants.

And then there it suddenly was.

The answer to her question, *what do I want?*

The clarity of Ormilu made the complex seem obvious. She wanted *to be needed.*

And then came the revelation. A thought so obvious that its delayed arrival was all the more powerful.

Of course, she was wrong for her husband.

She was terrible for him.

She wanted someone who needed her not as an accessory, but someone who needed her as an inalienable, non-negotiable fact of their existence. Someone who needed her strength, her stamina. Someone who would fold without her.

And he – Charles – wanted something similar. That was the whole problem. In his own way, he also wanted to be needed. He wanted a wife who was a little bit vulnerable, needed a little bit of propping up, while being eternally grateful for his strength. Someone who would play second fiddle to his sparkling career and his sparkling talents.

What he *didn't* need was a wife who had just been given an assignment he might have hoped for himself – but would never know about, because they could barely talk to each other about their own jobs.

Everything was so obvious, so clear. *Two strong people who both want to be needed.*

No wonder that, two months in, they had both been able to bear this trial separation.

Part of the magic of Ormilu – the strange, trance-like quality it produced in her – meant that she was experiencing this revelation not in a selfish way. There was no *Poor me* or *What a mistake I've made.* Instead, she felt a movement of pure pity for her husband.

She knew she wasn't to blame. She hadn't seduced him into this inappropriate future like some temptress with a plan. They had walked forward together, hand-in-hand. And somehow, with the passage of a few years – quite inevitably and without either of them noticing – the grip had slipped. Until they had become quite separate. She could see it clearly now. And so there he was, in a marriage that wasn't right for him.

Like the play of light within a crystal, the thoughts continued to dart round Elizabeth's head. And once again, Elizabeth wondered how she would ever sleep.

But the calmness of Ormilu prevailed.

Sleep overran her and sent her down, down, and down into its most refreshing depths.

22

Juckes had climbed to the 22nd floor.

The Zailan numerals on each landing meant nothing to him. Just squiggles. But he had been counting the flights. 22. He estimated the lowest ring of darkened windows, which he had earlier noted, were probably somewhere between the 20th and 25th floors and probably straddled more than one floor. Just a guess.

So he had climbed to the 22nd floor.

He took a few moments to gather his breath. It had been a slow climb; he had stopped on each landing. Three or four other humans had passed him on the way, casting furtive looks in his direction. Almost sympathetic. They knew what an electrocution looked like. Juckes felt like he belonged now.

He pulled the watch from his pocket. T+60. Fifteen of those minutes had been spent just dragging himself up the staircase. He pulled himself upright again and shook his joints. The agony of the electrocution had subsided, just a little, and the disabling stiffness was easing.

He looked at the door in front of him. *What was behind it?* Possibly a service corridor. Hopefully not a security barrier.

He pushed against it and entered.

*

In the event it was neither.

Because what Juckes had just walked into was the central control room of the facility. He could tell immediately. *Instinctively.*

This was the nerve centre.

Entirely open plan, the outer wall was an unbroken ring of windows. Sitting under the ring of windows was a ring of computer terminals, manned by upwards of a hundred operators, evenly spaced around the perimeter. The terminals flickered with activity. They were displaying video footage, radar images, location maps and technologies Juckes couldn't even guess at. He was tempted to walk once round the room. A single walk-past might get him close enough to one of those screens to confirm – finally – what exactly this facility was that they were so busy controlling.

But he checked himself. No-one seemed to have noticed his presence. The lack of security was puzzling. The easiness of it made him uneasy. He wasn't going to push his luck, not after the last encounter.

He continued to scan the room.

Just inside the ring of computers, managers were moving quietly to and fro, their footsteps cushioned by the deep pile carpet. They were passing messages, holding brief discussions, looking over the operators' shoulders to check the activity on their screens.

The whole place exuded quiet efficiency, *hushed power.* Definitely the control room.

Towards the middle was a raised dais, perhaps fifteen yards in diameter, with a low rope that discreetly restricted access. Exotic pot plants and some high-tech planning screens denoted this as a high-status area. Somewhere for senior managers to hold quiet meetings, while remaining half-visible.

Juckes was sucking in the dynamics of the room – kilobytes of information passing through his eyes – when he realised that another pair of eyes had fastened onto him. Through a narrow channel of vision, between the deep green leaves of a plant on one side and a swivel chair on the other, he saw a Zailan watching him. And not just any Zailan. This was the one from the elevator – *the boss* – the one who had electrocuted him.

Juckes didn't hesitate.

He turned as swiftly as his stiffened body would allow, headed back through the door and back down the staircase.

*

The Controller was nobody's fool.

He could sniff out risks with an almost feline sensitivity. He had a sixth sense for it. If you wanted to survive in the Caucus, you had to spot danger at the first whiff – it might be the only indication you ever got. By the second whiff, you'd be dead – knife in the back, body in the lake. Not literally of course. They weren't animals after all. But metaphorically – *career-wise* – dead.

And right now, the Controller's instincts told him there was something about that slave that was trouble.

As he stared – in the passing of a single moment – his brain recognised him from the encounter in the elevator. In the next nano-second, he figured

THE ZOO OF INTELLIGENT ANIMALS

something was amiss. The slave was half a yard from tripping the perimeter security. Slaves weren't allowed in here, of course they weren't. If he took one small step forward, the circuit in his ankle tag would be completed and another violent surge of electricity would pass through his body. The slave was taking this risk *minutes* after being electrocuted to within an inch of his life?

The Controller continued to stare. There was something else about the slave that made him uneasy. *But what?*

And then he put his finger on it.

The eyes.

A slave's eyes should look blank and brainwashed. But this one's didn't. They expressed quiet confidence. Intelligence even. *And that was after being electrocuted.*

The Controller didn't like eyes like those. Not in an underling and definitely not in a slave. In fact, they weren't the eyes of a slave at all, they were the eyes of someone who was *free.*

The Controller knew this one was trouble, just *knew it.* He was about to stand up and call out – when the slave spotted him and left.

The Controller stood up anyway. He started looking left and right for an underling, when a voice behind made him jump.

It was the morning Duty Manager with an urgent question.

It didn't do to look jumpy in front of staff. The Controller felt all the more embarrassed precisely because he *was* feeling jumpy. He re-focussed quickly onto what he was being asked.

The Duty Manager was reporting on the latest asset

to arrive in the facility. Abducted from London. 'Doctor Agustus Setiawan'. An interesting case this one. An anthropologist and also a member of the so-called 'Council'. Their intelligence sources reported the Council to be the only known group on Earth in regular contact with alien species. In other words, the only ones who might present a threat to the Controller's plans.

"So, how was the interrogation? Was the truth serum applied?"

"Yes."

"*And?*"

"Nothing. He's not even aware of the message from the Golgothans."

"And the mass abduction? The ten thousand?" The Controller's gaze flitted to the perimeter window. Through it he could see the new park. Fully constructed – still uninhabited.

"No. Not a thing. Blissfully ignorant." The Duty Manager smiled.

"Aah…" This was welcome news. The Controller paused for a moment as his brain rifled through implications and options. They'd been trying for months to identify and track down members of the Council. It wasn't easy. But if – *if* – the Council knew nothing about their plans, then perhaps there was nothing to worry about?

The Zoo Controller made his decision. And his mood lifted. "If the asset knows nothing, then he's no longer an asset. You can arrange for his exit – and make it colourful." The Controller winked at his Duty Manager. Colourful exits were what this facility majored in.

"Actually," the Duty Manager replied, "the human

we had lined up for this evening's spectacular has fallen sick with a fever. We could still use her, but she might not put up the same—"

"—resistance?"

"Exactly."

"Well then," the Controller replied, "your problem has just solved itself. Tonight it is." The pair smiled a final time before the Duty Manager turned and made his way to the elevators.

The Controller sat back down at his desk. He rubbed his eyes as he tried to re-focus on the task he had been working on before all the interruptions.

Interruptions…

Of course!

The strange slave with the confident eyes.

The Controller stood back up to hail his Duty Manager back. *Why didn't I mention it to him just now?* The Duty Manager had been one of the small group with him in the elevator…

But he was already back in that same elevator and the doors were already closing.

The Controller thought for a moment about fetching one of his other managers and asking them to investigate. But the slave could be anywhere by now. What information could he give? There were just over a thousand slaves in the facility. Probably over a hundred in the building right now. *"Find the one with the suspicious eyes."* He would sound like a fool. Or, even worse, a paranoid fool.

Meantime the task on his desk was pulling his gaze back. He sat back down. He had an important lunch appointment to prep. The Controller wasn't one to neglect a nagging problem – but if you have *two* nagging problems, then logically, you deal with the first one first.

And nagging problem number one was the Regional Governor.

*

The Regional Governor was one of the most powerful figures on Zil. So high in the Caucus, you could only go one higher. His was a career in the clouds – beyond the vision of ordinary Zailans – god-like. And in about thirty minutes he would be visiting the Controller for one of their informal lunches.

But when it came to the Regional Governor, there was no such thing as an informal lunch. Everything had to be perfect. Even the casual touches had to be perfectly casual.

The Controller carefully hinged open a small, polished wooden box on the table in front of him. As the lid swung back, it revealed several small, velvet-lined compartments.

Everything about this box looked expensive, everything about the Controller's movements looked reverential. He switched on a desk lamp and picked up an eyepiece like a watchmaker's loupe. He held it to his left eye with one hand, while his other took hold of a pair of tweezers, which he directed into one of the box's compartments. Very carefully, the tweezers closed around a small gemstone. He lifted it from the tiny scarlet cushion on which it had been perched.

As he started to examine the stone through his eyepiece, the Controller could feel the stress departing his body.

Obsequium.

Very rare. Not the largest piece you could find, but

flawless. Its faceted surfaces glinted and sparkled in different shades of crimson and ochre. One of the exceptional properties of this gem was the changeability of its colour. Under daylight, it took on a hue of soothing russet; but under indoor lighting, its colouring veered towards an intense scarlet. Almost priceless.

But not actually priceless.

After all, everything has a price. *Everyone.* In this case, 20 million Ziloti. A lot to pay, the Controller thought, but worth it. The stakes were high. *The highest.*

The Controller permitted himself a half-smile as he released it into the small brown pouch sitting opposite the gem box. He heard it clink as it nestled amongst the other stones.

And the best thing about this gift?

He wouldn't even tell the recipient what he was getting. The Controller knew how it would play out. The recipient would gather up the brown pouch discreetly, with only a thin smile of acknowledgement; a gem expert would be consulted – perhaps as soon as tomorrow – and the true value would be discovered. His guest would find out everything he needed to know soon enough and be even more impressed by the Controller's understatement.

The Controller loved precious gems, *loved them.* Most members of the Caucus did. It wasn't hard to see why. The Controller's tweezers hovered over the box for a moment, before descending again into the velvety depths and withdrawing another sparkling, many-faced stone. This time, *oleaginite.* Gems were hard, implacable, unchanging. Their character was dependable, unyielding, tough. But also – *being honest*

– a bit limited. This one might refract light one way, that one another. They didn't have character the way an animal does, or a pet – or a submissive. Their *real* character lay outside of them: in the reaction of the beholder. In the gasps of admiration they elicited, the excitement, *the awe.*

Without that admiration, what were gems in truth? Just stones. Polished pebbles. Faceted gravel.

But *with* it, what were they?

Everything. Gravel became gold, pebbles became power – ore became *awe.*

The Controller dropped the oleaginite into the same brown pouch – listened for the little clink as it landed – and looked up at the large picture of the Supreme Governor. It was hanging above the elevator doors, the one windowless section of the control room's perimeter. The Supreme Governor looked down on this room as he looked down on almost every room on Zil, with his enigmatic half-smile. It was a smile that might seem to the uninitiated – *to a submissive* – to hint at benevolence, at deeper wisdom. But the Controller knew, like every member of the Caucus, that this smile was enigmatic not because the Supreme Governor was an enigma, but because the Supreme Governor was only *pretending* to smile. He was lending to his psychopathic, flint-like core a hint of character. The enigmatic half-smile was pure theatre, a mask – *a faceted surface.* But how it worked among the submissives. They believed he cared about them; they believed he loved them. That enigmatic smile inspired admiration. Devotion.

Awe.

23

Elizabeth, it seemed, had passed the first two rounds of her training this morning. First up, a five-mile run through the forest – at pace – with a weighted knapsack on her back. This time, as they raced back into the clearing, she had lead Sir Claude by a couple of yards. Round one to Elizabeth. From there, straight into round two: shooting static targets from a standing position – at twenty yards. Sir Claude had lined up a variety of items in order of size along a fallen tree trunk. Elizabeth had started with the largest targets on the left and worked her way along the trunk to the smaller ones – like some kind of weaponised eye test. A single shot was all she needed for each – until she reached the Robertson's jam jar at the end of the line. She hit that with the second shot.

Elizabeth lowered the revolver, satisfied. The woodshed was a few yards to her right; the log cabin about twenty yards to her left. She thought she glimpsed Dr James passing one of the windows – or maybe she imagined it. She looked forward again. Beyond the targets, she could see the sparkling, snow-laden landscape stretching for miles and miles.

Day three on Ormilu.

Elizabeth was cold and her legs were aching. A

blister had started to form on her left heel. The snow was blindingly bright – the cold was intense – and the exercise was beyond demanding.

She was, in short, loving it.

She was waiting now for Sir Claude to set up round three. *Moving* targets. Although it wasn't at all clear to her how they were going to practice that. She was already missing her Browning 9mm. Light, accurate, and quick-firing, it was standard issue in her department. She looked at the gun in her hand. This thing, by contrast, was heavier, clunkier, and considerably more powerful. *The Webley Mark IV.* Sir Claude's service revolver from the war – the *Second*, not the First, thank God. Although the distinction seemed moot.

She'd asked Sir Claude earlier how much use an old service revolver was going to be where they were going? His reply was simple. *Lethal is still lethal.* Elizabeth had asked why Za-Farka couldn't get them something *more...* modern? But Sir Claude had repeated her rule: never to share technologies beyond what a civilisation already had.

"Right, I think we're ready." Sir Claude was back alongside Elizabeth.

"So what's the target?"

Sir Claude pointed to a contraption he had rigged up beyond the end of the fallen tree trunk. It looked like some kind of small, primitive catapult. Next to it was a pile of... *something.*

"Seedpods," Sir Claude said. "From the forest. That's what you'll be shooting."

He passed her one. It was spherical, the size of a large tennis ball, with layers of hard scales like a pinecone.

"Come on – let me show you how it works."

He went back over to his catapult, loaded one of the strange projectiles into it, levered back the arm – and released it.

T H W A M

The catapult's arm whipped the air and the projectile went hurtling upwards, briefly describing an elegant parabola across the face of the Ormilu landscape. The feathered scales meant it didn't fly as fast as a tennis ball – *but almost.*

"*There.* Simple." Sir Claude loaded a second one into his contraption. "Ready?"

"No."

"Excellent." Sir Claude released the catapult a second time and a second of his strange targets went arcing through the air.

Elizabeth fired.

C R A C K

She didn't expect to hit and – so far as she could tell – she didn't get anywhere close.

"Sir Claude," she called out. "This isn't a shotgun and those aren't clay pigeons. I'm not going to waste any more of your ammunition trying to hit *that.*"

"Elizabeth – where's your ambition?" Sir Claude called back with perfect good humour. "Here. Let's swap."

The two changed position. Elizabeth sat down beneath the trees and loaded one of the pinecone-like fruits onto the primitive catapult. Warily, she levered the arm back.

"All ready this end, Sir Claude."

"Very good," he called back. "*Pull!*"

Elizabeth released the mechanism.

Sir Claude's gun fired – and the cone deflected in mid-flight. A little shower of splintered scales fluttered down onto the snow beneath.

"*There.* You see? Perfectly possible." Sir Claude handed the gun back to Elizabeth. "Your turn."

Twenty times Elizabeth fired. And twenty times she missed. On her last attempt – with her last bullet – she tried to persuade herself she saw a slight deflection in the projectile's flight. But she hadn't.

"*Hopeless,*" she remarked, as Sir Claude joined her.

"Not at all," he replied. "This is why we train. Come on, let's get some more bullets. We store them in the woodshed."

*

Elizabeth stood at the doorway to the shed, while Sir Claude wen to the ammunition store in the far corner.

She was a little annoyed to have missed the moving targets, but not very. As far as she was concerned, they were an impossible ask. Except that Sir Claude had managed it. Now *that* was annoying.

As she loitered at the doorway, her eye picked out something curious. In the centre of the floor, directly below the storm lantern. She stooped down to pick it up. It was a small circular, domed object – the size and shape you might get if you sliced the top two inches off a football. Its colour was a dull, gun-metal grey. It was heavy. It felt both high tech and indestructible.

"Sir Claude, what's this?"

"Hmm?" Sir Claude turned to look. "Oh, I should

put that down if I were you," he replied. "Unless you want the steps to land on top of you?"

Elizabeth quickly replaced the object on the floor.

"That, Elizabeth, is what we call a *beacon*."

"A beacon?"

"Yes. It's what we use to navigate the library steps with precision."

Elizabeth shrugged.

"Well... When we pilot the steps, we enter spatial coordinates. *Seven-dimensional* coordinates as it happens. We'll get to all that when we do your navigation training. Point is, the coordinates will direct the steps more or less where you want to go. But they just won't be precise."

"Alright... So the beacon improves the accuracy?"

"Exactly. If there's a beacon within four hundred yards, then your problems are solved. The steps will land precisely on top of it."

"Four hundred yards?"

"That's the range. If the steps are out by more than that, the beacon has no effect." Sir Claude crossed the shed to join her. His ammunition pouch was full again. "Tell you what, shall we break for a cup of tea? Guaranteed to improve your aim."

"You think so? Worth a try."

*

The pair sat quietly on a couple of tree stumps, sipping tea that Sir Claude had produced from the thermos. Their chatter had faded away to a companionable silence, as they stared out over the far-reaching snowscape.

Elizabeth felt good.

She felt she had been accepted by Sir Claude in some undefinable way. Accepted for who she actually was and not just the person that C happened to send his way.

As for the shocking conclusions of the previous evening, even they didn't dampen her mood. *The opposite.* She felt a strange elation at her newly won clarity. She was seeing her life from a distance. Emotions and feelings that had previously seemed complex and boundless now appeared simple and defined. Where previously she would look into her emotional life as if staring into fog – now she felt more like a gemologist, dispassionately examining the contours of a small and uncut stone.

Maybe she would feel stress and anxiety once she was back in London. Maybe there would be a messy confrontation. Or maybe she would suppress the problem again – like she'd been doing for years.

But right now there was only right now.

Her eye drifted lazily back to the log cabin.

She saw Dr James again, passing one of the windows. The sight of him triggered another thought. More of an itch.

"Dr James… *Artemas…*" She started, not entirely sure where the sentence was going. "Why… Why isn't he taking part too?"

"I beg your pardon?"

"I mean…" Elizabeth was confused. She felt emboldened by their growing friendship to speak out, but now she regretted it. And it was already too late to turn back. "Since we got here, he… He hasn't—"

"—done much?"

"Well, yes."

"You'd be happier if he did a little more washing up

166

perhaps?"

"Perhaps."

"And maybe joined our training?" Sir Claude gestured with his elbow to the targets. His voice carried the faintest hint of hostility.

Elizabeth's cheeks were burning. She realised she'd just overstepped some invisible line and wished she hadn't. Her feelings towards Dr James weren't at all what Sir Claude was probably now supposing. But there again, she wasn't sure what they were. The clarity she was feeling about her life on Earth didn't – it transpired – apply to her life on Ormilu.

She did know, though, that at some point in the last couple of days she'd stopped wanting to irritate Sir Claude. And now she'd done precisely that.

"The reason that Artemas isn't out here with us right now, Elizabeth," Sir Claude started, landing on her name in a tone that was just the wrong side of frosty, "is because he's back in the cabin learning Zailan. He's got a total of four days, maybe five, to learn their script, so that at least one of us can read it. There's only one human alive who could master the grammatical niceties of an alien language and an alien script in under a week – and memorise two to three thousand words to boot. And that's Artemas. So that – *in summary* – is what he's doing."

"Of course," Elizabeth replied, shrinking inside herself. "I apologise, Sir Claude. My words came out wrong. I didn't mean to cast judgement."

Sir Claude looked sideways at Elizabeth and examined her critically. He nodded. "And I didn't mean to speak so harshly." He returned his gaze to the further landscape. "You know how I see it?" he asked after a pause.

"How?"

"We each have our own place in the universe and our own role to play. It's our job – the job of each and every one of us – to find out what that is. That's the single most important thing we can do." He paused for a moment. "I don't know if there is or isn't some kind of divine Providence guiding us. Adelaide's certain there isn't; I'm no longer sure. But I do know that Artemas' role is not to run marathons through the woods or shoot moving targets. Or to be a housekeeper. I'd no more ask someone to go against their nature than ask a pig to fly. Let the ducks fly and the pigs sniff for truffles."

"That makes perfect sense, Sir Claude. Thank you," Elizabeth replied. "*And me?*" she blurted out on one of her impulses.

Sir Claude looked at her sideways, quizzically, as he withdrew his pipe from his coat pocket. "Well, you're here, aren't you?" he replied, his response as cryptic as her question.

He searched his pockets for his tobacco pouch and matches. After some patting, he located them in an inside pocket. "Look," he continued, "I don't judge people by who they are or by what they do. *This person's a bricklayer – that person's an academic.* It's all well and good. No, I judge them by *the challenges* they overcome. And on that basis, Artemas is as fine a man as I've ever met. And I've met a lot of fine men in my life, believe me. And women too."

Elizabeth nodded and bit her tongue. She didn't trust it to say anything sensible.

"Artemas is a linguist. But I'll bet you're thinking he's rather inarticulate for a linguist? Am I right?"

Exactly that thought had crossed Elizabeth's mind

at least a dozen times. Probably more. But she shrugged her shoulders in a non-committal way. Dr James was inarticulate for a linguist – *true* – but she had a remarkably impulsive mouth for someone in her profession. *However was she going to stay in it?*

"You know that when Artemas first came to live with us – this was during the war – he was so traumatised, he couldn't speak? Not English, not any language. Literally, *could – not – speak.* Did you know?"

It was a rhetorical question. Of course Elizabeth didn't know. She shook her head anyway. Sir Claude grunted and took a pinch of tobacco from his pouch, which he started to prod into his pipe with a half-frozen finger.

Elizabeth watched him. She rarely needed much courage to open her mouth, but she did this time, at this moment.

"Would you tell me about it please, Sir Claude? I'd very much like to hear."

Sir Claude looked at her, his gaze drilling into hers.

"Yes, I believe you would," he said at length. He turned back to his pipe and continued to bed the tobacco down. Elizabeth found herself in an agony of suspense. *Is he going to tell it?* The conversation had already taken one uncomfortable twist, she wasn't sure where it might go next. Or even if it would go at all—

"It was late 1940, during the Blitz," he started. "Artemas' father – that was my nephew – had just been killed. He was on active service in North Africa – at Sidi Barrani. A ghastly business." Sir Claude paused again. As if his mind needed extra time to make the transition to another decade – *another planet.*

"Artemas' mother didn't take it well, not at all. She

was the gentlest of souls – a poetic creature if you will. She'd have done well in a Tennyson poem… But not alas in wartime London with a dead husband and a miserable son. She nearly lost her reason, that's the truth of it. We moved her to a cottage on the estate and arranged the best care that we could. But raising a child was no longer an option."

Sir Claude lit his pipe. In the stillness, Elizabeth heard first the scratch and then the hiss of the match. And then the faintest crackle as the tobacco came alight.

"So where did that leave Artemas?" she asked.

"Yes – exactly," Sir Claude replied. "The poor lad had been sent away to be schooled – some God-awful pile in the middle of a Yorkshire bog. Although 'schooled' was hardly the right word for it."

"What was the right word?"

"*Bullied*," Sir Claude replied without hesitation. "There he was, a fish completely out of water. Shy, inarticulate, sensitive – his father dead – no siblings to look out for him. With all those disadvantages you can imagine how the other boys treated him?"

Elizabeth wished it might have been kindness – or compassion. But that was the one word that no-one had ever yet associated with an English boarding school in the mid-20th Century. *Compassion*.

"It was merciless," Sir Claude resumed. "The boarding school, like all schools back then, was running on a skeleton staff. All the teachers under 40 had been called up. With most of them away, and surrounded on all sides by ten miles of moor, the boys had turned… They'd turned *feral*. You can imagine what they did to Artemas? Actually, you probably can't. I certainly couldn't. God knows, school had been rough enough in my day." Sir Claude shook his head sadly. "And here's the thing. When all those beefy farmers' boys found out about Artemas' mother, *it got worse*. I say again, you cannot imagine what they did to him."

Sir Claude stared straight ahead. Elizabeth watched his jaw muscles clench and unclench. Into the tense stillness, she watched the aromatic smoke curl slowly upwards from the end of his pipe – a motion so elusive, so exquisitely delicate, the merest breath of wind would have dashed it.

"Dr Bryce," he resumed at length. "He was the headmaster at the time. A 70-year-old scholar of classics. Thoroughly likeable fellow. But run ragged as you can imagine. He wrote me a candid letter about the situation. *Very candid*. As soon I got it, I showed it to Adelaide. We both knew what had to be done. We couldn't leave Artemas there.

"That same day, I got straight in the car. The ridiculous thing was, I'd used up my fuel ration. I had to fill the tank on the black market – from some ghastly spiv on Exmouth Market, would you believe?" Sir Claude released a mirthless chuckle. "Anyway, it got the job done. I brought Artemas back to Cleremont Avenue the next day. The bombing in London now became a risk for the poor lad. But far better a quick death like that than the slow death he was enduring up in that bog."

The two sat silently for a while. Elizabeth knew there was more to come. Her tea had turned cold in her hand. So still was the Ormilu air, the pipe smoke hung round them in strange, wistful layers of grey and blue and white, like low-lying clouds.

She waited.

"So now he was with us, at Number 55," Sir Claude re-started. "This stick-thin, bedraggled creature. *So thin...* You know, I detected something in him, something unusual. I'd seen it a few times in the trenches – more than a few times actually – but never in a seventeen-year-old. He was... *How should I put it?...*

"*Broken.* That's the word. Quite broken. You could see it in the eyes. The light had gone out. The misery was so intense, I wondered if the boy might do himself a mischief. A serious mischief. But Artemas is too gentle a soul for violence. I soon realised he had a different plan. He stopped eating, you see. And he stopped talking, oh yes. Another thing he had in common with the men from the trenches." Sir Claude gave another brief, rueful chuckle. "You had this feeling that he had come to consider life – I don't mean all forms of life, but intelligent, *sentient* life – to be a hideous aberration. A mistake. A ghastly cosmic error that must soon be righted."

As Sir Claude was speaking, Elizabeth detected the faintest flicker of movement from the corner of her eye. She glanced left. Through the window of the log cabin, she saw a figure pass into – and then out of – view. *Dr James.*

"How awful for him—"

"On the contrary," Sir Claude shot back, making Elizabeth start. "It was the making of him." He turned to her with a broad, unexpected smile on his face. His eyes were glistening.

"I don't understand?"

"I often wonder about those bullies, and where they've got to in life. I'll wager they haven't got the one thing that Artemas has got."

Elizabeth's mind raced. *A doctorate? A supportive family? A fine inheritance—*

"*Happiness*," Sir Claude continued. "Not the happiness of some happy-go-lucky character, with an easy disposition and a lucky station in life. Although I suspect that's what people assume when they meet him. *Did you?*" he asked, fixing his piercing gaze on her for a moment. "No need to answer," he added, waving his hand. "No, this was something quite different. This was a young man broken on the rack of this tough world. A boy whose spirit was crushed and who could walk no further, not one single step. But who somehow *crawled* to the far side of his misery. And then, contrary to all expectation, he reached a hidden garden. He did his time in the salt mines. And then he found his Eden. I doubt anything can ever touch him again." Sir Claude drew on his pipe and exhaled. "Do you know your Kierkegaard?" he asked, catching Elizabeth out again.

"I beg your pardon?"

"Kierkegaard. '*It belongs to the imperfection of everything human that... that...*'" Sir Claude's eyes narrowed as he recalled the quotation. "'*...that man can only attain his desire by passing through its opposite.*'" He looked up again. "Study Artemas, Elizabeth. Learn from him. I'm trying to."

Elizabeth nodded. "*Theodicy*," she said. Her turn to catch Sir Claude off guard. She was remembering her very first conversation with Dr James and Lady Danziger – at dinner on Cleremont Avenue.

"Theodicy? Ah yes. Artemas' obsession." Sir Claude looked sideways at her and smiled. "How to explain the presence of evil – of *suffering* – in a world overseen by a loving God... Well, I'm deuced if I know the answer. Back in the trenches, I lost my faith. But in the midst of the Blitz, Artemas found his." Sir Claude shook his head at the strangeness of it all. "Somewhere on his journey from the salt mines to Eden, he met his God."

"But how… *How* did he recover?"

"A good question," Sir Claude replied. "Well, Adelaide and I weren't much help. Two anxious faces – trying to draw him out – *busy* – but determined to give him all the time we could. No use at all. He got thinner and thinner. I'd like to say he got even quieter. But once a fellow's decided to say nothing, you can't get much quieter. No – salvation came from an entirely different quarter."

"Where then?"

"Mrs Carstairs, can you believe it? The housekeeper." Sir Claude laughed a quiet laugh of pure relief, as if the mere mention of her name was enough to roll back the clouds. Elizabeth found herself – irresistibly – laughing with him, while having no idea why.

"Mrs Carstairs, God bless her soul. It's certainly the kindest I've ever met." Sir Claude shook his head with happy disbelief. "Yes, she turned out to be the key to the door. Utterly patient – never judged, you see? Never told Artemas to eat, never asked him to talk. Quite happy to let him be exactly as he was. Extraordinary really. He would sit with her down in the kitchens for hours on end, watching her while she worked. After a while it just became natural that she'd ask him to do little jobs – *fetch me that rolling pin – pass me that pot* – that sort of thing. And he'd oblige. And then with all that food around, of course he started to nibble a bit of this or that. Almost with no-one noticing. And then words. *'Would you like a spot of trifle later?'* – *'Yes, please, Mrs C.'* That's what he called her. 'Yes, please…' When Mrs Carstairs told us later, she didn't even think it consequential. Of course the boy would talk, that was her view all along. *'Yes, please...'* The boy had *talked.* Adelaide was in tears."

Elizabeth stared. In that moment, it was 1940 and she was in Number 55 with them.

"After that, it got a little better every day. He started to heal. *Curiosity* seeped back in. There was no question of him going back to school of course. Artemas was ready to teach himself. You can probably guess by now what he wanted to learn?"

"Languages," Elizabeth replied, getting it.

"Exactly. He took a book from my library, sat down and taught himself Middle Egyptian hieroglyphics. I think he wanted to start as far from the present world as he could. Then one language after another. Gradually getting closer to the 20th Century. Of course, it doesn't matter what he's learning, his accent remains as British as a lemon drizzle cake. He'll never be a great communicator, Artemas. But he set himself the challenge to be a not-great-communicator in as many languages as possible, and by God he's achieved it. Twenty at the last count." Sir Claude had shifted his position on the log pile. He was no longer looking into the middle distance, but facing her directly, staring at her with the full force of his personality. "He chose to rise to his challenges, Elizabeth. To rise above his isolation, to overcome his disgust with humanity, to *communicate.* As it happens, I'm very proud he's my nephew."

*

That evening, as the three of them went about the business of preparing supper, Elizabeth realised that they had already settled into a pattern, a cosy routine.

They talked less and the quiet was almost more companionable than the lively conversations had been. Elizabeth felt like she fitted in. They were comfortable around each other. The awkwardness she experienced earlier with Sir Claude was like the resistance of a mechanical component in the moment before it clicks into place. Elizabeth had found her place within the intricate clock mechanism of the Cleremont Avenue household. Even here on Ormilu.

After supper, they moved to the sofas in front of the log fire. While Sir Claude buried himself in a book, Elizabeth asked Dr James how his language study was proceeding. *Very well, thank you*, he replied, *very well.* She gently encouraged him to tell more.

And so he talked and Elizabeth was soon lost – *happily* – somewhere in the interspaces of Zailan grammar. And as he continued to speak, she noticed through the curtainless window behind him that snow was falling outside, coming down from the Heavens in large generous flakes like a gift.

24

Juckes' heart was pounding. The way that Zailan – *the boss* – had looked at him. There was nothing innocent about it. It was a look of raw suspicion.

He had to assume he had been detected.

His adrenaline and cortisol levels had rocketed, as he flew down the single flight of stairs. It turned out that mixing physiological stress with the after-effects of electrocution was not pleasant. Like mixing bright sunlight with a hangover. His head was cluttered, a cold sweat had formed on his brow, every muscle in his body was trembling.

He made one smart decision. He didn't head for the building's exit. If the alarm had been raised, that was the first place they'd block. He wouldn't get out in time, not in his condition.

Instead – on a hunch – he descended a single floor. He pushed open the door from the staircase and found himself in a service area. *Backstage.* The province of junior staff and humans. No exotic plants or carpets here. Not much air con either. He stumbled along a featureless corridor, his breathing ragged and urgent, palming the wall to stay upright. He tried each door handle as he passed it – desperate for a quiet place to hide and recover.

Every door was locked.

A human came into view.

Juckes tried to straighten himself. The human, who was wearing the same clothing as him and carrying a large rattan backpack, brushed past, apparently taking no notice. Juckes breathed a sigh of relief. He remembered: *tortured* was a perfectly natural look for a human on Zil.

But he also knew that he was yet to fulfil either of his core objectives. *Find out the purpose of the facility – Find a safe place inside it to land.* He had the beginnings of an idea about the first. But nothing at all for the second.

He tried another door handle.

This one yielded. He peered inside: the room looked empty. Juckes stepped in and closed the door behind him. The door had an internal bolt, which Juckes slid gratefully home.

And then he collapsed with his back against the door and sucked in deep lungfuls of air.

*

Five minutes passed. Five minutes during which he expected to hear at any moment an alarm blaring or feet running urgently along the corridor outside.

But nothing.

Juckes dared to believe he might have got away with it.

Slowly, effortfully, he pulled himself to his feet to start investigating just what kind of place he'd stumbled into.

It looked like a storeroom of sorts, barely visited, long and thin. Against one of the walls were storage racks, piled up with boxes and assorted equipment, most of it covered in a film of dust. Juckes cautiously probed in a few of the boxes. Within seconds he spotted items that would be handy.

And it got better.

The wall opposite the shelving was long and gently curved with a waist-to-ceiling window running the full length. It gave a near-perfect aerial view of the facility. Juckes allowed the faintest smile of relief to filter up to his face. *This will do just fine.* He reached into his pocket and retrieved the round, metallic object that Lady Danziger had given him back in the forest. *The beacon.* He placed it on the centre of the floor, flat-side down, dome-side up.

Then he took a couple of steps towards the window. From his new angle of elevation, he could stare down over the top of the giant archways he had seen earlier in the plaza below. And the huge walls that he had seen earlier through the field glasses.

The facility was at last revealing its purpose.

25

High up on the hillside, Elizabeth was getting her first proper view of Ormilu. And she was getting it from a sleigh.

Day 4 on the safe planet and it was her most exhilarating yet.

Quite how she had ended up on a sleigh pulled by huskies, coursing through fresh powder on the snow-covered wilderness of an alien planet, was still a bit of a mystery to her.

The morning had been devoted to navigation training. As soon as he'd seen the huge overnight dump of snow, Sir Claude had – uncharacteristically – relented. A fifteen-mile run through two feet of powder daunted even him. So they had a theory session instead. He had pulled out pencil and paper – made a diagram of the controls on the library steps – and proceeded to instruct Elizabeth in the basics of seven-dimensional navigation.

It was after lunch that he suggested she head out with Artemas on the sled – an experience not to be missed, especially in fresh powder. She'd cautiously asked whether Dr James was experienced with husky sledding? Apparently – came the reply – he'd been out with them a few times before. And anyway, it was a short trail, only ten or twelve miles, and the huskies knew it well. Elizabeth then ventured that, prior to heading into the alien wilderness, perhaps they should both be accompanied by someone *who actually knew what they were doing?* To which Sir Claude had roared with laughter. *Let go* seemed to be the core of his advice. "And anyway, the beasties will take care of you," he'd added with a wink. "I've never met a creature yet, who didn't want to look after Artemas."

And so here Elizabeth was – on a sled – in the wilderness – *letting go.*

As she looked out from the trail at the Ormilu landscape stretching away to her left, she was entranced. The bright coldness, the sense of freedom. It was like her homeland at its glittering best but brighter – illuminated by the mystery of the unknown. The training runs with Sir Claude had always stayed deep in the forest; now at last she was following a trail across wide open vistas. Elizabeth was doing something spontaneous and irresponsible and fun and to her amazement it was exactly that – *fun.* She felt refreshed and alive. More alive than she had felt in years.

She turned to look at her companion. Dr James looked impossibly slight and fragile inside his huge furs. She glanced at the reins hanging loosely from his mittens and noted gratefully that the huskies were guiding themselves – just as Sir Claude had promised.

Steam had fogged Dr James' spectacles. She watched with concern as he put the reins down on his lap and tried to wipe his spectacles. "Here, Dr James," she said briskly, as she took off her own mittens, "you take the reins back and let me take those." Before he could protest, she had taken the spectacles from his nose.

She cleaned both sides with a tissue until the lenses were refracting the Ormilu light with a perfect sparkle. She leaned across, just for a moment putting her face directly in front of his. As she slipped the spectacles back onto the end of his nose, her lips were parted in concentration. Her fingers brushed his cheek as they carefully curled one end of the spectacles over one ear. And then over the other ear too. The faintest whiff of flirtation passed from her to him on the breeze.

Elizabeth turned back to look at the trail ahead. About a mile away, she could see they were going to twist down the hillside, into the forest proper. She wanted to ask Dr James about all the things Sir Claude had told her the previous day. About his past. About his school. But she knew that this was too soon. She looked at the scenery around her, the space – the peace. *Tell me about theodicy*, she asked instead.

"Ah!" His eyes lit up with delight. "Well, it mostly comes down to the difference between religions with one god and religions with many. Do you see?"

"No," she smiled back with equal delight. "I don't see at all."

"Ah, yes. No, it's not obvious, is it? Well, religions with one god – monotheistic religions... Naturally, they imagine their god is loving. So all the suffering in the world is a constant affront, *hmm?* That god may be the Christian God or even the modern god of science."

"Oh, so science is a god too now?"

"Oh, I don't know, *haha!* But we do put a lot of faith in it, don't we? To make us happy – to lift the suffering. *Hmm?* In any case, the same point applies. In the religious age, we tried to pray our suffering away. In the scientific age, we try to *research* it away. But still the suffering remains."

Elizabeth nodded, intrigued. It felt strange to be discussing God and religion at such a moment in such a place – but natural too. This was a landscape that invited the bigger questions – that seemed to speak of infinity. In any case, Dr James didn't traffic in small talk; she had worked that out from the start. "So are you saying... Polytheistic religions have it easier?"

"Religions with many gods? Oh, indeed yes... *and no.*"

"Please explain?"

"Well, they have naughty gods as well as nice – so suddenly, suffering makes more sense. Don't you think? When things go wrong, people think, *oh, that's just the naughty gods doing their work. I must pray harder to the helpful gods!*" Dr James tilted his head down and looked at Elizabeth, mole-like, over the top of his newly cleaned spectacles.

That gesture. Elizabeth felt something stir inside her—

"But it's not all plain sailing for them."

"No?"

"No. They the problem of *order.*"

Elizabeth shrugged.

"Yes – order. Why should Hades respect the same rules as Jupiter? Why should Kali obey the same rules as Brahma? The polytheistic universe may explain the presence of suffering, but it's a lot more chaotic—"

Just at that moment the sled swung sharply. The huskies plunged down and round a hairpin bend in the trail. Elizabeth lurched against Dr James. For a short second they were a clumsy tangle of reins and mittens and fur-lined sleeves. And for a short second, Elizabeth felt embarrassed as she tried to extract herself.

The sled straightened out and Elizabeth started to laugh.

"My, my, Dr James – you werenae making a pass at a young lady, were you?" she asked, slipping into Scots brogue and prodding his shoulder with her mitten.

"*Me?* No, I… That's to say, it was you, who…" Dr James stuttered. He glanced at her again over the top of his spectacles. And then smiled. "Oh! *Haha!* You're teasing me. Yes, very good!"

"Ignore me." Elizabeth smiled and gently took the reins from him. "You were saying?"

"Hmm? Ah yes, about polytheistic religions…"

Elizabeth half-listened as Dr James elaborated on the problem of order and chaos. *Have I just been flirting with him?* she wondered. With a man she deemed a mere simpleton a few days ago. *Yes, I have.* The wilderness – the exhilaration – had unlocked a door within her. Elizabeth wasn't normally the flirting kind. Not before she was married, and certainly not after.

She felt a spasm of guilt – and quickly pushed it down again. *What harm can a little flirting do?* Dr James was hardly the type to make a pass at her. She'd caught him staring at her over dinner the night before. When she'd returned his gaze, his eyes had hurried back down to his plate.

She looked at him again now.

She marvelled at his near-boundless curiosity. At the way he spoke about things with the enthusiasm of someone discovering them for the first time. She wondered if he was always this happy. She wondered if she could be too.

The childlike state he seemed to inhabit – fragile

and wonderful – fused in her mind with the fragile, wonderful landscape around her.

*

The sled descended round several more hairpin bends until the trail levelled out. They were now off the hillside and passing through deep forest. They were still in the same landscape but, in the briefest of transitions, their perspective had changed utterly. The trees were taller and thicker; the view had shrunk from a boundless horizon to less than a hundred yards in any direction; the light reduced to a cathedral gloom. By degrees, they had both fallen silent. For the first time, Elizabeth became aware of the huskies' heaving breath as they hauled their payload forwards.

They continued in silence through the sepulchral quiet of the forest.

As furlong after furlong of dark, unchanging woods passed her – and quite without wanting it to – Elizabeth's mood darkened. Her thoughts changed direction. She cast another sideways glance at her travelling companion. Just for a moment she was seized by a dismal vision.

She saw Dr James, years in the future.

He was alone in the house on Cleremont Avenue – Sir Claude and Lady Danziger long dead – Mrs Carstairs vanished and Juckes moved on – the whole vibrant household dispersed like a circus that's left town. The enchantment gone. Just a few photos and mementoes on a counter somewhere as a reminder of a time that could never return.

In this vision, Dr James remained exactly who he must always be – still childlike, still thoroughly impractical, and still smiling his fragile, indestructible half-smile – even as the layers of dust gathered around him, and the visitors stopped coming, and the house started to fall apart in the myriad little ways that neglected houses do.

The force of the vision lay in its accuracy.

Elizabeth knew it was completely accurate and it made her sad.

*

That evening a new note entered their previously cosy supper gatherings in the log cabin. Sir Claude was noticeably tense.

According to the arrangement he had made with his wife, there was a window of time when they could expect her and Juckes to return to Ormilu. And that window started now, tonight. If things had gone well, they might arrive anytime during the evening. The window ended at the same time the next night. If they weren't back by then, it meant something had gone wrong. Elizabeth didn't need reminding about the consequences of that. Both groups stranded on two different planets, with time passing 40 times faster on one than the other.

Sir Claude tried to hide his tension. But he was no poker player.

The clock was ticking.

26

Elizabeth watches the projectile hurtle out of the undergrowth and up and up—

C R A C K

The report of the revolver shatters the brittle Ormilu air. She's fired. And missed.

Day 5 on Ormilu.

She and Sir Claude have just completed a three-mile run at breakneck speed and launched straight into target practice. As they ran back into the clearing, she was a clear fifty yards ahead of Sir Claude. But the satisfaction was fleeting.

Sir Claude releases a second target. Another miss.

Her breathing is still ragged.

Up goes a third target.

A third miss.

"Never mind," Sir Claude bellows. "Back round we go." She throws the gun into her knapsack and sets off after him.

Another three-mile circuit through the woods.

*

This time, Elizabeth, this time.

She is back in position. The woodshed a few yards to her right, the log cabin off to the left. Sir Claude promised this morning would be their toughest yet. He wasn't lying, the old bastard.

Elizabeth stands, chest still heaving, legs shaking, arms outstretched, two hands on the revolver's grip.

Up goes the projectile.

C R A C K

Missed.
And again.
And a third time.
"Back round we go," Sir Claude bellows.
Elizabeth throws the gun back into the knapsack.
And they're off. Another three-mile circuit through the woods.

*

Elizabeth is back in position, next to the woodshed.

She's run nine miles at full tilt. She's not had a drop of water. With each circuit, the possibility of hitting the moving target seems more remote than ever.

Somewhere in her fogged mind, she has a theory why Sir Claude's turned this morning into a living hell. He's trying to distract himself from thinking about his wife. About the steps that haven't returned. He's trying to distract himself, and yet he can't help bringing them back round to the woodshed. Again and again. So he can keep checking it. He's worried about his wife and she – Elizabeth – is paying the price—

"Focus, Elizabeth, focus."

Sir Claude is next to her. She didn't seen him approach from behind.

"You need to focus. You need to control your breathing. And you need to relax. Focussed and relaxed. It's the only way to live your life." Elizabeth looks at him. "Raise your gun," he says.

His head is just behind her, a few inches from her ear. She raises the revolver.

"When the next target is in the air... You need to believe the bullet in your gun and that projectile are connected. That they belong together. Does that make sense?" It doesn't. "You need to *see* it. And believe it. Really believe it. Once you believe it, it'll happen."

He goes back to his den.

He launches the projectile into the air.

This time – *somehow* – Elizabeth sees it in slow motion. She follows the target's trajectory with the revolver, as if the barrel of her gun is a pen, drawing its path across the sky. She squeezes on the trigger. The gun fires. The projectile explodes in mid-flight.

She has hit it dead centre.

Sir Claude says nothing. Before Elizabeth can begin to think, or congratulate herself, a second projectile is arcing through the air.

She fires a second time. This time a glancing hit. The damaged projectile falls at a new angle towards the ground, spinning erratically.

He launches a third one and she hits it again.

"Bravo, Elizabeth!" Now Sir Claude is on his feet. "Three out of three—"

*

At that moment – literally that moment – the woodshed

to her right gives a brief and silent shudder. They both turn. It's the sort of shudder which suggests repressed energy. Not violent, but powerful. Like being on a boat far out at sea as a tidal wave – still just a moving mass of energy – passes underneath. The tremor passes beneath the feet of the pair and disperses out across the Ormilu forest. A little snow is shaken from the lower branches and falls around the forest clearing like sparkling dust.

Sir Claude knows immediately what has happened. He strides across to the shed.

His wife has returned.

And she isn't alone. She has brought with her one butler (rather heroic) and one German (very confused).

27

Juckes unloaded the stolen kit in front of the others.

"I'll be deuced, Juckes," Sir Claude exclaimed. "However did you manage to bring all that back?"

"Well, sir, among the various roles humans seem to have over there is portering." Juckes held up the strangely primitive rattan backpack. "Bringing the kit back was easy. Aroused no suspicions at all. The miracle was finding an unlocked storeroom."

The group were standing round the dining table looking at Juckes' haul. Night was falling outside. The debrief was almost at an end. Elizabeth had been hearing about Zil and the Zailans. She had learnt about tall obelisk at the centre of the facility and the enormous, unexplained spacecraft on the distant launch site. She heard him describe his infiltration – his electrocution – his sighting of Dr Setiawan. She learnt that Setiawan was on the 55th floor of the obelisk – *probably* – and that the control room was on the 22nd floor – *definitely*. Finally, his story had reached the storeroom on the 21st floor.

As Elizabeth listened, a tumult of emotions was churning beneath the calm surface. She was sorry they were about to leave their simple life on Ormilu but excited about the adventure ahead. She was fearful of confronting the Zailans but felt an unexpected confidence in the team. As the debrief continued, she looked at the faces around the table – at Juckes, at Dr James, at Lady Danziger and her husband. The saboteur – the linguist – the pilot – and the leader. They were formidable. When she had first arrived on Ormilu, her mind was spinning out of control as events and revelations swirled. Now, as she contemplated leaving, she still wasn't in control, but she felt a hundred times calmer. The spinning had stopped and so had the confusion.

She was ready.

*

"You said there were two classes of human on Zil." Sir Claude spoke. "You're wearing the supervisor's outfit. What do the slaves wear?" He looked down at the indistinct heap of clothes on the table in front of them.

"Well…" Juckes started, a little embarrassed, "*These.*" He held up one of the caveman outfits.

"Good God – are we going to have to wear those?" Sir Claude asked.

"Darling, whatever's the matter" – Lady Danziger's eyes twinkled – "I think it'll suit you."

"You do, do you?" Sir Claude took the outfit from Juckes. "Well, that changes things, naturally. How do I look?" He modelled the caveman skins against his body, one hand pressing a strap to his shoulder while the other held the opposite side against his waist. He turned around on the spot. "Fetching?"

A muffled guffaw escaped from the gagged German by the fireplace.

"That good, eh?" Sir Claude grunted, turning to

look at their hostage.

Dr Nussbaum was sitting next to the fire, bound hand and foot to a chair. He was awake now, but as uncooperative as Juckes had predicted. For decency, they had dressed him again in a shirt and trousers. They had all agreed they couldn't leave him alone on Ormilu. He'd have to return with them to Zil.

"Actually, sir, I've brought several of each type of clothing. We can carry spares in the backpack. It's just I thought we might stand out if we were all to wear the same."

"Fair enough, fair enough. So what else is in your bag of tricks?"

Juckes showed them the translation earpiece that they'd retrieved from the German. Elizabeth thought the library steps had made her immune to the wonder of advanced technologies – but they hadn't. Juckes invited her to try it on. She was awestruck as she listened to Dr James speaking Latin through one ear, while a perfect translation arrived in the other.

Next, Juckes showed them the ankle tags. He had brought back five from the storeroom. "You already know what these do," he continued. "I'm afraid it's essential we all wear one. If the Zailans don't see one round your ankle, with the green diode flashing, you'll be stopped immediately."

"But is it that simple?" Elizabeth asked. "Don't they include a tracking device?"

"That's what I assumed at first, ma'am," Juckes replied. "But I don't believe they do. They're not sophisticated. I honestly think their main job – apart from inflicting pain – is to humiliate. To remind humans of their place."

"So how do you fit them?"

"Relatively easily. With the right tools." Juckes explained how he was able to remove the tag from the German and attach it to his own ankle.

"But if it's that easy, couldn't the slaves just remove and replace the tags at will?" Sir Claude asked. "It sounds to me that security is lax over there. Is it?"

"I wouldn't say lax, sir..." Juckes started cautiously. "The system depends on brainwashing. The slaves *don't want* to leave, as far as I can tell..."

The group glanced at the sullen figure of Dr Nussbaum.

"That and the fact they've nowhere to leave to. After all, no human can get within a million light years of Zil. Apart from us, of course. So why should the Zailans worry?" Juckes paused to think. "Overall, the Zailans have a number of precautions to stop humans leaving. But very few to stop them *entering*. I think we have a chance."

The group fell silent. They were encouraged by Juckes' assessment. But they also knew they had been skirting around the *real* issue. They knew humans were there to serve as slaves and menials. But serving *who exactly?* And *how?*

What was the facility actually *for?*

"So, you estimate about a thousand humans in the facility?" Sir Claude asked.

"Actually, sir, it might be rather more than that."

"I don't follow? Are you saying there are more than a thousand slaves?"

"No, sir."

"Well, what then?"

"There aren't just slaves there, sir. There are other humans as well. They fulfil... a *different role*."

"A different role? What role? And how many

more?"

"At a guess, another ten thousand, sir," Juckes replied, answering one question and avoiding the other.

"Good god!" Sir Claude exchanged a horrified look with Elizabeth. "Well, whatever are they doing there?"

"That's... That's a little hard to explain, sir..." Juckes was not given to hesitation. His replies were normally pauseless and reassuring, delivered like the breakfast tray into the morning room – somehow quick and unhurried at the same time. The merest tinkle of crockery as tray touches mahogany.

But not now.

He stuttered hopelessly in front of his employer.

"Well, tell us this then. What conditions are they being kept in?"

"What conditions, sir?"

"Yes. Come on, man, spit it out?"

"The conditions are, err, variable, sir."

"Variable?"

"Yes, sir."

"You mean *universally awful?*"

"No, sir, no," Juckes replied. "Variable, sir. Some are living in, well, modern comfort – or an approximation of it. Others are living in conditions that are more... *medieval.*"

"Exactly, you mean awful."

"No, sir, I mean medieval."

Sir Claude paused and tilted his head slightly to the side as he fixed Juckes with the kind of stare too long exposure to which might give a man internal bleeding.

"Exactly what kind of facility is this?"

Finally.

The question that must be answered.

Juckes cleared his throat with the relief of a man

whose interrogation has reached the point of final confession – a moment that's both daunting and cathartic.

"They appear to be in a sort of zoo, sir."

"A *zoo?*"

"Yes, sir. A zoo."

"What manner of zoo?"

"I would call it a kind of theme park. One in which humans are the star attraction."

28

The Regional Governor levered a large mouthful of grilled porcubus tripe into his colossal mouth. His palate immediately caught the distinctive, earthy aroma of the seasoning.

"Has this been flavoured with... With, *you know?*"

The Regional Governor spoke with one side of his mouth, while the opposite side continued chewing indulgently. The Regional Governor might be uncommonly fat and, frankly, a little repulsive – but he was certainly a connoisseur.

The Zoo Controller nodded back with knowing discretion. "Yes, Governor. It is."

Powdered unibuck horn. The perfect accompaniment to grilled tripe. And said to enhance the male body parts to boot. Unibuck had become very rare on Zil – almost extinct – the Regional Governor was very impressed.

So far, lunch had been going well. The Governor had only arrived half an hour late, he was enjoying the food and the informal setting on the raised dais at the centre of the control room – all of it pitch perfect for the occasion. To be powerful was a pleasure; *to be seen* to be powerful was pure joy. The underlings at work in the control room could see them now and again through the thin scattering of office furniture and pot plants. The Zoo Controller noted with gratification how they lowered their heads with deferential shock when they saw who he was dining with.

Power was in the room.

The conversation, it was true, had been a little stilted. Caucus Zailans in general could only manage a small amount of small talk; they were always itching to move on to business. The more psychopathic the individual, the briefer the small talk. And the better the career prospects: it didn't pay to be too chatty.

Equally, it was important not to be unfriendly either. The trick was to show just the right amount of chattiness. If talking to someone senior, fractionally more chattiness than them. If to someone junior, fractionally less. It was both important to get it right – and difficult.

Somewhere inside his head, the Controller sighed. Just another daily challenge for the psychopathic mind trying to navigate a social world. Constantly studying the rules of interaction, constantly pretending to have a personality – *to give a damn*. How he preferred the simple pleasures. The gratification of status, of spending more money than the Zailan next to him – or occasionally torturing an innocent animal.

Still, the Controller felt he had been getting the conversational balance about right. The Regional Governor seemed happy and had cast his eyes more than once – he had noticed – at the small brown pouch perched on the empty chair. He glanced at the Governor's hands. Nine different rings nestled in the folds of his fleshy fingers. The metal bands were largely enveloped by skin, but the gemstones shone proud like beacons.

"So I wonder if you could help me with a small something?" the Regional Governor asked, apparently still casual. Although the Zoo Controller could tell from the way he twiddled his knife that it was anything but casual. "A little favour?"

"Of course," the Zoo Controller replied without hesitation. *Favours mean leverage.* "Anything."

"My son. He's dropping by here tomorrow night. With a few friends, you know. You'll see that he has a good time?" The Regional Governor sent a lascivious wink sliding across the table.

"Naturally." The Zoo Controller maintained the same outward bonhomie, while a small alarm bell started tinkling in his head. "Not a problem."

The Regional Governor's son was an extreme psychopath. Rare in the general population but common among the offspring of Caucus Zailans. A 'baby psycho' in the parlance. Even the Zoo Controller winced at some of his more outlandish pleasures. The whole pressure of running a theme park like this was to keep raising the thrill bar. It was hard enough with the general public, without catering to the rising expectations of the VIP visitors as well. *The high rollers.* And with the Regional Governor's son, those expectations had moved skywards – or Hell-wards. Give him the free rein he wanted, and the zoo would have no humans left.

Still, this was an opportunity to keep the Governor in his debt. With the right supervision, he could keep the collateral damage limited to a few inmates, a dozen tops.

"I'll see that he gets the best possible entertainment," the Zoo Controller replied smoothly. "Depend on it."

"Thank you. It's what I tell everyone about your little zoo. The best entertainment in the galaxy," the Regional Governor said, managing to compliment his host and patronise him at the same time. And then his voice dropped. "So, there's something we need to discuss."

It was time for business.

The Zoo Controller's smile slipped from his lips like an eel sliding into mud at the first whiff of danger. Because if the Regional Governor's new expression was anything to go by – and it was, as far as the Zoo Controller was concerned, the only thing to go by – then this wasn't just business, this was *serious* business.

"You're aware of the top priority in the Caucus right now?" the Regional Governor grunted as a gassy burp escaped his lips.

"Of course," the Zoo Controller replied, bluffing. *Which one does he mean?* At any given moment, there were always three or four. He needed to tread carefully.

"Admission to the Intergalactic Council."

Yes, that one, the Zoo Controller thought to himself. He could guess where this conversation would go. He had initiated purchase negotiations for the Earth precisely to provide diplomatic cover for the zoo's activities. It was standard practice for intelligent zoos across the galaxy. First you find an intelligent, defenceless species; then you follow the playbook: *abduct – exhibit – make money... And buy their planet if cover is needed.* He had been careful to seek all the necessary permissions on Zil before starting. Of course, abductions and forced incarceration remained, technically, illegal under the laws of the IGC. But like all these things, there was generally a gap between the rules and the reality. *Generally.*

"Now the risk that your little zoo poses," the Regional Governor continued ominously. "I have it from the Supreme Governor himself that you're to be extra vigilant."

Both of them looked up with reverence at the Supreme Governor's portrait above the lift doors. Whenever his name was mentioned, it was customary among Caucus Zailans to pause and stare at the nearest portrait of him – there was always one within eyeshot – and look wistful for a few moments, as if one could somehow see his monumental achievements sitting there like a classical temple in the middle distance. Only as the Zoo Controller dutifully stared, his wistful reverence was now tinged with one or two degrees of fear.

"Of course, Governor," he started speaking. "But I don't see what risk this facili—"

"Watch out for any visits from the Za-Nakarians," the Regional Governor continued speaking as if the Zoo Controller hadn't been. "Or any other members of the IGC. Snap inspections, that kind of thing. They don't like seeing slaves or abductions, you know their rules. Do-gooders, every one of them. *So squeamish.*"

The Regional Governor smiled. This was the Zoo Controller's cue for an ingratiating laugh – which he managed thinly, even while his guts churned.

"So, you see how it is. We don't want to see the Supreme Governor's diplomatic priority jeopardised by anything… *How should I put this?* … Anything *illegal.*" The Regional Governor pressed the tips of his sixteen fingers together under his chin as he landed on the word 'illegal'. The Zoo Controller squirmed.

"After all," the Governor continued, wiping his mouth and smiling with bonhomie, "we wouldn't want you ending up inside one of your own exhibits. *Hahaha!*"

"Haha." The Zoo Controller joined in the merriment with all the enthusiasm of a Christian in the Coliseum. *Why would the Regional Governor even crack that joke?*

The Zoo Controller leaned forward and spoke in an urgent whisper. "But what about the new park? You know, *the planned abduction...*" He dropped his voice even lower "*...the 10,000?*"

The Zoo Controller's insides were melting. He didn't want to press the question, but he had no choice. He had to be sure he still had the Regional Governor's support. The new zone was the biggest investment the zoo had ever made. An entire city district had been re-created. Regent's Park, London. It was perfect – *it was expensive* – it was ready to go. It just needed the humans to populate it. And for that he had hired one of the largest bulk carriers Zil had ever seen. *More expense.*

"Hm, what? Oh, that little plan," the Regional Governor answered, his voice loud and ostentatious, as if he couldn't possibly be involved in anything underhand. *Even though he explicitly approved the plan*, the Zoo Controller thought. *And was richly bribed to do so.* "Well, better be quick about it, hadn't you? And discreet."

"I intend to," the Zoo Controller replied leaning back, fractionally relieved. "The bulk carrier leaves the day after tomorrow. At dawn."

"Good," the Regional Governor replied, laying down his napkin to indicate their lunch was at an end.

"Well then, you have nothing to worry about, do you?"

You? The Zoo Controller tried to suppress the fear and anger that the Governor's emphasis on *you* was generating inside the tripe-region of his own guts.

"Would you like a tour of the new park before you go?" he asked with forced casualness. They always finished these lunches with a tour – a stroll – a chance to see and be seen. *And by the way it's 'we'*, the Zoo Controller's head was screaming. *If anything goes wrong, we're both going down.*

The Governor and the Controller.

Power and Money.

You and me.

Us.

"No, sorry, have to go. *Busy.* You know how it is." The Governor's brusque reply set off yet another bell in the Controller's head, which was already ringing like a fire station in a bombing raid. "Nice lunch though."

*

A few minutes later, having seen the Regional Governor off at the lift, the Zoo Controller returned alone to the table uneasy – angry – anxious.

He reflected on the risk – *alleged* risk – the zoo posed to the Supreme Governor's plans for Zil. *Be rational*, he thought, trying to calm himself, *nothing will go wrong.* He made a mental note to get one of his people to photograph the next set of Za-Nakarian visitors – try to tempt them into one of the VIP suites. The more compromising the photos the better. *Every damn race visits this zoo*, the Zoo Controller thought. *The whole galaxy is up to their eyeballs in it.*

And, anyway, even if there was a snap inspection, he was ready. They had prepared for it – the staff were trained – they had *Protocol 34.*

So there's nothing to worry about, right?

The Zoo Controller made a couple of hand gestures at one of the large screens. Immediately a crystal-clear video channel came to life. *Feeding time in Forest Park.* He watched as a caveman in a colourful tribal outfit – *a 'Penan' from Borneo* – was lowered into the wild animal enclosure. Always a great way to unwind from cares or worries. Such as *why the Hell is the Regional Governor inserting distance between us?*

He had seen it done plenty of times before. First some distance – then dissociation – *then the knife.*

He looked across at the spare chair, the one on which he'd left the small brown pouch.

It hadn't even been taken.

29

Zoo…

Or theme park?

Elizabeth was studying the landscape before her with rapier intensity. She was deploying all her training and her formidable memory to paste the layout of the facility into her mind.

Her left eye was glued to a telescope – the one she had found that night on Cleremont Avenue, in the corridor outside her room. Quaint, but surprisingly effective, especially when mounted on the wooden tripod they had brought with them. Sir Claude was next to her, scanning with his pair of field glasses. Behind them both were the library steps and beneath the steps was the beacon, that Juckes had planted earlier. They were in the storeroom, every inch of it exactly how he had described.

They had arrived on Zil.

*

When they had landed about a half hour earlier, Elizabeth had – *this time* – been the first to come to. Once she had shaken the others awake, there had been a rushed ten minutes. The first job was to connect Dr

James with the telescope. They had him study the plaza below and translate the signage into English. This quickly confirmed the facility was what Juckes had said. Besides that, it yielded a number of other unexpected – *explosive* – details about the Zailans and their taste in entertainment.

But here had been no time to dwell on them. Sir Claude dispatched Dr James and Juckes to the 55th floor. They knew Setiawan had been there about three Zailan hours ago; they had no idea if he was still there. Time was pressing. Juckes was chosen for his familiarity with the building; Dr James for any translation. Plus, they were the only two dressed in supervisor clothing. The regulation charcoal-grey trousers and light-grey shirt.

Elizabeth and Sir Claude remained behind in the storeroom to study the zoo below. They needed to commit the geography to memory as quickly as possible. The next time they saw it, they would likely be at ground level and the others would be depending on their recall.

To make sure they were ready to move at a moment's notice, Elizabeth and Sir Claude had already dressed in the caveman outfits that would help them blend in. They'd also attached an ankle tag to the base of their left leg, the same as Juckes and Dr James.

The only two who would be staying behind in the storeroom were Nussbaum and Lady Danziger. Even so, they'd attached an ankle tag to Nussbaum – just in case he got any ideas – and given the control pad to Lady Danziger.

Elizabeth glanced behind. Nussbaum was in the far corner of the room – trussed, muffled, and sullen. Lady Danziger was stood at the shelving racks, rifling through the stores to root out anything else that might be useful.

Elizabeth returned her gaze to the telescope. She kept in mind the objectives they had agreed for the mission. First and foremost, rescue Dr Setiawan. And then secondly, try to locate the other abducted academics. If Dr Setiawan was being kept on the 55th floor, perhaps the others were too? Sir Claude hoped to set up an air-bridge between the storeroom and Ormilu to spirit away as many as possible. Which struck Elizabeth as a fantasy, but they had to try.

*

The first thing Elizabeth focussed on was the spacecraft at the far end of the facility. It was every bit as huge as Juckes had described – by Elizabeth's reckoning, four hundred yards long and over fifty high. *What was it for?* The temptation to blurt the question out was overwhelming. But she and Sir Claude had agreed to work in silence.

Elizabeth bit her lip and kept scanning. Every minute was precious. As soon as Juckes and Dr James were back, they would likely have to ship out. And those two might be back any moment.

Or never at all.

Elizabeth shuddered. The operation was live – they were in the field, on an alien planet, and every action was consequential. One wrong move could blow everything.

Elizabeth shuttered her attention back onto the zoo – *theme park* – before her. Immediately below their eyrie on the 21st floor, she could see the central plaza of the zoo, filled and thronging. Spread in a horseshoe around the outer edge of the plaza were seven giant gateways each one leading to a different 'zone' of the zoo. Dr James had already translated the names that were emblazoned across the gateways – names that left her imagination twitching. 'Headhunters of the Forest' – 'Swords of the Samurai' – or 'Medieval Mayhem'.

Elizabeth's initial scan revealed the same basic layout in all seven zones. Each was made up of two parts. After visitors had passed under the giant gateway, they entered first a sort of mini-plaza, themed to that zone. Here the visitors could buy stuff, eat stuff, ride stuff. In 'Headhunters of the Forest' (sub-title: 'Forest Park'), the buildings were all grass huts and longhouses. The staff were wearing the same clownish caveman outfits that Elizabeth was. In the neighbouring 'Arabian Safari', the staff were dressed as Bedouin and the buildings looked like the set of Aladdin.

But this was only the warm-up area.

Elizabeth could see the main attraction was at the far end of each mini-plaza. Here a long line of visitors were dutifully queueing to enter the park proper.

They were queueing to pass under – or sometimes *over* – the wall.

The wall.

Elizabeth hadn't needed the telescope to take this in. The wall – or rather *the walls* – snaked in long sinuous curves across the landscape before her. Built along high ground, they enclosed and divided the seven different parks. The seven parks varied in size from large to massive. The smallest was probably about a square mile; the largest – this was the Classical Park – closer to ten square miles. And the wall ran round them all. Sheer and sinister, it was twice the height of the tallest tree in the Forest Park, it was higher than the dunes in the Arabian Park – or the hills in the Classical Park.

The whole scene before her was breathtaking – unfathomable – unimaginable. And yet imagination wasn't required; it was all laid out for the eye to see. As she scanned one of the walls, Elizabeth saw a tropical forest on one side, a barren desert on the other. On the other side of the desert, another wall. And on the other side of that wall, a medieval landscape of strip farming and windmills. And on and on.

But Elizabeth didn't have the luxury to gasp or to fathom the unfathomable. She needed to study, record, remember.

She leaned back into the telescope. She was scanning the Arabian Park. Inspired by the crusader era, it was a landscape of low, rolling sand dunes, sprinkled with palm-fringed oases. Near the oases she could see camels and Bedouin-like figures going about their business.

She re-focussed the telescope to the near end of the park. Sitting among the dunes was a walled town. The ramparts were cratered and pock-marked with what looked like *battle damage?* Warriors with curved scimitars patrolled the crenellations.

The town itself was a maze of narrow streets, domed mosques and minarets. Elizabeth saw ornate Islamic arches and filigree stonework so fine, it looked like lace. White-robed townsfolk moved, antlike, through the streets in what seemed like a vision from One Thousand and One Nights. But again, as she looked more closely, she saw large divots in the walls; a few of the buildings were crumbling.

Stranger than that, some sections of the houses were

made not of stone but... *frosted glass?* In the main town square, one whole side was a single large sheet of it. Elizabeth guessed this glass – *if that's what it was* – concealed viewing platforms. For visitors to see without being seen. There must be a tunnel system beneath the park, spiriting visitors between viewing points.

She spotted the same kind of glass in the Forest Park. In this park, there were no glass buildings, but there was a long, wide glass tube, snaking between the trees. She followed the tube to its source and, just inside the mini-plaza, she could see visitors queueing on a station platform.

All throughout the zoo, there was a dizzying variety of ways for visitors to watch without being watched. Trains in the Forest Park, personnel carriers in the Arabian Park, a covered travelator in 'Medieval Mayhem'. In 'Swords of the Samurai', there was even a gondola. Visitors could travel in giant loops across the park, grazing the forest canopy and brushing past Shinto temples.

The park Elizabeth studied last was the one furthest to the right. 'Zootropolis'. She swapped places at the window with Sir Claude to get a better view.

This park was different, that was immediately clear. It was small and mostly urban. A small city. Or a section of a city. The buildings looked new – brand new – and a couple of cranes were still in evidence. *Why have they called it Zootropolis?* It looked familiar to Elizabeth, more like a part of... *London?*

But that wasn't the strangest part about it. What unnerved Elizabeth was the absence of people. There must be housing there for 10,000 souls at least. A gleaming city district that was perfectly constructed –

and perfectly empty.

An unexplained shiver went down Elizabeth's spine.

On a hunch, she swung her telescope back round to the giant spaceship, sitting on its launch pad.

And then the penny dropped.

Of course...

She stood up to speak to Sir Claude. But he was already next to her.

"The seventh park, Sir Claude, it's new..." Elizabeth started. "And it's empty."

"I know."

"And you've seen the spaceship? The one Juckes told us about?"

"Yes."

"I think they're going to..." Elizabeth could barely bring herself to say it out loud. "They must be planning a—"

"—a mass abduction? I fear you're right."

Tap – Tap – tap-tap – Tap

Elizabeth started. She turned to look and saw Lady Danziger was already at the door. Elizabeth watched her unbolt it, pull it cautiously ajar, and then open it fully.

Juckes and Dr James were back.

*

Their eyes were bright.

"You've seen him?" Sir Claude asked, as soon as the door was closed behind them.

"Yes," Juckes replied, still out of breath.

"And?"

"Dr Setiawan's alive, sir," Juckes replied. "That's

the good news."

"And the bad?"

"He's being moved. To one of the parks. We were just in time to spot him leaving the 55th floor."

The group had gathered around the library steps. Elizabeth had perched herself on one of the upper steps. Lady Danziger and Sir Claude were standing below.

"To which park? Did you find out?"

"To the medieval one, sir. To the *err…* What's it called again?" Juckes turned to Dr James.

"*Hmm?* 'Medieval Mayhem'."

"To 'Medieval Mayhem', sir," Juckes repeated.

"And why the devil are they moving him there?"

Juckes turned to Dr James for guidance. It was clear both knew and didn't want to say. Dr James took Juckes' hesitation and raised him a dither.

"They've dressed him up in a…" he started. "In a very unusual fashion, sir."

"Whatever for?"

"Yes, sir. That's what we were wondering. I managed to pick up a short snippet through the earpiece." Juckes gave a quick tap on the device in his ear. "But it was brief. I can't be absolutely sure—"

"Come on," Sir Claude rumbled. "We haven't got all day."

"Indeed, sir." Juckes drew in a deep lungful of air. "I believe he's about to be sacrificed."

The room stopped.

Lady Danziger's throat sucked in an involuntary gasp of air. Elizabeth's hand went to her mouth. Sir Claude's normally ruddy cheeks drained white.

"So we're too late?"

"Possibly not, sir. Actually, I think we may still

have a chance," Juckes replied quietly. "If we're quick."

"How can we possibly get to him? *How?* Surely one of you needed to trail him. I don't blame you for coming back here. But how can we possibly find him again?"

"Actually, sir," Juckes replied, "locating him shouldn't be any trouble at all."

30

Dancers cartwheeled and somersaulted. Their long, naked limbs spun like the sails of so many windmills, while the slanting light of the late afternoon sun flashed on their bronzed, moist skin. Their routine was relentless, mesmerising. After advancing a few more yards, two joined hands together, creating a small platform onto which a third dancer elegantly landed. They then launched the dancer into a somersault – sending her onward to the next pair of hands.

And on they went. A blur of motion – spinning, twisting, somersaulting – that disguised the fact they were advancing at a very measured pace along a very precise path. They were leading a parade through the crowded centre of the main plaza.

There must've been about a dozen of them. It was hard to count, they didn't stay still for long enough. The Zoo Controller couldn't remember which species, but they were good. *Pros*. Great eye candy at the front of the parade.

He was idly watching on one of the large planning screens, while sifting through some routine paperwork on his desk. The Controller was multi-tasking, trying to stop himself brooding over his lunchtime meeting. He watched as the parade approached the centre of the plaza. Behind the dancers came a line of twelve soldiers, marching two abreast. Zailans this time, but dressed up as medieval – *human* – soldiers. They looked squat and aggressive. On their heads they wore great clunky helmets, with a single, thin rectangle of iron extending down to protect their noses. In their hands they held tall, menacing halberds. *Bit daft*, the Zoo Controller thought, *but not too bad.*

He was less sure about what came next. Four knights on horseback in full chivalric costume. For sure, there was nothing wrong with the costumes. Shining suits of armour – colourful pennants flying from lances – extravagant plumed helmets – visors raised jauntily. All very well presented, same as the large white chargers they were riding, which had been abducted at enormous expense...

Which was all fine.

Except they'd used Zailan actors again.

Short and plump, did they look a bit ridiculous on the large white horses?

The Zoo Controller pondered the issue for a moment with some irritation. *Urgh.* If they could just close their visors, no-one need know who was underneath.

Like every high-ranking Zailan, the Zoo Controller was pin-sensitive to anything that might compromise the dignity of Zil. He'd have a word with Parades. Make sure they used a different race next time – humans if necessary.

Still, that was a mere quibble compared to what came next.

The float.

The main attraction.

Gliding a foot or two off the ground, the float

carried the sacrificial victim. They had prepared him in the usual way. He had been stripped naked, except for a loincloth, and covered in body art. His ankles and wrists were manacled. On his head he wore an elaborate headdress – full of flowers and fruit and animal bones and bells – and, on his face, a wooden mask. The headdress was fun, the mask a regrettable necessity. In the past some of the younger visitors had been upset by the sight of raw terror. But that was all fine, no big deal. The executioner standing behind him, he looked fine too.

No, the problem wasn't them. The problem was elsewhere. Parades had built four turrets on the four corners of the float, creating a kind of mini-castle, and in each turret stood a medieval maiden. All four were perfectly dressed in a medieval gown that flowed freely at the base and grasped tightly at the bosom; they wore cone-shaped hats – a *hennin* was the word, apparently – with a veil floating behind in the wind. Exactly like the pictures in the fairytale books the humans seemed so keen on.

The only problem was that under these hats, and inside these dresses, they'd put a Zailan. *A submissive.* As they dabbed their eyes with white lace handkerchiefs with one hand – and threw out confetti with the other – they looked comical. Ridiculous. *Couldn't they have found some other species?* The Zoo Controller made a mental note to fire someone.

After that, he merely glanced at the remainder of the parade. Eight more Zailans marched behind the float dressed in the scarlet tunics of Beefeaters. And behind them, sweeping up the litter, came a rabble of human slaves. *Pond life.*

*

My God, they're ugly, Elizabeth thought to herself, as her gaze fastened onto the 'maidens' in the four turrets.

Any other time, she might have checked herself from such a sweeping generalisation. But right now, right here – walking at the back of the parade with the other slaves – she wasn't in command of her thoughts.

The dancers and the soldiers and the crowd swirled before her eyes, they swirled inside her head. Through the earpiece Sir Claude had given her, random snippets of conversation crowded in through her ear, like impatient travellers at a railway turnstile. She felt nauseous. She was taking quick, shallow, panicky breaths, like she had been thrown into ice-cold water. Any moment, she expected a hand to take hold of her shoulder and pull her away for questioning. The alien beings, the blaring music, the sacrificial victim – the sheer mad danger they were all in – the cacophony of sights and sounds and risks – it was overwhelming.

She glanced up ahead at Dr James. He was blending in with the other supervisors well enough. Their job was to keep the crowd at a distance. Meantime, she and Sir Claude were with the other 'cavemen' at the back, collecting the litter into their rattan backpacks.

Elizabeth was worried about Juckes – or rather the lack of Juckes. Sir Claude had dispatched him towards the spacecraft, the bulk carrier, to scout for sabotage opportunities. They'd all agreed that four of them couldn't trail the parade. It was too many, the risk of detection too high. But Elizabeth felt his absence keenly.

And then she was worried about Sir Claude. How long could a six-foot, ruddy-cheeked Englishman with a razor-sharp moustache and an imperious manner blend in amongst these cowed-looking slaves?

The answer, she hoped, were the ridiculous caveman outfits. The Zailans were using clothing to dehumanise, obviously. Same as they were doing to Setiawan. So long as they wore these, any suspicious Zailan was likely to underestimate them. How could anyone who looked so stupid travel from another planet, infiltrate their zoo, and stage a rescue mission?

Elizabeth glanced left and right at the crowd. Some were excited, some were bored, some were snacking, some were taking photos. But none were interested in the slaves. She felt less exposed now.

She started to realise she was, in fact, invisible.

The parade passed under the giant archway into the Medieval Zone. About a hundred and fifty yards ahead was a fairytale castle. Large, cheerful, silly. And about fifty yards beyond it, the wall.

The wall.

They advanced slowly towards the castle along an avenue lined with kiosks and shops disguised as medieval cottages. Zailan staff dressed in peasant costumes were standing at the open windows, selling food and souvenirs across the counter.

Elizabeth went back over the plan in her head. It was simple. Blunt even. They hadn't had time to come up with anything clever. Concealed at the base of Sir Claude's backpack – beneath the litter, beneath the spare clothes – were three pieces of equipment. A revolver, a beacon, and one of the two short-wave radio handsets. Lady Danziger held the other back in the storeroom. They figured at some point the procession would have to stop somewhere quiet, somewhere backstage – probably just before the execution – to prepare the victim. At that point, they would radio to Lady Danziger, tell her their location. She could direct the steps towards them and onto their beacon. That would give them a chance to wrench Setiawan free from his captors and escape on the steps. It wasn't much of a plan, but they'd at least have the element of surprise. And a revolver.

The procession reached the castle entrance. She looked up at it. The castle had crenellations, pointed turrets, the whole nine yards. Elizabeth's last thought, as she headed over the drawbridge, was how strangely sanitised it all was. *Fake.* Like a Disney parade.

Except the sacrificial victim at the centre really was about to be sacrificed.

31

Once across the drawbridge, a large part of the parade started to melt away. They disappeared like spilled water round concealed corners and through obscure doorways.

There was a new crowd of onlookers inside the castle, watching as the remainder of the parade started to mount a monorail just outside the castle keep.

All three carriages of the monorail were open; it was a kind of show train. The four maidens mounted the front carriage, continuing to sob and dab their eyes and throw confetti. The second, central carriage was for the victim. The two remaining soldiers used their halberds to prod Setiawan onto it.

These halberds – if that was the correct name for the weapon, Elizabeth wasn't sure – were not the Disney version. They were long spears or pikes, but with a kind of axe-head mounted just below the sharp pointy bit for extra medieval-ness. Just in case the Zailans wanted to slash Setiawan as well as gore him.

Not that they needed to do any slashing. Elizabeth saw a trickle of blood had started to run down his back.

The third and final carriage was for the slaves. A number of them mounted it, sitting back-to-back on two lines of outward-facing seats. Elizabeth, Sir

Claude and Dr James found spare seats at the very end.

All the other slaves seemed to know what they were supposed to do and where they were supposed to go. For the first time, Elizabeth saw a couple of them glance in their direction – anxious, furtive glances. *Who are you? What are you doing here?* their looks seemed to say. *Please don't get us punished.*

And then the monorail started to move.

The two large gates of the castle keep opened and the monorail was swallowed into the gloom inside.

*

The ceiling inside the keep was wood-beamed. The walls either side were made of stone and lined with flaming torches. Those were the medieval touches – everything else was high tech.

As Elizabeth peered over the heads of the Zailan onlookers, she realised they were now travelling through an entertainment arcade. Some visitors were staring at large video screens; others were sitting in flight simulators. They appeared to be controlling *actual* drones that were *actually* flying through the Medieval Park. The deeper into the keep they travelled, the dimmer the lighting. She saw iron cages hanging from the ceiling with human figures caged inside. The sound of torture reached her ears. The figure in the first cage was so lifelike, she initially thought it *was* a human. Until she saw the same thumbnail being plucked a second time. She exhaled with relief. Frighteningly lifelike, but just a dummy.

Every ten or twenty yards, a pair of slaves would jump down from the slow-moving train and set to work sweeping up the confetti and other detritus that their procession had created. The further they went, the more the numbers on the final carriage thinned out, and the narrower the arcade became. Until it was nothing more than a corridor, half-lit by flaming torches on the stone walls.

"We're not going to be able to use the radio," a voice whispered into her ear. It was Sir Claude. "Not in here." Elizabeth had already figured this out. The stone walls would flatten the signal to nothing.

"*What do we do?*" Elizabeth whispered from the side of her mouth.

"Wait 'til we know where they're going to execute Setiawan. Then you slip away. On foot. Get back to the storeroom as quickly as possible."

Elizabeth nodded. She watched another two slaves slip from the carriage. There were only a half dozen of them left now.

"You'll be able to tell Adelaide roughly where to go," Sir Claude continued. "The beacon will do the rest. Does that make—" Sir Claude was interrupted by a new sound that had seeped into the arcade. "*What's that?*"

Elizabeth heard it too.

It was some kind of… *chanting*. It was echoing along the corridor like a rush of unexploded gas. A moment later, the train passed through a checkpoint and started descending downwards.

Elizabeth looked up above her head. The beam ceiling had disappeared, replaced by an arched stone roof. The air was becoming cooler and damper. Corridor was becoming tunnel.

They approached a large sign, written in Zailan and hanging from the ceiling. Elizabeth reckoned they were about ten or fifteen yards below ground at this point.

"*What does it say?*" Elizabeth whispered to Dr James on her other side.

"Hmm? '*You are now passing under the Medieval Park,*'" Dr James translated.

"So we're passing under the wall?"

"I think so."

The chanting was getting louder. Elizabeth could sense they were reaching their destination.

And then suddenly they were *at* their destination.

32

Elizabeth felt taut inside as if each minute spent in the procession had somehow ratcheted the string of a crossbow.

The next few moments passed, however, with the swiftness and horror of the bolt being released.

They had arrived at the base of a large underground theatre. Up to her right, about two, maybe three hundred Zailan spectators were sitting, cinema-style, in a steep auditorium. The monorail paused beneath them. The sight of the sacrificial victim below amped up the atmosphere. The crowd was restless – aggressive – volatile. They were chanting, beating their arms in the air.

But it wasn't this set of spectators that really caught Elizabeth's attention. It was the other set.

The audience of Zailans were facing towards an enormous vertical sheet of plate glass. Beyond the plate glass was a semi-circular amphitheatre. It was filled with a baying throng of human – *medieval* – peasants. On the stage below them, only a few feet from where she was sitting, Elizabeth could see a large, tidy stack of logs at the centre of the stage. And at the centre of the log stack was a single stake.

A funeral pyre.

This was where they were going to execute Dr Setiawan and this was how they're going to do it.

They were going to burn him alive – *out there*.

A half-dozen medieval soldiers were standing guard in a semi-circle around the funeral pyre. And beyond the soldiers, a priest was striding around the edge of the stage, facing the peasants, whipping them up. He was holding a long wooden staff in one hand, while his other hand was holding a large brass crucifix outstretched towards them.

Dishevelled, noisy, angry, the medieval peasants had come to watch an execution. And the Zailan spectators had come to watch them watching it.

And they were all loving it.

Humans and Zailans were all joined in the same chant:

"BURN - THE - DE-MON
BURN - THE - DE-MON
BURN - THE - DE-MON
BURN - THE - DE-MON—"

Elizabeth shuddered.

She slipped from her seat to the ground. She only hoped she had enough time to get back to Adelaide. She turned to head back the way they'd come.

But her nightmare was about to turn a darker shade of black.

At the moment she started moving, she saw a set of guards pull shut a barricade behind them. They were sealed inside their underground theatre.

She exchanged a despairing glance with Sir Claude. She slid back onto her seat on the monorail. Her mind raced and spiralled. *How can we rescue Setiawan without Lady Danziger and the steps? In the middle of all this, how can we—*

And then the world shook.

The chanting stopped. The audience stopped braying, the priest stopped striding, and Elizabeth stopped despairing. Everything – everyone – froze.

"*B E – Y E – S I L E N T*"

A voice thundered like no voice Elizabeth had heard before. The voice pealed across the air, it shook the floor beneath them, it vibrated through the glass separating the Zailan world from the human. The Zailans in the audience – violence junkies, who had paid two month's wages for a ringside seat – gasped like children in dread. The peasants beyond the glass cowered, physically cringing in their seats.

"*Y E – S H A L L – C A S T E – O U T – T H E – D E M O N – F R O M – A M O N G – Y O U.*"

Elizabeth looked towards Setiawan in the carriage ahead, dreading to see him collapsed and broken.

"*S E E – H O W – M E R C I F U L – Y O U R – G O D – I S – T H A T – H E – O F F E R S – Y O U – T H E – M E A N S – O F – Y O U R – S A L V A T I O N.*"

To her surprise, a little stiffness had returned to his body. He had actually turned his head. His mask shrouded his expression, but she could see he was looking in their direction.

B U R N – T H E – D E M O N – A N D – K N O W – T H A T – Y O U R – S I N S – W I L L – B E – C L E A N S E D – B Y – T H E – F L A M E S – O F – H I S – S U F F E R I N G."

A brief clicking sound could be heard. Then…

Silence.

Utter, formless silence.

Seconds passed, untouched by noise or motion.

And then, striking out across the air, a single rhythmic banging sound. It coursed through the silence like the prow of a boat breaking the waters of a motionless sea.

THUMP – THUMP – THUMP – THUMP...

It was the priest in the amphitheatre. He was banging his staff against the ground. As the thumping accelerated, the crowd took up their chant again. Quiet at first, and then with increasing force—

"Burn - the - de-mon
Burn - the - de-mon
BURN - THE - DE-MON
BURN - THE - DE-MON..."

*

The monorail started to move again.

Passing the plate glass on the left, and the Zailan spectators on the right, the train glided forward and passed through a set of double doors. As soon as the train was through, the doors slid shut behind it.

Elizabeth was disorientated.

Any moment, she was expecting to watch them thrust Setiawan – *somehow* – onto the amphitheatre stage.

But it hadn't happened yet.

The monorail turned right, branching into a large, concrete tunnel. It drew to a gradual halt.

As she looked around on her seat, she now found herself in a very different place. It was a half-lit, subterranean world of concrete tunnels and ventilation shafts. Empty and bare. Elizabeth was now backstage at the zoo.

She didn't have long to take it in.

Two Zailans had climbed down from one of the other carriages and walked past her. She hadn't noticed these two before. They wore a nondescript, dark-green uniform. They weren't soldiers, they weren't slaves either – *perhaps they're zookeepers?* Directly behind them came Setiawan, his arms still tied, his back bleeding profusely now. Behind him came the two soldiers, halberds outstretched.

Elizabeth watched this group of five starting to walk down the impossibly long tunnel. *Why are they walking? Where are they heading?*

And then she figured it out.

About twenty yards behind the train, she could see a pair of thick, curved glass doors protruding from the left-hand side of the tunnel. This was no ordinary doorway – the doors looked high tech, bulky, impregnable. This must be the doorway leading onto the amphitheatre stage. This must be Setiawan's route to the Medieval Park. To death.

Just as Elizabeth figured this out, the monorail started to move forward in the opposite direction. Elizabeth glanced ahead. In about twenty yards the tunnel branched three ways. Their monorail was about to disappear into the labyrinth.

She glanced back again.

Setiawan and his entourage were already disappearing.

33

"*Now!*"

Sir Claude's voice was low and urgent, as he slipped from the moving monorail and stumbled to the ground.

Dr James followed him an instant later, staying effortlessly upright.

Elizabeth jumped last. The train was accelerating. Unable to control her momentum, she tumbled onto all fours. She looked up just in time to see the train pass out of sight down the right-most of the three branch tunnels.

She waited a moment, expecting it to stop. To start reversing back towards them.

But it didn't.

Sir Claude had timed their jump perfectly.

"*Come on – quickly – catch up!*" Sir Claude whispered.

He was already striding back down the tunnel, back the way they had come. Towards Setiawan and his entourage, now about twenty yards' distant. Sir Claude didn't want to run, not yet. The guards still didn't realise they were being followed.

Dr James was striding next to him – or rather *wafting*. His upper body was at a slight tilt; he looked as if the merest puff of wind might blow him clean away. He glided along, while Elizabeth was half-running to keep up.

The gap between them and Setiawan was down to fifteen yards. The bulky glass doors lay a further fifteen years ahead.

"Come on, faster now," Sir Claude whispered as he quickened his own pace.

"Shouldn't we get the revolver out?" Elizabeth asked.

"No time. Too noisy."

Sir Claude broke into a run.

The gap was just ten yards as Setiawan's entourage reached the airlock.

At that same moment, the two soldiers turned round and finally noticed the threat.

Slaves were running towards them.

This wasn't in their manual. They were just actors after all, not real soldiers. A slave – *a brainwashed slave* – turning on his Zailan masters? It didn't happen. And definitely not three at once.

They lowered their halberds tentatively towards the one at the front. They never expected to use these weapons *to defend themselves*.

Their uncertainty cost them dear.

Sir Claude met their hesitation without hesitation. He turned smartly sideways, stepping between the two halberds. In a single, sideways stride, he put his body past the danger end of both weapons, rendering them useless. He brushed the left-hand one to the side with his left forearm, while his right hand grasped the shaft of the other with such force, it came clean out of the hands of the Zailan holding it.

Elizabeth was just a yard or two behind.

She watched as Sir Claude closed with the soldier on the right and punched him just beneath his nose guard, his fist crashing into the soldier's mouth.

Elizabeth ran straight at the one on the left, kicking him in the groin. *That's got to hurt*, Elizabeth thought as her foot connected with his body in the manner of a goalkeeper punting a football.

Elizabeth was certainly right about one thing. Every Zailan has a groin with dangly bits.

But not, alas, located in the same place as a man's.

Elizabeth's foot had actually landed in one of the most padded and least sensitive areas of the Zailan anatomy – a bit like kicking a pig in the thigh.

Unhurt, the Zailan used his spare hand to pull from his pocket a small plastic box. It had a single large red button on it, covered by a clear plastic casing.

A control pad.

Elizabeth knew immediately this small box had the power to cripple her. She lunged towards it with both her hands, clawing at his eight wriggling digits, trying to stop them from hinging back the safety cover and plunging her into agony.

And then just for a moment he got distracted.

And so did Elizabeth.

Unnoticed by anybody, Dr James had walked behind the Zailan and neatly plucked his helmet from his head. He held the helmet directly behind the soldier's skull.

Confused, the Zailan swivelled his head to see who was behind him.

"A punch perhaps, Mrs B. *Hmm?*"

"Eh?"

"*His face?*"

"Oh. Yes. Right." Elizabeth released her grip and, in

the instant before the Zailan could electrocute her, she slammed the heel of her hand into his exposed face, aiming for a point six inches beyond the nose. First contact didn't knock him out – she didn't quite have the force for that – but it sent his head careening against his own helmet, which did.

The Zailan soldier collapsed unconscious at Elizabeth's feet.

She turned to look at Sir Claude. He had just dispatched the other soldier in like fashion.

Two down.

But still two to go.

*

The Senior Zookeeper and her assistant did not stand idle during this fight.

The zookeeper's first thought had been to electrocute the slaves. But electrocution was a blunt instrument. If she activated her control pad, it would electrocute the nearest ankle tag – and that was on her prisoner, not the three that were fighting.

Meantime her prisoner – 'Dr Setiawan' – was now struggling like his life depended on it. Which of course it did. She tightened her grip on his arm. Her priority was clear: to get him through the glass doors and into the amphitheatre. At all costs.

Nothing like this had ever happened in her long career at the zoo. *Brainwashed slaves rebelling? A rescue attempt?* They had protocols for both, of course they did – they had protocols for *everything* – but they were covered in dust. Humans could barely reach their own moon, never mind travel across galaxies. Why waste time preparing for something that would never happen?

But now it was happening.

With her spare arm, the zookeeper reached into the large pocket at the side of her uniform. This was not the pocket of some tidy- and tiny-minded soldier. This was the busy pocket of a busy zookeeper. It was filled with all sorts. Her eight digits sought restlessly for the thing they needed. They brushed past the control pad – they accidentally knocked her protocol manual out onto the ground – and then they fastened gratefully onto their target.

Her security pass.

She yanked it out and slammed it against the card reader on the wall.

An instant later and the large, curved glass doors started to open at the centre. The glass doors didn't provide immediate access to the amphitheatre – entry and exit to the human parks was far more tightly controlled than that. They were the outer doors of an airlock. On the opposite side of the airlock was a second set of reinforced steel doors, which would only open once the glass doors were shut again.

The zookeeper and her assistant dragged their prisoner towards the growing gap in the glass doors. His legs were dragging and his body writhing, but he was a small one and his hands were still tied. No match for the vice-like grip of four Zailan hands. They forced him through the opening and into the airlock.

The zookeeper looked over her shoulder. To her horror, the first of the two soldiers had just crumpled to the ground.

She had scarce seconds to play with.

She slammed her pass against the reader a second time. The glass doors shuddered to a premature halt –

and started to close again. Facing the prisoner, the zookeeper blocked the opening with her body to stop him escaping. She glanced over her shoulder a second time and saw the second soldier fall to the ground. She yelled at her assistant to raise the alarm.

The assistant didn't need a second invitation. He ran off in a clumsy lolloping gait, his hands occasionally pawing the ground for support. The Senior Zookeeper saw it from the corner of her eye and winced. Even in an emergency, the indignity of it was painful.

A moment later, from the same corner of the same eye, she saw one of the slaves – the female – take off after him.

The irony of the situation was not lost on the Senior Zookeeper. Her whole career had been devoted to the Medieval Park and its strange, angry, self-hating inmates. And she had spent the best part of that career trying to ease their lot, often against the orders of the psychopaths in the Obelisk. When the harvest failed, she sneaked in extra supplies; when the adults got injured, she provided modern medicines; and when too many children were born, she falsified the records. As far as the Obelisk was concerned, famine, injury, and infanticide were all box office. Where she saw suffering, they saw ratings. Subverting their instructions had been a nerve-wracking game. When a fire broke out a couple of years ago in the slum quarter, she had gone directly against orders and dispatched an aerial crew to put it out. That act of charity nearly cost the zookeeper her job.

And now, here she was in a life-or-death tussle to make sure a prisoner got executed on time. Maybe if she had a few more moments to think about it, she'd let the unthinkable happen – she'd let the prisoner escape.

She'd fluff an execution.

But she didn't get a few moments to think. Not about that nor anything else.

A boot landed against her back.

It struck with a force that expelled the air from her ventral lungs and propelled her directly through the remaining gap in the glass doors. Her body flew through the airlock and her face slammed up against the unforgiving steel doors on the far side. For a moment she stood there, winded and panting, her eye frozen on the vertical hairline that marked the point where the two steel doors met. The moment that hairline became a crack – and then an opening – her life would be as good as over.

She spun round in time to see her prisoner being pulled out of the airlock to safety. He was being rescued by the tall slave. The older one, with the silver hair. He was now standing guard, blocking her exit through the glass doors that continued to whirr shut.

They were just two feet apart.

She knew what she had to do. In a single fluid motion, she pulled the control pad from her pocket, flipped the safety cover, and slammed the button.

She pressed it down and held it down and watched the slave's body start to shudder and wobble as 500 volts were delivered in ten-microsecond pulses through his ankle.

Still pressing the control pad, the zookeeper placed her shoulder into the diminishing gap between the doors, and turned her head sideways to squeeze through. As she did so, her eyes locked onto the slave's.

Nothing but nothing in her soon-to-end life could prepare her for the sight before her.

She watched in disbelief as this man – with 500 volts coursing through him – and with his legs still somehow vertical beneath him – met her gaze, raised his fist, and knocked her back through the doorway.

She landed on the floor of the airlock as the glass doors clunked shut in front of her.

An instant later, she heard a second whirring sound as the steel doors on the other side of the airlock started to move. The vertical hairline between them had become a crack. A few seconds later, it became a gap and, a few seconds after that, the gates of Hell opened.

*

Elizabeth returned, panting, to the airlock.

She had just tried to chase down the second zookeeper. Ordinarily, her speed would've easily outstripped a Zailan. But the keeper had left the main service tunnel, ducked down a side-tunnel – and then down another. A maze of tunnels started to open up. Elizabeth had enough wits about her to realise that if she followed the zookeeper any further into the labyrinth, she might never get back out.

So she'd turned around and let him go.

She returned to the airlock, to find a desperate scene. Sir Claude was on his knees in front of the glass doors, his chest heaving, his hair pointing in every which direction. He had been electrocuted.

On the other side of the glass doors, she could see the other zookeeper – the older one – pawing at the glass with all sixteen fingers. The zookeeper's face was stretched taut in a look of unmitigated terror. The door to the amphitheatre behind her had opened fully and the noise of the medieval crowd had erupted into the service tunnel. Not a recording, not piped – but the real, live braying of a crowd desperate to see blood spilt.

And then came the medieval peasants and soldiers.

Coarse, warted faces thrust their way into the airlock. They grasped the long, flailing arms of the Zailan and yanked her viciously out of her world and into theirs.

Those humans were expecting a demon to be delivered up to them and – when they saw the Zailan face and the eight-digit hands – a demon is what they believed they had been given.

This sight that could never be unseen crashed against Elizabeth's retina. Then the airlock was empty again, the steel outer doors slid shut, and the horrific vision ended as abruptly as it began.

*

"Dr Setiawan, I presume?"

Elizabeth held out her hand to Dr Setiawan, seeing his face for the first time. His hands were unbound, his mask was off, the headdress gone. A diminutive and bedraggled figure, dressed only in a loincloth and body paint.

"Indeed, it is," Dr Setiawan smiled back at her, courteous but weak. He extended his hand in reply. "It was most thoughtful of you to come and rescue me."

"Oh, think nothing of it."

"But who exactly," he replied, shifting his gaze between her, Dr James and the stricken Sir Claude, "is going to rescue *you?*"

34

As the Senior Zookeeper emerged onto the stage and saw the funeral pyre waiting for her – the funeral pyre that her own team had built the night before – she felt the full flood of panic course through her body like an uncontrolled power surge.

She levered her long arms, ripping them clear of her captors' grip with a wild strength that only confirmed to them her demonic nature.

"The Beaste is among you! SATAN HAS RISEN!" the priest cried from the other side of the stage.

The zookeeper looked up towards the voice. Behind the priest, she could see a set of steps that ran upwards through the auditorium, between the crowd.

Just make it out of the amphitheatre. At some level of her brain, somewhere beneath the blind panic, she knew that if she could just get past the crowd, get out into the open, an exfil crew would surely rescue her.

So she did something that was unthinkable – unforgiveable – *taboo*. She dropped to all fours and ran. Not the occasional motion of hand to ground – but a full-blooded quadrupedal run. She headed straight for the priest and the steps behind him.

"WILL NO-ONE AMONG YOU STOP THE *BEEEEEEEE—*"

Words blurred into a panicked shriek in the priest's throat as he saw the zookeeper charge towards him. Thinking he was the target, he started sprinting round the edge of the stage terrified, his knees pumping high, his arms flailing.

And so, miraculously, a path started to clear before the zookeeper.

Panic drove her forwards and panic drove the peasants and soldiers backwards.

The zookeeper thought she had been thrust into the jaws of Hell. They thought she had been drawn from the jaws of Hell. Two species that ought to have been separated by hundreds of years of time and millions of light years of distance were clattering against each other violently, unpredictably. Two stonemasons in the audience would later recreate her image as a gargoyle on the church they were building.

"BEHOLD ITS TRUE NATURE!" the priest screamed, his voice all the louder to compensate for his cowardice. His anger all the greater. "*Simeus dei* – the ape of God! See how evil has corrupted its face! See how it cleaves to the ground like a beaste of the field. WILL NONE AMONG YOU STOP IT?"

But it didn't matter how much the priest thundered. The crowd continued to part before her like the Red Sea. She was almost at the top of the amphitheatre.

She dared to believe she could make it.

Only a few more yards to go.

And then a spear.

Straight through the chest.

Just as she was cresting the final step, one of the soldiers, who had concealed himself, stepped forward with an outstretched spear, its point positioned exactly on the Zailan's flightpath.

239

The zookeeper, with no time to react, impaled herself on the spear with all the force of her own powerful momentum. Her chest was pierced just off-centre.

Exactly where a human heart lies.

But not the Zailan heart.

The spear had gone through the zookeeper's digestive tract. Her guts. It would probably kill her, but not for a few hours.

The zookeeper and the soldier looked at each other for a few seconds in a moment of ghastly intimacy. The whole amphitheatre fell quiet. Even the priest.

And then – with an eerie slowness and deliberacy – the Zailan placed her hands on the spear and slowly withdrew it from her chest.

The soldier dropped his own hands from the spear in shock and terror.

He watched as the creature removed the spear from its chest and dropped it harmlessly at their feet.

The pair remained frozen in front of each other.

"SEE!" the priest resumed his thundering. "See how Satan protects it! Let not this creature escape into our world. ONLY BURNING CAN KILL SUCH AS THIS!" Then he resumed the chant and the crowd quickly picked it up too:

"BURN - THE - DE-MON
BURN - THE - DE-MON
BURN - THE - DE-MON—"

Something changed in the crowd.

They feared her escape now more than her capture.

They surged forward. The peasants at the top of the amphitheatre came together to block her exit. The zookeeper turned back around and started running back down towards the stage.

But it was all up for her.

In a few seconds, she was swamped by the peasants, as they unleashed the fury of their own cursed existence onto her.

They bore her up on their shoulders and streamed down towards the funeral pyre. It was as if they'd found a channel to vent all the anger of their own benighted lives. All the torments that were mysteriously and inexplicably visited on them, all the frustration of being promised a world of love and living in a world of suffering – they found expression in their bellowing rage as they bore their demon towards its death.

Her body was lashed to the stake by a dozen hands; her legs and wrists were bound by a dozen more. And then a dozen torches were plucked from the edge of the stage and thrust into the log pile beneath her.

The flames started to lick at her feet and the Senior Zookeeper – a submissive, whose career had been secretly devoted to improving the lot of her human captives – screamed curses at their God and her own as her soul was dispatched into the afterlife.

*

The Zoo Controller exhaled a ragged breath. Shallow and panicky.

He couldn't bear to watch – he couldn't tear his eyes away.

He was paralysed.

As he stared at the video screen before him, his own hands were covering his face. He was watching the execution between the gaps in his sixteen digits. Something he hadn't done since he was a child.

Something he didn't even realise he was doing now.

A half-dozen of his most senior managers were round the table with him, stuck in the same craven posture.

They all knew the protocols. They knew the emergency response times. A ground intervention would take twenty-five to thirty minutes. An air intervention ten to twelve. There wasn't a team on Zil that could save that zookeeper now.

Despite the vast arsenal of tricks and interventions available to them at the push of the merest button – despite *the God-like power* – there wasn't a single thing they could do. She was toast.

The Zoo Controller enjoyed watching an execution, of course he did. And he was relaxed about the odd accidental death, of course he was. Lax safety standards meant three or four keepers died every year in the wild beast enclosure alone. No big deal.

But a Zailan dying at the hands of another intelligent species – the humans? And for it to happen on one of the zoo's own TV channels, *live?*

Never.

The humans weren't animals, but they were scum. *Inferior.* To see a zookeeper running *on all fours...* And then to see her executed by humans in his own zoo...

It was humiliating.

The loss of face was unimaginable.

What would the Regional Governor say? *The Supreme Governor?*

The Zoo Controller was struck dumb.

Paralysed.

How the Hell had it happened? Had they got their timings confused? The Zoo Controller reasonably thought he could rely on his zookeepers' basic sense of self-preservation not to wander through a double-skinned, failsafe airlock when it was feeding time in the human enclosure.

If only someone had got a warning out – if only they'd switched off the video feed a short while earlier. Two minutes earlier – nothing more than that. *Two minutes.* Two minutes in which his life had changed. Two minutes that would live forever on video. Two minutes that could never be undone.

He felt as if he could see his career evaporating. Vanishing. *If only they'd... If only I'd—*

NO

No

No.

Pull yourself together, a voice spoke inside his head.

Self-pity is for losers.

The Zoo Controller had seen it destroy others often enough. Seen how quickly its tendrils could spread over a Zailan's character, like a vine on a trunk, sapping their strength.

No.

You rose from nothing, you have achieved too much, he told himself. *Think. Act. A way will be found.*

"Cut the video feeds to the Medieval Park," he whispered. His voice was faint. Hoarse.

"Boss?"

"I said, *Cut all video feeds to the Medieval Park. NOW!*" he barked, suddenly staring one of his underlings full in the face. "Get Media to redirect the live channels to the Classical Park."

"Yes, boss – on it."

"And you – get Recreations to clear all the live

243

viewers from the theatre in the C-Zone. Take them to the holding pen." Orders started issuing from his mouth in an unrelenting stream. All the talent and all the skills he had built through his career came to serve him now, as complex instructions were delivered with automaticity. "And get Legal on it too. Every one of those visitors gets coupons – but only *after* they've signed a Non-Disclosure. What happened this evening didn't happen. They don't talk about it in public, they don't talk about it to their friends – *it did not happen*."

"Right away, boss."

Another manager dashed from the planning area into the main control room, grinning and re-energised. The Zoo Controller's team started transforming around him from rudderless shipwreck into the well-drilled crew he knew them to be.

"Who's still here? Right – *you* – get a SWAT team down to Airlock C-144 so fast it's already happened. We need to find out what went wrong on the other side of it."

"No problem, sir."

There were now just two of his senior managers left near him. "Anything I can do to help, sir?"

"*Yes…*" the Zoo Controller replied absently, as his brain rippled through options and scenarios. "Yes! Get onto the keepers and get a clean-up team ready to roll. They're probably all blubbing about their fallen comrade. Let's keep them busy, it'll be good for them. As soon as the fire has burnt itself out, I want them in there. We don't reconnect the video feed until all evidence has been removed."

In time, the Zoo Controller would have the entire amphitheatre razed, but he could get to that later.

That left just one Duty Manager with the Zoo Controller. His best. The one who'd been with him earlier that morning, when that strange, defiant slave had all but wandered around the control room.

That slave…

Almost from the off, the day had felt different, out of joint. The strange slave with the confident eyes, who had wandered into his lift and then into his control room.

Then the disastrous lunch with the Regional Governor.

And now this.

"Sir?"

Of course, these events weren't connected. How could they be? That's paranoia, the Zoo Controller chided himself. They were separate.

And yet—

"Sir?" the Duty Manager repeated, more insistently. "I've had a thought."

"*Eh, what?*" the Zoo Controller started. "Yes – what is it?"

"There's probably a live video feed to that service tunnel. We've got most of the backstage area wired. I think we should take a look – maybe spool back to when the incident occurred?"

Of course. The Zoo Controller slapped his forehead. "Yes, bring it up now."

The Duty Manager made several hand gestures at the screen in front of them. A menu appeared. He air-tapped his fingers in quick succession, drilling through a sequence of menu options.

And then, just a few seconds after the Zoo Controller commanded it, there was a clear, live, full-colour video feed from Airlock C-144, spread lavishly across the 120-inch planning screen.

It showed the service corridor in its usual tone of concrete grey but – uncharacteristically – smeared with a few points of colour.

The Zoo Controller and his Duty Manager gasped.

There in the foreground of the image they could see two bodies lying crumpled and motionless. They wore the unmistakable tunics of soldier-actors from the Medieval Zone and – with both their helmets removed – they were unmistakably Zailan.

And over in the background, movement.

In a corridor that would normally see nothing for hours on end, except the occasional passing of a rail cart or forklift truck, there were three, maybe four, figures – *were they humans?* – scurrying about.

"Zoom in on them, those figures. Have you got another camera angle?" the Zoo Controller asked.

"On it, boss," the Duty Manager replied.

They *were* humans.

The Zoo Controller leant forward to scan their faces…

No – he's not there. The Controller felt a strange relief that the slave from this morning wasn't among them.

He studied the four figures in front of him.

They were faces he would see a lot more of over the next 36 hours.

35

Elizabeth looked anxiously at Sir Claude.

The great man had slumped to the ground. His back was propped up against the glass door of the airlock and he had wrapped his arms around his knees. Suddenly, he looked his years. His face was sagging and his limbs trembling. Livid rings on his skin either side of his ankle tag betrayed the electrocution.

"Sir Claude?"

"Hm?"

"Sir Claude, what happens next? How do we get out of here?"

"Ah yes. Well... Well, I was rather hoping..."

Sir Claude's voice trailed off, leaving an uncharacteristic, vacant face behind it.

Elizabeth's anxiety was intensifying. She glanced up and down the service tunnel. It remained quiet – *for now*. Meantime she had one rescued hostage descending into shock and one expedition leader emerging from an electrocution.

She looked again at Sir Claude.

Elizabeth hadn't been there to see it but, for a few moments, he must've seemed *indomitable*. Staying on his feet through an electric shock that would have floored any other man – that *had* floored Juckes – and still finding the strength to dispatch the zookeeper into the airlock.

Only now he looked all too domitable, while precious time was draining away.

The authorities would surely send in a search team in seconds, minutes at the most. And even if they didn't, one or other of the Zailan soldiers lying nearby might regain consciousness.

"*Sir Claude*," she repeated, "what's the plan?"

"Yes, yes – what was I hoping?... Ah yes, I was rather hoping Adelaide would show up. You see?"

"I don't understand?"

"Pity we couldn't get a message back to her earlier... But she's bright. Through the telescope, she must've seen roughly where the procession went. Don't you think?" Sir Claude was about one hundred times more hesitant than usual. "If she sets the coordinates to that position, the beacon should draw her to us." Sir Claude weakly patted the rattan backpack next to him. "It's a chance, isn't it?"

Elizabeth thought for a moment. As a plan, it was plausible – but passive.

She stared at the airlock for a moment. On the far side of it, flames would now be engulfing the zookeeper. Might that draw Lady Danziger's attention? But the amphitheatre was sunk into the ground. The most she would see from the obelisk would be a plume of smoke – which could signify anything. Or nothing.

It was clear to Elizabeth that no help was coming. They were on their own.

This jolted her to action.

"Sir Claude?"

"Yes?"

"Please extract the revolver from the backpack. And

the spare ammunition. We might need it."

"Of course, good idea." Sir Claude started to sift effortfully through the contents of the rattan backpack.

"And while you're in there, please pull out the spare clothes." She looked at Sir Claude's colleague. His body was trembling – possibly from shock – possibly from cold – probably both. "Dr Setiawan will need them. And it's time you and I got out of these skins too."

"From the tone of your voice, young lady – do I detect a plan forming?" Dr Setiawan smiled weakly as he took a pair of charcoal-grey trousers from Sir Claude.

"I wouldn't go that far," Elizabeth replied, distracted. Turning her back to the three gentlemen, she had just pulled off the hated animal skins and slipped her arms into one of the grey shirts. As she buttoned it up, something on the ground ahead caught her eye. A book. It looked like a small manual. One of the Zailans must have dropped it during the struggle. She picked it up and leafed through the pages. "Dr James – could you keep this? Perhaps you'll get a chance to leaf through it later? Might be useful?"

Dr James took it from her.

"Meantime," she continued, pulling on a pair of trousers, "you and I need to check the two soldiers."

"*Hmm?* Of course, happy to help," Dr James replied, as if he'd just been asked to organise tea for the village cricket match. "What are we looking for?"

"Our ticket out of here."

36

Lady Danziger was scanning the zoo urgently and methodically.

Her short-wave radio lay on the sill next to her. Her husband hadn't radioed in and he hadn't responded to her call.

Ten minutes ago, she was still relaxed about the radio silence.

Five minutes ago, she was pretending to be relaxed.

Now she was sure something had gone wrong.

The telescope was her only other tool. As her husband had predicted, she had used it to follow the route of the procession. She had watched as the large float carrying Setiawan disappeared through the portcullis and into the outer ward of the castle.

From that point, she had lost visual contact – the walls of the castle were too high. Now the telescope was telling her little more than the radio, which was nothing.

However, what her husband had not correctly predicted was her next move. She was not about to breach protocol. Their expedition rules were quite clear: don't risk moving the steps unless you're certain where you're going.

She knew the others could be anywhere by now.

They might still be under the castle, where the beacon would guide her in. Or they could have been spirited to the opposite end of the zoo. In which case, the beacon would be useless and the steps might land in the worst possible place. She didn't have a gun to defend herself; her husband had one revolver and Juckes the other. The only weapon she could bring was a fire-axe, which she had spotted on one of the shelves behind her – and that was scarcely going to be much help.

No – if she landed the steps in the wrong place, it would be game over for all of them.

So she did the only sensible thing.

She watched.

And she waited.

It was just a matter of time and patience.

*

Unfortunately, she wasn't the only one watching and waiting.

Lady Danziger may have forgotten all about Dr Nussbaum. But he hadn't forgotten about her. He too was biding his time.

Large regions of his brilliant mind had been drained empty by the Zailan brainwashing program – and then re-filled in quite unrecognisable ways. 'Re-education' had robbed him of a lifetime of loyalties, values, and goals – and re-programmed him solely to the service of the zoo and the Zailan state. Part of the brilliance of the re-education program was to persuade him that his *previous* condition was the brainwashed one.

But while he may have lost his values, he hadn't lost his reason.

After all, reason has no goals or values of its own.

What is reason except mental machinery that can be turned to good purpose or evil? Dr Nussbaum's own words. Back on Earth, back in Germany, he was often asked to give talks in schools about his wartime experience. In the darkest depths of the 1940s, he and his extended family had learnt all too painfully in the darkness of Treblinka and Birkenau how reason could be deployed for both fair ends and foul.

Ironically for him, fair and foul had now been switched in his mind. His undeviating goal was to report his fellow humans to his Zailan superiors and to restore order at the zoo.

And to do that he needed to get free of the bonds in which they'd tied him.

And to do that, he just needed to deploy his reason.

And reason was telling him…

Time and patience.

He picked his moments carefully.

Only when the woman was staring through the telescope – and even then, only when she'd raised her hand to the side of the eyepiece to shield her eye from the sun – only then, sometimes just for a few seconds at a time, he rubbed the bindings.

The bindings were strong and the awkward motion of his hands behind his back was weak.

But bit-by-bit, rub-by-rub, the bindings must surely start to loosen.

It was just a matter of calmly waiting for the right moment.

Time and patience.

37

"Which tunnel do you think we should take? *Hmm?* I was thinking the, err, the left one looked more inviting. What do you think?"

"Yes. Yes, err, alright. Branch left," Elizabeth called back. She found Dr James' calm both calming and alarming. She had a feeling it was either going to get them through this mission – or get them killed.

The group were making their way down the main service tunnel. Dr James was at the front, Sir Claude and Dr Setiawan were behind him.

Sir Claude had struggled to his feet with difficulty and struggled into his new set of clothes with even more difficulty. Now he and Setiawan were shuffling along next to each other, one arm over each other's shoulder to prop themselves up.

Elizabeth was at the rear, shepherding them forward, and glancing back at the long straight tunnel behind them. She had hurriedly grabbed all their gear from Sir Claude. There wasn't time to think or re-pack. The beacon had gone straight in one pocket, spare ammo in the other. In one hand she held Sir Claude's service revolver and, in the other, the rattan backpack. It contained the remainder of their equipment: the radio and a small amount of food.

At least they were all now wearing normal clothing – shirt and trousers. She found it a little easier to believe in their chances.

Just five yards ahead, the tunnel branched three ways. *Left* would do fine, Elizabeth thought. Dr James had called that right. It was the direction that would get them furthest away from the Medieval Park. Not much of a reason, but good enough.

She glanced back over her shoulder again.

Lights.

Flashing lights.

Some kind of vehicle was heading in their direction. Probably still two or three hundred yards away but moving fast.

"Run, Dr James, *run!*" Elizabeth called out.

"*Hmm?* Run, you say?"

"*Yeees!*" she cried back, praying that some her urgency might find its way through to his legs. "Sir Claude, Dr Setiawan – they're coming. We have to hurry now."

The pair broke into a stumbling jog.

Dr James had already rounded the corner ahead and was out of sight.

Just as Sir Claude and Setiawan were rounding the same corner, a flash was suddenly visible to Elizabeth's right. She turned to see a beam of light – straight and blinding – stretching from a point on the wall all the way back down the tunnel. A second later, the light went out.

A laser had just been fired.

For an instant, the wall remained unchanged. And then, just as she ran past it, a great chunk of concrete collapsed away in a cloud of dust. *Vaporised.* It left behind a divot the size of a man's head.

She wasn't fooled. If they had wanted to hit her, she'd already be dead. It was a warning shot.

A moment later – just as she rounded the corner – a second warning shot. Elizabeth looked down and saw the rattan backpack glowing an infernal red beneath her hand. She dropped it in horror. On hitting the ground, the backpack disintegrated into a small pile of grey ashes.

Damn – Damn – Damn, her mind screamed, as she flew round the corner, breaking line-of-sight with her pursuers. The radio was gone. *Damn – Damn – Damn.*

She tried to force her anguish into a separate compartment of her mind. Up ahead in the branch tunnel, she saw the exact thing she was hoping to find.

"*Hurry!*" she screamed at the others. "Over *there!* Do you see? Twenty yards ahead on the left. *Another airlock.*"

"But how—"

Sir Claude was interrupted by the sound of voices shouting. Still distant, but getting closer.

"*But how do we get through?*"

"We've got a security pass!"

Dr James waved it above his head. He had found it a few minutes earlier on one of the unconscious Zailan soldiers. The soldier was clenching it in his fist. Only the smoothness of the plastic had made it possible to pull it from the vice-like grip.

"*Marvellous!*" Sir Claude exclaimed, a hint of vigour returning to his voice.

Dr James placed it against the reader. An instant later, they all heard a faint clunk and the sweet, sweet whirr of the curved glass doors starting to open.

Just above the doors was a sign in Zailan.

"What does it say, Dr James?" Elizabeth asked,

panting, waiting. According to the layout imprinted in her memory, they should be about to enter the Classical Park.

"*Hmm?* 'Park D – The Revenge of the Gods'."

"Is that what they call it?" Elizabeth shook her head. "Sounds about right. Come on – *follow me!*"

Taking the bewildered Setiawan by the hand, she stepped into the airlock. Sir Claude stepped in behind.

Dr James placed the card against the reader a second time. He slipped through the doors as they started to close again.

Feeling exposed in their glass bubble, the group looked back down the short length of tunnel to the junction. They were willing the glass doors to close before their pursuers rounded the corner.

And then the rail cart appeared. It screeched around the corner at an unfeasible speed and careered towards them just as—

C L U N K

The doors had closed.

The rail cart halted in front of the airlock. Six members of a Zailan SWAT team trained their weapons on Elizabeth and the others. Sighting lasers shone through the glass and danced across the fugitives' faces.

But the SWAT team didn't fire.

There was no point. The airlocks were germ-proof, bullet-proof, laser-proof and had a better-than-even chance of surviving a nuclear blast.

W H I R R R R

The massive steel doors on the other side of the airlock were starting to open.

The group were through to the other side.

Although the gods only knew what lay in store for them there.

38

As soon as the steel doors had clunked shut behind them, Elizabeth ran across grass to a spot ten yards away and wheeled back round to face the doors.

"*Go!*" she cried to the others. "I'll cover you."

She was standing with her feet planted shoulder-width apart – both hands on the revolver's grip – arms outstretched – aiming straight at the closed doors.

If this was to be their final stand, she was ready.

But the three gentlemen, standing just to one side of the steel doors, didn't move.

"Go," she repeated, "*now!*"

Sir Claude, however, didn't go. Or at least not in the direction she wanted. Instead, he started walking towards her, still limping, but calm.

Elizabeth was confused. Alternating her gaze between the door and Sir Claude, she felt her panic rising.

"You don't understand," she said, almost crying, but determined not to. "The radio. It's *gone.* They destroyed it. Don't you see? We've got no way of contacting your wife now. She can't rescue us. This gun—" she nodded at the revolver "—it's all we've got."

Sir Claude stopped just a yard from Elizabeth.

"I understand," he said with an uncanny kindness in his voice. "How about the beacon?"

"No," she replied. "I've still got that. In my pocket."

"Good," Sir Claude replied. "That's good. And don't worry about the radio. We'll work something out."

"What do you mean, *don't*—"

He placed his hand on the top of the revolver and gently – *firmly* – lowered her aim.

"Hang on a sec— Wait. What are you—"

"Look at us," he said. "I'm still recovering. Setiawan is wounded. And this gun." He glanced down at the revolver, which was now pointing into the soil. "It's a toy compared to those lasers. If we try to fight them, Elizabeth, we die."

She looked at Sir Claude. His hair was still spiked; there was a lingering air of frailty about him. But there was also calm certainty in his eyes.

"But we can't just give up," Elizabeth said, even as she loosened her grip a little.

"We're not," he said, gently taking the gun from her hands. "In the next 60 seconds, they'll either come through that door. Or they won't." He looked back up at her. "My guess, however, is not."

"But how can you know that?" Involuntarily, she started counting the seconds.

"Ah, but would you smell that?" Sir Claude said, turning away. He paused to drink in a deep lungful of air. His eyes were half-closed. "I could almost believe myself in Tuscany."

Elizabeth could almost see the strength seeping back into him as he breathed. She smelt the air too. He was right. After the concrete dampness of the tunnels, it was sweet. Fragrant even.

"Sir Claude," Elizabeth persisted, still counting the seconds. "I don't get this."

"Agustus?" Sir Claude called his friend over his shoulder, while returning his gaze to Elizabeth. "Tell us. Would you agree that we make rather good viewing. Now we're out in the open?"

"Quite so, Sir Claude," Dr Setiawan replied, as he made his way towards them. "Just a pity you're no longer wearing the caveman outfit. You looked most fetching in animal skins."

"True," Sir Claude replied, "But I suspect I'm still a specimen that you wouldn't want to kill off *too soon*. Am I right?"

"I think that's fair."

"Hang on…" Elizabeth stammered. The 60 seconds must be up and the steel doors had remained firmly shut. "Are you both saying we're now part of… *the entertainment?*"

"I'm not saying anything," Sir Claude replied. "I'm just guessing. Agustus?"

"Oh, we're part of the entertainment alright. *Part of the zoo*. No question."

"But who's watching us. And *how?*"

"Cameras everywhere," Setiawan replied. "In the trees, the walls, the buildings. On large drones the size of birds. On tiny ones the size of insects. Everywhere."

"My God—"

"The zoo has probably closed by now for live visitors," Setiawan continued. "But it's always open for the TV networks. All day, all night."

"And when is peak viewing?" Sir Claude asked.

"Well, I believe they have something equivalent to 'a weekend' over here on Zil." Dr Setiawan pronounced 'weekend' as if he wasn't particularly comfortable with the concept either on Earth or Zil. "So, tomorrow night would be my guess. That's their 'Saturday night', if you will."

"So, are you basically saying... The Zailans won't try to kill us *yet?*"

"That's right," Setiawan replied. "My guess is we're safe until tomorrow night. Honestly, the best thing we can do is make ourselves as visible as possible. We have become – *how would the Americans put this?* – box office."

*

The Zoo Controller leaned back, euphoric.

Good news was always welcome. But when it displaced dreadful news, it could be intoxicating.

And the Zoo Controller was intoxicated.

Sabotage.

He curled his long, undulating lips around the word, mouthing it silently to himself. How sweet it sounded.

Sabotage.

Sabotage perpetrated by *outsiders.*

Sweeter still.

To lose the life of a zookeeper to the humans through error or accident... That would have been humiliating.

But to lose one because the zoo had been infiltrated? That was a different matter.

Very different.

This wasn't a disaster anymore. This was *a gift.*

Even now the comms team on the 20th floor were turning his hapless zookeeper into a planetary hero – putting out on the wires the tale of a diligent, hard-working Zailan, loyal to the Caucus unto her last breath

– the victim of malevolent, interfering human scum. *Outsiders.*

The Zoo Controller brought all sixteen of his fingers together under his chin, fingertip to fingertip. The feeling coursing through him was one of pure joy – joy heightened by relief.

Because it got better.

The human infiltrators – all three of them, along with the friend they had 'rescued' – were now wandering as defenceless as new-born children in one of the most controlled environments in the Universe. One of the most controlled – and the most hostile.

His zoo.

Thank the gods that the SWAT team *hadn't* managed to capture them down in the service tunnels. Truly he felt blessed by Providence. The humans were now walking across the open, gentle hills of the Classical Park. As he watched them, he was toggling between the half-dozen different camera views on offer. A small fleet of surveillance drones was circling the fugitives. They were the very latest models: unheard and unseen – hearing everything, seeing everything.

The Zoo Controller could now do what he wanted with the fugitives, and he could do it *in full view of Zil.* Media were already reporting a ratings spike. The Zoo Controller had no doubt the ratings would grow and grow as word spread. That soon no-one on Zil would be watching anything else. *Doing* anything else.

He was tempted to bring things to a head today, this evening.

But *no* – better to wait.

Build the ratings for an extra day – slowly, *deliciously.*

Tomorrow night the Regional Governor's son would be visiting the zoo with his friends. Let *him* deliver the coup de grâce. Then the Regional Governor would be in his pocket – all of Zil would be enthralled to him – and the Supreme Governor himself would surely call to offer his congratulations.

And it would all happen the night before the bulk carrier – the largest ever seen on Zil – was due to depart to the Earth to effect the mass abduction.

The timing couldn't be better. From chaos, order was being re-established. From disaster, triumph.

A career born in the sunshine was about to reach a dizzy zenith.

The gods favoured him still.

39

Elizabeth was breathing more freely now. As she strode through the long grasses up the gentle slope, she drank in the sights and sounds and scents around her.

It was almost like she was back on Earth. And in a particularly lovely corner of it.

The low sun illuminated the yellowing grass around her feet in the golden hues of late summer. The meadow scents filled her nostrils, powerfully, and in the strange stillness she became aware of birdsong. The trilling of goldfinches in the evening air and the chiffchaff's urgent call.

It was all artifice of course. Biologically real, yes, but artificial on every other level. *Fake*. A Zailan construct. Saccharine, not sugar.

But right now, Elizabeth didn't care. Between a real Hell and an artificial Heaven, she'd take the latter, every time.

She looked up ahead.

Sir Claude was back at the front of their group, thank God, recovering his strength with every footstep. Behind was Dr James, gliding up the hill as effortlessly as a leaf on a breeze. Dr Setiawan came a pace or two behind, gamely trying to keep pace. *The poor man must be exhausted*. His wound was weeping again. She could see a dark, drooping stain, gluing his shirt to his back.

Elizabeth glanced over her shoulder.

The door they had come through – the *airlock* – was disappearing from view. A barely discernible rectangle in the great wall behind them.

The wall.

It was over forty yards high. She had known that theoretically from her observations through the telescope. But to see this massive structure, curving behind her, was a different matter. Over past her left shoulder it stretched away for miles, forming the boundary between the Classical Park and the Medieval. Over past her right shoulder it formed a boundary with the central plaza of the zoo. Beyond that, it bordered the Japanese Park. *Maybe?* That was her best guess. Right now, the only thing she had to orientate herself was the great white obelisk, about two miles behind her.

Elizabeth refocussed on the hill ahead. They were approaching the crest about thirty yards away.

"I have a question, Agustus." It was Dr James' voice. "Why did they make those airlocks so secure, *hmm?* So bulky? Was it to stop the spread of disease?" His face expressed the curiosity of a child on a geography field trip.

"Oh perhaps, Artemas, perhaps. But that's not the main reason," Setiawan replied like his indulgent geography teacher. "They're really there to stop the spread of something far more dangerous."

"What then?"

"Ideas!"

"Oh, very good!" The pair started chuckling.

"But why?" Elizabeth asked. "Why would they care

about the spread of ideas?"

"Many reasons," Setiawan replied. He was still doing his best impression of cheerfulness as he visibly weakened. "But mostly this. You see, none of the humans in these parks realise they're in a zoo."

"*They don't?*"

"No. No idea at all."

"*But*... But what about the walls?"

"Indeed. Strange, isn't it? I guess as generation followed generation, the walls just came to be accepted as part of their universe. They built it into their mythology, I imagine. That's what humans do, isn't it?" Setiawan stopped talking a moment to catch his breath. The walking was taking its toll. "There's one exception, though."

"Who?"

"The Victorians."

"The Victorians?"

"Yes. Park F. 'The Engineers of Empire'. They've only been here 50 years or so. 50 *Zailan* years. The oldest ones still remember life on Earth. They know this place isn't home... But even they don't understand it's a zoo."

"Ah…" Elizabeth replied, trying to take it all on board. "So, is that why the Zailans have built a triple wall around their park?" She recalled what she had seen from the 21st floor.

"In a way. But perhaps not in the way you're thinking," Setiawan replied. "Yes, they're always trying to escape. Good old Victorians and their relentless endeavour. *But*..."

"But?"

"But the Zailans have turned it to their advantage. Do you see?" Dr Setiawan heaved. "They've turned the

Victorian attraction into a… A giant 'escape room' is what they call it. Visitors pay extra to watch them escape over or under – or *through* – the first wall, only to find another wall in their way. And if they manage to get past that, *another*. And so on."

"And if they do make it over the third wall?" Elizabeth asked Dr Setiawan.

"Oh, believe me," Setiawan replied, "they *never* make it over the third wall."

"But what if they—"

Elizabeth stopped in mid-flow.

They all did.

They had just crested the hill.

There before them, unfolding like the canvas of a Dutch master, was a scene of Elysian beauty.

*

It was hard to take in.

The valley before them presented a sight so beautiful, it was painful to the eyes – seeing it as they were after so much violence and ugliness. Like sunlight glimpsed after darkness.

Stretching away to their left, they saw a patchwork of fields, a small river undulating between, rows of cypress trees flexing in the gentle breeze like so many feather quills. Elizabeth could see peasants working in the evening sunshine, gathering in the harvest. Just a half-mile away she could see a cart, half-loaded with hay, hitched to a couple of ponies – *actual ponies* – champing in their harness. Some way beyond them she spotted the distant outline of a small temple. Rectangular, with a classical portico, Elizabeth could make out a small parade of figures in flowing white robes in front of it.

It was a scene of bucolic classical fantasy. Just for a moment, Elizabeth forgot the cares and worries of their predicament. She forgot the wall behind her and the dangers ahead of her, she forgot the tunnels and the amphitheatre and the funeral pyre.

Yes, this might all be artifice – but then so was a painting – and this scene was better than any painting. This scene was *alive*. It was also, Elizabeth now admitted to herself, to some degree *real*. If only because the characters within it thought it so.

She looked to her right.

Here she saw slightly wilder country. A spring gushed from the hillside. Elizabeth knew the water was being pumped there by Zailan engineers, but so artfully done. Water cascading over rocks; the sidelight of the setting sun sparkling and shimmering on the spray. Just to look at it was to feel refreshed. She could see a few figures bathing in a rockpool at the base.

Dr James was standing next to her. Elizabeth touched his arm and pointed wordlessly in their direction.

He stared in wonder.

They all did.

Just for a moment, Elizabeth found her view of the Zailans softening. If they could recreate such a scene in their zoo – and do it so perfectly – were they all bad?

A groan brought Elizabeth back to their present reality. She spun to her left.

Dr Setiawan had collapsed to one knee.

"My dear chap…" Sir Claude rushed to grab one of his arms and steady him. "You need some rest. Urgently."

"I'm fine, really, I am. Please don't make a fuss,"

Dr Setiawan replied. He looked worryingly pale to Elizabeth.

"There!" Sir Claude pronounced. "You see that folly on the far hillside?" Elizabeth followed his gaze. Up on higher ground beyond the stream, perhaps a mile and a half away, was a small, marble-white folly or rotunda. An elegant, domed building, supported on a circle of a dozen perfect columns. Sir Claude placed a hand on his friend's shoulder. "Rest here for a few minutes, old man. Then we'll head over. We should be able to shelter there." He turned to Elizabeth. "And then we can set about trying to get a message to Adelaide."

"Sir Claude—" Dr Setiawan started weakly.

"But how can we get a message to your wife?" Elizabeth spoke over Dr Setiawan.

"Well, interesting that you ask," Sir Claude replied. "Actually, I've had an idea—"

"*Sir Claude*—" Dr Setiawan tried to interrupt.

"—You see what we could do is—"

"*SIR CLAUDE!*"

"*What?* What is it? My dear fellow, don't excite yourself—"

Dr Setiawan, still down on one knee, was gesturing insistently – one moment pointing at the sky, the next at his ear again.

"Oh. You mean…" Sir Claude gestured to his own ear. "They're listening too?"

"Yes!"

"*Even here?*"

"Particularly here," Dr Setiawan replied. "Every word."

*

The group seated themselves in a small circle on the crest of the hill, while Elizabeth did her best to tend to Dr Setiawan's wound.

It was still weeping. Elizabeth tore off a strip of material from the hem of her own shirt and pressed it to his back. It was all she could do. "We'll wash it when we cross that stream, Dr Setiawan." He nodded in reply. "I'll try to fashion a bandage for you later."

The group couldn't speak openly – at least, not about anything confidential. And they had nothing to write with. Their only pen and jotter pad had been turned to ash ten minutes earlier.

But Elizabeth saw Sir Claude was whispering into his nephew's ear. They were trying to maintain a neutral expression, but she could see the excitement lighting their eyes.

Dr James moved across to Elizabeth and crouched next to her.

"*What?*" she whispered. "*What is it?*"

Dr James leaned into Elizabeth's left ear. His voice was faint, even at half an inch, his lips almost brushing her skin.

"*Claude has an idea for getting Adelaide's attention. For summoning her.*"

"*But how?*" Elizabeth whispered, "*How can we possibly signal to her?*"

"*Fire, of course,*" Dr James whispered back. "*Fire. In the dead of night.*"

40

Lady Danziger didn't take any breaks. Equal supplies of stamina and anxiety were keeping her hunched over the telescope.

The short-wave radio still lay on the windowsill just to the side of the telescope, still inert. Every ten minutes, with metronomic precision, Lady Danziger tried to raise her husband on it. *Nothing.* She kept her call signal short and brief. No emotion, no detail. If her husband wasn't listening, she had no idea who else might be.

She re-focussed the telescope. To avoid distraction by the many, many distracting things in the zoo, she kept reiterating her mantra. She was looking for a small group: one woman and two, possibly three, men. Clothing: two of them very likely still in caveman skins, one in supervisor clothing, and one – Dr Setiawan – half-naked. Possibly. All of them would be – *should be* – trying to draw attention to themselves.

She had been focussing her efforts on the Medieval Park. Logic and experience dictated they would re-surface somewhere close to where she'd last seen them. Which was the entrance to the castle.

But, theoretically, they could re-surface anywhere in the zoo.

Or nowhere.

Lady Danziger tried to stop herself dwelling on that possibility. All through her life, she had made a conscious effort to be guided neither by pessimism nor optimism. Just by reason. She continued to hold fast to this pillar, even as the tide of anxiety swelled at its base, like floodwater in a temple.

She had had a couple of leads. A couple of *maybes*. The first had been a plume of smoke rising over the top of the great wall, just inside the Medieval Park. She had spotted it fifteen minutes earlier. *Where there's smoke there's fire*, she thought. *And where there's fire, there's usually my husband.*

But she hadn't been able to see where the smoke was coming from. The wall blocked her view. So, she scanned the area just beyond. There was a small town. But nothing looked untoward. There were very few people about, nothing much seemed to stir. Or nothing that she could see.

Her second lead had followed about five minutes later.

She had been scanning the Classical Park, focussing on the area nearest her, and had spotted a promising-looking group. Four tiny figures, about two or three miles away, wandering across the open grassland. She watched them for several minutes.

But none of them were stripped down or wearing caveman skins – they weren't visibly drawing attention to themselves – and they had been walking *away* from the obelisk, not towards it.

Still, it was a lead.

She decided to have another look. She started to swivel the telescope back towards where she had last seen them.

That was when she heard a clink of metal. She assumed it was the tripod.

But the tripod was made of wood. She looked up.

Movement flashed in the corner of her eye.

And then she saw him.

Their hostage.

Nussbaum.

Herr Doktor Yuval Nussbaum was running towards her with a fire-axe. He was holding it outstretched above his head. The very image of a madman.

Lady Danziger screwed her eyes shut and reflexively raised her arms above her head. Fighting didn't occur to her.

He had an axe, she had nothing.

She was going to die.

It would be an exaggeration to say Lady Danziger's entire life flashed before her eyes in the moments before Nussbaum reached her and swung the axe. But a surprising amount of cognitive activity did take place.

She wondered how he had managed to slip free of his bindings and cursed herself for not checking them. It had seemed impolite to be trussing up a distinguished academic – so she cursed herself for that thought too. And she cursed herself for leaving a fire-axe so visible and reachable.

And her final thought, as the axe swung down, was why her head made a splintering sound. She imagined the sound might involve some splintering, yes, but would otherwise be much more – *well* – squelchy.

She opened her eyes.

The axe was not, after all, between them.

And Dr Nussbaum was not directly in front of her. He was about five yards away, at the top of the steps. He had run straight past her and, in a couple of giant bounds, had propelled himself up the eight steps to the small platform at the top. Once there, he had plunged his axe into the bench under which the controls were located.

The madman was acting rationally. He had no intention of killing her. Or at least, not right away. He was going to do something far worse. He was going to destroy the steps – their one means of escaping from this planet. He was, in effect, going to kill them all. Or at least condemn them to remain forever on Zil, which came to the same thing.

And because Lady Danziger had left the small bench open, he didn't even need to waste a half-second hinging back the seat. She felt sick as she looked at the axe, buried in the controls inside.

Her sheer fury with herself prised open the door to courage.

She launched herself from the window and started scrambling up the steps behind the mad axeman. *Who's the mad one now?* When she reached the third or fourth step, she realised the axe-head had lodged itself in the wooden bench. It was stuck. It delayed Nussbaum by a couple of seconds, as he struggled to free it. Just enough of a delay so that when he did free it and wheeled round to strike her, he was himself panicked. He lashed out, sinking the axe-head into the banister four inches from Lady Danziger's right hand.

Her right hand didn't waste its reprieve.

Still standing a couple of steps below him, she punched directly between his legs. In the groin. Happily, the German groin, unlike the Zailan one, did indeed sit in the cleft between the thighs.

Very much so.

Professor Nussbaum howled with pain and released

his grip on the axe.

This presented a second opportunity. With force and speed, she grabbed hold of his upper arm, stepped to one side, and sent him cartwheeling past her and down the steps.

Without looking to see how he landed, Lady Danziger flew up the remaining three steps to the small platform at the top. The axe-head *wasn't* buried in the controls. By the grace of a God she didn't believe in, the axe had buried itself in the wooden side of the bench – that and Sir Claude's leather notebook, which had been cleaved in two.

She rifled desperately through the jumbled contents of the small compartment – *Where is it? Where is it?* She was looking for the one thing that could save her now.

She glanced behind.

Nussbaum was back on his feet. He was advancing back up the steps – a little slower, a little buckled – but every bit as brainwashed as before. The axe was still lodged in the banister. She saw his hand land securely on the handle and, with a single wrench, pull it free.

Desperately, she turned back to the bench compartment. *It must be here, it must be.* She heard the creak of wood, as he advanced another step. He was in striking distance of her now. She imagined him raising the axe—

And then she saw it.

The control pad.

She grabbed it with her left hand and flipped back the plastic safety cover with her right. As her thumb plunged down on the red button, she spun round to face Nussbaum.

She watched as 500 volts coursed through the

German's body. He crumpled and fell, his head landing just a few inches from her feet, and the axe just a few inches from that. Instinctively, she withdrew half a pace back, her waist pressed against the banister at the back of the small platform.

The German was lying perilously close to the step's controls. She didn't dare release the button. She watched as his mouth frothed – as his muscles jerked uncontrollably – as his body writhed and careered towards death.

And that's the destination he seemed to have reached, when a knock on the door snapped Lady Danziger out of her panic.

Tap – Tap – tap-tap – Tap

She released the button.

The German continued twitching, not unlike a chicken's corpse in the seconds after its neck has been wrung.

My God – have I killed him?

And then a second, more insistent knock on the door.

41

The howl of a wolf struck out across the valley with the clarity of a church bell but none of the friendliness.

Elizabeth and the others looked at each other across the top of the small fire that lay flickering between them.

Wolves – seriously? Elizabeth's expression said to the others, whose eyes replied in kind. If the Zailans felt the need to abduct nocturnal mammals from Earth, how about badgers?

Or hedgehogs?

The wolf howled again.

Unless of course it was a different wolf responding to the first. It certainly sounded a little closer.

Night had fallen and their pastoral idyll was at risk of turning into something more sinister. So far, Elizabeth had counted three moons in the sky, two of them full. For all she knew, there were more on the other side of the folly, on the *obelisk side*. But the two windows – more just ventilation slits – only covered two points of the compass and didn't give a view of the obelisk. Elizabeth remembered the name of the park – *The Revenge of the Gods* – and promptly tried to forget it again.

"Well, the good news," Sir Claude spoke first, "is

that whatever else they throw at us, they won't be getting us with wolves. Not tonight anyway."

He gestured with his head towards the trap door through which they had climbed – the only route into their first-floor eyrie. Only one way in and one way out. They had pulled the ladder up behind them and bolted the trap door. It wouldn't exactly stop aliens with lasers. But it should stop wolves.

Theoretically.

Elizabeth smiled and prodded the fire with the poker, sending a flurry of sparks circling upwards. She watched them swirl towards the small round opening at the top of the domed roof. They had found their folly to be – in the circumstances – well suited for their purposes. It was a single upstairs room, almost certainly used by shepherds. There was a stone hearth in the centre and a good supply of logs, stacked tidily against a section of the curved stone wall. The thick stone offered some shelter against the surprisingly cold night that had fallen outside. That and the small fire they had laid.

The moment they had arrived in the folly – while Sir Claude laid the fire – Elizabeth had set about tending to the puncture wound on Dr Setiawan's back. It was deeper than she had feared. She did her best to clean it and dress it. She tore more strips of fabric to create a bandage long enough to wrap around his torso. She suspected a fever would take hold soon. All the while she had found herself warming to this unusual man. He never once complained, remaining exquisitely courteous even in pain.

And now they were playing a waiting game.

They had a plan – to signal to Lady Danziger by laying a fire outside – and to do so an hour before dawn. The hope would be for her to get the steps in and out before the Zailans could realise what was happening. Try any other time of day, and the Zailans would likely vaporise them into the next life. So, they were all agreed: it had to be done in the darkest hour of the night.

Elizabeth felt conflicted. At one moment, the plan seemed hopelessly ambitious. *What if Lady Danziger is asleep? Or doesn't spot the fire?*

Or misinterprets it?

And then the next moment it seemed hopelessly unambitious. *Is that it?* Were they just going to make off with Setiawan and leave the thousands of other humans here to their miserable fate—

The wolf howled again, interrupting Elizabeth's spiralling thoughts.

Sir Claude clapped his hands, breaking the nervous silence inside the folly. "Well, there's no sense in us just sitting here getting the jitters," he said. "I'm sure there are some things we *can* talk about. Setiawan – how are you bearing up?"

"Perfectly well, thank you, Sir Claude," his friend lied.

"Good. So how about a fireside story?"

"Of course. How may I entertain you?"

"The story of your abduction should do."

*

And so Dr Setiawan shared his story.

He didn't have much to say about the early part. He had almost no memory of the abduction itself. And none at all of the initial interrogation – he had been drugged. The story came to life when he was moved to the 55th floor of the Obelisk.

The 55th floor was part of the 'high value suite'. Where the Zailans kept the academics who were helping them understand humanity: the scientists, the historians, the anthropologists, the engineers. Their lodgings, Setiawan discovered, were comfortable. They were even permitted a certain amount of freedom – in the sense they could mingle and chat and draw books from an extensive library.

But the Zailans were always listening, of course. And studying.

While there, Setiawan had befriended a morose but talkative French economist. The Frenchman had freely shared much of what he knew about the zoo. He'd also described the kind of fate an academic could expect when *the day* arrived. The day the Zailans didn't need his or her expertise anymore. A very few – those who proved susceptible to brainwashing – were trained as slave supervisors. Dr Nussbaum had been one. Others were released into the parks to see how they fared. Normally into 'Headhunters of the Forest' or 'Arabian Safari', where the chance of survival was lowest. Watching middle-class intellectuals from the 20th Century integrate – or fail to integrate – into remote cultures was essential viewing on Zil. As the French economist explained it: if the Zailans found the suffering of an intelligent being pleasurable, they found the suffering of a very intelligent being very pleasurable.

But those were the lucky ones.

The less fortunate provided the raw material for *'Feeding time at the zoo'* – the star attraction at the end of every day. Today's victim was to have been an Italian zoologist. But she had fallen ill with a severe fever. The authorities were worried she wouldn't offer enough fight. So, after Setiawan had 'failed' his interrogation, they had earmarked him instead.

"But my dear fellow – surely they needed you?" Sir Claude asked. "There isn't a man alive who knows more about the tribes of Borneo."

"Ah yes, the Penan in the Forest Park. You're very kind, Sir Claude." Dr Setiawan smiled. "But they already have plenty of anthropologists. No, I don't believe they abducted me for my expertise."

"Why then?"

"Because I'm a member of the Council."

"Ah…"

"When it turned out that I knew nothing of interest to them, they decided to terminate me."

Dr Setiawan, suddenly dizzy, put a hand out on the ground to steady himself.

"Dr Setiawan, please let me help you." Elizabeth was worried. "Please try lying down."

"Of course, of course."

Elizabeth helped manoeuvre him into a lying position. She had fashioned a primitive pillow from hay and an old sack. She cradled his head as he slowly lowered it.

"You know the ironic thing?" he asked rhetorically, a sheen of sweat on his forehead from the effort of moving. "After a lifetime of probing at other cultures and studying them, it seems almost fitting that I should end up in a zoo."

"Come now, Agustus," Sir Claude remonstrated, "I think you're being a little harsh."

"No, no, it's true. I shall never look at my job the same way again."

42

Lady Danziger was still shaken – but no longer shaking. She knew that because the barrel of the revolver she was pointing was no longer wavering. Or at least, not as much.

She was covering Juckes as he bound Dr Nussbaum. She watched him secure his wrists with a second cable tie – they weren't taking any chances this time – and then approach his legs with a length of rope.

"I apologise for this, sir, but I think we'll need to bind your legs as well. Would you mind?"

"Not at all, young man, not at all," Dr Nussbaum replied in near-faultless English. "I would do the same."

"Very good, sir. So I'm just going to pass it under your knees like so... And then back round..." Juckes talked through the actions, like a dentist soothing a patient through the worst part of the procedure. "You see? Nowhere near your ankle."

"You are very thoughtful, ja?"

Lady Danziger and Juckes found themselves in a very strange position. They were worrying if Dr Nussbaum would be alright – and they were worrying if he would try to kill them. They had made him as comfortable as they reasonably could, before binding him hand and foot.

It had been a half hour full of reversals.

Despite what Juckes insisted, Lady Danziger – in her mind – did *not* have the situation under control when he'd arrived in the storeroom.

Thank God he did arrive.

He had a talent for that, Juckes. For being there when he was needed and scarce when he wasn't. When Lady Danziger had opened the door to him – *shaking* – the control pad still in her hand – all words were stuck in the back of her throat. But he immediately grasped what had happened.

He had rushed across to the German, lying prostrate at the top of the steps. The extended electrocution had stopped the man's heart. Juckes performed CPR and brought him spluttering to life. After that, they had given Nussbaum water, they'd applied salve to the burns around his ankle – although most of the damage was likely sub-dermal – they'd propped his head on a pillow... And then bound him hand and foot.

At one level, Lady Danziger's survival instincts left her paranoid about a second attack. But at another level, she was certain none of the precautions were necessary.

Why?

Because Dr Nussbaum was himself again.

The electrocution had somehow freed his mind – it had washed away the brainwash. As Nussbaum himself calmly explained, this was a rare but known effect of electrocution. This was why the Zailans sent slaves for re-education – whenever their ankle tags logged a longer-than-normal electrocution. They were 're-brainwashed'. Just in case.

"I should try and rest now, sir, if you can," Juckes

said, as he finished knotting the rope. "But if you need anything, just ask?"

"Thank you," Nussbaum replied. "I appreciate that."

Juckes walked to the other end of the room to join Lady Danziger, who was at the window, her eye back on the telescope.

"I don't think we'll have any more trouble from him tonight, ma'am," he said in a low voice.

"No, I think you're right."

"Let me do a shift on the telescope. You should get some rest, ma'am."

"Are you sure?"

"Yes. Quite sure."

Lady Danziger moved gratefully away from the window. He was right. She *did* need to rest. She looked at her watch. She'd take over again in four hours. "So tell me. How was your mission? To the bulk carrier."

"Not good, I'm afraid, ma'am. I think it's a bust."

"That bad?"

"Yes. Tight security all round the perimeter. Security lights every twenty yards, armed guards. No chance of sabotage. But…"

"Yes?"

"I did gain access to the hold. Slaves were being used to help load provisions. So I managed to plant a beacon. In an unused stowage area. I'm afraid that's the best I could do."

"Still, not bad," Lady Danziger mused. "It means we could land the steps on board at any point."

"At any point while the bulk carrier is still there. *Before launch.*" Juckes paused for a moment, looking for his words. "Because I did find out something else…"

Lady Danziger was immediately on edge. She was

certain that carrier was intended for a mass abduction – to populate the new city park. *Zootropolis.* She gestured to him to continue.

"I overheard two supervisors talking – in English. About the launch schedule."

"Yes?"

"I think they said – and I might be mistaken of course…"

Lady Danziger gestured again.

"In just over a day. At dawn."

43

The folly was silent again.

The group were all starving but refusing to mention it. What was the point? They knew there was no chance of food that night. Elizabeth looked from face to face in the flickering light. Sir Claude was prodding the fire with the poker. Dr James was quietly reading the manual they had retrieved in the tunnels. Dr Setiawan was lost in thought. *Or pain.*

"So how about the others, Agustus?" Sir Claude broke the silence. "How did the slaves end up here? Were they abducted like you?"

"Don't you think we should leave Dr Setiawan in peace?" Elizabeth protested.

"No, no," Setiawan protested back. "Sir Claude is quite right. We must talk, young lady! Information is everything. Sir Claude must extract every last ounce!"

He paused for a moment, recovering from the effort of his cheerfulness. "The answer, Sir Claude is, *more or less.* Apparently, the Zailans choose the slaves carefully too. They pick only waifs and strays. People whose absence won't be missed."

"Ha! So they pick from the very top and the very bottom of society."

"I suppose you could put it that way."

"And what about the zoo inmates? I mean the ones in the actual parks?"

"Ah, the third and final group of humans. They're different. They were abducted – *yes* – but not by the Zailans. That's the extraordinary thing. Most of them were taken generations ago."

"So they're from *real* communities?"

"Oh, yes," Setiawan replied. "The oldest community are the Romans of course. They were abducted 1,000 Zailan years ago."

"2,000 Earth years?"

"Just so. Of course, they haven't always been held in this location. No, no. They were sold from one place to another."

"Sounds peculiar?"

"Isn't it? Rather like the way they shuttle a prize panda from one zoo to another. But the Romans have been here – I mean, literally right *here* – for a hundred years at least."

"You bothered to find all this out?" Elizabeth asked. "Didn't it seem a bit pointless, with your execution scheduled?"

"Oh, I guessed that Sir Claude would come and get me," Setiawan replied with a twinkle. "And when I saw Juckes' face at the lift, I knew it."

The group all stared into the fire for a moment. Amazed and aghast. All except for Dr James, who remained absorbed in the manual.

"So, which is the most popular park then? With the visitors, I mean?" Sir Claude asked. "This one?"

"Apparently not," Setiawan replied. "The Classical Park is popular, yes. But I'm told the Medieval Park wins the crown."

"Why?"

"It's right up the Zailan street, of course." Dr Setiawan shivered as he recalled his brush with death. "The vigorous medieval lust for executions, the fights, the rape, the brutality – *the sermonising priests*. Fantastic theatre." Dr Setiawan paused for a moment. "Only the Victorians come close in terms of popularity. Of course, the Victorians don't relish a public execution quite so much. But they offer something else the Zailans find irresistible."

"The belief that they can escape?" Elizabeth ventured.

"*Exactly*. They keep trying and trying, and devise ever more ingenious technologies. They're very different to the medieval peasants. But also the same. Do you see?"

"You're talking in riddles, old man," Sir Claude shot back. "Whatever do you mean?"

"The Victorians, the medieval peasants... They share the same outrage at their present circumstances – a refusal to accept things as they are. But while the medieval peasants just get angry about it, the Victorians try to do something. *To escape*. The Zailans love it of course. They find increasingly cruel ways to raise their hopes – and dash them again. It really draws in the crowds. Poor Victorians."

"It's barbaric."

"Ah well, it's partly your own fault, Sir Claude. You Christians. You just won't accept things *as they are*."

"But surely the other peoples here are just as outraged? Just as keen to escape?" Elizabeth asked.

"That's the thing you see. Not according to what I was told. The Moslems seem to have settled much better within the weird confines of their illusory world.

Makes sense if you think about their faith. The very word 'Islam' means—"

"—surrender."

"Exactly so, Mrs B. They *surrender* themselves to God's will. No questions asked. The Romans, apparently, are the same... Well, we're in their park. We may yet get a chance to see for ourselves. But remember: none of them realise they're in a zoo."

"So it's the Christians they really want to see?" Elizabeth pressed the point.

"Oh yes. The Christians just can't seem to settle within their walls. So angry – never satisfied with what they've got – always wanting to escape. Or – to use the polite term – *to progress*. Onto the next thing and the next thing. Things that are up-to-date one day are obsolete the next. Honestly, Mrs B, I find it quite shocking how quickly the past arrives in your country."

Sir Claude poked the fire in irritation. "So that's why they're going to do this mass abduction from London?" he asked. "Because they want more restless Christians in their zoo?"

"Exactly."

"And there was me thinking it's because they wanted a new zoo."

"I don't understand."

"Weren't you aware?" It was Sir Claude's turn to be in the know. "They've recreated Regents Park. Including *London zoo*. There'll be a zoo within a zoo. Probably the Zailan idea of humour."

"My goodness... and my—"

"Your house?"

"Yes."

"Oh yes, they've copied that too," Sir Claude replied. "At least, a freshly painted version of it. Saw it through the field glasses. You know when we get back, you really must attend to the stucco."

"*If* we get back."

The pair chuckled, as if this was somehow funny – until Dr Setiawan gasped in pain. The laughter had pulled on his wound.

"Come on, Agustus. You must be all done in. It's time to sleep."

"I agree," Elizabeth added. "We need to rest while we can. Who knows when we'll be disturbed."

"I'll take first watch," Sir Claude said, picking up a small three-legged stool – the folly's only piece of furniture. He placed it next to one of the ventilation slits.

"And I'll take second," Elizabeth added.

She was already on her feet and took hold of the two blankets they'd found in the folly. Coarse and large, they smelt of wood smoke and soil. She laid one over Dr Setiawan, doubling it back over him again.

She carried the other to Dr James.

"Dr James…" she said, "it's time to rest."

"*Hmm?*" He looked up from the manual. "Ah yes, yes, thank you, Mrs B." He smiled as she started to lay the second blanket over him.

"Spread it wide, Elizabeth," Sir Claude spoke up. "You two are going to have to share that blanket."

"Pardon? I don't—"

"I'm not having you do a sacrifice act here," Sir Claude cut her off. "You need your rest too."

He was right of course.

44

Elizabeth found herself lying under the blanket next to Dr James, a narrow gap in between. Their heads were propped up on makeshift pillows, both of them staring up at the domed ceiling above. He with his hands tucked up under the back of his head; she with her arms down by her side.

Elizabeth's body was rigid, even while her mind was filling with tenderness towards this slip of a man. Scarcely a natural fighter, he had done his bit according to his own style and never once complained. He had helped them fight their way out of the tunnels and now, here in the folly, he had started fighting his way through a book *in Zailan*—

"One last question, Artemas." Sir Claude's voice glided into the calm dark of the folly like an owl from its perch. "That manual. Did you discover anything useful?"

"Ah, the zookeeper's manual, *hmm?* You know, this and that."

"And?"

"Well... There are feeding instructions. And emergency protocols. What to do in the event of a fire, an outbreak of disease, that sort of thing."

"Anything we need to know?"

"*Hmm?* Not really, no. But… But there was, err… There was one thing…"

"Yes?"

"At the back of the book…"

"*Yes?*"

"Ah, yes…. Well… Protocol 34, you see? Very interesting."

"Come on, Artemas, spit it out." Sir Claude's voice hovered over the room, like an owl that's heard a rustle in the undergrowth.

"Well, it's a protocol for evacuating the zoo – all the inmates. Very interesting."

"You mean all at once?"

"Yes, it seems so."

"But whyever would they need to do that? Surely they'd only ever need to evacuate a part of the zoo. If there was a fire or some such?"

"That's the interesting thing. The manual doesn't say why. It just says *how*. Do you see?"

"Alright. And?"

"Well…" Dr James started. "The airlocks will all be opened – simultaneously across all seven parks… And the humans will make their way into the tunnels, where they will be directed to a single rendez-vous point, *hmm?* Underground. Somewhere beyond the Japanese Park."

"But *how?* How could they persuade all the inmates to pass through doorways that have been strictly forbidden to them?" Sir Claude asked. "Makes no sense."

"Hmm, yes, yes – no sense at all. But that's the clever bit," Dr James replied. "The voice of god, you see? Their gods will instruct them – over some kind of speaker system I imagine."

"Like we heard in Medieval Park? At the amphitheatre?"

"Yes, I imagine so."

*

Quiet descended on the folly, as the pair lapsed back into their own thoughts.

But *quiet,* as Elizabeth's father often used to say during long spells in the hide, was rarely the lack of noise. Quiet was the sounds you don't normally hear.

And as she listened now, she heard a single bird sing outside – igniting the night air with a shrill innocence, like the light of a child's sparkler. A nightingale. They had brought *nightingales* to the park. This one was perhaps twenty yards away.

And then the wolf howled again. Plaintive and foreboding.

Elizabeth's attention retreated quickly back inside the folly. She thought again about the calm, still presence next to her under the blanket. Dr James. She became aware of his every breath, his every micro-movement. As his chest rose and fell, she felt the blanket give a barely perceptible tug on her own chest.

A few moments later, he removed his hands from behind his head and laid them by his side. As he did so, his right hand brushed Elizabeth's left.

Her hand thrilled to the touch.

Before she knew what she had done, she had reached out under the blanket and taken hold of his hand in her own.

She was acting on impulse again.

She lay back, her eyes fixed on the ceiling, scarcely daring to breath. It was an innocent gesture, she told herself. Just one human wanting the reassurance of another.

She expected him to pull his hand away at any moment.

But he didn't.

She felt his skin beneath her own. Smooth as a young girl's – and cold. She could only imagine how warm hers must feel. She felt like her heart was in her wrist.

On an impulse – *another one* – she tilted her head fractionally to her left to look at him.

He was already looking at her, sideways.

Somehow, she met his gaze, there in the three-quarter darkness of the folly. Firelight flickered on his face. Her eyes were wide, anxious, uncertain. His calm, steady, elusive.

And then – just for a moment or two – she felt his fingers squeeze against her hand. And the faintest hint of a smile on his face.

Elizabeth turned her gaze back upwards, towards the domed roof above them. She didn't know what to think. She felt alarmed, excited, soothed. She was holding his hand. Such a small gesture, freighted with so much meaning.

Deep down inside – somewhere too deep for words to reach, nor thought nor even emotion – Elizabeth knew that everything had just changed. She knew that her life – whatever was left of it – was pivoting.

Her conscious mind was starting to drift down towards this truth, when the thought of her husband entered her head, like a door being blown open in a gale. She rushed to shut it again. She wasn't ready to think about change, to confront the gale.

Instead, just for these few moments, she squeezed

her mind into the narrow, liberating confines of the present. She existed purely in physical space. She was just one human in danger, she told herself again, reaching out for the reassurance of another. She drank in the comfort of being connected to another person – of two hands warmly entwined – their union the still centre of a universe in motion.

A short while later, Dr James fell into a quiet, quiet sleep. She could tell from his touch and the lightest change in his breathing.

A few short minutes after that – far fewer than she was expecting – she followed him there.

45

The passing hours had already carried Lady Danziger deep into the calm of the Zailan night. The nightscape before her was a brighter one than on Earth. There were four moons, that she had been tracking as they shifted by imperceptible degrees across the night sky. They cast a radiant, silver light over the zoo. The deserts and forests and grass plains of the different parks – existing as they did in a world before electricity – looked serene beneath it. Bewitching.

She rested her eye from the telescope. If she was going to see any signal – a flashlight or a fire – she was as likely to see it with the naked eye.

In the depths of her fatigue, she clung to her three-step routine, which she rotated through every ten minutes. Try to raise her husband on the radio. *Done.* Nothing to report. Visual scan of the park. *Done.* Nothing to report.

And the new step three. Check the room.

She turned around. She looked first at Nussbaum. His erratic breathing and small involuntary spasms persuaded Lady Danziger he was unconscious. And then Juckes. He was asleep too, his head propped up on his rattan backpack and his arms slung protectively around the fire-axe.

That was another of his talents, Juckes – falling asleep whenever he was given the chance. And waking up just as quickly when needed. He deserved the rest. A couple of hours earlier, he'd completed his own four-hour shift.

And so Lady Danziger turned back around, glanced at the loaded revolver for the umpteenth time, and ran back through her routine.

Radio check. *Nothing.*

Visual scan of the parks. *Nothing.*

*

About three miles away – in the folly – Elizabeth was also checking her revolver for the umpteenth time and also staring into the Zailan night.

Her turn on watch.

Her mind kept rotating around the question: could they do anything for the other humans incarcerated here? Even if only the hundred or so academics? Objectively, she knew they'd be lucky to escape with their own lives. And to rescue Dr Setiawan as well would be an honourable outcome.

But still…

She had felt groggy when Sir Claude first roused her. But – after a few minutes sitting on the three-legged stool and staring into the cool blue of the Zailan night – the grogginess subsided and a calm clarity replaced it.

The doors of her mind stood open. Surely there must be something they could do for the other humans?

But what?

She felt alert, her senses sharpened. She attributed it to the quietness of the folly, to the pressure of survival

297

in a hostile environment. She didn't want to connect it to Dr James. The feeling that life now seemed larger and freedom more important.

She turned back to the ventilation slit in the curved stone wall. Through her narrow field of view, Elizabeth looked out into the nightscape. Zil's moons illuminated the park with a beguiling softness. She could see an open, grassy hillside and something like a corral perched on it. The gate was open and the corral empty. Elizabeth imagined the shepherds used it from time to time. As protection from the wolves. Somewhere to pen their flock at night, while they slept in the folly. The corral was maybe fifteen yards by fifteen yards in size, with a high, sturdy fence and only narrow gaps between the planks. They glinted silver against the dark blue of the night.

Beyond the hillside her view V'ed outwards to take in woodland on a more distant hillside and the faint outline of the classical temple they had spotted the evening before. Beyond that the view faded into the night.

She turned to look at the sleeping figure of Dr James. Such stillness. He had barely moved the whole night. She could just discern the outline of his slim body beneath the heavy blanket.

She turned her eyes back to the park outside. Her gaze lingered again on the corral.

The corral…

Of course.

The corral!

It was so obvious.

Elizabeth was jerked out of her reverie. *The corral.* That's how they could do it. A plan started to form in her mind, take shape. It started to grow – she probed it from different angles. Tested it.

This was a way to rescue…

This was a way to rescue *everyone*. Themselves, the academics in the high-value suite, the slaves and supervisors, the Romans here in the Classical Park – *all* the humans in *all* the parks. *Everyone.*

She checked Sir Claude's watch. She was due to wake them in fifteen minutes to light the fire.

She wanted to jump up and wake them now— But restrained herself.

She went back over the plan in her mind – testing it – not believing it – testing it again – and then believing it again.

46

Lady Danziger had allowed her attention to wander.

Her gaze was resting on the bulk carrier. Over beyond the Japanese Park. Security floodlighting made it stand out larger than ever in the nightscape. She thought with dismay about the mission it was about to undertake. The plan she'd agreed with her husband had been to come here, rescue Setiawan and as many of the missing academics as possible – and get back out. Now her husband and nephew were missing, Setiawan was probably dead, and there was every likelihood the Zailans were about to end up with more abductees, not less. *A lot more.*

Lady Danziger turned back to the telescope, trying to interrupt her spiralling thoughts.

She trained it on the Classical Park. In the depths of her fatigue, her methodical approach was starting to break down. Her mind was rotating back to the four figures she'd seen on the hillside. They'd been her best lead and she was ready to clutch at straws. So that's where she rotated the telescope to.

And then...

Something.

She wondered if she had imagined it?

She was close to the hallucination stage of

exhaustion and she knew it.

But no.

There it was.

A sign. A flicker – literally, a flicker.

Her exhausted adrenal glands squeezed one more pulse into her body. She refocussed her eyes.

She could see smoke.

And fire.

And where there's fire, there's usually my husband.

She put the control pad in her pocket, picked up the Webley – and slipped across the storeroom to wake Juckes.

*

The Zoo Controller woke with a start.

He looked at his alarm clock. Still another half hour to go.

Why have I woken? He looked around. His apartment was noiseless. The floor-to-ceiling window, which he always left uncovered, was still a large, not-quite-black rectangle, framing the stars and the moons.

And yet he felt wide awake.

Strange.

He stretched, stood up, and slipped on a pair of padded slippers and a towelling robe. He stepped a couple of yards towards the window and stared out through it.

He was on the 144th floor. The control tower was at its narrowest at this height and the apartment occupied the entire floor. The full-length window described a gentle arc as it curved around the large expanse of the Zoo Controller's bedroom.

His juniors, whom he had never invited in, imagined

the apartment to be a place of unimaginable luxury. *Fine.* Let them think that. Something to inspire their jealousy. Something to inspire their *ambition.*

The truth, however, was very different.

This was an apartment without ornamentation. The walls were blank, the fittings were simple. The sitting room was furnished with a single reclining couch and a single cinema screen, tuned always to one of the zoo's network channels. His study contained more screens and consoles and comms equipment – but none of it was personal.

The apartment manifested nothing of the Zoo Controller because, as far as he was concerned, *the whole zoo* was a manifestation of him. Of him, his career, his *ambition.* Living space was just a distraction. He wondered at colleagues, who spent so much of their energy adorning something so inconsequential.

In the entire apartment, there were only two personal touches. There was his copy of *The Little Black Book*, which he kept always at his bedside, next to a glass of water. This contained the thoughts of the First Governor, the founder of the Caucus. This book was the Zoo Controller's creed and his religion. He knew every word *by heart.* Here was the philosophy that guided him in all things. Here were the words that had taught him the proper relations between *Power* and *Money* in the well-balanced state. Here was the wisdom that explained the one true force in the universe: the mind of the Caucus Zailan. *His imagination.*

The other personal detail was the curved, floor-to-ceiling window in his bedroom, the installation of which he had supervised himself. He stood before it now, framed by it. Here he could see his zoo at any time of the day or night. Not via the dry reports that he would read before sleeping; not relayed through a video feed or some other medium – but actually *see* it. In the entire facility, this window had the only view of the entire facility.

In short, this wasn't somewhere the Zoo Controller came to revel in wealth. This was somewhere he came to focus on *his career.*

He padded through to the kitchen to fix himself a glass of water. He liked to sip warm water, always heated to between 60 and 65 degrees.

He owned 21% of the common stock. Through an arrangement with the other stockholders, he exchanged his extravagant remuneration package each year for more shares. Every year, his ownership increased by one to two percentage points. A trivial change, year on year. But a massive one, decade on decade.

The day would soon dawn when he would be the majority stockholder in the most profitable entertainment facility in the entire galaxy. That was a day he longed for, one he could *see* right before him.

How things would change on that day.

He would own the zoo and all its inmates; he would own the other investors; he would teach the Regional Governor how *Power* should talk to *Money.* He was going to be the richest, most successful Zailan on the planet and he wasn't going to let any frippery or extravagance distract him.

Glass in hand, he returned again to his window.

His thoughts drifted back to his earliest days in the zoo. The Controller had worked here since he was a teenager, shovelling dung in the wild animal enclosure. After a violent, delinquent childhood, he had been sent to work in that enclosure on a court order. *Shovelling shit*. Even the slaves weren't forced to do that – a Zailan couldn't sink any lower. It was the moment of total failure.

It was also the moment he decided to make something of himself.

His rise had been slow at the start. Long hours devoted to educating himself, observing the ways and manners of the rich and successful. Then, bit by bit, he had gathered momentum – until, like a meteor, he had reached the top and was pulling the whole zoo forward in the wake of his ambition. He had transformed this facility more than any other controller in its history. He had introduced cybernetics and the avatar program; he had built the VIP suites, being the first to see the potential for after-hours entertainment for the high-rolling elite. He had re-branded all of the parks, building new rides and jazzing up the dowdy old ones. The Forest Park had become 'Headhunters of the Forest', the Classical Park 'The Revenge of the Gods'. And now 'Zootropolis' was about to be added to his list of achievements. During his time in charge, visitor numbers had doubled, revenues had quadrupled, and profits had increased tenfold.

More than anyone else, this was *his* zoo.

And more than anywhere else, the Zoo Controller could stand at this window and feel at one with his creation.

Dawn was starting to break. He could already see a few figures moving back and forth across the main plaza below. Human slaves performing the early morning chores. He loved to stand here and watch the life of the zoo play out beneath him, the antlike creatures moving around parks he had designed for them, following journeys he had ordained, enjoying pleasures he had invented – witnessing punishments he had commanded.

His eye took in the bulk carrier on the horizon. It wandered from there to the Classical Park.

The park where the fugitives were spending the night.

The Revenge of the Gods.

His mind crunched on a small sand-grit of irritation. He remembered learning the previous evening that the first floor of the folly was the one area where they had no cameras or microphones. *How could Parks have been so stupid? How could they not install surveillance tech in what was just about the most obvious hiding place in the entire park?* They'd asked if they should send the drones inside the folly? But he forbade it. He didn't want to risk the humiliation of the fugitives catching one during the night.

Still, no harm done.

The fugitives were cornered. They wouldn't be moving from there this night, not if they wanted to avoid the four different wolf packs he had prowling round a one-kilometre radius. Them and the numerous other control measures.

The Zoo Controller took a meditative sip of water, as he tried to pick out their night shelter in the darkness.

And then he saw it.

The folly.

And he saw it because it was illuminated by…

Fire.

On the crest of the hill, just next to the folly.

Why would the humans light a fire outside?

And then the Zoo Controller struck his own

forehead with rage and panic.

*

Down in the control room on the 22nd floor, the Night Manager was sitting in the central planning area, his feet up on a neighbouring chair, while he snacked on a porcubus burger and soda drink. His glazed eyes drifted lazily across the planning screen, where a dozen video feeds were displaying in three tidy rows of four.

The night shift was drawing to a close.

He and his team would soon be relieved and – frankly – not a moment too soon. The massive flow of stress hormones at the start of the shift had left them all feeling leaden by the end.

He knew the next night shift was likely to be explosive. He wanted his crew out of here as soon as possible to rest up through the day.

The intercom on the table started buzzing. *Probably one of the submissives in Parks wanting permission to wipe their arse,* the Night Manager thought. *Idiots.* He took another bite of his burger as he leaned across the table and pressed down on the green button.

"Yep – 'sup?" he asked, mouth full of food, and released the button.

The intercom exploded at him.

Exploded.

The Night Manager bounced out of his chair like a toy on a spring. His burger flew across the planning area and impaled itself on the cactus spike of a nearby plant. His soda went spewing across the table, small bubbles skittling over the expensively polished surface.

The voice belonged to the boss – and right now it could be heard across the entire control room. The

Duty Manager yanked a headset around his ears and slammed the headphones button.

At least he was the only one being shouted at now.

"Video feed from the folly roof? On it now, boss."

Shit – how had he not got that video feed on his planning screen? He gestured frantically with his hands and brought up the folly's roof camera.

Nothing.

Just blackness.

He made a couple more gestures and switched to night vision.

Still nothing.

"Can't see anything, bo— Right, *the other direction*. On it now."

He made some more gestures and the camera view started rotating through 180 degrees.

And then he saw it.

Fire.

Someone had lit a fire. No, not a fire – a whole damn *bonfire*. About fifteen yards beyond the folly.

"I can see it now, boss. Maybe they were feeling cold, maybe they—"

The second explosion in his ear made the first one sound like a gentle throat-clearing.

But it wasn't the way his boss was talking that terrified the Night Manager. It was *what* he was saying.

Seconds later the Night Manager was on his feet, running through the main control room, shouting – *screaming* – at his team. He wasn't just in fear of his career, he was in fear *of his life*. And he was making damn sure they were too.

They had seconds, minutes at most, to save the situation.

47

Elizabeth picked up a small, dry cypress branch and threw it over the fire. As it landed it sent a cheerful cloud of bright orange sparks swirling up into the still-dark Zailan-Tuscan sky.

She turned to smile at Dr James.

She couldn't help herself. Wherever she stood, she was conscious of where he was standing. Whenever she looked round, she looked for his face. Whatever she thought about, she wondered if he was thinking it too.

Dr James was carrying a couple of old planks for the fire. He'd picked them off the ground where they'd fallen from the corral. He smiled back at her.

And so here they were, building a fire together again. Just like on Ormilu. Same principles but bigger stakes – *higher* stakes.

The idea was to spend as little time as possible outside the folly. While Dr Setiawan had stayed inside next to the beacon, the other three were building the fire. Elizabeth's role was to light and establish it, while watching out for danger. She had been given the revolver and their small supply of spare ammunition. Dr James was searching for dry branches and loose timber on the ground outside; Sir Claude was ferrying armfuls of hay down from the store in the folly. Anything that could produce an intense blaze quickly. They needed to get the fire roaring within a couple of minutes – get straight back into the folly – and wait for Lady Danziger to spot it. *Pray* for Lady Danziger to spot it.

But like every plan it had one unavoidable flaw: it was just a plan.

Elizabeth looked over Dr James' shoulder and saw—

"*Wolves...*" she said unbelievingly.

"*Hmm?* Oh yes, they've been howling all through the ni—"

"No. Wolves – here – *now.*"

A wolf was flying through the air towards them, leaping out of the darkness towards the light.

Elizabeth reacted on instinct. She didn't even know what she was doing until she'd—

C R A C K

In a single fluid movement, she'd raised the revolver, aimed just above Dr James' shoulder, and fired into the animal's chest. It collapsed in mid-air, the momentum sending its stricken body in cartwheels towards them. It came to a halt inches from their feet. Elizabeth saw blood pulse from its chest three – four – times. And then the animal was inert, the rich dark pool ebbing into the Zailan soil.

"Dr James – please get behind me!" she cried, putting her left arm out protectively even as her right was extended outwards, gun in hand.

Elizabeth squinted towards the folly, trying to understand what was happening. She could see a whole pack of wolves had materialised out of the darkness. They started howling with rage. Their alpha had just been killed.

Worse, they were positioned between Elizabeth and the folly. There were about a dozen of them, pacing an imaginary line that exactly bisected the path back to safety. Silver grey shadows passing back and forth across each other. They were snarling. Illuminated by the infernal, dancing light of the bonfire, Elizabeth could see white teeth revealed by raised, flickering lips. They weren't attacking and they weren't retreating either.

A moment later, Sir Claude emerged through the trapdoor and onto the ladder. Elizabeth could see his silhouette through the ring of pillars that supported the folly. Immediately, three or four of the wolves broke from the pack and ran onto the ground floor of the folly. They started launching themselves at the ladder. She heard their feet scuffle against the wooden steps; their jaws snap as they lunged at Sir Claude's legs. But Sir Claude was just out of their reach – *thank God* – and the steps were too narrow. The wolves couldn't get any purchase on them.

Meanwhile, Sir Claude – unarmed – was staying on the ladder, kicking ineffectually. Every kick gave them an opportunity to grab his leg. *What's he trying to do?*

"*Dammit, Sir Claude, get back inside…*" Elizabeth muttered under her breath. "*Get inside and close the trapdoor…*"

Elizabeth raised her revolver to shoot. Her brain was racing. She had enough ammunition to kill these wolves, *just*. But only if she hit each one first time. And the wolves near Sir Claude… *How?* Her mind went back to the training on Ormilu. *What did Sir*

Claude say? Something about stilling her mind, about believing the bullet and the target are already connected... *Hopeless.* Her mind was close to panic as she looked through fifteen yards of darkness at moving, leaping targets. *Dammit, Sir Claude, close the trapdoor—*

Elizabeth felt a small tap on her shoulder. She started. It was Dr James – his arm was raised towards the fire. Or maybe to something beyond? Elizabeth tried to look in the direction he was pointing. Her eyes watered; their fire-laying had been only too successful. The tinder-dry hay was flaring – blazing stalks were rising in the updraught and drifting towards her on the wind. She squinted, narrowing her eyes against the heat. To begin with all she noticed was that the first grey light of dawn had started to spread over the horizon like a bruise.

And then she saw it.

More wolves.

Another pack was approaching in single file up the slope. They were running in that lolloping wolf gait that can eat large distances fast and short distances like this even faster. They couldn't be more than thirty seconds from reaching the folly and the fire.

The situation looked hopeless.

She turned back around. Sir Claude at least had retreated back inside the folly. He'd left the ladder out – presumably so she and Dr James could fight their way back up it. *But how are we going to do that?* Four wolves remained at the base, prowling around the ladder, leaping at it. One even managed to clatter up three of the steps – before slipping and falling.

Elizabeth looked up at the narrow ventilation slit above them. She was willing Sir Claude to appear.

Praying he'd appear, tell them what to do.

And then something strange happened.

The two wolf packs started to *cooperate.* Leaving their previous patrol route, the first pack merged with the second and suddenly 25 or 30 wolves were circling the fire, closing off any escape route for Elizabeth and Dr James, either to the folly or to anywhere else. The pair inched backwards, closer to the flames behind them.

And then something even stranger happened.

A face appeared at last at the slit. But it wasn't Sir Claude.

Elizabeth felt her heart leap.

It was Juckes.

*

As soon as he'd seen the fire from his bedroom window, the Zoo Controller had guessed what was happening.

There must be an accomplice out there, elsewhere in the zoo, and they were signalling to him. Or her.

After screaming instructions at his Night Manager over the intercom, the Zoo Controller had flown out of his apartment and into the elevator. He didn't even stop to change.

If some kind of craft or spaceship materialised in or near the folly, they had to stop those fugitives getting on it.

Fool, he upbraided himself as he thumped his hand against '22' on the lift panel. He had been complacent. As the elevator started to hurtle downwards from the 144th floor, his mind went back to the slave he had seen the previous morning – the insolent one – the one who *hadn't* shown up in the footage in the service tunnels. He had been so wanting to believe there wasn't a conspiracy, that there weren't any more saboteurs, that he had blinded himself to the possibility that actually *there were.*

That was stupid assumption number one.

Stupid assumption number two was that the humans had reached Zil via a first- or second-generation teleportation device. In other words, that they had arrived via one of Zil's hyperspaceports and would have to leave via one too. It hadn't occurred to him that a civilisation that primitive somehow had access to *third*-generation technology. That they might have their own teleportation device. *Fool again.*

Well, he wouldn't be making any more assumptions.

He looked at the panel: 57th floor – 56th – 55th…

He drummed his fingers impatiently on the handrail.

So if the fire is a signal to an accomplice, his thoughts raced along a steep, downward-descending track, *where might that accomplice be? Where else in the zoo has a line of sight to the fire?*

The lift juddered to a halt at the 22nd floor.

The abrupt deceleration of the lift – and the realisation that had just dawned on him – left the Zoo Controller's stomach several floors above his body.

Their accomplice is right here – in the Obelisk. In my own control tower.

Or perhaps worse: *was* right here.

The Zoo Controller swept out of the lift and strode across the control room, his towelling robe billowing around his legs.

*

Elizabeth could see Juckes' face through the ventilation slit, darting back and forth. He was trying to figure out the best way to shout through it.

In the event, he pressed his cheeks into the cleft in the stone, pushing his lips as far forward as possible.

"DOO.. 'RRY. COMIIING... YOU."

Juckes and Sir Claude were planning to bust out of the folly. She knew Juckes and Lady Danziger must have brought the second revolver with him. Two revolvers, two wolf packs. It was just about plausible except... A *third* wolf pack had now arrived. A few seconds earlier. Another dozen or more wolves had poured up the slope and immediately merged with the others. They had no chance. Not with two guns – not even if they had three or four.

The heat was now singeing the clothes against Elizabeth's back. There were forty-odd wolves, snarling and howling and circling the fire. Juckes was shouting something again from the folly, but she couldn't hear what. It didn't matter. It was all over, it had to be. She turned to look at Dr James. Her eyes spoke desperation – an apology even – there was nothing she could do to save them now.

Dr James looked back at her. His face at that moment – which she would remember for the rest of her life – was calm. Here amidst the panic and the noise and the chaos. The smile had gone, but it hadn't been replaced by fear. Just by a calm confidence. She felt him take hold of her left hand with his right. And then he did smile at her – his calm, elusive smile – and in that moment she seemed to lift out of her own body. She detached from the chaos. She was looking down on them. Their two hands entwined at the centre of the maelstrom.

And suddenly it all made sense.

Why they hadn't been killed already.

She released her hand from his and passed her revolver to him. Of course the wolves weren't going to attack them. Not her and Dr James. She cupped both hands to her mouth and yelled towards the ventilation slit.

"*JUCKES,*" she yelled, "*YOU MUST LEAVE NOW WITH THE OTHERS. SIR CLAUDE WILL TELL YOU THE PLAN.*" She waited for a moment for a reaction, but nothing came. She resumed. "*THEY'RE NOT GOING TO KILL US. WE WILL BE ALRIGHT.*"

She watched as Juckes alternated between pressing his ear to the ventilation slit and looking at her in disbelief.

"*REPEAT: WE WILL BE ALRIGHT BUT YOU… YOU MUST LEAVE NOW!*"

A fourth wolf pack had arrived. The snarling and baying and howling had reached a crescendo. But Elizabeth wasn't afraid anymore. It was so obvious. They – the zoo psychopaths – were controlling those wolves in some way. And they – the psychopaths – wanted her and Dr James alive. For entertainment later. *To save face.* Elizabeth wasn't afraid for herself anymore.

But for everyone in the folly, she was terrified.

"*GIVE ME A THUMBS-UP IF YOU'VE HEARD?*"

Juckes' face disappeared for a moment and then his fist thrust through the gap. His thumb was pointing resolutely down.

"Can't he hear?" Dr James asked.

"Oh, he can hear me alright," Elizabeth replied over her shoulder. "He just doesn't want to."

315

Juckes disappeared from the window. Elizabeth dreaded seeing Sir Claude's face in his place. She knew he'd tell her they could still rescue the situation. Try to persuade her they could still link up.

But she was wrong. It wasn't Sir Claude who appeared next. It was his wife. Elizabeth could only see half of Lady Danziger's face through the narrow gap – an elegant nose, a hint of mouth, first one eye, then the other, dark and pleading. Every half-glimpsed line on that face was imploring her to come up with some other plan.

And Elizabeth might have cracked.

But a new factor came into the equation. She spotted something else approaching up the hill, from a different angle. Beyond the folly, slightly to the right of it, she could see some kind of vehicle. It was wide and dark and squat and looked very like the ones she had seen yesterday in the Arabian Park, through the telescope.

This was exactly what Elizabeth had feared.

"*YOU MUST LEAVE NOW!*" Her shouting was approaching a cry, a scream. "*PLEASE TRUST ME. WE WILL BE ALRIGHT.*"

Lady Danziger remained at the window for one more heartbreaking second and then disappeared.

A few seconds later Sir Claude appeared at last. But he hadn't come to argue. Elizabeth saw him stretch his arm through the narrow gap. She squinted. His hand was holding something small and round and metallic, but she couldn't tell what. Constrained by the narrow gap, she saw Sir Claude lever his wrist back and forth to build momentum before releasing the object into the air.

It was the beacon.

The one she had saved from the SWAT team.

She watched it fly towards her like a frisbee, round – spinning – aerodynamic.

And she was still watching it as an intense beam of light sliced across the grey light of early dawn. It reached from the armoured vehicle to the beacon in mid-air, connecting them as if their destinies had always been entangled. A perfect shot. *Bam.* The beacon's flight dissolved into a small cloud of ashes, that blew a yard or two forwards with the momentum before sprinkling harmlessly down over the wolves beneath.

Elizabeth didn't have time to mourn its destruction. *What if the Zailans turn that firepower on the folly?* Elizabeth stared at the building, speechless with anxiety. *Surely Sir Claude saw that? Surely they realise they have to leave. Surely – surely – surely—*

And then it happened, three, four seconds later. Exactly what Elizabeth most feared. A second beam of light, more intense than the first, passed from the vehicle directly into the side of the folly. The building – the *whole* building – started to glow. And then, after a couple more seconds, it crumbled. Just like that. Not into broken stones, not even rubble, just... *powder.* The building slumped to the ground and Elizabeth saw a huge dust cloud billowing up from the base of where it had been in a great expanding circle. A couple of seconds later, the doughnut cloud had enveloped the wolves. And a second after that, her and Dr James too.

Elizabeth and Dr James dropped to their knees, coughing, spluttering, holding each other in the dust cloud, that was glowing a demonic red from the fire behind them, and wondering, *did they survive? Did they get out in time?*

Elizabeth kept telling herself that they must have done. Sir Claude saw what happened to the beacon. He had enough time to react – *just*.

But she couldn't know. There was no way of knowing.

She thought about her own situation. And her thoughts spiralled in a different direction. Her stunned mind rotated around three things. Three *absences*. She had *no* beacon – *no* radio – *no* library steps. And yet a fourth: even if her friends were alive, they had no way of helping Elizabeth.

Events had rushed past in a torrent. She couldn't yet see what they all signified. But one simple and quite awesome fact was clear.

She and Dr James were on their own.

48

Are they dead? Or did they get out of the folly in time?
The Zoo Controller watched the dust cloud spread
across his video screen and mulled the probabilities.

And then he considered the issue from another
angle. *Doesn't matter*, he said to himself. *If they're
dead, good. It's what we'll announce anyway. But if
they're alive...* his thinking continued. *If they're alive,
there's no way I'll give them the space to mount a
second rescue attempt.* The Zoo Controller wasn't one
to make the same mistake twice.

The main thing, as far as he was concerned, he still
had two of the fugitives in the Classical Park – the
younger man and the girl. Alive and vulnerable and so
very, very telegenic.

The Zoo Controller slumped back against his chair.

That had been close.

Too close.

Way too close.

He waved off the Night Manager with a dismissive
flick of the wrist. That same manager, instead of
getting the rest that he urgently needed, would now
spend the day contemplating the fragility of his career,
which he had correctly guessed was hanging by a
thread.

In his place, the new Duty Manager arrived – the Zoo Controller's most trusted lieutenant.

The Zoo Controller permitted himself a thin smile of relief. And then issued a stream of instructions in a subdued, almost casual voice that the Duty Manager knew to be anything but casual. *Comply or die* was the motto singed onto the tender minds of the Controller's managerial team. And this Duty Manager was going to make no assumptions and no mistakes.

One. Two packs of wolves were to be left circling the site of the folly until they could get an investigation team in there. He wanted the team to search for any signs of biological life – of *death* – among the vaporised remains of the building.

Two. The other two wolf packs were to trail the remaining fugitives, one pack on their left, one on their right, three to four hundred yards distant.

Three. The armoured personnel carrier was to trail behind at four to five hundred yards. Far enough away to stay out of shot for the network channels, but close enough to stay within eyeshot for the fugitives. The Zoo Controller wanted to make the authorities' presence – *His* presence – felt.

On which point – *Four* – he wanted a minimum of eight surveillance drones forming a box around the pair at all times. Again, it didn't matter if they got so close they could be seen.

Finally – *Five* – just in case – he wanted three hovershoots with combat teams airborne and on permanent standby. They should stay one mile distant, on a thirty-seconds-to-engage basis. Any more rescue attempts would be crushed before they started.

The Zoo Controller had every intention that the fugitives should ultimately escape the Classical Park.

But not until tonight and only in bodybags.

"Anything else, boss?"

"Yes – one thing. Make sure you 'guide' them towards the town. Discreetly of course."

"Towards the town? No problem. On it already. Is that it?"

"Yes, that's it."

The Zoo Controller watched his manager leave.

The two fugitives might think they were making a set of free choices. But it would be pure illusion. By occasionally making their presence known, the wolf packs would 'steer' them wherever the Zoo Controller wanted. And where the Zoo Controller wanted them was in the Classical Park's only town, New Herculaneum. The town was covered, gable to sewer, in fixed camera points. It would provide a stunning backdrop to their final demise tonight.

The Zoo Controller got up to leave. He still needed to shower and dress.

As an afterthought – just before leaving – he made a couple of hand gestures at the large planning screen. The network numbers dialled up in front of him. And, just as he thought, the morning's drama had proved a hit. A massive hit – possibly the highest weekend breakfast viewing figures Zil had ever seen. And anyone not up early enough to see it live would be watching on catch-up through the day, he was sure of that.

Tension was building nicely. That little scare with the bonfire was turning out to be the perfect curtain-raiser for the day's events.

The Zoo Controller breathed in deeply – and exhaled – calming himself.

The saboteurs, the failed rescue attempt. Every slip-up was turning out to his advantage.

Truly, the gods favoured him.

Tonight, everybody but everybody would be watching. Every submissive on Zil, every Caucus member, the Regional Governor, the Supreme Governor. *Everybody*.

As his underlings watched him stride back across the control room in his slippers and towelling robe, they even heard him whistle a little tune to himself.

49

Lady Danziger, it transpired, was not dead.

Nor were her husband, her butler, and the Drs Nussbaum and Setiawan. Although the latter was giving it his best shot. Just as Elizabeth had predicted, he had developed a fever overnight and his face had taken on a shade somewhere between verdigris and bonfire ash. But nonetheless Setiawan was still alive, same as the others, and gamely pretending he was fine. The group had managed to teleport out of the folly even as its walls started to glow a hellish red from what they correctly assumed was a laser blast.

Lady Danziger's mind moved from the hellish red to the dingy room she was now in. Unending grey. She looked around with dismay. There were a half-dozen grubby strip lights on the ceiling; a couple of them weren't working and a third was blinking annoyingly. There were odd boxes and crates lying around, as well as a surprisingly large number of hospital gurneys, which made no sense at all. To look at the place, she could be in some kind of backroom at a British Rail station in London.

But she wasn't. She was at the hyperspaceport on Za-Nak.

Another planet, another storeroom.

This was the room to which Za-Farka, her husband's contact on Za-Nak, had hurriedly taken them about ten minutes earlier. Za-Farka was now sitting in front of them and looking stressed. She was stressed about this unscheduled visit to her workplace, which ran every risk of blowing her cover. She was stressed about Dr Setiawan who, if he died, really would land her in trouble. And most of all, she was stressed about the plan that Sir Claude had just described to her.

Za-Farka thought the plan was mad and had no chance of working and Lady Danziger was, privately, inclined to agree. Za-Farka had suggested she escort the group somewhere more comfortable – somewhere *outside* the hyperspaceport – where they could have a rest and take some time to think things through. Then they could all get together again for a nice chat – *tomorrow, say* – when things would doubtless seem clearer. Sir Claude had replied, very politely, that things were already perfectly clear, that *now* was always the best time, and that he was sure the plan could work. It had sounded like bluffing to Lady Danziger, and pretty feeble bluffing too.

Za-Farka turned directly to Juckes. "You've always been the sensible one. Are you going along with this?"

"Of course," he replied.

More bluffing.

Because the plan – *Elizabeth's* plan – was, frankly, madness. Brilliant – but mad.

"Alright, let's get this straight," Za-Farka continued. "So you've discovered the facility is a zoo, a *human* zoo. I'm prepared to believe that bit at least. Knowing the Zailans, it makes sense. But what evidence have you got? If you want to persuade the Za-Nakarians… You've got to believe me, they're *lazy*. They're going to need not just evidence, but evidence they can't ignore. Let's think. If it's a zoo, there should be brochures – leaflets and fliers. Did you manage to collect any?"

"No," Sir Claude replied.

"Alright then. Do you have any documentation – zoo records, that kind of thing?"

"No."

"Any video footage?"

"No."

"Photographs?"

"No."

"Of course we don't." Lady Danziger dived in with a confidence she didn't feel. "Photographs can be faked. We've got better than that."

Even more bluffing – it must be catching.

"What then?"

"Eye-witness testimony."

"Pah!" Za-Farka's legendary politeness failed her.

"Technology can fake anything. Photographs, video, anything," Lady Danziger replied with a hint of ice. She and her husband exchanged a quick glance. "It's eye-witness testimony that counts most in the courts of the IGC. You know that." She turned sideways to Dr Setiawan. "And right here we have a man who was abducted by the Zailans, stripped naked – *tortured* – and nearly executed. Show her, Agustus."

"Hmm? Excuse me?"

"Your shirt. Show her."

"Oh right. Yes. My shirt." Dr Setiawan was too feverish to resist. As he unbuttoned his shirt, his confused mind reflected – accurately, as it happened – that he probably hadn't exposed his body so much in a single day since his 0th Birthday. He reached the last button and started to pull the shirt away. His blood had glued the field dressing to the fabric, and as he pulled the shirt, the dressing came away too. He winced with pain, turning his bare back towards his hostess.

Za-Farka placed a hand to her mouth, nearly retching from the sight of the open wound. It turned out that ruined flesh was recognisable anywhere in the Universe.

"Alright, alright. Enough already. You have a wound. That's something, I grant you." Za-Farka gestured at Setiawan to put his shirt back on. "But that's all you've got. It could have happened anywhere."

The group stared back at her. Lady Danziger, Sir Claude, Juckes, Dr Setiawan. They felt like they had played their ace – and were being told it was a jack.

The situation was desperate.

'The plan' – *Elizabeth's* plan – involved several extravagant leaps of faith, but before they could even get to those, they needed to persuade their own contact to go along with it. This was first base and it looked like they couldn't even get past it.

And then the one person who'd said nothing spoke.

Herr Doktor Yuval Nussbaum.

Someone whose presence had become so self-effacing, so inconspicuous, they'd almost forgotten they'd brought him.

"I was abducted by the Zailans four Earth years ago," he started, his voice flat and emotionless and uninterruptable. "I was brainwashed and held in bonded slavery for all of that time. I was made to undertake menial tasks unpaid. During this period, I would electrocute, torture, and coerce my fellow human beings – while also being tortured and electrocuted myself…"

Professor Nussbaum carried on talking, listing the salient details of his abduction and enslavement with a chilling calm. *Forensic.* His words flowed fluently and rang true. He was eyewitness *gold.*

Za-Farka was speechless.

They all were.

"…and in case you are still doubting out story, here is further proof." Professor Nussbaum extended his right leg outwards to reveal the ankle tag and rings of burn marks above and below it. "An examination will reveal this ankle tag to be an instrument of torture."

Za-Farka stared at his leg with a transformed expression.

Automatically, Sir Claude, Setiawan, and Juckes extended their legs outward too. Za-Farka's eye moved from one to the other, taking in the fresh burn marks on all three.

And then Nussbaum delivered his *coup de grâce.*

He pulled back his sleeve and revealed a number tattooed on his forearm. "They brand each slave," he said, concluding his speech with the minimum of words and the maximum of impact.

"That brand is in human script. *Arabic* numerals. Not Zailan?" Za-Farka asked, pointing at a tattoo. But her voice was no longer hostile – it was the voice of someone *wanting* to be convinced.

"Not that one," Nussbaum replied. Lady Danziger exchanged another glance with her husband. They both recognised the style and composition of the mark. 'A-75025'. Nussbaum had received that tattoo from abductors right enough, but not on Zil.

"*This* one," Nussbaum said, pointing at a second tattoo further up his forearm.

This one *was* in the Zailan script.

"Alright… Alright…" Za-Farka threw her hands up in surrender. "Maybe we can do this… Maybe we've got enough to take this to the Za-Nakarians."

"Good," Lady Danziger replied. "What's next?"

50

The Duty Manager was studying the progress of the three fugitives across the Classical Park. Sitting here in the control room, he had a dozen angles to choose from. Eight drone-mounted lenses, one zoom on the armoured personnel carrier behind, and three fixed cameras on the town wall that they were currently approaching.

These humans couldn't so much as scratch their backsides without the Duty Manager seeing it first.

With a few tweaks from the wolf pack – the odd snarl, the occasional flash of fangs – he had shepherded them nicely towards the gates of New Herculaneum.

The next few minutes would need some careful finesse.

Some *artistry*.

He knew exactly what the main challenge would be. Two innocents approaching a fortified Roman wall in barbarian clothing – dirty, wretched, covered in dust. It was obvious. They looked like a gift from the gods. *What else were the Roman soldiers supposed to think?* He pulled on a headset and clicked a switch on one of the earpieces.

"Ops Team Delta – are we live and connected?"

Check buzzed through his headset six times. They

came from control-room staff, positioned at different stations around the perimeter of the room. He had picked the best.

"Alright – the operation is now *Go*. Intervention systems are live. Please stand ready." The Duty Manager's voice droned with the calm authority of an airline pilot, operating in an environment where any number of things could go wrong, but rarely did. He watched the pair of fugitives on his screen as they approached the imposing gates of the town and stopped. The male – the one they called 'Dr James' – took two steps closer to the gates. "The subjects have stopped in front of D-Gate-3 and... *we have contact.*"

The Duty Manager watched as one of the two Roman soldiers standing duty on the ramparts hailed the fugitives. Even now, he could see the soldier was starting to laugh.

But he couldn't hear it.

"*Ears* – talk to us – what's happened to the audio?"

"On it, sir. The gate mic is offline. Am switching to one of the drones."

The male fugitive had started speaking. The Duty Manager could hear it, which was an improvement. But it was muffled – and was coming through in Latin. "Amplify the signal," he ordered. "Clean out the static – switch on live translation."

"On it, sir."

The soldiers on the gate were laughing again.

"Well, sunshine" – it was the second soldier speaking now – "you can tell that little story to the Prefect... *From the town dungeon!*"

Yep, the Duty Manager thought to himself, *right on cue.* It had been obvious the Romans would want to enslave these two. *Fair enough* – the zookeepers had been supplying the Romans for years with excess population from the other parks. They got a full memory-wipe, a short journey through the tunnels, a shove through the airlock – and from there to enslavement.

Except these two needed to be kept out of the dungeons. That wasn't at all what the boss had in mind.

"We might need some firepower here. *Weps* – I want you to bring the APC online. Primary armament. Train it on that soldier's shield. The one on the left."

"Right away, sir."

Back in the park, a brass bell was ringing. It was the first soldier, the one on the left – he was giving the bell a vigorous shake in its wooden housing.

"*Open the gates! Open the gates!*" he shouted as the ringing died down. He called down to someone behind the gates. "Two arrivals. Please escort them in. They would like to be taken to Hades' waiting room," he added with a leer. "Oh and watch out for wolves."

The Duty Manager listened and watched.

"*Eyes* – get us a visual behind the gates please."

One of the smaller planning screens, just to the Duty Manager's right, lit up. A moment later, he found himself looking at a small detachment of twelve Roman legionaries, who were forming up behind the gate as it started to inch open.

"Right, Weps, now's your moment. Go easy please. No-one needs to die," the Duty Manager pressed the mic to his lips as he spoke. "But you are hot to fire. Repeat: you are hot to fire."

A moment later a weapon mounted on the armoured personnel carrier fired a one-second laser pulse onto the soldier's shield.

Another second or two passed during which the

large rectangular shield glowed an infernal red – and then promptly vaporised – falling away from the soldier's arm in a cloud of dust.

The soldier on the gate screamed – and looked in horror at his arm – unable to tell whether he was in shock or pain or both. His arm in fact was untouched.

"Good shooting. Now take out the other one too."

Another laser pulse and the second shield was vaporised.

The Duty Manager watched as the two soldiers dropped to their haunches behind the ramparts and started whispering to each other. Their conversation came through the headset as little more than static.

"Come on, team, I want ears on this please…"

In an instant, a drone dropped six feet through the air. The audio feed crackled and then turned clear.

"…*I've seen this happen once before I tell you*," the first soldier was whispering. "*These people – they are protected by the gods…*"

"*But what about those wolf packs?*"

"*The wolves aren't chasing them, idiot. They're guarding them!*"

"*Alright, alright, I believe you,*" the second one replied. "*So what do we do?*"

"*How about we do what they want?*"

"*You mean…?*"

"*Yes, I do.*"

A couple of seconds later, the two soldiers had returned to their feet, hesitantly. "On behalf of the Prefect and people of New Herculaneum," the first soldier started speaking, his voice quavering between formality and fear, "I bid you welcome. Please step through the gates. We shall escort you to the Prefect."

The Duty Manager watched as the male fugitive, Dr

James, turned to his companion. A moment later, both started approaching the gates, which were three feet ajar.

"Alright..." the Duty Manager started speaking. "And three – two – one... They are *through the gates.* Repeat: they are through the gates and on their way to the Prefect. And the gates are closing – closing – *closed.* Alright-y, good work, nicely done." The Duty Manager released a sigh of satisfaction and some celebratory whoops rang back towards him over the intercom. "Right, Cyber, you can stand the wolf packs down," he instructed. "We won't be needing them for a while, let them rest. Weps, you can return the APC to base. Have the ground assault team switched to foot – we're still gonna need them on standby *beneath* the town. Move them to Airlock D-89. The rest of you, take five. Good job, everyone."

He ripped off his headset, and stood up to start clapping, looking around the rest of the control room as he did so. Scattered around the curved edge, the half-dozen members of Ops Team Delta likewise stood up to celebrate. The faint sound of their clapping could be heard for a few seconds tinkling and circling the perimeter.

The Duty Manager felt a hand clasp his shoulder. He looked behind with a start.

It was the Zoo Controller.

"Great operation," he said. "Nicely handled." His hand gave the Duty Manager's shoulder a friendly squeeze, every one of the eight pressure points communicating *promotion.*

"Great job."

And then he disappeared again.

51

It turned out, Lady Danziger reflected ruefully, that when Za-Farka had told them her role on Za-Nak was humble, she hadn't been lying.

She worked as a hostess at the principal hyperspaceport in Za-Nak's capital city. Her job was to greet VIPs and, occasionally, escort them on to their next destination.

The role had its advantages. It put her close to power. She knew all the important political and business types, she picked up snippets of gossip about the workings of the Intergalactic Council, the IGC. But while the role may have provided her with information, it didn't provide her with influence. *None.*

Lady Danziger and the others followed politely as she guided them through the twists and turns and corridors of the hyperspaceport. Her eye took in the Za-Nakarians – the master race, the founders of the IGC, on whom their plan now utterly depended. A semi-aquatic species, the Za-Nakarians were gliding about in purpose-built vehicles that looked a bit like – *well* – large bins on wheels. Or 'aquapods' to use the correct term. They had green skin, smooth like a seal, long necks, and large luminous eyes. The digits on each of their two hands were webbed.

Za-Farka was now on board with the plan that Elizabeth had devised. But the most she could suggest was to submit themselves formally to the immigration department at the hyperspaceport. Apply for political asylum and claim to be escaping from an intelligent zoo on Zil. There was a chance – admittedly only a small one – that it would get red-flagged up through the hierarchy and bypass the usual sclerotic processes.

Zil, after all, was currently applying for membership of the IGC. And Za-Farka happened to know there was, within the circles of power on Za-Nak, a growing faction who were becoming wary of granting this once-given-never-rescinded privilege to the Zailans.

They reached the immigration office.

As Lady Danziger calmly waited in the queue, her rational mind alighted on one other point on their side: Za-Nak ran on Standard Universal Time (SUT), the same as Earth. By contrast, Zil was running at 0.5x SUT – so for every hour that passed on Za-Nak, only half an hour passed on Zil. In simple terms, for every hour she wasted drumming her fingers in the immigration queue at Za-Nak hyperspaceport, only half an hour was passing on Zil. *Small mercies.*

But two times a small number of hours was still a small number of hours. The clock was ticking. The bulk carrier was due to leave Zil at dawn the next day for its journey to Earth.

The timeframe was tight, but at least it was known.

What was completely unknown to Lady Danziger and her husband was how long Artemas and Elizabeth could stay alive, trapped inside the most hostile environment that imagination could create. That imagination *had* created.

52

Elizabeth watched as her Roman host dropped a grape into his mouth.

Is he in on it? she wondered. *Is he in league with the Zailans?*

And then: *did he seriously just drop a grape into his mouth, while reclining on a couch?*

She looked her host up and down. He was the Urban Prefect of the small town they had entered a few hours ago – *New Herculaneum*. Presumably in his mid-forties, he was now getting a little plump, with a touch too much rosiness in the cheek and nose. But, to be fair, he probably passed as quite the athlete a few years ago. And beneath the bonhomie and the excess of grapes and wine and toga – he had a sincere look about him. He didn't *look* like someone who would knowingly host a dinner party for people he was about to slaughter.

It was just a few hours ago that they had been granted entry into the Roman town. Somewhere between Dr James' accented but quite brilliant Latin and an uncanny intervention from the armoured vehicle behind them, a small miracle had unfolded. The gates had opened and soldiers had escorted them to the house of the Prefect – the town mayor in effect. He had accepted their flimsy cover story – that they were two friends, two travellers from the Province of Britannia – with a surprising lack of questions. He was the image of cordial hospitality. They were given separate rooms to rest in and food to eat – *at last*. They were given fresh clothes to wear, while their own clothes were cleaned and pressed. Elizabeth had even been able to wash.

In amongst all the strange and wondrous details she had seen as she passed through a real, living, breathing Roman town, Elizabeth had noticed one strange and less wondrous detail. The town was, in its own discreet way, battle-scarred. Some of the walls were pockmarked, a few houses were burnt out and unrepaired. All of the soldiers she saw looked like they knew how to use the weapons they were carrying.

Why?

Elizabeth hoped she'd get an answer over dinner. And she hoped she wouldn't.

As of right now, they'd reached the dessert stage of their meal. The Prefect held the bunch of grapes above his head and plucked another with his teeth.

"Hadrian you call him, eh?" The Prefect spoke to Dr James out of one side of his mouth. "And this Hadrian, was he a wise Emperor? Effective? *Strong?*" The Roman filled the empty side of his mouth with a slurp from his goblet, as if wine consumption and strength were somehow connected.

"Oh yes. Very much so, yes," Dr James replied with enthusiasm. He had spent the last hour filling their host in on Roman history. "He travelled widely through the Empire. In Britannia, he sorted out all our problems at the northern border. He pulled the border further south and built a—"

"*What?* Retreated you say?"

"Oh. Err, yes. But only a little," Dr James added quickly. "And then to, err, to keep the barbarians out, he built a wall, you see? A big one. It was terribly impressive."

"A *wall?*"

"Oh. Yes. A wall." Dr James fidgeted. Perhaps walls weren't the ideal topic of conversation here. In a park at the zoo.

"Haha! Good for him!" the Prefect replied, clouting Dr James on the shoulder. "We like walls here, we do."

"Oh, you do? Haha. Yes, good." Dr James moved on quickly. "So after Hadrian came Antoninus Pius…"

And so their conversation continued.

Elizabeth had to pinch herself again.

The scene was coloured in twenty shades of weird. She was, so far as she could tell, looking at a middle-aged – *ancient* – Roman, hosting a Roman dinner party, complete with Latin and grapes and silver goblets being lavishly refilled with red wine by wordless slaves. Stranger still, she was able to understand it all, courtesy of the translation earpiece which she was still wearing. Although she still *pretended* not to understand the language – so no-one expected her to speak it.

And then their clothing. Dr James was dressed, implausibly, in a toga and she was in a *stola*. Traditional clothing for a Roman lady. Better than animal skins, but scarcely practical clothing for the trials that surely lay ahead.

She knew her dress was a *stola* for the same reason she knew the dining room was called a *triclinium* – because Dr James had told her. He was sharing a couch with their host, while a second couch was occupied by their host's wife and teenage daughter. The wife was a pale and pinched-looking creature, the daughter a shy beauty with a cowed look. Every time she tried to speak, her mother immediately scolded her.

Elizabeth meantime was on the third and final couch, which she shared with their host's oldest son. He was a reedy, spotted confection, barely eighteen years old with a downy lip and a deep conviction that he was Cupid.

The three couches were positioned around three sides of a low, square table. Across the table was spread every Roman indulgence she had ever seen in picture books, and a few more besides. Etiquette apparently required that you lie on your left side, leaving your right hand free to pinch delicacies from the table or – indeed – your neighbour's bottom. Elizabeth had slapped the spotty youth's hand away three times already.

Elizabeth wished Dr James had told the Perfect they were a married couple.

In case the sheer mad Roman-ness of it all wasn't already clear to her, Elizabeth had a full view of a fresco depicting Bacchus surrounded by, yes, more grapes and wine. The Romans were supposed to be dead and gone. But here they were, a final surviving pocket, apparently leading an authentic Roman lifestyle for the last 1,000 Zailan years – or 2,000 Earth years.

As the minutes ticked by, Elizabeth felt increasing tension *and* increasing relief. It was strange. Like mixing beer and wine. Or eating sausages with sorbet. She felt growing relief because they had one job only now: *survive*. The clever work had passed to Sir

339

Claude and Lady Danziger. Every minute she managed to survive on Zil bought her friends two extra minutes to succeed. Always assuming her friends were still alive – which she had to believe. *Had to.*

But as each minute passed, the apocalypse drew closer and Elizabeth's tension grew higher. She had no idea what the Zailans had in store for them, but that it would arrive tonight she was in no doubt.

"May I ask you a different question…" Dr James wanted to change the subject. He had reached 193 AD and stepped into more deep water as he tried to explain why Rome had consumed five emperors in a single year. "How did your, err, your *people* – how did they first arrive here?"

Elizabeth shot him a look. *Does the Prefect really want to discuss this?* But their host, as always, seemed quite unconcerned.

"We're not fools, Artemas," he replied. "We know we're not in Italy. We know that Rome doesn't lie on the other side of the great wall. Haha!"

Do they know? Elizabeth wondered. *Do they realise they're in a zoo?*

"No, we're not fools" the Prefect continued, still chuckling. "No, no. The reality is quite clear to us—"

Ah, they do *know*, Elizabeth thought, *what a relief.*

"—we've been chosen by the gods. To live nearer to them."

Oh.

Their host gestured munificently towards the open door. Elizabeth turned on her couch to follow the direction of his arm. Framed dead centre of the doorway was a view of the Obelisk.

"Behold Olympus!"

That's Olympus?

"You must understand," the Roman continued, "that here, in our world, the gods speak to us *directly*. I don't mean with signs and symbols, but *with voices and words*. Oh yes, and they have told us. One day judgement will come. And on that day, we are to proceed through the divine gate and Elysium will open before the virtuous. Ah yes, the Elysian Fields... Which lie just beyond the great wall..."

A dreamy, drunken look came over their host. "The gods have chosen us to live nearest to them. And now they've chosen you too. We welcome you amongst us. You take your place among the exalted!"

The host raised an unsteady goblet to toast his guests, who raised theirs in reply.

During the toast, the spotty youth had leaned forward and, thinking Elizabeth couldn't understand, whispered something quite unrepeatable in her ear. At the same time his hand landed, again, on her backside. If there was one thing Elizabeth found unimpressive, it was lecherous men. She looked towards Dr James – someone she doubted had ever committed a lecherous act in his life – and swung her heel back sharply towards the spotted youth. Sadly, it missed his groin, but landed with satisfying force on his knee cap.

He yelped.

She smiled.

"And the moment that your people were chosen by the – *ah-hm* – by the gods ..." Dr James was talking again. "Do you have a record of it? Within your mythology?"

"Oh, there are no myths here. We have it all written down in our annals. Annals that stretch back a thousand years, mark you. We come from Herculaneum. In the Bay of Naples. I imagine you have heard of the eruption of Vesuvius?"

"Yes, of course."

"Well, that's where your history and ours parted company." Their host smiled.

"I don't understand?"

"Vesuvius was erupting – disaster was raining down on our ancestors' heads. The annals record how the gods came to rescue them. With sky chariots. Oh yes, don't look shocked. It's all quite true." Their host waved his goblet towards the Obelisk. Wine sloshed over the lip and splattered on the floor. "The chariots drew our ancestors up to safety and as they left, they saw the eruption surge across the Bay of Naples – rock and ash and fire. As if the realm of Hades had spilled into the mortal realm."

The host paused to slurp more wine. Elizabeth wondered for a moment if the abductors actually started the Vesuvius eruption? Or merely took advantage of it?

"How strange it must all have seemed to our ancestors," the Prefect mused. "Of course, we see the sky chariots all the time now."

"But do you not the find the Zai— I mean the, err, *the gods* a little, *hmm*... A little *capricious?*"

"Of course!" The Prefect bellowed with laughter. "They're gods after all! What would you have them be?" He playfully poked two fingers into the cleft of Dr James' shoulder. "Little cats that purr and nudge us gently? *Haha!* What strange notions you have. From Britannia you say? *Haha!*"

"Yes," Dr James replied, "yes, we do rather expect our gods to be a little kinder…"

"My good fellow. Life is cruel, life is savage, *life*" – the Prefect clapped Dr James round the shoulder – "*is magnificent!* Some gods send us trials, others send us blessings. And I tell you," he said, gulping more wine, "what blessings they send us. How about that, *eh?* Looking forward to a few blessings now you're amongst us? You should be. You'll get a whole lifetime of them." He winked encouragingly.

Elizabeth made eye contact with Dr James. At that moment, they'd have settled for surviving the night.

"We live with the bounty of all Elysium just an arm's length away. When our harvests fail, the gods supply us. When our slaves die, they send us new ones. When illness ravages our more important citizens, healing herbs are provided. Such bounty."

"Life here is a blessing indeed. We're, err, we're, very much looking forward to it," Dr James stammered. "But the walls that surround your world..." He paused, trying to find the right words. "Do you not find them a little... *strange?*"

"Strange? Why should we find a fact of life strange? They're no stranger to me than my own arm. What *we* find strange is the notion of *not* living behind walls. The boundlessness. The uncertainty. How did our ancestors cope? But there we are – it's recorded in the annals – I must accept that theirs was a life without walls."

"Except Hadrian's wall."

"*Haha!* You are a wit, Artemas. Yes – except Hadrian's wall." The Prefect slurped happily from his goblet again.

"But are you not curious to see over them?" Dr James persisted. "Maybe to climb up them?"

"*Why? – How?*" In the midst of his drunkenness, the Prefect looked thoughtful. "Here's how I see it," he continued, his finger chasing a piece of pastry round his plate. "There are walls everywhere in our lives. *What happens after we die?* Eh? We can all guess, but we can't know for sure. It's a wall. *What lies beyond the stars?* No idea – it's a wall. *How do our bodies work?* I mean, *really work?* Even Pliny in all his wisdom couldn't tell us that. Another wall." The Prefect looked up at them. "The great wall outside. It's just more visible. But we get on with our day, mostly ignoring it, the same way we – *you* – ignore the other walls."

There was a pause around the table as the Prefect looked from one to the other.

"Come now, enough serious talk. Let us toast ignorance." He lavished wine into Dr James' goblet. Or rather, he tried to lavish wine into his goblet, but it was mostly full. Dr James, like Elizabeth, had kept a careful check on his consumption. "I say we drink to ignorance. Not because we choose it, but because we can't avoid it. *To ignorance!*"

"*To ignorance!*" Dr James repeated the toast.

As Elizabeth raised her goblet to her mouth, one overriding thought struck her.

My God, they're happy.

This single observation stopped all other thoughts.

These Romans, they're actually happy here.

"You know the only problem with it all?" the Prefect continued, his good humour flowing freely.

"No?"

"*Too much* bounty sometimes. I thank the gods for the trials they send us too. Else we'd grow soft with all this fine living." He paused to take a slice of honey cake.

"What kind of trials?" Dr James asked.

"*Eh*, what's that? *Mm?* What kind of trials?" the

Prefect replied, as some cake crumbled from his mouth. "Well, beasts mostly. We're forever losing shepherds and country folk to the beasts. Some nights even in the town…"

Elizabeth noticed his wife direct a scowl in his direction. But the words were out and it was too late to re-cork them.

Elizabeth nodded at Dr James, urging him to keep asking.

"You mean wolves?" Dr James clarified.

"Wolves, yesh… Yes!" the Prefect slurred. "But beasts too. *Beasts.*"

"Do you mean that…" Dr James started to falter but Elizabeth again nodded encouragement. "Do you mean that, err, *mythical beasts are brought to life?*"

"Not mythical, Artemush – *real*," the Prefect replied with overblown pride, slurring his words now like a pub bore on his favourite topic at the end of long session. "They may have been mythical to our ancestors. But here – in New Herculaneum – they're quite real, I can a— a-zure you." The Prefect slammed a drunken palm down on the table for emphasis.

Dr James and Elizabeth looked at each other.

"Yes, the gods are a very real presence," the Prefect continued, oblivious to their anxiety. To his wife's scowl. "And we welcome them. We *honour* them. The high godsh and, and… the low err… *the low*. The kind ones and the, err… the cruel. I suggest another toast to the animals that, um, the animals that, err—"

"Enough, Publius my dear," the host's wife intervened. "Why, you'll scare our guests." She stood up from the couch. "They've had a long journey. We should let them rest, *darling*."

His wife landed on the word 'darling' with all the

warmth of a bedpan being dropped on a stone floor. *Let them rest*, Elizabeth figured, was code for *stop drinking.*

"*Eh?* You think so? But we were, umm, just, umm… You know, getting sharted—"

His wife replied by removing the goblet from his hand.

"Yes, yes, you're quite right, Fulvia dear. We must err… We must, um… *Exactly.*"

Their host tottered to his feet. He held up an unsteady arm, directing them to the doorway.

*

"Well, it's been a fine evening. And may there be many more such evenings!" the Prefect proclaimed, raising a single, happy – *drunken* – finger.

They had reached the corridor outside. Oil lamps lined the windowless wall behind. "Your brooms have been repaired… I mean, your rooms have been, err…"

"Thank you," Dr James replied. "Your hospitality has been, um, *exceptional*, Publius Vallius."

"Good, good. Well, my wife and shun will sow you the way. I mean they will, err… *Yes.*"

Elizabeth whispered in Dr James' ear.

Dr James looked back up at their host. "Just, err, just one last question before we go," he said. "Do you have armed men guarding the house? Do you keep weapons here?"

"*Hahaha!*" their host bellowed. "Whatever are you afraid of, Artemush? Robbers? *Brigands?* You don't look the nervous type? Allow me to a-zure you, you have no need of weapons. Or soldiersh neither." The Prefect stumbled a yard or two towards Dr James and placed a familiar arm around his shoulder. He spoke conspiratorially into his ear, as if they were old friends. Elizabeth could smell his breath at five yards. "My men at the gate told me, *eh?* You are favoured by the gods. *Yesh!* You lucky…You luckeee… *Protected!*" He pulled away and gave Dr James a hearty slap on the back. "No power under the stars can harm you while you enjoy their protection, *eh? Hahaha!*"

53

Something, finally, had gone right.

Bureaucratic wheels that might have taken weeks or months to grind round, were spinning like well-oiled rotors.

There were very few things that might have shaken the average Za-Nakarian immigration bureaucrat from his usual torpor. But the one thing that could be relied on to motivate him, or any of his colleagues, was job security. Backside-covering being about the most powerful force at work within this bureaucracy – or any other on Za-Nak.

And nothing put job security more at risk than an Executive Order. Or, to be more precise, an Executive Order that has not been followed. And this Executive Order had been quite explicit: any refugees from Zil were to be taken straight to a Supervisor. For some months now the order had been in place. Only there had been no refugees from Zil.

Until today.

The Za-Nakarian immigration official knew exactly which side his bureaucratic bread was buttered. He only needed to hear half Lady Danziger and Sir Claude's story before handing out top-spec translation earpieces to them and the other three refugees and

348

referring them straight up to his Supervisor.

The Supervisor, who might also have reacted with torpor to the presence of illegal aliens, likewise sat right to attention. His instructions gave more detail. They said in effect: "If this is a Zailan refugee seeking better economic prospects on Za-Nak, refer them back to the initial case officer and allow bureaucratic inertia to resume its normal course. But if, on the other hand, these refugees are claiming political asylum and might have useful intelligence on Zil, they should be referred straight up to the Duty Director."

And so, in the course of just a few hours, they found their case being referred up and up through an organisation that normally guarded its higher echelons with the sophistication of a Kafka plot.

But there it was.

Within a few hours, the group found themselves in front of an actual decision-maker. An actually intelligent life-form. Through the day, they'd been upgrading from dingy to more swish offices until they now found themselves in an executive suite that looked much more like the future as they expected to find it. An automated droid offered them nibbles that looked classy and tasted disgusting. Their chairs self-adjusted around their bottoms to grasp their hips gently and squeeze their backs into a better posture. Dr Setiawan – *impressed* – yelped in pain.

Better than all that, the Duty Director in the immigration department had called into the meeting a representative from the Legal Directorate of the Za-Nakarian Government *and* a representative from the IGC itself. These were people with an agenda of their own regarding Zil. These were people with previous experience of intelligent zoos on other planets. These were people *keen* to listen to what Lady Danziger had to say.

And so she told them.

She told them what had happened to Nussbaum and what had happened to Setiawan. She told them about the dozens of abducted academics and the hundreds of abducted vagrants. She told them about the slavery, the electrocutions – the brainwashing. And most of all she told them about the parks: the communities living behind walls, their every movement on camera, their lives being led purely to entertain the zoo visitors and to enrich its psychopathic management team.

After she was done, the Za-Nakarians opposite whistled quietly.

They disappeared from the room to confer.

They returned a few minutes later.

"Of course, we can offer you temporary asylum here on Za-Nak," the immigration director said. "But I suspect you would rather get home to Earth. Why is it that you're really here? And what do you propose?"

Lady Danziger looked at her husband. She liked this Za-Nakarian. This was someone she could do business with.

She thought of the psychopaths running the zoo on Zil. She thought of the sport they made of other people's lives – partly for their own gratification and partly, she suspected, because of their own insecurities.

And so she told him what they really wanted.

54

It took a lot for any self-respecting Caucus psychopath to admit that another Zailan was more psychopathic than he. But in the case of the individual standing in front of him, the Zoo Controller had no hesitation.

The Regional Governor's son was malignant, vicious, psychotic and – worst of all – out of control.

Of course, he cut an unimpressive figure. And precisely that was the problem. Shorter than average height, already vastly overweight, and with no discernible talents, he was a dumpy little idiot.

Pathetic.

If he hadn't been the Regional Governor's son, he'd be nothing. And the brat knew that and hated himself for it. And he hated other people for knowing it too. Inflicting pain and misery on other creatures would never adequately compensate him for that knowledge – but he was sure as Hell going to try.

"Through here, please," The Zoo Controller said unctuously, as he opened the door for his hated guest. "We've prepared the VIP suite for you."

*

The VIP suite at the zoo was, for a certain kind of

Zailan, their vision of Heaven.

Luxury was the first impression the room made on any visitor. There were couches to lie on and plush armchairs to lounge in. There was a bar manned at all times by three of the most comely submissives in the whole facility. Here guests could choose from a vast list of cocktails popular on a dozen different planets. Or have gourmet food whisked up at a moment's notice from the kitchens in the basement floors – almost every dish guaranteed to push some endangered species or other a little closer to extinction.

But guests didn't come here for the luxury or the cocktails or the food.

They came here for the *fun.*

Fun was the VIP suite's speciality. It was one big games room – a mini-control room, where the big spenders could come and, for an exorbitant fee, play god.

From any one of a dozen huge screens, or several dozen VR headsets, they could watch anything they liked in the zoo. They could link up to over 50,000 different cameras or – using the courtesy set of joysticks – control a private fleet of drones. Some were the size of a large bird, that could sweep effortlessly over the large parks. Others were as small as insects, that could intrude in any place at any time to watch the humans doing – *pretty much* – anything. Guests could soar like a bird – or they could creep like a peeping Tom. They could look down from above as humans scurried about like ants. Or they could look up from beneath as they talked, argued, or danced – as they made friends, enemies, or love.

But that was just the kids' stuff.

The Zoo Controller stepped deeper into the suite,

guiding his guests towards the serious equipment at the far end.

Here several banks of control decks were located, looking not unlike the mixing desks in a recording studio. But these decks weren't controlling the sound output in the zoo's parks, they were controlling *everything*. With the merest flick of a button, any number of horrors could be unleashed in any number of ways. Imagination was the only limit. And if they did want to say something directly to any of the humans... Over against the wall, there was a soundproof booth. Here – at specified times and in specified parks – the guests could provide the 'voice of God'. The *actual* voice of God.

But always under supervision of course.

And, from the Zoo Controller's point of view, exactly that was the problem.

Supervision.

Given power without responsibility, the Zoo Controller found the Zailan elite were hard to rein in at the best of times. And none more so than the Regional Governor's son. Which is why the Zoo Controller himself was on hand to supervise this evening.

And he had another problem.

The *wow factor*.

The story of the human fugitives had been playing out wall-to-wall across Zailan media for the last two days. The occupants of the VIP suite tonight would get the chance to bring that story to a close. Any other guests would be honoured to fulfil this task at this moment.

But not this brat.

"So what's new, hmm? Same old – same old – and" – the Regional Governor's son pointed at the various entertainment points around the room – "*same old*." He looked at the two companions he had dragged along with him. They all dutifully returned a bored look towards the Zoo Controller.

"Haha!" the Zoo Controller laughed ingratiatingly, and with quiet confidence. "Don't you worry. I have something special lined up for you and your friends this evening."

And he did.

He swept his hand towards a corner of the suite that had been overlooked. The guests turned to see three body suits mounted on specially adapted treadmills.

"Something very special."

55

Elizabeth lay on her bed, motionless, listening through the window to the nighttime sounds of a Roman street.

She had changed out of her *stola* and back into the supervisor clothing: grey shirt and trousers.

Dr James had too.

They had quietly agreed this in the corridor last thing before they were escorted in different directions around the house. Dr James was shown to a room on the second floor. Elizabeth had been taken to the *cubiculum* – she assumed it just meant 'bedroom' – on the first floor.

The window had a pair of shutters, which she had left open, but no glass. Just a rectangular hole in the wall with a sturdy set of iron bars. The sounds of the street filtered up through the bars like a nighttime aroma. The distant barking of a chained dog. A drunk slurring his way through a shanty. The occasional banging door or clank of pottery from the house opposite. Some giggling.

As Elizabeth lay on her back, with her hands tucked up under her head, her eyes strayed across her room. An oil lamp remained lighted on the small table at the far end of the room. It was an Aladdin-style lamp. The modest flame danced on the top of the spout, pushed and pulled by the gentle draught coming past the open shutters. The light skipped erratically across the frescoes that decorated the walls.

An oil lamp.

For a moment Elizabeth was back at Number 55 Cleremont Avenue – in her small room overlooking the conservatory. *How many days has it been?* The answer, she reasoned, depended on which planet you were talking about. In Earth days, *maybe two or three?* She wasn't sure. In terms of her actual, lived experience – hour by hour – *maybe closer to seven?*

But in terms of how much she'd seen, how far she'd come...

Lifetimes.

She thought about Dr James, who every minute lingered higher in her consciousness. Closer and closer to the surface. Could she really be feeling what she was feeling? This affection, this protectiveness...

But this wasn't actually *love*, was it? When she had fallen for Charles, affection and protectiveness had nothing to do with it. There was passion – a sense of possession – ambition even. Very different feelings to now. Therefore, this couldn't be love. *Could it?*

Perhaps this was more like a holiday infatuation – an emotional alibi. Real enough at the time but sure to evaporate at the first return to normal life.

But that was the point. She couldn't picture a return to normal life. Not now. Not anymore. There would be things – a lot of things – to confront when she returned home.

If she returned home...

Some barking – loud and insistent – snapped her back into the room. *What a luxury to think about normal life*, she chided herself. She would be lucky to

356

survive the night.

She distracted herself with the frescoes. She picked out the images in the flickering light. There were nudes – *lots* of nudes, she could see that now – a half-clothed Venus pouring water from an urn – young girls bathing – a young man hiding behind rocks, spying on them – stags running.

A new sound was slipping through the window. Elizabeth's attention latched onto it. Her ears traced the sound back out of the window, following it to its source. The giggling from the house opposite had morphed into something more insistent. Between the window bars, the soft moan of a young woman was seeping in. She couldn't be more than ten, maybe fifteen yards away. At a guess, downstairs.

Elizabeth smiled to herself. Their lovemaking wasn't yet loud enough to drown out the barking of the dog. Nor the street drunkard, who had just crashed into a crate of pottery and was mouthing filthy curses in Latin.

A moment later and the dog gave a strange yelp – *had he been spooked by the drunk?* – and fell silent.

Elizabeth strained her ears.

Something wasn't right. Into the midst of this strange – and yet also *un*strange – soundscape, a new note entered.

A low, bass snarl.

Was that the dog again?

If it was the dog, Elizabeth could swear it must've escaped its tether. The noise was getting closer. Elizabeth thought about going to the window to look.

She tried to persuade herself she was overreacting. *It's just the dog and it's wandering down the street. No big deal.* And anyway, the lovemaking was

357

intensifying. The timbre of the girl's moaning had deepened and widened, adding a febrile energy to the atmosphere of the night. She didn't want to be seen at the window like some voyeur.

And then below her window – undeniable, unmissable – something was amiss. She heard a bass growl so menacing, so powerful, she could virtually hear the drip of saliva from jaws.

The drunk stopped his singing and exclaimed with surprise and confusion. A second later, there was a brief and savage snarl – a clattering of crates – a sickening gurgle – and then the drunk too fell silent.

Elizabeth was on her feet now.

She pressed her face to the bars, and gripped them with her hands, reflexively testing their strength again. The house was heavily constructed – *thank God* – from the massive oak front door to its walls to its barred windows.

But the window offered limited visibility. The bars were recessed inside the window socket. The walls beyond them were so thick, she had only the narrowest field of view. She thought she saw a flash of movement – there was another clatter – and a scraping sound, like claws dragging against stones. And over it all, the sound of passion approaching its peak, a young woman in the grip of delirium.

Elizabeth strained and strained to see what was happening.

She heard more snarling – the sound of things – household things – being broken.

Then the door to her room opened behind her.

She wheeled round in alarm.

She hoped it was Dr James – but it wasn't. It was that oaf from supper. The pimply son, holding an oil lamp. He was standing on the far side of the room in some kind of nightgown, the bed in between them.

"*What the Hell are you doing here?*" she snarled at him in a language he didn't understand.

"I, err... thought..." Some stuttered phrases came through her earpiece as she eyeballed him with impatient ferocity.

They were still staring at each other when it came.

A final, orgasmic, ear-shattering scream from the house opposite pierced the night air.

"*Is that... Was that...*" The youth giggled and stuttered ineptly, half in shock, half in gormless amusement. "Was that what I think it was?"

Elizabeth ignored him. She grabbed the revolver that was concealed under the clothes next to her bed. She didn't bother checking at the window again. She wouldn't see anything there. She needed to link up with Dr James, fast. *Dr James...* She had to get to him before anything else did. Gun in hand, she strode round the bed, towards the youth – *what actually was he doing here?* – and towards the doorway behind him.

"*That*," she said as she brushed past him, not caring if he understood or not, "was the sound of someone dying."

56

The Zoo Controller quietly watched his young guests.

Two of them were still suiting up, bickering with each other like children as they struggled to pull the rubber suits over their flabby, unfit limbs.

The Regional Governor's son, however, was too impatient for any of that. He wanted to be first into the fray. He had gone straight to one of the control decks – a technology he was all too familiar with – and his long arms had started moving across the kaleidoscope of dials and switches with practised fluency.

The beast that he was controlling from that deck was notionally a cyborg. Created by the zoo's state-of-the-art genetic engineering program, its movements were cybernetically controlled by chips implanted in its brain. Born of technology, permeated by technology, this creature was controlled by technology.

Theoretically.

But, in reality, it was a living, breathing monster. Better than anyone, the Zoo Controller knew that. From the moment it had been born – even as it lay there with toothless gums, eyes shut, wriggling and defenceless – even then, it had scared the life out its handlers. Its limbs, its muscles, *its shape*. As it grew, so did the fear that surrounded it. It killed its first handler before it even reached puberty. The creature had a life of its own, appetites of its own, an agenda of its own.

After puberty, it had somehow become aware of its own uniqueness – and that it would never find a mate. Its fury had been unquenchable ever since.

In the brain of such an intelligent, demented animal, the digital-neural connection was unstable at the best of times. And these were not, from the beast's point of view, the best of times. Starved of food for the last two days, hunger and hormones were coursing through its body, leaving it stressed, confused, and only partially responsive to digital signals.

The Zoo Controller watched as the Regional Governor's son tried to steer it towards the front door of the Prefect's house. The animal resisted at first... And then responded. A lascivious smile spread across the face of the Governor's son. *He's enjoying himself,* the Zoo Controller thought with relief.

The Zoo Controller looked up at the three large screens above the control deck, and the speakers next to them. Here the operator could share the beast's point of view, see with its eyes, hear with its ears. This was both an advantage – and a disadvantage. The image was grainy and dark. It lacked the full colour range. And the image shook and shuddered with the beast's movements.

Good, the Zoo Controller thought, *it increases the challenge.*

Right now, the three screens were showing a massive wooden door that was starting to buckle under repeated assault. The brat worked a few levers on the control deck and the beast hurled itself once more against the obstacle.

Truly, these two were the perfect match.

The son of the Regional Governor and the three-headed hound of Hades.

The psychopath and *Cerberus*.

In human – *Roman* – mythology, Cerberus guarded the gates of the underworld. It was said that his job was to stop the dead leaving. The Zoo Controller chewed this thought over in his mind for a moment. And smiled. To the fugitives, Zil probably was Hades, and they certainly wouldn't be leaving it. Cerberus' mythological role would tonight be made real. *How perfect.*

And the fugitives wouldn't be the only ones to die tonight.

Three had gone already.

The Zoo Controller had had to step in a few minutes earlier to stop a full-scale rampage through the streets of Herculaneum. The drunk he didn't mind losing – *free meat* – but the copulating couple was a different matter. A noisy copulation was ratings gold and a couple in their prime could perform night after night for the audience. True, the brutal murder of the couple had produced a ratings spike – but it was scarcely repeatable.

So, the Zoo Controller had stepped in. He had reminded the Governor's son about the mission. Not to tear up half the town, but to kill the fugitives. And when the brat had resisted, the Zoo Controller reminded him what a hero he was about to become on Zil. The one who slayed the saboteurs and avenged Zailan honour. *The saviour.*

And then the brat got it. He started to realise that killing the fugitives might bring him something he'd never known before. Respect. Not because of who his father was – but because of something *he* had done. Respect.

And perhaps even a little love.

57

The pounding against the front door shook the entire building. The Prefect's house was extensive, with long colonnades and corridors and two internal courtyards. Elizabeth had found Dr James on a first-floor landing. On seeing him – ambling contentedly along – relief had washed through her for a moment. And then the pounding. They were some distance from the front door and *still* she felt the floorboards shake. She grasped a ledge to steady herself.

She looked at their host, who had just appeared alongside them in his nightgown, oil lamp in hand. In the heat of his fear, all the alcohol had evaporated from his system. No longer drunkenness but terror creased his face.

Worse than the pounding was the sound of splintering wood. The sound of time running out. When they had first arrived at the Prefect's house – half a day and half a lifetime ago – she had taken note of the front door with approval. Its construction was sturdy. Two-ply of heavy wooden boards, braced and bolted with solid wooden cross rails at the back. Three flat-iron bolts locked the door shut. It was a door that could keep out a whole platoon of soldiers.

But it was a door that was about to succumb to

whatever creature lay on the far side.

"Ask him what's wrong," Elizabeth said to Dr James. "What's out there?"

Dr James translated. But the words failed to penetrate the Prefect's fear.

"How could they do this... Never before..." The Prefect was muttering incoherently, his eyes lolling about like a madman's. *"Never before..."*

"'Never before'?" Elizabeth, understanding the Latin but unable to speak it, alternated her gaze between Dr James and their host. As Dr James translated again, she took hold of one of the Prefect's shoulders and shook him. "Never before *what?*"

He looked at her hand, eyes wide, doubtless shocked he was being man-handled by a woman. It injected a fragment of sense. He fixed his eyes on her. "Never *here*, do you see? Always others – *the plebs*. Never in *this house.*"

"Yes – but never *what* in this house?"

"It must... *It must be...*"

"*Yes?*"

"They must have sent *the—*"

"FATHER! FATHER!"

Their host's pimply son had appeared at the far end of the corridor, running. His sour-faced mother heaved into view just behind him, and his timid sister behind her. The trio halted when they saw the guests. Elizabeth dropped her hand from the Prefect's shoulder.

"What is it? What is it my boy?" the Prefect asked, feigning the thinnest veneer of calm in front of his first-born.

The mother whispered something in the boy's ear and pushed him forwards. She eyed Elizabeth suspiciously, as the boy approached his father. He whispered in his ear.

Elizabeth didn't have time for their parlour games. "Ask him this, Dr James. Is there another way out of the house? A backdoor somewhere?"

As Dr James translated, some tiny spark of courage ignited in their host. Not enough to stop his trembling – nor undo the stains on his nightgown where he had soiled himself – but just enough to recover the power of speech.

"Yes… *Yes.* Down the stairs. Yes – down the stairs into the atrium. Turn right through the *tablinum*, pass straight through the—"

The house heaved to the sound of another crash. No front door could survive this kind of assault for long. Their host looked away again, his features sagging with fear, his face muscles quivering. He didn't even look like the man Elizabeth had met a few hours earlier.

"Through the *what?* Speak, man!" Elizabeth had both hands on his shoulders this time.

"*Eh?* Through the *peristyle* of course. Yes, the garden. There's a small door on the far side. It leads to the street. Yes. You must go there. Yes – you must. *Both of you.*"

The Prefect's tone had changed. He was staring at them in a strange, hypnotised way. Elizabeth wondered if he was losing his mind.

"Dr James, did those directions makes sense to you?" Elizabeth asked as she flipped the cylinder of the revolver and checked all six chambers were full. Dr James nodded. "*Good.* Then please lead the way. Oh, and ask the Prefect if he's coming? Him and his family?"

"No!" he replied to Dr James abruptly, placing his arms out wide, shielding his wife and son behind him. Then more gently: "No. It's you, who… *You* must go."

"Very well," Elizabeth replied, looking at him for a moment sideways, suspicious. And then she left – following Dr James along the corridor and down the staircase to the ground floor.

*

A moment later and Elizabeth found herself in the atrium at the entrance to the house. When she had passed through it a few hours earlier it had been a scene of grace and tranquility. A colonnaded courtyard, with a pond and a small fountain at the centre.

Now, in the darkness, it had acquired the complexion of a nightmare. Just as they stepped into the atrium, the beast outside had crashed against the front door. Illuminated by two torches hung on the wall either side, Elizabeth watched as this mighty door jumped on its hinges. The three massive iron bolts were starting to buckle. One of the three keeps had all but fallen away from the door frame.

In the atrium itself, a half-dozen slaves were standing in a horseshoe around the door, spears in hand, their faces half-illuminated by the torches that were mounted on the pillars all around. Elizabeth recognised one – he had helped wait on them over dinner.

Elizabeth was about to ask what was outside, when another crash reverberated across the stonework. The timbre was different this time. The beast hadn't crashed against the door, it had crashed against one of two small windows set either side of the door.

Elizabeth started. Just for a moment, illuminated by the torch beneath, everyone in the atrium could see an enormous head, jaws thrust up against the window grill. The grill had buckled and Elizabeth saw a mesh of white teeth, iron bars, dark pink gums – and blood. Elizabeth had never seen jaws so massive. *Is it some kind of over-sized panther? Or a hound even?*

But that wasn't what unnerved her. It was the beast's indifference to pain. It had just crushed its own muzzle against cast iron bars, and yet still its assault continued.

There was a clattering of iron on stone. The slaves had dropped their spears and were fleeing. They had seen enough, they knew what it was. Half fled up a staircase opposite, the other half sprinted past her, heading up the staircase she had just come down. The last spear was discarded at her feet.

Why up the stairs? Why aren't they fleeing through the backdoor—

"It's this way, I believe?" Dr James' voice interrupted her train of thought. He was already striding along the colonnade at the edge of the atrium. Elizabeth hurried to catch up. They passed through a doorway directly opposite the front door. Some small voice in her head kept repeating over and over – *keep Artemas in your sight – keep Artemas in your sight.* They were running now. Through a room of some kind. A vague impression of desks and scrolls and parchments flashed past her periphery. A moment later she was running between more columns – Dr James still a couple of yards ahead – and then out into a cloistered garden. The house's second courtyard.

They reached the far side of the garden and stopped. "Somewhere here," he said, gesturing with his arm.

"The backdoor should be somewhere here."

They were beneath another colonnade. Behind them was the garden, in front was a row of rooms. One of them presumably led to the backdoor.

"Alright…" Elizabeth gasped. "Let's check them in turn."

They found what they were looking for at the third attempt. "Here, Dr James, look!" she called over her shoulder.

Elizabeth had entered a storeroom. A single lamp was burning on the wall. The fragile flame danced as the door shut behind Dr James, its quivering light illuminating a clutter of crates and shelves and barrels and amphorae. Unmistakably, on the far side, was another heavily bolted door. The tradesman's entrance to the house. *The backdoor.*

Elizabeth crossed the room and took up position, both hands tight on the revolver, arms lowered and outstretched "Dr James – could you open it?" she asked. "I'll cover you. We don't know what might be out there." She recalled the strange look on the Prefect's face as he directed them downstairs—

"Ready?" Dr James asked.

"Ready."

Elizabeth watched him pull back the three bolts. One – two – three. Then he lifted the heavy iron latch. Straining with both hands, he started to pull the heavy door inwards. It ground against the dusty stone floor like a flour mill.

*

For what Elizabeth sees next, nothing on this mad, infernal journey – nothing in her life – could have prepared her.

Beauty.

Radiant and utterly compelling.

She sees thick, lustrous tresses tumbling either side of a face lit by moonlight – a face *like* moonlight. The fine, classical nose, the pale luminous skin, the high cheekbones. She sees two milk-white mounds rising from a chest in a perfect curve of taut skin. The lower half of the breasts are covered in downy feathers, soft and chaste. She is reminded of Lady Danziger. Lady Danziger as she must have been in her youth, the lines gone, the eyes hypnotic.

From far away she hears a voice calling. '*Mrs B!*' it says. And then, '*Watch out!*'

"*What?*" Elizabeth replies, distracted.

'*Watch out!*' the voice – Dr James' voice – cries again.

The radiant face in front of her is alarmed. *Of course she is.* And the face contorts itself – from serenity into a snarl. Elizabeth starts to anger. *Why is Dr James shouting? Why must men always assume violence?* Then something flaps, almost like a wing – a claw stretches out – her revolver is knocked from her hand and scuttles across the stone flagging.

Elizabeth is confused now. A body dives past her legs. *It's Dr James.* He appears to grab the revolver. And then—

A shot rings out.

Loud as death.

The report echoes around the stony interior of the storeroom. The radiant – snarling – figure in front of her bucks and recoils.

A second shot is fired.

Dark red blood starts to pulse and gush over the

silver-pale skin of the creature's breasts. It spills down the unresisting mounds until it reaches the soft white feathers below, staining and defiling them.

A moment later and Dr James is back on his feet. He hurls himself at the door. It crunches shut. He presses his back against it, jamming his slim shoulders into one of the cross rails.

"The bolts, Mrs B, *the bolts!*"

She obeys, unthinking, and slides the bolts home – one, two, *three.*

The door is secure again.

And Elizabeth snaps out if it.

*

Dr James sat collapsed against the large door, his slim chest heaving. Elizabeth looked at him in horror at what she'd done. Failed to do.

His eyes stared into space. "*They always come in threes,*" he said to no-one in particular.

Elizabeth continued to stare at him, ashamed of herself. His smile was gone, the calmness too, the serenity. She didn't even think to ask *what* always come in threes. "My God, Dr James, I'm so sorry…"

For the first time since she'd met him, he looked frightened. His face was drawn, characterless. *And all because of me.* She felt like she'd picked up a talisman of rare and unique power and smashed it to the ground. Broken it. It would be days before she worked out that Dr James wasn't frightened at all – but dismayed. Distraught to have killed a living, sentient being.

"It's alright, Mrs B," he replied, briefly looking at her, "it's alright."

"I promise that won't happen again." As she spoke,

she made a commitment in her mind far stronger than he could know.

"Thank you," he replied, managing the faintest flicker of a smile. "So, what's the plan now?"

"To the roofs," she replied without hesitation. "It's our only hope." Elizabeth extended her hand and started to help him to his feet. "But just one question…"

"Yes?"

"What *was* that thing – that creature?"

"That, Mrs B, was a harpy."

58

Harpies.

The head of a maiden, the wings and claws of an eagle. Said to be the snatchers of the underworld, tasked with carrying off the souls of the wicked to the realm of Hades.

They always come in threes.

The Zoo Controller was enchanted by the poetry of it. The beasts that all of Zil was now watching faced both ways at the gates to Hades. The harpies were there to drag the wicked in; Cerberus to stop them from leaving. The *three*-headed hound. *Three* harpies. And *three* psychopathic guests. But of course the trio that really mattered: himself and the two fugitives, locked in their remote duel. He hadn't exactly planned it this way. But that was life for you. When things go right, they go really right. Connections are made, circles are closed, pieces fit together with previously unimaginable perfection.

And what perfection.

The ratings were *soaring*.

Right here, in the VIP suite, he was creating TV that was going to be watched again and again *forever*. But this wasn't just TV. This was entertainment – and justice – *and art* all rolled into one.

He had to hand it to the genetics team. Their avatar program had exceeded all expectations. To create beasts and monsters and gnashing teeth – that was all great. Actually, it was their job. But to generate beauty as well? That was inspired. Even to a Zailan, that harpy looked gorgeous.

Until she snarled, of course, and did that snatchy thing with her talons. That was just nasty.

But so fun.

The Zoo Controller looked across at his three guests. One had just lost his avatar, shot through the chest – *tough* – and was just now clambering clumsily out of the rubber bodysuit. The second was still in his avatar suit and still in the game.

And then there was the Regional Governor's son.

The brat had chosen to go with the cyborg and not the avatar – and now he looked put out. He had paused hurling Cerberus against the front door and switched his camera view to watch the backdoor. He had watched the strange clinch between the female fugitive and the harpy. And how the harpy – *his friend* – had managed to wrestle the gun from the fugitive's hand.

He looked annoyed.

He had just been upstaged.

Good, the Zoo Controller thought to himself, *he's angry. Let's see what he does next.*

59

Cerberus retreated into the street, extending the length of his run-up. He turned back around towards the house, his three heads tossing and twisting, and launched himself forwards.

Five yards from the door, he leapt.

This time he crashed against his target with all the momentum of his run-up and all the force of his full weight. Flank, shoulder and heads all landed in the same instant against the beleaguered timbers. There was a brief splintering of wood, followed by a soul-shattering *bang* as the door landed flat against the stone tiles of the Prefect's vestibule.

He was in.

*

Elizabeth and Dr James were at the foot of the staircase at the moment the front door collapsed.

She had just grabbed a discarded spear from the floor and given it to Dr James. "It was a trap", she'd said. The Prefect had sent them to the backdoor to be killed. To be sacrificed. "Now we have to get to the roofs." Dr James had nodded. His confidence in Elizabeth hadn't been shaken, despite her near-fatal lapse in front of the harpy. Elizabeth no longer shared that confidence. *And after the roofs, then what?* she had asked herself silently. *How can we possibly get out of this?* But she checked herself. She wasn't going to unnerve Dr James a second time. *Just survive,* she repeated to herself, *one minute at a time.* And hope for a miracle. She had to believe that Juckes and the others were alive, that they had succeeded in their mission. She had to hope. *What else is there?*

And then the front door collapsed.

The crash echoed around the atrium behind them like an artillery piece. She and Dr James made the mistake of turning to look.

It was, quite simply, the ugliest creature Elizabeth had ever seen. A parody of nature. It stood now at the doorway, rearing on its hind legs, its three heads twisting and bucking. Its sleek black coat glinted in the torchlight with the colours of an oil slick.

"The three-headed hound... *Cerberus...*" Dr James's voice sounded distant and monochrome. Hypnotised. Like Elizabeth, three minutes earlier. "*They re-created Cerberus...*"

"Don't look, Dr James – *run!*" she yelled at him, grabbing his spare hand and pulling him away. Out of his trance. She was delivering on the promise she'd made to herself a little less than three minutes earlier. "*Run!*"

And run they did.

They channelled their fear into energy and the energy into their legs. Elizabeth hurtled up the staircase to the first floor, turning constantly to check Dr James was never more than one – two – yards behind. They sped along the first-floor landing, careering into walls as they rounded corners. They flew past the door to the *triclinium* – and past the spot where they'd last seen the Prefect and his family – all now vanished.

As Elizabeth was halfway up the next flight of stairs, she heard a noise that, again, threatened to immobilise them. Part howl – part bark – part roar – she correctly guessed that all three heads of the beast were venting in unison. An instant later she felt a thumping shudder through the building as the beast made its way up the first of the staircases.

They pressed on. A second or two later, the pair spilled out onto a second-floor landing. At the far end, Elizabeth spotted a slave disappearing through a concealed doorway. Too breathless now to speak, she gestured with her arm and, the air burning in their lungs, they ran to the spot.

It was a door disguised as a wall panel. Only a small handle gave it away. She pulled it open. They heard a thumping beneath. The beast was somewhere below on the first floor. Elizabeth slipped through the door and Dr James pulled it quietly shut behind him.

Ahead of them, barely discernible in the dark, was a wooden staircase that must surely lead up to the roof. Moving more quietly now, they made their way up it. They rounded a final corner, passed through another door and stepped out into the night.

*

They had arrived onto a kind of roof garden, or terrace.

Elizabeth's eye darted left and right, absorbing her surroundings. The terrace was maybe fifteen yards square. A single, thick rope looped from post to post around the perimeter. Within the roped area, she saw plant pots and decorative amphorae, low tables and couches, all of them illuminated by the soft, yellow light of some oil lamps that were positioned on the perimeter posts. On two sides of the terrace, there was a sheer drop to the ground below. On one side, down to the Prefect's garden; on the other, the street outside. On the remaining two sides of the terrace, the roofline continued in haphazard fashion, following the row of buildings up and down the street.

It was to one of these sides that Elizabeth's eye was drawn. She saw the last slave disappearing over a ridgeline. Dr James set off to follow him.

"*NO!* Dr James... No."

Dr James turned back around, confused.

Below, they heard a low growl – a snarl. The beast was prowling the floor beneath, looking for the staircase up. Dr James pointed to the obvious escape route, over the roofs.

"No," Elizabeth repeated. "We'll make our stand here. *Look* – it has to come through that doorway. I'll have a perfect shot when it does. We may never get a better chance."

Dr James nodded – still compliant, still trusting. He joined Elizabeth where she was standing, ten yards from the door. She shifted a little, placing herself protectively in front of him. She glanced at the wooden shaft of the spear which he held in his hands. It gave little reassurance. As if to confirm her fears, the noise of splintering timber echoed from below. *Has the beast found the staircase to the roof?* A low growl confirmed it had. She quickly re-filled the two empty chambers of the revolver from the small supply of bullets in her pocket. She closed the cylinder shut and looked back up. She couldn't see it, but she knew the animal was advancing up the narrow wooden staircase. The menacing, telltale creak of the timbers crept ahead of it and leaked through the terrace doorway like the promise of violence to come.

Elizabeth adjusted her stance. She raised the revolver with both arms outstretched; she lined up the front and rear sights with the doorway. She thought she was ready.

But she wasn't.

Commotion broke over the roof terrace.

A piercing, screeching sound fractured the night air. A second harpy had flown up over the edge of the building. Framed by a moon either side of her shoulders, they saw her hovering for a moment, ten yards above the terrace doorway.

Elizabeth angled her gun upwards at the harpy and this time – *this time* – she didn't hesitate. She fired.

Immediately the harpy recoiled. And then fell away, to Elizabeth's right – below the roofline and out of sight. *Did I hit it? Maybe the wing?*

Elizabeth waited for a second.

But she didn't hear the *thud* she was expecting of a dead creature hitting the ground. She alternated her gaze anxiously between the still-empty doorway and the edge of the roof terrace. Cerberus still hadn't appeared. The last thing she wanted was for a wounded harpy to stage a dramatic reappearance just when the hound was attacking. She made a snap decision. She gestured to Dr James to stay where he was and ran to far side of the terrace to look over the edge.

She reached the perimeter rope and peered down into the garden courtyard below. In the gloom, she saw nothing. Anxiously, she glanced back at the doorway, now ten yards to her left. She was checking she'd still have a good view of Cerberus when he appeared.

And then Cerberus *did* appear.

And so did the harpy.

In an assault of perfect coordination, Cerberus burst through the doorway at the exact moment that the second harpy reared up out of the shadows where she'd been hiding below. Hound and harpy were both attacking.

As the harpy flew up the side of the terrace, the beat of one of her wings knocked Elizabeth's gun hand. It was almost a perfect repeat of the incident outside the backdoor. The revolver was almost struck away. *Almost.* But not quite. Elizabeth spun round 180 degrees from the blow and landed heavily on the floor tiles. But her gun was still in her hand.

Now lying on her back, Elizabeth saw the harpy directly above her – about to plunge. Elizabeth's right hand raised the revolver directly above her head, her left hand went up to join it—

C R A C K

She'd fired a single round directly into the heart of the creature, directly between the breasts. The second harpy released a strangled shriek, the noise struggling to bubble through the blood that was filling her lungs. Her body collapsed onto the terrace just a yard to Elizabeth's right, her dishevelled wings scattered awkwardly either side.

Elizabeth found herself entangled under the bones and sinews and skin of the outstretched wing as if under a giant, broken umbrella. She thought of Dr James on his own with Cerberus. *Dr James...* She thrust her way up through the tangled mess of the fallen harpy. She looked across the terrace. She saw the hound was now just a couple of yards from him. The spear in his hands looked no more lethal than a piece of driftwood – and the best was snapping at it.

Elizabeth dropped to one knee, revolver outstretched. Positioned as she was to the side of Cerberus and behind him, she couldn't get an angle on any of his heads, nor even on his heart.

Instead, she fired into his side once – *twice*.

The bullets left two small red punctures in the vast muscular flank. But they achieved their purpose. Cerberus howled with pain and checked his advance on Dr James. He turned instead towards Elizabeth.

It was a victory, but only a small one. A temporary delay of the inevitable. Elizabeth saw the animal's mud-black pelt close back over the puncture marks like a bog closing over footprints. The flesh seemed to suck the bullets in like nourishment, the pain feeding his anger.

And his confidence.

Now knowing her gun to be useless, Cerberus advanced towards Elizabeth with slow steps. Elizabeth felt faint, nauseous with fear. She could see his six eyes all had a famished look. Saliva spilled from his mottled black and red gums, dripping down over slack, ill-fitting lips. Elizabeth had the impression of quivering restraint. Of flickering violence and unbounded appetites just a hair trigger – just a tiny command – from being unleashed.

It would have been so easy to freeze at this moment. It was so tempting to give in to her fear. Elizabeth could hear a voice inside her telling her to do so. *To let go.* To let him sate his appetite. *Let him.* Everything would be over so much faster. *Maybe they'll let Dr James live a little longer.* Elizabeth could see no way out of this for herself. She was backing towards the edge of the terrace, her legs taking her there without her even knowing. What she did know was that the revolver was useless, utterly useless. Unless she managed a direct hit to the creature's brain – and he had three of those.

And, worse – much, much worse – she only had two bullets.

She fired one of them anyway.

Just for a moment, one of the animal's heads was still and she fired straight between the eyes. Cerberus' right head flopped against his side.

Shocked – enraged – Cerberus cast aside the shuddering restraint that had been holding him in check. Like releasing the brakes on an engine in full throttle, he reared onto his hind legs, his two remaining heads tossing and writhing and foiling Elizabeth's aim.

She stumbled backwards. As she did so, she tripped on the outstretched wing of the dead harpy. She took rapid, panicky steps backwards, trying to regain her balance, until her right leg snagged on the perimeter rope. She felt the rope ride up the back of her thigh, and then up to her waist.

The rope held – it checked her fall – but it was only delaying the inevitable. She was now leaning out over the edge of terrace. Death lay beneath her – death lay in front of her – and there was only one bullet left in the gun.

Elizabeth was certain it was all over.

Except for one thing.

The one thing she had never expected.

She had spent so much energy wondering how to protect Dr James, it never occurred to her that he might protect her.

He appeared now, near the beast's left flank.

Holding his surely-useless spear, he jabbed it decisively into Cerberus' left neck. Just for a moment the left head was immobilised.

Elizabeth fired her last bullet at the static target

A second head toppled.

And then Cerberus started to back away.

The hound was howling in agony and disbelief from his central head, the last surviving one. Still alive, a mere parody of himself, the creature shuffled backwards towards the terrace door – his other two heads flopping and lolling with hideous redundancy against his flanks. His steps were faltering and erratic. His last surviving head tossed and twisted, as if in conflict with itself.

*

Elizabeth listened to the howling of the animal, fading and fading as he retreated down the staircase.

She walked four or five yards across the terrace to join Dr James, who was sitting now, heaving deep lungfuls of air. She sat beside him and placed an arm around his shoulders. She was shaking, jubilant.

"We've done it… We've done it, Dr James!" Then, as she registered the unresponsive look on his face, "*Haven't we?*"

"Have we?" He spoke between breaths. "We've slain two harpies and two heads of the dog is what we've done."

60

The Regional Governor's son thumped hard against the console – his sixteen digits crashing against the levers and dials in outrage against beast and machine.

Above the control deck, two of the screens had gone blank – the grainy video feed replaced with black and grey static that danced tauntingly before his eyes. And while the third screen – the central one – *was* still operational, it was not showing what its operator wanted to see. It was looking down a staircase. The staircase leading *away* from the roof terrace.

Cerberus was retreating, hideously wounded, and there was nothing the Regional Governor's son could do to stop it.

He stood up, ripped off his headset, and threw it against the control deck in disgust. He glared at the Zoo Controller as if this failure was somehow his fault.

The Zoo Controller returned his glare with an even gaze. He gestured to the avatar suit. As far as he was concerned, this was going well. *Really* well. The last thing he wanted was a quick ending. The way the fugitives had dispatched Cerberus was perfect. The longer they stayed in the game, the better the ratings.

He leant casually over the now-vacated control deck and pressed the home switch. This fired a neural impulse into Cerberus' one remaining brain, instructing him to return to base. Or, to be more specific, to return to the airlock located in the Temple of Jupiter. It was located in the forum, at the end of the Prefect's street. Not that Cerberus needed much encouragement. He was probably heading there already.

The Controller looked across at the Regional Governor's son. The brat already had his legs inside the rubber bodysuit and was pulling it over his chubby torso. He wanted to get back into the fray as quickly as possible. *How sweet.* His friends were already out of their bodysuits and looking round for fresh devices to kill the fugitives. For sure the brat would have to hurry. It would take a little while to get the suit fully clipped up, establish the interface – and then get his avatar from the holding pen to the fugitives.

That said, the Zoo Controller was now backing the fugitives to survive these clowns.

But was he worried?

Hell no.

If the humans survived the next phase, he had hundreds – no, *thousands* – of ways to dispatch them. He had ground assault teams, air assault teams, drones, missiles, lasers – literally limitless ways to snuff them out. Heck, he might even let them survive to the morning. *Why not?* He idly toyed with the beacon in his hand. With ratings this good, why not let the good people of Zil wake up to the best entertainment of their lives?

The Zoo Controller felt replete with joy, power, *gratitude.* He looked again at the beacon in his hand. An hour earlier, one of his team had finally found the fugitives' lair – in a little-used storeroom on the 21st floor. When he heard, he experienced a moment of rage – the fugitives had been operating directly beneath his own control room. The insolent slave from yesterday, the saboteur, had based himself *a few yards below him*. He had felt mocked. Humiliated.

But the anger quickly subsided when he was given their beacon.

He wondered where to leave it. *Here in the VIP suite?* That would be fun. If they tried to teleport back to the Obelisk, they'd find themselves face-to-face with the Regional Governor's son, right here. *Or down in the basement levels?* Probably more sensible. *Why waste time escorting them to the detention cells, when they can fly in themselves?*

Flying. The Zoo Controller's thoughts drifted to the bulk carrier. It was waiting to take off the next morning to commence the mass abduction. *Perfect.* What a perfect time to launch a new park at the zoo. The reception would be ecstatic.

And it was all thanks to these fugitives.

The Zoo Controller, now reclining indulgently on one of the loungers, had his hands behind his head, as he let his daydreams wander. It was late after all – the end of another long day. He turned his head lazily as the door to the VIP suite opened and shut.

Strange, he thought, *why's he down here?*

It was the Duty Manager, his favourite.

Technically, this was a breach of protocol. A Duty Manager should always remain in the control room during a shift. After all, the Zoo Controller was being kept up to date with all developments via his private console. The live feeds from Media, Ops, and Parks were all green. If anything needed to be said, he was contactable.

Ah, to Hell with protocols, the Zoo Controller

thought. He could forget them for one evening. He'd earned it. They both had. The Zoo Controller waved his manager over with bonhomie. It would be nice to have the company of a non-idiot for a while. They could watch the humans' final demise together; have a quiet laugh at the ineptitude of the brats.

The Duty Manager continued walking towards the Controller. His expression gave nothing away. *Why isn't he smiling?* The sheer professionalism of his Duty Manager gave the Zoo Controller his first squirm of unease. A small flutter in the guts. His Caucus reflexes, honed over years of political manoeuvring, started whispering one word.

Trouble.

Reaching him, the Duty Manager leaned over and discreetly delivered into his boss's ear the news that could only be conveyed in person.

And as he whispered, the Zoo Controller's world and life and career started to crumble.

61

Elizabeth held out her hand. Dr James took hold of it and she led him across the Prefect's roof terrace towards the neighbouring roof. Now was the time to follow that last fleeing slave. Now was the time to scramble up the roof tiles towards the ridgeline, the highest point on any of the roofs.

But they weren't going any further than that. The plan was simple. To wait it out up on that ridge. To wait and watch.

After Cerberus' retreat, she and Dr James had dragged the couch and every other bit of furniture across the terrace and blocked the doorway. Elizabeth had reloaded the revolver with the last of the ammunition. Whatever came next up that staircase was going to have to push through a lot of rubbish and – hopefully – offer itself as a clear target in the process.

Elizabeth reached the top of the adjoining roof. She grasped the ridge tiles with both hands and hauled herself onto them. She twisted around through 180 degrees and extended a hand to help Dr James up next to her. The pair now had seven or eight yards of elevation above the terrace. From here they had a clear view of the doorway – the one through which Cerberus had first burst and then retreated – they had a clear view of the street below, a clear view of the sky, a clear view across the town. When she stood up and stretched a little, Elizabeth could even see the forum at the end of the street, and the temple which dominated it.

Elizabeth lowered herself again and carefully slid a yard or two down the far side of the ridgeline. There she lay, chest downwards, head and arms resting on the ridge tiles. She now had a perfect view back down onto the roof terrace. She indicated to Dr James to shift to the same position.

Yes, they were visible. *Exposed.* But Elizabeth figured that, with all the technology around them, they were visible to their enemies wherever they went. The point about this spot, their enemies would be visible to them too.

Elizabeth turned to look at Dr James as he settled into position next to her. She noticed he was shivering. And then she noticed she was too. Probably from the cold – from the sweat drying on them – from the adrenaline sapping – from the shock.

She shuffled a little closer to him and placed her left arm around his shoulders for warmth. It had been about ten minutes since Cerberus had disappeared. Elizabeth turned her head and allowed her eyes to sweep over the roofscape around them. *Just survive*, she repeated to herself, *one minute at a time.*

62

The Zoo Controller sat in front of the Za-Nakarian inspector, doing his best to maintain an even face, while inside his guts were melting.

"Let me get this straight. You're saying this facility covers about 40 square miles?" the Lead Inspector asked.

The Zoo Controller nodded.

"Including towns and villages and parks and agricultural systems."

The Zoo Controller nodded again.

"And that all this is just a... *a theme park,* as you call it. Somewhere visitors can go and see how humans live—"

The Zoo Controller nodded a third time.

"*—but without seeing any real human communities?*"

"Not one," the Zoo Controller replied maintaining the even face. "Because that would be illegal under the Articles of the Intergalactic Council", he added blandly.

The Za-Nakarian leaned across in his aquapod to eyeball the Zoo Controller. "You seriously expect me to believe that you have built a 40 square mile facility dedicated to showcasing the lives of an obscure species from an obscure galaxy, *without abducting a single one of them?*"

"Of course. Because that's the truth."

"And these leaflets that my team picked up—" the inspector waved a flier in the Zailan's face "—these leaflets, which just happen to promise safari rides, fights, torture – *executions.* I suppose they are all just—"

"—re-enactments. Exactly. We couldn't possibly show any real executions because, like I said, that would be illegal." As the Zoo Controller spoke, he even managed to inject a little boredom into his voice – which was quite extraordinary given the fear and fury he was actually feeling. "Of course, you will find *some* humans here. We get visitors from almost every planet, you understand. *Including your own,*" he added with an ingratiating – *sly* – smile. "And for some of the re-enactments, we use human actors. But they're paid. They're free to come and go."

"Actors?"

"Actors." The Controller folded his hands in his lap.

The Lead Inspector looked at him with disdain. "You know that at some point my investigations team will break through your firewall—"

"Not a firewall. A regrettable systems outage. We hope to get the servers back online as soon—"

"—and when they do break through, they'll find the video footage. They'll get to see for themselves what goes on here. The abuse, the executions—"

"Deepfake."

"Excuse me?"

"Naturally we use synthetic media for the more graphic re-enactments," the Controller intoned. "We would never risk the actors being accidentally harmed.

That would be unacceptable. *Immoral*. This is a family park."

"*This is a family park*," the inspector repeated, leaning back in his aquapod, contempt seeping from his voice like battery acid.

"Of course. And I shall be delighted to give you a tour in the morning. I would do it now, but everything is locked dow— Locked *up*. My staff are in bed."

The Zoo Controller was playing for time.

Time – time – *time*.

That's what he needed right now.

That's all he needed.

As soon as his Duty Manager had brought him up to speed on the snap inspection – as soon as he'd seen the aquapods for himself through the window in the door to the control room – he had done the unthinkable.

He had activated Protocol 34.

Never before had it been invoked in the entire history of the zoo. It was a momentous decision to take in a stairwell after only two minutes' consideration.

But that was the whole point about Protocol 34. It was designed to be used in a hurry. Miss your moment, and you might as well forget it. The inspectors would be all over the shop and your backside would be well and truly busted.

Protocol 34.

Step one: cut the video feeds to the control room, lock down the servers. *Done.* Step two: get the academics out of the control tower, down into the tunnels and across to the rallying point. That was priority. Of the three groups of humans in his zoo, they were the only non-brainwashed ones. The ones most likely to blab. Even now – as the Zoo Controller sat there bluffing – his team would be shepherding them into the service elevators. *Good.* Step three: direct the thousand-odd slaves out of their underground dormitories to the same rallying point. This bit was straightforward. In progress already. They just had to be moved from one underground point to another. No-one need know they'd ever existed. *Easy.*

Step four was the big one. The final group of humans. The *zoo inmates.* Any moment, the night shift in the Parks team would play the Protocol-34 pre-recordings from every tannoy in every park. They *had* to get the humans out of the parks – under cover of night – into the tunnels and across to the rallying point.

But it was noisy. Unavoidably so. That's why the Zoo Controller had to keep the inspection team with him in the Obelisk, sealed off from any noise outside.

That's why he was playing for *time.*

"Out of interest, how many inspectors have you brought with you?" the Zoo Controller asked, feigning innocence.

"Enough," the inspector replied, monosyllabic. He saw straight through the question. The question was, the Zoo Controller had to concede, pretty transparent.

He needed to know if there were any other inspectors, snooping about elsewhere. The small inspection team in front of him had all arrived via the zoo's own hyperspaceport. His intel told him that no other Za-Nakarians had passed through that night. *So far.* But you could never be sure. Others might have arrived using a teleportation device. For certain, there would be swarms of them by the morning.

"I ask only so I can alert the hospitality team." The Zoo Controller flashed an unctuous smile. "So they can provide you with food, with accommodation. So they can look after you."

"I thought you said your staff were all in bed?"

Touché. The Zoo Controller smiled back. *Smarmy little shit.*

"In any case," the inspector continued, "there's no immediate need for accommodation. My team here will be working through the night."

The Zoo Controller gave a vague wave of the hand in a gesture of understanding. *Pompous shit too.* What gave the inspector the right to sit there in judgement? He'd seen Za-Nakarians visit the zoo over the years. Not many to be sure, but a steady trickle. They were big spenders too – mostly bored rich kids, as keen as any Caucus Zailan to blow some cash and play god for a couple of hours. Everyone knew about his zoo. *Everyone.* And now it was being turned into a political football? Just like that? Just because some politicians on Za-Nak had got jealous of some politicians on Zil?

The sheer injustice of it tugged at the Zoo Controller's insides. It made him want to scream, to explode, to tell the inspector a few home truths about his own race, *the sanctimonious*— Just for a moment, he fantasised about tipping the inspector's aquapod over and watching him slide helplessly across the floor.

But he reined his thoughts in.

The situation was recoverable. *Just.* It all depended on how well his team remembered the drills. If they could somehow get all the humans to the rallying point... *But how long can I keep 11,000 humans penned together in an underground hangar?*

And then it came to him.

A brainwave.

The underground rallying point was almost directly beneath the bulk carrier. The bulk carrier that was scheduled to depart in the next few hours. It had been fitted out to hold a human cargo. It was suddenly *so obvious.* Kill two birds with one stone. Load the humans onto the bulk carrier – get them into the air – into *space* – get them out of here. At least for a few days, a week or two, until the whole thing quietened down.

I just need to deny them the hard evidence. Any brain-dead moron could tell this was a human zoo. Any half-witted inspector could soon get their hands on the security footage, watch the executions on catch-up. But – as everyone knew – busting an operational zoo was one thing. But busting a place that *used to be* an intelligent zoo... Well, that's different. That's just an anti-climax. Apologies would be made – everyone would *tut-tut* for a while – the issue would fade away.

I just need to deny them the hard evidence. Without that – without any humans – they would be bogged down for days gathering the *forensic* sort instead. And that would provide enough time for the political cover to arrive. *Hopefully.* Some help from the Regional Governor. An intervention from the Supreme Governor, a deal of some sort. This could still be rescued.

He just needed more *time.*

*

And now he had a new worry.

Over the Lead Inspector's shoulder, the Zoo Controller had noticed a single video screen that was still live. About ten inches by eight, it was his personal video feed – a small screen mounted on a small robotic arm next to his desk. *Why's it still on?* the Zoo Controller asked himself. *Of course...* He gave himself an imaginary kick. When the Duty Manager and his team cut the main video feeds, they hadn't cut this one precisely because it was designed never to be cut. It operated on a bombproof backup circuit, intended to give the Controller a visual link to the facility at all times, even if there was a power outage, a power-down, a fire, an earthquake, a plague, *anything*.

At least there's no audio, the Zoo Controller noticed with relief. He glanced at the inspector, who was busy talking to one of his team, and glanced back at the video feed. It was showing one of the cameras in the Classical Park.

In a few minutes it would show a stream of humans – probably distraught, confused and panicking – thundering past.

But right now, it was showing something quite different. To the right of the picture was the row of buildings which included the Prefect's house – in the centre of the frame was the open space of the forum – to the left was the Temple of Jupiter, looking serene under the moonlight.

Now, as he looked, he could see a lone figure running across the forum.

Running – running – *flying*.

It was the Regional Governor's son – or rather his avatar. *The third harpy.*

The Zoo Controller, despite the mess he was in – despite everything – smiled.

63

B O O M

Elizabeth started. *"What is—"*

B O O M

Dr James looked at her. *"I wonder if—"*

B O O M

Silence.

The pair were still lying prone on the roof tiles, looking down onto the Prefect's roof terrace. They glanced at each other. Each *boom* sounded like a thunderclap – but the sound repeated itself too perfectly. The intervals were too regular. This noise didn't come from nature.

But from where then?

In her logical mind, Elizabeth knew the noise was generated by some kind of PA system. But the effect was momentous, thrilling. Like the sound was not generated by individual speakers, but somehow rising from the land itself.

Elizabeth couldn't know it, but the reason the sound

felt like it was coming from all around was because –
in point of fact – it was. Walls and trees and rocks,
connected to the zoo's system, acted like so many
synchronised diaphragms, vibrating in unison and
radiating sound unlike anything ever heard on Earth.

*"ROMANS – PEOPLE – OF –
HERCULANEUM – YOUR – GOD
JUPITER – SPEAKS – TO – YOU.
JUDGEMENT – IS – UPON –
YOU."*

Elizabeth looked again at Dr James and he looked
back. The joy rising in their two hearts was as
synchronised as the sound they were listening to.
Surely this announcement must mean—

*"MAKE – YOUR – WAY – TO –
MY – TEMPLE. MAKE – HASTE –
AND – PRAY – JUDGEMENT – IS
– SWIFT – AND – GENEROUS.
THOSE – LEFT – BEHIND –
WILL – SURELY – BE –
DAMNED."*

Then the message was repeated.
And then—

BOOM

It *was* true.
This could only mean one thing.
The Zailans had activated Protocol 34.
And that in turn must mean Lady Danziger and Sir

Claude and the others had been successful.

They'd done it.

They'd persuaded the Za-Nakarians to visit. To lift the rock under which this zoo had been hiding.

The pair stared at each other. Too stunned to speak or celebrate or even move.

Down in the street, Elizabeth heard the first sounds of reaction filtering up to their rooftop perch. The mirror image of the joy and relief she was feeling. Sounds of distress and disorientation. Shutters flapping open and closed. Doors banging. The clattering of household possessions being grasped and dropped again. Babies crying. A woman started wailing.

Elizabeth stood up. She wanted to peer down into the street. To watch the miracle unfold. Dr James stood up too. After a night of relentless risk, they moved gingerly, checking their weight before each step. After what they'd just survived, neither wanted to end their story with a silly slip on a broken tile.

Peering down, Elizabeth saw the first bewildered figures stepping out into the street. Most were still in nightgowns. One, for no obvious reason, was carrying her bed linen. Elizabeth smiled and nudged Dr James gently and was about to point with her arm.

And then it happens.

*

Elizabeth hears a ferocious shriek and wheels around to look. A third harpy has swept down from above.

They always come in threes.

In a single fluid motion, the creature's talons grasp Dr James by his shoulders and pull him from the roof.

Elizabeth turns and sees Dr James still facing her,

his body hanging from the feet of the harpy. He is disappearing over the roofs, his arms sticking out awkwardly to the side like a scarecrow.

She looks at the revolver in her hand – senses the impossibility of it – and she screams.

All her strength and ferocity and desperation – all the passion she didn't realise she was feeling – is channelled into a single word, a name that she is saying for the first time in her life:

"A R T E M A A A A S !"

And then a small voice.

Amidst the mayhem and the horror, a small voice in her head. *Raise the gun, Elizabeth. It's just another target. Raise the gun.* She wants to argue with it – with herself – but there's no time.

She raises the revolver, her left hand joining her right, half a yard in front of her chin. Past the gun sights, she sees Artemas, trailing beneath the harpy like the tail of a kite – now fifteen yards above the roofs, fifteen yards distant and disappearing fast, rising fast. *But this is* not *just another target*, her mind screams back at herself. This is a moving target, at nighttime, at the end of an exhausting battle.

A bullet first to the wing, the voice says – the other voice. *It's a large target, aim for its wing.*

It's true, the wings *are* a large a target. It calms Elizabeth, this thought. She lines up her shot and…

She fires.

Elizabeth sees the harpy react – and then a shriek reaches her ears. The right wing has been hit.

But it's not fatal. She's still flying and she's still holding Dr James in her claws.

With her wings now beating arrhythmically, the harpy is spiralling in mid-air. She's no longer flying forward, in fact she's starting to lose height, yard by yard. *If they land on the roof below, what will she do to Artemas?* This thought pollutes and panics Elizabeth's mind. She remembers the vicious power of a harpy's claws.

She knows she needs to take a second shot – to the harpy's body – but she hesitates. She can't do it. She can't risk hitting Artemas.

And then the voice again.

For a moment, there is stillness in her mind. She's back on Ormilu. With Sir Claude. The lesson. *You have to believe, Elizabeth*, the voice says. *The bullet and the harpy belong together, they deserve each other. Believe it. See it.*

And Elizabeth does start to see it.

She lines up the front and rear sight of the revolver with the small, indistinct shape of the harpy's body as it descends erratically towards the rooftops. She holds her breath. She holds her body. She wills every fibre to stillness – until the only motion in her universe is the infinitesimal shifting of the revolver's barrel, tracking this shape downwards. She squeezes the trigger—

C R A C K

Another shriek.

Harpy and man fall entwined, through ten yards of air. There's a sickening thump as they hit the roof tiles, some thirty yards away – accompanied by another shriek of pain.

This time, the cry is human.

64

Control.

That's what he lived for.

And now, as in a nightmare, it deserts him.

As the Zoo Controller starts to shuffle out of his own control room in his own control tower, he is experiencing a total loss of it.

Control.

As he passes by the equipment, he wants to reach out to pull the familiar levers, press the responsive buttons – to command legions and change destinies. All of it so close to his touch.

But so far from his reach.

His arms are bound behind his back. Marshals he doesn't recognise walk on every side of him. His movements aren't his own. His decisions aren't his own. He is underwater. He is being carried along by the flood. Everything he passes swims and dances in his vision, remote, untouchable.

The reversal in his fortunes has overwhelmed his mental systems.

It will take him weeks in a Za-Nakarian detention cell to process how so much could go wrong so quickly. How the Za-Nakarians did indeed send a second inspection team and found the underground hangar to which he'd sent all the human inmates. How the Supreme Governor on Zil did indeed a strike an emergency deal with the Za-Nakarian inspectors, but one that sacrificed the zoo in order to protect Zil's political priorities – entry to the IGC. How his zoo was finished, how his career was over, and how the remainder of his life would be spent in prison. Behind bars. Behind *walls*.

But these reflections would be for later. Right now, his mind is elsewhere, fixating on something it can grasp. On the fugitives. The slaves who have outwitted him.

As he passes by his personal video feed – the one screen that is still working in the control room – he sees the female fugitive clambering across the rooftops. She reaches the fallen harpy. The harpy is inert – *dead.* But the male fugitive, the one the harpy was carrying is... *alive.* The fallen fugitive is on his feet now. He seems to be holding one arm with the other. *Is it maybe broken?* Like an addict, the Controller's mind grasps for the faintest evidence of misfortune. But the satisfaction is fleeting. The injury to the fugitive's arm is minor. He sees the two humans, the male and the female, embracing.

It is over.

*

Elizabeth has folded her arms around Artemas. With a hushed, wordless tenderness, she has cleaved him to her. Cheek against cheek, chest against chest. There is no dissembling now about her feelings. Not to herself. Nor to anyone else.

403

She can feel Artemas' right arm bound around her waist. His left arm – the injured one – hangs at his side. She still watches the skies, Elizabeth. She knows Artemas is too. But deep down inside, she *knows*. They both know.

Elizabeth starts to withdraw. Very slowly – as if opening the most precious present she has ever been given – she unwraps her arms from Artemas. She looks at his face to see how much pain he is in. But on his features, she sees his timeless smile has returned and knows that he is alright.

She looks beyond his shoulder. She can see the Temple of Jupiter. In the light of Zil's four moons, its high, pillared portico looks resplendent – like an immutable dream untouched by the restless, mad reality of the night's events.

She shifts her gaze. She sees townsfolk streaming, antlike, along the street below, towards the forum. Her ears pick up the sound of their panic. The commotion of the world below reaches her again on the rooftops.

Elizabeth is not going to cry. She controls her breathing. She stills her heart rate. And when Artemas asks if they should move, her voice is calm as she directs them back over the roofs to the Prefect's house. But tears slide down her cheeks anyway; small translucent droplets that clear quiet channels through the dust on her skin.

The pair pick their way back to the roof terrace – over the tiles and ridges, back along the valleys and gutters. They reach the terrace and cross it, passing the stricken body of the second harpy. They head through the small doorway, down the narrow wooden staircase where they last saw Cerberus, and back into the Prefect's house.

The house is in commotion.

Stripped of their servants and slaves, the Prefect's family have emerged from their hiding place and are running from room to room, grasping possessions, dropping them to grasp other possessions, panicking. They don't even see Elizabeth and Artemas.

The pair make their way to one of the bedrooms. There Elizabeth finds fabric to make a sling for his injured arm. They continue their journey. They make their way down the staircase and back into the atrium. They see the front door, flat on the vestibule floor, its timbers clawed and splintered. They see the open doorway and – through it – the river of terrified Romans washing past.

The pair pause. They are wary. They are wary of the panicking townsfolk. They are wary of Cerberus or another harpy or whatever else might be thrown at them. But deep down inside, they *know*.

They know their ordeal is finished.

It is over.

65

The preceding hour etched itself into Elizabeth's memory. Years later she would be able to pick out each detail from her memory – turn it round in her thoughts – and put it back in its precise place, the order of events undisturbed. Horrific details, yes, but not just horrific. She felt like Fate – or the Zailans – or whatever force one might care to call it – had hurled her first one way and then another, but ultimately had thrown her and Dr James together. And that had added another tint to the adventure. Tinged it with a golden light.

The next hour, by contrast, would remain forever an indistinct blur.

As the adrenaline ebbed and safety beckoned, her passage through the underworld of the zoo became a distorted smudge of impressions – a painting in which the colours have run.

There was the moonlit flight to the Temple of Jupiter, amidst the heaving, panicking population of New Herculaneum. There was the crowd in front that held them back, and the crowd behind that pressed them forward. Elizabeth vaguely recalled passing up the front steps, under the classical portico, whose calm serenity she had admired just a few minutes before, and into the inner sanctum, its tranquility now violated by the urgent press of bodies.

And there was the sheer inevitability of it all. No choice, only one way to go. A vast tide of souls in motion, pressing and pressing. She couldn't have gone a different way if she had tried. Yard by yard, she shuffled forward, flotsam on a tide of floodwater. She felt the crowd trying pull her and Dr James apart. But she didn't let them. The one choice she seemed able to make in the otherwise ineluctable motion of events. She clung to him and he to her, his right hand always in her left. Together, they approached the airlock. Both pairs of doors had been thrown completely open, thank God (or the Zailans). They passed through the airlock that was no longer an airlock in the temple that was barely a temple. Then they were in the grey concrete passageways beneath the zoo again – illuminated arrows on the tunnel walls directing them where to go.

And there was the strange equality of it too. Stripped of their weapons, without food or money or even identity, they were swept along with prefects and peasants, Bornean tribesmen and Japanese warriors, Christians and Muslims, towards their shared endpoint.

She could dimly recollect the same emotions playing out across all the many and varied faces. Mixed together – *thrust* together – in the dead of night, for an event they had all separately been warned about, but none had truly expected, they looked at each other with disbelief and fear and – given the sheer incomprehensibility of it all – wonder too. There were gasps and wailing, some voices were ululating, others sobbing. A few were singing.

After trudging what felt like miles – what *was* miles – Elizabeth would later remember spilling out into a vast underground hangar. A holding pen, in which all the races and peoples mingled and shivered and wailed and prayed. They were all looking to their different mythologies for guidance and the mythologies, in all their colour and variety, all pointed by different means to the same thing: that a moment of judgement had come.

To Elizabeth, of course, it was just *Protocol 34* – a panicked response by the psychopathic owners of a quite unconscionable zoo.

But, to her horror and dismay, there was a judgement to be made – not exactly the judgement of God, selecting souls for damnation and salvation – but almost. At the time it felt more like a decision than a judgement. And it was one that would have to be made by Elizabeth and her friends.

The pair muscled forward through the distressed horde, their wretched and ragged condition provoking gasps of fear and parting the crowd in front of them. At the front of the hangar, they reached some kind of barrier. Here the abiding memory was the disarray of the Zailan zookeepers on the far side. If they were supposed to be the guardians of the gateway to Heaven in this strange Passion play, they were making a poor fist of it. They looked as traumatised as the souls they stood before. And then behind the line of gatekeepers, some other alien race. A series of figures – perhaps a half-dozen – riding in contraptions that looked like… Well, large bins on wheels.

And then Elizabeth sees them. Beyond the barrier.

Sir Claude and Lady Danziger.

They're smiling at her. Just like the first time she saw them together, that night on Cleremont Avenue. A single harmonised force, powerful and quite irresistible, welcoming her and Dr James back from the jaws of Hell.

There is a shout. A greeting. An almost unbelievable rush of relief that briefly, like a rogue wave, overruns the harbour wall of fatigue Elizabeth feels. Hands reach out to hands over the top of the barrier, awkwardly – a clatter of strangely antique-looking keys – a gate opens before them and closes behind – and then they are through. Lady Danziger is throwing her arms around her and Dr James. She feels Sir Claude's hand on her shoulder. She glimpses Juckes – Setiawan – and sees they are smiling.

Elizabeth and Dr James have left the realm of the zoo inmates on one side of the barrier and joined the realm of the zookeepers on the other. More than that, they are reunited with their friends who – in the strangest reversal of all – somehow seem to be directing events.

They are safe.

The nightmare is over.

But the judgement is still to be made.

66

Lady Danziger, Sir Claude, and their three companions had arrived from Zil two hours earlier.

Travelling on the steps, Lady Danziger had set the coordinates to land inside the bulk carrier. The beacon, which Juckes had secreted there, guided them in.

Minutes after they had landed, a Za-Nakarian intervention team followed them in on a teleportation device of their own. The Za-Nakarians had wasted no time making their authority known and set about taking command of the vessel from a profoundly startled captain and his crew.

And they immediately alerted the Lead Inspector, who was over in the control tower – the Obelisk – interviewing the Zoo Controller.

The quickest of searches revealed the human cargo they were expecting to find. Down in the hold of the bulk carrier, they found that the Zailans had already embarked their 'high value assets'. The academics. Moving lower through the carrier, they found human slaves. Hundreds of them in the process of being embarked. Just as Elizabeth had predicted, the Zailans were going to use the bulk carrier to 'hide' the evidence of their zoo.

And then, pursuing the evidence trail further and

lower, the inspectors found the hangar beneath the carrier. For the inspection team, this was far from being their first bust. But none of them had blown open an intelligent zoo of this scale before. Here in the hangar, they found thousands upon thousands of inmates – of varied races, cultures, age and gender. They knew the Lead Inspector needed hard evidence. Well, this evidence was diamond-hard and, cameras in hand, they beamed it across to him.

And so they came to the judgement.

*

Sir Claude and Lady Danziger had already had a discussion with the Za-Nakarian inspection team about the 'after game' as they called it. How to dismantle the zoo. *Whether* to dismantle the zoo. There were two very different options. The decision was always left with the victim species.

Lady Danziger explained it to Elizabeth and Dr James as calmly as she could. *The Za-Nakarians have experience.* They had busted several dozen intelligent zoos in recent centuries. The biggest issue was always how to handle the inmates. And for this, they had developed an off-the-shelf solution – provided everyone was in agreement.

At this point, Elizabeth was starting to chafe. Her emotions were overwhelmed on every front – she was running on fumes – she was wondering what there was to discuss. The plan had worked, they should embark all the humans into the bulk carrier, *and go home.*

Lady Danziger politely agreed that that remained the default option. The other option looked very different.

411

The guiding principle of the Za-Nakarian team: only repatriate those with a living memory of their original world. For any community held for more than a generation: it could be more cruel to return them to a changed world than to leave them in their unchanged one within the zoo.

Under this option, the zoo would be passed to IGC supervision. All degrading punishments would be banned, along with all visitors, media channels, merchandising and other forms of exploitation. The host planet, as punishment for this violation of intergalactic law, would have to maintain the facility *ad infinitum*, at their own expense. A living deterrent to anyone thinking of setting up their own intelligent zoo.

Sir Claude and Lady Danziger, to their own astonishment, had found themselves backing the Za-Nakarian view. *The inmates should stay*. All the other humans – the academics, the slaves – should be embarked, but not the zoo inmates. They should be led back to their respective parks, back to their respective worlds. And left alone.

Elizabeth had shouted, she had cried, she had – so she was later told – even screamed at Sir Claude at one point. She couldn't accept it – she wouldn't accept it. That they should be left in such a cursed existence.

"But they're *happy*. You said so yourself, Elizabeth."

"The Roman Prefect and his family, yes. But what about the others? We have no idea. And the peasants in the Medieval Park – they looked *miserable*."

"You don't know that. Subjectively, maybe they are miserable. In which case, you can bet your bottom dollar that moving them won't help. But *objectively*... Think about it – if they stay here, they'll live in a world without disease – without want or famine. And under IGC supervision, it'll get *better*. It'll become a world without torture, wild beasts, or tourists."

"I don't care. We cannot knowingly leave humans behind *on another planet*."

"Then try to imagine taking them with us. Imagine re-introducing the Borneans to their forest island that's being stripped of its forest? Imagine returning Romans to a city that's been stripped of its empire? The Christians to a country that's been stripped of its Christianity? The Muslims to a world where they won the crusades and lost the peace? How could that possibly make them happy? The world has changed beyond all recognition and they won't have the chance to adapt."

In the end, she had turned to Dr James.

They all did.

For no reason any of them could put their finger on, they agreed he should have the final word – and make the final judgement.

He looked back at their anxious faces, his own face calm and unwavering.

"If you gave me the chance," he'd said simply, "I'd stay here. In the Classical Park, I fancy, *hmm?* But some of the other parks look rather tempting too."

And then Elizabeth had said she'd sooner kill him than leave him behind and started beating with her fists against his chest in a fury of confusion and affection, before collapsing against it.

And so the judgement was made.

The inmates would stay.

*

Lady Danziger was able to convey the judgement to the Lead Inspector in person.

He and his team had just come over from the Obelisk, bringing four captives with them. They had brought the captives to the underground hangar to confront them with the evidence – the *human* evidence – of their crimes. Now they could see the thousands of zoo inmates wailing and praying, perhaps they might want to change their statements prior to being charged?

It was a memorable moment. Watching the Zailans – heads hung low, arms manacled – being brought face to face with their guilt. For Lady Danziger, it brought to mind photos of Nuremberg. But what she most remembered about this moment wasn't the manacles or the underground hangar or memories of the war. It was her butler. The look on Juckes' face. The man was staring intently at one of the captives.

And that same captive was staring back.

Juckes' face was calm, motionless, inscrutable. On the captive's face, though, emotions flickered across his mobile features like a restless flame. Lady Danziger thought she saw anger – fear – disbelief. Perhaps even admiration.

"Who is that?" she asked.

"The boss, ma'am. The controller of this facility."

"The one who…" Lady Danziger glanced down at Juckes' ankle.

"Yes."

Lady Danziger nodded slowly. "And the other three prisoners – who are they?"

"Don't know, ma'am. I'm sorry."

Lady Danziger approached the Lead Inspector. The inspector explained the other three were zoo guests. They had been caught terrorising the humans in the

Classical Park from one of the so-called 'VIP suites'. They'd been using fighting avatars – *harpies apparently* – which, at that moment, made no sense at all to Lady Danziger.

*

It made sense to Elizabeth, though.

As she watched her tormentors begin the long process of facing justice, the small knot of incomprehension within her started to unravel. Seeing the controller of the facility being frog-marched away to a life behind bars – *behind walls* – gave her the first inkling that perhaps they had made the right judgement. Perhaps the zoo would become a better place and the zoo inmates better off within it.

A short while later, she and her friends embarked on the bulk carrier, the last to do so, and the vast cargo bay doors were sealed shut behind them. The bulk carrier lifted off from Zil, and Elizabeth sank into the deepest sleep of her life.

67

Sir Claude was cooking again and Elizabeth found herself – again – in the unlikely role of chef's assistant. Lady Danziger was with her too, providing a welcome ally.

They were back at Number 55 Cleremont Avenue and down in the kitchens on the lower ground floor. As she passed Sir Claude a colander brim-full of vegetables, her mind tripped lightly over a thought: it was exactly the same time of day as when she had first arrived on Cleremont Avenue.

Then, a storm was brewing, and the wind had all but blown her through the front door.

Now, a beautiful low sun was bathing the house in light.

She couldn't see the street, the windows were set too high in the walls. But the evening sun flooded in above their heads, illuminating the space in a luminous, chalky golden light.

The kitchens were open plan and roomy, with pillars here and there, shelves stacked with crockery, great wooden sideboards and a great wooden table, piled high with produce. All the equipment and all the fittings were old-fashioned, of course, but clean and well cared for and built to last a thousand years.

It turned out that they had developed a little tradition at Number 55. After each adventure, there would be a celebratory dinner and – for one evening only – roles would be reversed. Sir Claude and his family cooked and served, while the staff were waited on.

Elizabeth noticed the staff hadn't taken many risks, mind. Much of the dinner was already prepared – the vegetables peeled, the potatoes scrubbed, the pie prepped.

Elizabeth felt an unexpected lightness within her. A lightness in her tread, and in her mind. Behind her, on Zil, lay pain and confusion and fatigue. Ahead of her, on Earth, lay more turmoil – *emotional* turmoil – there could be no doubt about that.

But right now was right now. Elizabeth was holding shut the doors to the past and the future, to regret and to worry. She was enjoying being alive in this present moment as only someone who has confronted death can.

And so this feeling – whatever it was – couldn't be denied. This *lightness.* She felt that if someone asked her to dance right then, she'd swing them off their feet. And if they didn't ask her, she might do it anyway.

Dr James was sitting at the large kitchen table, humming to himself, looking as reliably happy as he always did. His left arm was now in plaster and supported by a much tidier sling than the one Elizabeth had fashioned for him on a rooftop one unbelievable day ago and many unbelievable galaxies away.

She smiled at him, as she reached for a tea towel. She couldn't help it.

If she had been expecting her feelings for him to diminish, now they were back in London and he was

417

back in tweeds, then she'd been mistaken.

She stopped for a moment to imagine him in 1940. He must have sat in that exact spot, watching Mrs Carstairs bustle around him. A young schoolboy, sheltering from an infernal boarding school and from a war that was still raging. She could understand now how he might have healed here. It made sense.

"Come on, Elizabeth, don't dawdle!" There was a twinkle in Sir Claude's eye, as he barked. "We'll be serving in a few minutes. Here, take this to the dumbwaiter."

"Leave the poor girl alone, you big bully," Lady Danziger chided. "Elizabeth, let me show you."

Elizabeth was now holding a large bowl of new potatoes, as Lady Danziger gently guided her by the elbow through the kitchens. "Tell me this," Lady Danziger asked as they walked. "However did you come up with the plan to rescue the whole zoo? It was so audacious—"

"No! It was simple. It was the corral, of course."

Lady Danziger tilted her head to one side, not understanding.

"Outside the folly. There was a corral where the shepherds could gather their sheep – to protect them from wolves." Elizabeth paused to let Lady Danziger pass through a doorway first. "Artemas did all the hard work really," she resumed. "Translating the zookeeper's manual. Once we knew they had a protocol to gather all the humans into a single location, I just had to figure out what could possibly make them do that?"

"I think I get it… You'd probably already learnt that Za-Nak was wary of Zil…" Lady Danziger spoke slowly as she re-traced Elizabeth's thought processes.

"You knew Za-Nak didn't want to admit them to the IGC?" Elizabeth nodded. "And you knew that, according to the laws of the IGC, the zoo was technically *illegal?*"

"Right again."

"So you figured that a snap inspection of the zoo would trigger Protocol 34 and—"

"—all the humans would be rounded up into one place. Just like sheep into a corral!"

"I see it now, it's so obvious!" The two women smiled. They were standing, paused, next to the dumbwaiter.

"And, of course," Elizabeth concluded, "with that enormous spaceship just sitting there, the bulk carrier, it seemed inevitable they'd try to embark the humans on it. Get them out the way. It's what I would've done."

Elizabeth loaded the food into the small elevator as Lady Danziger shook her head in happy disbelief.

*

It had been a whirlwind of a day.

Absurd as it already seemed to Elizabeth, they had returned from Zil just that morning. The bulk carrier had emerged from hyperdrive into a near-Earth orbit and Elizabeth, having travelled across who-knew-how-many galaxies nor how many dimensions, had awoken from her sleep.

The first stop was Cleremont Avenue for a quick change of clothes. From there, she and Sir Claude made their way straight to C, her boss. They needed to report back and they needed to engage the authorities. Fast. Even if the zoo inmates had been left behind, they were still returning over a thousand abductees: the traumatised and the brainwashed.

But while the conversation with C and Sir Claude occupied Elizabeth's head, something very different took hold of her body. Rising tension – rising emotion. Her husband was based in this building, same as her. Would she bump into him in one of the corridors? Perhaps in the entrance lobby? If not, she'd have to try to call. Perhaps he would be back at his flat? Or even *their* flat?

Towards the end of the meeting C had interrupted the dialogue. He had a way of knowing what people were thinking, C. It was his job after all. "Charles is away on assignment, Elizabeth," he'd said. "Middle East. A week – possibly longer. Quite uncontactable I'm afraid."

"I understand, sir."

"Elizabeth – would you excuse Sir Claude and me for a few minutes? I have a couple of private matters to raise with him."

"Of course."

It was kind of C. It was his way of giving her space, she knew that.

She quickly sought out her own office, almost running to it. Alone inside, Elizabeth didn't know what to think. Here in the building she shared with her husband. Where so many things reminded her of him. *Of them.* She felt relief – and shame – and love – and desolation. All at once. She started sobbing. That door in her mind, the one behind which she had placed her marriage, had burst open and the gale was blowing in. And, this time, she let it blow. She let the thoughts flood in like rainwater. *The future.* Charles' pain – his family's dismay – her mother's disapproval. But as the anxieties paraded past her, there was never any doubt in her mind. Change was coming to her life. Change *had already come.*

And then – as minutes passed – her tears diminished. Composure returned, bearing a single, simple thought. *Judgement has been made*, the thought said. *The decision has been taken.* The trial separation would be permanent. It was always going to be permanent. They'd used the word 'trial' to lessen the pain, to move by degrees – she could see that now.

A wave of relief washed through her. There would still be so much to say, so much to confront, but the way forward was clear. The path was steep and difficult, but it was a path. And so a huge, crushing weight, which Elizabeth hadn't even realised she had been carrying, started to lift.

She got up from her desk. She started to tidy herself in front of the small mirror by the coat pegs. Her steps felt light, her head clear. As she dried the tears from her eyes, another thought ran round and round her mind. *Maybe it's meant to happen this way*, this second thought told her. *Maybe you're meant to have another week.*

She went back to re-join Sir Claude and C. Her nose was mostly dry, her eyes only a little bloodshot, a composed smile on her face.

Sir Claude and C welcomed her back. And then – in a motion that ripped all thoughts and feelings from Elizabeth's mind – the three of them were catapulted into a frantic round of shuttling across Whitehall.

*

The main dilemma was clear.

421

The abductees couldn't just be sent home. Some of them didn't even have homes. And all of them needed to be debriefed, de-programmed, re-acclimatised.

There were discussions about where to accommodate the returning humans. Logistics came up – *a lot* – as air bases on remote island archipelagos were identified and debated. There were discussions about how to debrief the abductees – how to inform their families – how to maintain secrecy. But as the discussions wore on, and as more military personnel joined the conversation, along with psychologists, planners, and other experts, so – bit by bit – there had been less and less need for either Elizabeth or Sir Claude.

To her own surprise, Elizabeth didn't mind being sidelined. She quickly tired of the busy, self-important people she was encountering, who – on learning the great secret – seemed to become increasingly busy and self-important. She started comparing them unfavourably in her mind with Dr James who, in his childishness, seemed infinitely more grown-up. And she found that all she wanted to do was to get back to Cleremont Avenue. To see him and to feel his eyes upon her.

And so towards late afternoon, she and Sir Claude had quietly – unnoticed – peeled away from the proceedings and returned to Number 55.

68

And so here Elizabeth was, in the kitchens under 55 Cleremont Avenue, putting the finishing touches to dinner.

And somewhere in the sunlight of her mind a little cloud of confusion was starting to form.

Dr James and Lady Danziger had both disappeared upstairs. Perhaps to stand at the receiving end of the dumbwaiter, but she wasn't sure. Sir Claude, meanwhile, had disappeared down into the basement – *how big was this house, actually?* – saying he needed to fetch the wine. But that had been minutes ago.

Alone in a strange kitchen, Elizabeth was feeling, frankly, abandoned.

The final item to take upstairs was the main course. She carried the huge pie to the dumbwaiter, carefully placed it inside, closed the hatch, pressed a button and dispatched it upwards.

She was now at the foot of the stairs. She caught sight of herself in a full-length mirror. She was wearing a dress that Lady Danziger had lent her – it fitted perfectly, hugging the contours of her body. In a self-conscious gesture, her hands moved to smooth it down over her hips, and then she set off up the wide, windowless staircase.

At the top of the stairs, she turned left and passed into the butler's pantry. There was no sign of the butler in his pantry, nor Lady Danziger, nor anybody else. She peered into the dumbwaiter and saw the pie sitting there patiently.

Tutting ever so slightly to herself, Elizabeth reached in and pulled it out. She carried it towards the large, padded swing door that led into the dining room. She turned around, placed her backside to the door, and pushed her way through backwards.

"For she's a jolly good fel-low..."

She was in the dining room.

And confused again.

There must have been a dozen and a half people. They already seemed to be half drunk—

"For she's a jolly good fel-low..."

—and singing.

She placed the pie down on the table, dazed, mechanical.

"For she's a jolly good fe-el-looooow..."

And then she realised they were singing about *her.*

"And so say all of us!"

Lady Danziger, mid-song, gestured her towards the spare seat next to her. In a trance, Elizabeth obeyed.

"And so say all of us,
And so say all of us..."

Dr James was on her other side. All three were sitting with their back to the windows.

"For she's a jolly good fel-low..."

And on and on.

The whole room was in uproar, singing and banging the table. As she looked around it, she noticed that no-one was sitting at the head – both ends were clear. In between, a jumble of faces flashed before her disorientated mind. Sir Claude was on the opposite side, a few places away, orchestrating the singalong. Dr Setiawan was directly opposite her. She saw three or four faces she didn't recognise and Daniels, the maid, and Miss Wainwright, Dr Setiawan's maid, and Juckes and Nussbaum. The whole shooting match.

It was all so hard to process. Her mind catapulted back, involuntarily, to her first dinner here – a nightmare of stiff formality and staccato conversation. And now… As she looked around the table she saw revelry, celebration, delight.

The singing stopped. Sir Claude was already on his feet. He clinked his glass.

It took some while for the table to come to order.

"My friends, I propose a toast—"

"Aren't toasts supposed to be done at the end of the meal, darling?"

"Ah yes, Adelaide…" Sir Claude raised his voice to speak over the renewed table-banging. "But this is a night of reversals. And anyway, I want to propose this toast while I'm still capable. Now – you all see before you Elizabeth Belfort…" Sir Claude gestured towards her, as Dr Setiawan of all people gave a wolf whistle. "This is the young lady who was sent some days ago to this very house to abduct me—"

"Abduct you? You ended up abducting *me!*" Elizabeth retorted in a flash. The table shook with laughter and Sir Claude's face flushed.

"*Touché!*" He turned to the rest of the company, one arm stretched theatrically towards Elizabeth, palm open. "You can all see now why I was so intimidated by this lady when I first met her—"

"*Rubbish!*" several voices called out, including his wife's.

"—and, frankly, still am! Anyway, to the point. Please could you all raise your glasses to our intrepid, fearless and quite indispensable explorer. To the instigator of the cunningest plan we ever did have. To the newest member of our team, to Eli—" Sir Claude corrected himself. "To *Mrs B!*"

The name *Mrs B* echoed round the table, as the assembled throng drank and Sir Claude sat back down.

Carried along by the next round of shouting, and with two hands at her back pressing her forward, Elizabeth found herself on her feet. She was supposed to reply. Now everyone was looking at her. A respectful quiet crept into the merriment. Elizabeth found the hush more intimidating than the hollering.

"Thank you for your kind words, Sir Claude..." Elizabeth started, wondering where she would go next.

Then she decided to just say it how it was and lodged her accent firmly north of the border. "You know, when I first arrived here, I feared I'd been sent to bring in a chauvinistic, misogynistic old dinosaur..."

The room went quiet. Elizabeth pressed on regardless.

"But then, as I got to know Sir Claude better," she continued, "I realised *those were his good points.*"

The stillness of the room dissolved into a bellowing clamour. Elizabeth had found the right tone. She had found the right audience. She had found the right everything.

She didn't remember what else she said. As she sat back down afterwards, Lady Danziger touched her arm.

"Wonderful speech. You know," Lady Danziger spoke into her ear, competing with the din in the room, "when you first arrived here, I did think you a terrible stiff."

Elizabeth laughed.

"It's only fair, I was a bit... *uptight*," Elizabeth replied. "But to be honest, "I thought—"

"—that I was too?"

"*Yes!*"

They both giggled, like old friends.

"Sir Claude and I..." Lady Danziger's face assumed a more serious expression as she spoke. "We're really very grateful to you, Elizabeth. For looking after Artemas. If you hadn't been there... He wouldn't have had a chance." Elizabeth flushed. Dr James was just the other side of her. *Can he hear?*

And then – unexpectedly – Lady Danziger placed one hand on Elizabeth's. She spoke again, no louder nor quieter. "You know you're exactly what Artemas needs, Elizabeth. *You'll be perfect for him.*"

Lady Danziger immediately turned away and started chatting to someone several places away, leaving Elizabeth flushed and confused – all the more so, when she saw Dr James was looking at her.

Did he hear?

An ornery instinct in Elizabeth sent her on the attack. "It wasn't a great advert for God, was it?" She spoke abruptly, not quite sure where she had dragged that thought from.

"Excuse me?"

"The zoo, I mean," Elizabeth clarified. *He can't really have heard, can he?*

"*Hmm?* How do you mean?"

"The way the zookeepers, invisible to humans... The way they treated the humans. Didn't it remind you of Fate? *Of God?*"

"Ah yes, yes. But *no*. I don't think it did. We must

remember, Mrs B, it was just a zoo."

"*Still*... The zoo kind of goes to the essence of that problem you study. You know, theodicy?" Elizabeth was starting to regret her confrontational tone. *So what if he did hear?*

"That's right. Theodicy. How to justify a loving God in a world of suffering."

"Yes – *that*." She softened her tone. "But what if God isn't loving? What if... What if God is *like the Zailans?*"

"But Mrs B" – Dr James lowered his glasses to look at her over the top of them – "God *is* loving."

Elizabeth looked back at him. Something about the way he looked at her over his spectacles left a hole in her stomach. It always had done. Since the very first time. "Alright, alright. Just supposing that's true..." *Actually, I hope he did hear. I truly hope he did.* "But I'd still like to know. How *do* you deal with the problem of evil? Do *you* have an answer? A justification for God?"

"Oh yes, I think so."

"Oh." Elizabeth was happily flummoxed. "Wonderful. Will you tell it to me one day?"

"I'd be delighted."

And they sat in companionable silence. Elizabeth didn't want to hear it now. In her head, she was imagining they would have all the time in the world to discuss that – and everything else. And whether that would prove to be the case or not, the mere thought of it felt wonderful.

Elizabeth's eyes swept around the table again, a little calmer this time. She saw Sir Claude regaling the young footmen and maids around him with the tales of their adventure. A little further down the table, Juckes and Miss Wainwright were locked together in a quiet conversation that had just a hint of promise. And opposite her, next to Dr Setiawan, Mrs Carstairs was looking at her through kind watery eyes, smiling.

*

The rest of the evening passed in a haze of wine and good humour. As the outdoor light faded to darkness, toasts continued to be parried across the candlelight. Lady Danziger toasted Dr Nussbaum for not quite killing her with the fire-axe. In reply, Dr Nussbaum toasted her for freeing his mind by means of 500 volts. Dr Setiawan toasted his maid, Miss Wainwright, and the others for keeping the homefires burning.

And then, music.

Next door, in the main hallway, Sir Claude had wheeled out his gramophone and music was playing. He stepped back into the dining room, announced that their revels were now starting in earnest, and approached Mrs Carstairs for the first dance. The poor lady was still protesting as he led her away.

And so the dancing started. The house that had seemed so stiff and stuck-up when Elizabeth first arrived now seemed unbuttoned and bohemian. Between the orchids and the pot plants and the wooden panelling and the ancestral suit of armour, they danced and twirled and span around the main hall. All of them did, all except Dr James, whose arm was bound up and whose legs probably weren't the dancing kind anyway. The music never got past 1955, and the dancing never got more modern than lindy hop and Elizabeth liked it that way. She danced with Sir Claude, she danced with Juckes – when he wasn't spinning Miss Wainwright round the floor – and she danced with a footman whose name she learnt and then forgot again. She even did a spin with Lady Danziger.

Boundaries were dissolving. Elizabeth felt as if the gap between them all had been shrinking and shrinking all evening. In their conversation, in their dancing, they were flowing into one. It must be the wine of course, Elizabeth thought. And the excitement of the adventure just undertaken. And maybe love. From where she was spinning round the hallway, Elizabeth looked across to Dr James. *Yes, love.*

And something else besides. Elizabeth tried to put her finger on it. *Something else besides.*

She felt supple and fit and alive. She wanted eyes to be upon her, to be admired. She felt attractive. It was one of the few moments in her life she understood how a woman could become addicted to the feeling, why some of her friends fussed so much with make-up and shoes and handbags. But it wasn't any pair of eyes she wanted to attract. *Just his.* If he had seen it, it had happened; if he hadn't, it hadn't. After each spin on the dancefloor, she glanced towards him to check he was still there and still watching – with his happy, slightly vacant, slightly mysterious, impossible-to-grasp gaze.

Until at some moment, late into the night, he wasn't there. And at that moment, even though the music was still playing and the wine was still flowing, the light – for Elizabeth – had gone out.

And she slipped quietly away.

69

Elizabeth was back in her old room, overlooking the conservatory.

A nightgown and slippers had been laid out for her, just like last time. And an oil lamp was burning quietly on the dressing table – just like last time.

She checked the switch and found the electric light in perfect working order. She smiled to herself – the oil lamp was probably Daniels' sense of humour – and switched the electric light off again anyway.

She breathed in deeply. The room still had that faint guest-bedroom mustiness, it still had the crazy wonderful view of the conservatory outside. It was still perfect.

Before she pulled the curtains shut, she noticed the two cockatoos were on the same perch. The large black palm cockatoo with the red cheeks that might live to a hundred years and, just nearby, the smaller white cockatoo with the red crest.

So much was the same as last time. So much had changed in between.

She wasn't yet ready to reflect about that in-between. That could come later. Right now, she was living through a night that wasn't ready to end.

She slipped out of her clothes and laid them over the

back of the chair. She unclipped her bra, she pulled off her underwear and her stockings. She caught sight of her body in the dressing table mirror. She stopped for a moment. Looking down at herself, she could see a library of bruises, cuts and abrasions. She had taken a battering the last few days. But looking in the clouded mirror, by the light of an oil lamp, she didn't see blemishes. She saw a body toned by exercise, athletic and young.

She slipped her nightgown on and sat at the dressing table. She started to brush her hair. She felt... *young*. She thought to herself, *My Goodness, I'm actually young.* She laughed for a moment at the ridiculousness of thinking this. At the ridiculousness of *not* thinking this.

All the seriousness was sloughing away like an old skin. She felt that if friends asked her to join them for a day at the beach, or an evening at the pictures, she'd say yes without hesitation.

Which made sense, because spontaneity was exactly what she had in mind.

She felt nervous and excited. Any other time in her life, she'd pause and equivocate and think and probably delay. She'd fixate on all the reasons not to do what she was about to do. But her mind was made up. It had been made up since that unrepeatable moment on a distant rooftop, when she had watched her future almost being snatched away from her. There would be no more dissembling. The truth of who she was, who she was meant to be with, and what she had to do was clear to her.

The last few days had given her a lot of practice at overcoming fear, at moving forward, at seizing her only moment. Elizabeth felt no doubts at all. Not the slightest one.

She laid her brush to one side. She picked up the lamp and went quietly to the door. She opened it a fraction and listened. It was dark and quiet beyond.

Wearing just her nightgown, she slipped into the corridor, closing the door behind her.

Her heart was beating fast again – like the last time she had slipped into this corridor at night. The night of the storm, the night she had met Dr James.

That time, panic and fear ruled her emotions.

This time, excitement. And love.

She advanced a few yards and saw that Dr James' door was ajar, just by a fraction.

She looked at the sideboard in the corridor. The old telescope was back from its travels, back in its old position. She placed the lighted lamp next to it.

And then she slipped into his room.

EPILOGUE

Elizabeth wakes up.

Sleep has blanketed her for hours on end, hugged her tight in a dreamless and healing embrace.

And so once again she wakes up, disorientated.

She pats the bed next to her. She is alone. She looks at a clock on the bedside table. *No wonder*, she thinks.

She smiles to herself and stretches comfortably. She sits up and reaches towards the curtain, which she pulls back, just a fraction. Between the palm leaves and the fronds and the flowers and the mid-morning sunlight, she sees Artemas sitting at the round, wooden table. The angle is different from her own room: she sees him almost directly below. He's breakfasting with the others in the conservatory.

For a moment, she watches them talk and eat and sip coffee and laugh. Then she sits back on the bed. She leans against the pillow, closes her eyes. She starts to open the door in her mind. *That* door. The one she's been using to shut the future out.

No gale blows in this time.

She walks through the door. She looks at the future directly, in the face. When she set out on this adventure, looking at the bewildering ordeal ahead, she felt her mind was in a raft, spinning out of control through canyons unknown. Now, as she looks forward, her feet are firmly on the shoreline. Below is a raging river. This is the turmoil that she and Charles must confront. But she can see a bridge across. She knows what she must do. She must guide all three of them across to the different places they're meant to be. That will be her job – to do it calmly and kindly – and that work will start soon. Not now, not today, perhaps not even this week, but soon.

Elizabeth gets up and slips next door to her own room to throw on some clothes. She knows now that when she first came to this house, she entered some kind of chrysalis. Change – confusing and turbulent – was upon her. *Metamorphosis.* And when she emerged, nothing would be the same. Perhaps she is already emerging. Because the strange thing is, new certainties are already replacing the confusion. *New certainties.*

She brushes her hair swiftly, straightens her clothes a little. She washes her hands with the beautiful-smelling, botanical soap. She splashes her face and dries it. She looks vaguely decent, good enough. There's nothing on her feet, but that's deliberate. The bohemian spirit of the previous evening is lingering on her body like a scent. She wants to feel the floor beneath her toes.

New certainties. She is certain she is never leaving this house again. No, nor Artemas neither.

*

As she moves through the house, it seems more than a house. It cloaks her, protects her; it feels like an extension of her.

She walks along the first-floor corridor – past the telescope – past the oil lamp which she left out last night. Beneath her toes, she feels the thread of the rug, old and pronounced. Her nose draws in the scent of fresh polish from the rich, dark wooden panelling.

She's got that same feeling she had yesterday at dinner. She still can't put her finger on it. *What is it?* A feeling that's running through all her veins, tingling the surface of her skin, emptying her head of thought.

She starts to descend the broad staircase into the main hall – the scene of the dancing last night – the place she first met Sir Claude.

"Morning, ma'am." Daniels, carrying a breakfast tray, greets her at the foot of the stairs as if it's the most natural thing in the world.

"Morning, Jane," she replies, just as naturally.

She wonders why the Scottish lilt has been returning to her voice. Is it because she's rejecting this privileged world? Or because she feels comfortable here – can finally be herself again?

At the foot of the stairs, she passes the suit of armour on her left and, just past it, turns left to walk through the central archway. The front door is directly behind her, the large drawing room is directly ahead. As she walks, she has this thought. She knows that she could live like this for the rest of her life. Forever.

In a life where she rarely planned more than a year ahead, she now finds herself thinking often of *forever*.

She feels the encrusted layers falling away from her. She turns right and passes into the small drawing room, the one that leads to the conservatory, where she and Artemas had tried – in the dead of night – to spy on Sir Claude's mystery guest. Now in the daylight, the room is transformed. It is a place of large mirrors and glass doors and greenery and white fabrics on beautiful, white painted furniture.

And then she is walking between the trees and flowers in the conservatory, along the woodchip path. Through the vee-shaped cleft in the two trunks of the palm tree she sees the back of Artemas' head. Sir Claude is opposite him; three or four others are seated there too.

"Morning, ma'am." Juckes greets her cordially as he heads in the opposite direction. He's carrying away an empty coffee pot. They've just been on a life-or-death adventure together, and he greets her as if nothing remotely strange has just happened. *The adventure was then, and this is now, and both are fine*, his voice seems to say.

"Morning," she replies, startled – happy.

It's a conjuror's trick, Elizabeth thinks to herself. The household has closed its chest of treasures and, with a small theatrical sweep, is laying a green baize cloth back over the top. *And this is the cloth settling comfortably back into position.*

And then she realises what this feeling is that's come over her.

It's joy.

Quite simply that. *Joy*.

She walks up behind Artemas and places a hand gently on his left shoulder. He turns round to look up at her.

"Ah, Mrs B!" He extends his right hand, the unwounded one. She takes it and keeps it in hers, their two hands now resting on his shoulder. She stands behind his chair – tall and protective. None of the others at the table show any surprise.

She is no longer Elizabeth Belfort. She knows that for certain. But she hasn't become Elspeth McBey again either.

The creature emerging out of the shell – out of the *chrysalis* – is neither of them. And both.

And something new entirely.

Mrs B.

HOW TO BUY A PLANET

Find out what happens to Mrs B and Dr James in the next adventure in The Cleremont Conjectures *series.*

"Totally *mesmerising*" – *Oxford Daily Info*

"Entertaining and fast-paced" – Una McCormack, *USA Today* bestselling author

The Earth has been sold. *What could possibly go wrong?*

It's the Year 2024.

Drowning in debt following the pandemic, the world's leaders have taken the only logical decision.

They've sold the planet.

Offering the same mix of satire and adventure as *The Zoo of Intelligent Animals,* this novel is perfect for fans of Douglas Adams, Terry Pratchett, or Neil Gaiman.

Get a FREE sample (Chapters 1-3) at this link: www.squirrelandacorn.co.uk/buy-a-planet

SQUIRREL & ACORN PRESS

FOR MORE THOUGHTFUL FUN...

You can follow D.A. Holdsworth on

Email: Sign up to his monthly newsletter at this link
www.squirrelandacorn.co.uk/subscribe

Goodreads: D.A. Holdsworth

Twitter: @D_A_Holdsworth

Facebook: www.facebook.com/squirrelandacorn

From: The Glossary of Modern Life

art *n.*

All art is either great - or someone else's fantasy.

ACKNOWLEDGEMENTS

This novel started with a conversation. It was the summer of 2020 and *How to Buy a Planet* had just been published into the midst of the pandemic. Claire, my marketing guru who had helped organised the launch with me, suggested I now write a short story – something to grow the world of 55 Cleremont Avenue. *Maybe set it in 1977,* she suggested, *at the time of the Wow! signal.* I was sceptical, I had a completely different writing project in mind. *Yeah, but what exactly?* I replied, not getting it. I parked the idea at the back of my mind.

Move forward a couple of weeks and I found myself in the Cotswold Wildlife Park with my wife and daughter. As I stared at the many wonderful creatures, a simple question came to mind: what's the most interesting animal here? *Duh* – the humans of course. And then *Bam*, the idea of a human zoo meshed in my mind with Claire's suggestion and this novel was born.

Which was a long way of saying, my first acknowledgement goes to Claire. For lighting the fuse of this novel, and also for helping launch the first one. Perhaps most significant of all, she taught me how to be a self-published author – the steps I'd need to take, the challenges I'd need to overcome. I have a debt there that I'm not sure I can ever repay.

My second acknowledgement goes to my reviewers. Steph and Una in particular have been involved almost from the start, reviewing early drafts of the early sections – and sticking with me through the end. They must've read some chapters three or four times. Mike and Severine joined the project midway, sacrificing almost as much of their time. Finally, Lewis and Jenifer joined when the typescript was complete. The care and detail and insight they both put into their reviews was humbling – and utterly invaluable. I thank all my reviewers with profound sincerity.

And then my family.

My nieces, Lucy and Eliza, have had a tough year. Their father, Richard (my brother), died at just about the time I was starting on this book. And yet they've gone out of their way to offer me love and encouragement in my new career. Lucy in particular, who is an accomplished writer herself, joined in the reviewing effort and provided some of my most valuable feedback.

Lastly, my wife.

This book is dedicated to her and I doubt anyone has earned a dedication the way she has. This new life I lead as a writer must have tested her patience sorely at many moments. But her support for me has never wavered, not one jot. I have debts to many people but to no-one more than her.